ACT OF MERCY

ACT OF MERCY

A Celtic Mystery

Peter Tremayne

St. Martin's Minotaur
New York

www.minotaurbooks.com

ISBN 0-312-26864-5

First published in Great Britain by
HEADLINE BOOK PUBLISHING
A Division of Hodder Headline Group

First St. Martin's Minotaur Edition: November 2001

10 9 8 7 6 5 4 3 2 1

For Christos Pittas, whose music has always been inspirational but who, as skipper of the *Alcyone*, navigated Fidelma's course to La Coruña; also for Dorothy who shared my trip to Santiago de Compostela; for Moira for her suggestions and David for his sympathy.

I will rejoice and be glad in Thy mercy
for Thou hast seen my affliction
and hast cared for me in my disaster.

Psalm XXXI. 7

HISTORICAL NOTE

The Sister Fidelma mysteries are set during the mid-seventh century A.D.

Sister Fidelma is not simply a religieuse, formerly a member of the community of St Brigid of Kildare. She is also a qualified *dálaigh*, or advocate of the ancient law courts of Ireland. As this background will not be familiar to many readers, my Historical Note is designed to provide a few essential points of reference to make the stories more readily appreciated.

Ireland, in the seventh century A.D., consisted of five main provincial kingdoms; indeed, the modern Irish word for a province is still *cúige*, literally 'a fifth'. Four provincial kings – of Ulaidh (Ulster), of Connacht, of Muman (Munster) and of Laigin (Leinster) – gave their qualified allegiance to the *Ard Rí* or High King, who ruled from Tara, in the 'royal' fifth province of Midhe (Meath), which means the 'middle province'. Even among these provincial kingdoms, there was a decentralisation of power to petty-kingdoms and clan territories.

The law of primogeniture, the inheritance by the eldest son or daughter, was an alien concept in Ireland. Kingship, from the lowliest clan chieftain to the High King, was only partially hereditary and mainly electoral. Each ruler had to prove himself or herself worthy of office and was elected by the *derbhfine* of their family – a minimum of three generations from a common ancestor gathered in conclave. If a ruler did not pursue the commonwealth of the people, they were impeached and removed from office. Therefore the monarchical system of ancient Ireland had more in common with a modern-day republic than with the feudal monarchies which had developed in medieval Europe.

Ireland, in the seventh century A.D., was governed by a system of sophisticated laws called the Laws of the *Fénechus*, or land-tillers, which became more popularly known as the Brehon Laws, deriving from the word *breitheamh* – a judge. Tradition has it that these laws were first gathered in 714 B.C. by the order of the High King, Ollamh

Fódhla. But it was in A.D. 438 that the High King, Laoghaire, appointed a commission of nine learned people to study, revise, and commit the laws to the new writing in Latin characters. One of those serving on the commission was Patrick, eventually to become patron saint of Ireland. After three years, the commission produced a written text of the laws, the first known codification.

The first complete surviving texts of the ancient laws of Ireland are preserved in an eleventh-century manuscript book. It was not until the seventeenth century that the English colonial administration in Ireland finally suppressed the use of the Brehon Law system. To even possess a copy of the law books was punishable, often by death or transportation.

The law system was not static, and every three years at the Féis Temhrach (Festival of Tara) the lawyers and administrators gathered to consider and revise the laws in the light of changing society and its needs.

Under these laws, women occupied a unique place. The Irish laws gave more rights and protection to women than any other western law code at that time or since. Women could, and did, aspire to all offices and professions as the co-equal with men. They could be political leaders, command their people in battle as warriors, be physicians, local magistrates, poets, artisans, lawyers and judges. We know the names of many female judges of Fidelma's period – Bríg Briugaid, Áine Ingine Iugaire and Darí among others. Darí, for example, was not only a judge but the author of a noted law text written in the sixth century A.D. Women were protected by the laws against sexual harassment; against discrimination; from rape; they had the right of divorce on equal terms from their husbands, with equitable separation laws, and could demand part of their husband's property as a divorce settlement; they had the right of inheritance of personal property and the right of sickness benefits when ill or hospitalised. Ancient Ireland had Europe's oldest recorded system of hospitals. Seen from today's perspective, the Brehon Laws provided for an almost feminist paradise.

This background, and its strong contrast with Ireland's neighbours, should be understood to appreciate Fidelma's role in these stories.

Fidelma was born at Cashel, capital of the kingdom of Muman (Munster) in south-west Ireland, in A.D. 636. She was the youngest daughter of Faílbe Fland, the King, who died the year after her birth. Fidelma was raised under the guidance of a distant cousin, Abbot Laisran of Durrow. When she reached the 'Age of Choice' (fourteen years), she went to study at the bardic school of the Brehon Morann of Tara, as did many other young Irish girls. Eight years of study resulted in Fidelma obtaining the degree of *anruth*, only one degree below the highest offered at either bardic or ecclesiastical universities in ancient Ireland. The highest degree was *ollamh*, which is still the modern Irish word for a professor. Fidelma's studies were in law, both in the criminal code of the *Senchus Mór* and the civil code of the *Leabhar Acaill*. She therefore became a *dálaigh* or advocate of the courts.

Her role could be likened to a modern Scottish sheriff-substitute, whose job is to gather and assess the evidence, independent of the police, to see if there is a case to be answered. The modern French *juge d'instruction* holds a similar role.

In those days, most of the professional or intellectual classes were members of the new Christian religious houses, just as, in previous centuries, all members of professions and intellectuals had been Druids. Fidelma became a member of the religious community of Kildare founded in the late fifth century A.D. by St Brigid.

While the seventh century A.D. was considered part of the European 'Dark Ages', for Ireland it was a period of 'Golden Enlightenment'. Students from every corner of Europe flocked to Irish universities to receive their education, including the sons of the Anglo-Saxon kings. At the great ecclesiastical university of Durrow, at this time, it is recorded that no fewer than eighteen different nations were represented among the students. At the same time, Irish male and female missionaries were setting out to reconvert a pagan Europe to Christianity, establishing churches, monasteries, and centres of learning throughout Europe as far east as Kiev, in the Ukraine; as far north as the Faroes, and as far south as Taranto in southern Italy. Ireland was a byword for literacy and learning.

However, the Celtic Church of Ireland was in constant dispute with Rome on matters of liturgy and ritual. Rome had begun to reform itself in the fourth century, changing its dating of Easter and aspects of its liturgy. The Celtic Church and the Eastern Orthodox Church refused to follow Rome, but the Celtic Church was gradually absorbed by Rome between the ninth and eleventh centuries while the Eastern Orthodox Churches have continued to remain independent of Rome. The Celtic Church of Ireland, during Fidelma's time, was much concerned with this conflict.

One thing that marked both the Celtic Church and Rome in the seventh century was that the concept of celibacy was not universal. While there were always ascetics in the Churches who sublimated physical love in a dedication to the deity, it was not until the Council of Nicea in A.D. 325 that clerical marriages were condemned but not banned. The concept of celibacy in the Roman Church arose from the customs practised by the pagan priestesses of Vesta and the priests of Diana. By the fifth century, Rome had forbidden clerics from the rank of abbot and bishop to sleep with their wives and, shortly after, even to marry at all. The general clergy were discouraged from marrying by Rome but not forbidden to do so. Indeed, it was not until the reforming papacy of Leo IX (A.D. 1049–1054) that a serious attempt was made to force the Western clergy to accept universal celibacy. In the Eastern Orthodox Church, priests below the rank of abbot and bishop have retained their right to marry until this day.

An understanding of these facts concerning the liberal attitudes towards sexual relationships in the Celtic Church is essential towards understanding the background to this novel.

The condemnation of the 'sin of the flesh' remained alien to the Celtic Church for a long time after Rome's attitude became a dogma. In Fidelma's world, both sexes inhabited abbeys and monastic foundations, which were known as *conhospitae*, or double houses, where men and women lived raising their children in Christ's service.

Fidelma's own house of St Brigid of Kildare was one such community of both sexes during her time. When Brigid established her community at Kildare (Cill-Dara = the church of the oaks) she invited a bishop named Conlaed to join her. Her first biography, completed fifty years after her death, in A.D. 650 during Fidelma's lifetime, was written by a monk of Kildare named Cogitosus, who makes it clear that it continued to be a mixed community.

It should also be pointed out that, demonstrating women's co-equal role with men, women were priests of the Celtic Church in this period. Brigid herself was ordained a bishop by Patrick's nephew, Mel, and her case was not unique. Rome actually wrote a protest, in the sixth century, at the Celtic practice of allowing women to celebrate the divine sacrifice of the Mass.

To help readers locate themselves in Fidelma's Ireland of the seventh century, where its geo-political divisions will be mainly unfamiliar, I have provided a sketch map and, to help them more readily identify personal names, a list of principal characters is also given.

I have generally refused to use anachronistic place names for obvious reasons although I have bowed to a few modern usages e.g. Tara, rather than *Teamhair*; and Cashel, rather than *Caiseal Muman*; and Armagh in place of *Ard Macha*. However, I have cleaved to the name of Muman rather than the prolepsis form 'Munster' formed when the Norse *stadr* (place) was added to the Irish name Muman in the ninth century A.D. and eventually anglicised. Similarly, I have maintained the original name Laigin, rather than the anglicized form of *Laighin-stadr* which is now Leinster, and Ulaidh rather than *Ulaidh-stadr* (Ulster). I have decided to use the anglicised versions of Ardmore (*Aird Mhór* – the high point); Moville (*Magh Bhíle* – the plain of Bíle, an ancient god) and Bangor (*Beannchar* – a peaked hill).

In this following tale, set in A.D. 666, Sister Fidelma embarks on a pilgrimage to Santiago de Compostela, to the Holy Shrine of St James. Some readers might point out that it was not until A.D. 800 that a Galician monk named Pelayo, guided by the light of the stars (*campus stella* = field of stars), was believed to have discovered a site called *Arcis Marmoricis* where the marble tomb of the saint was found.

James, the son of Zebedee and Maria Salome, and brother of John, was killed in Palestine in A.D. 42, the first apostle to die as a martyr to the new faith. But, according to early Christian tradition, he had already made a missionary journey to the Iberian peninsula and so his followers took the body, placed on a marble bier, on board a ship and sailed for Galicia. The ship came ashore at Padron. When the author and his wife visited this lovely little town, an old man, cleaning the church there, showed them a deep recess under the High Altar. In this recess was an ancient white marble stone marked with Latin letters, which was claimed to be the original stone on which the corpse of St James had been conveyed.

The body was taken to the place which is now Santiago de Compostela (St James of the Field of Stars). Knowledge of the resting place of the *locus apostolicus* became confused with the passing of the centuries and with the schisms within the Christian movement. It seemed that those churches, now retrospectively called the Celtic Church, which clung to the original liturgy and rites of the Christian movement long after the Roman Church had begun to reform its theology and practices, continued to respect Santiago de Compostela as a last resting place of James.

There is nothing anachronistic about a pilgrimage to Santiago by Fidelma. Indeed, we are told in an early Christian text that ten thousand Irish *peregrinatio pro Christo* visited Santiago with the benediction of Patrick himself in the fifth century. The twelfth-century *Liber Sancti Jacobi* (Book of St Jacob) speaks of the long tradition of the pilgrimages and says that the symbol of James, one of the Galilean fishermen, was a scallop shell. Archaeologists have turned up many scallop shells at Irish sites, mostly buried with corpses at ecclesiastical sites, dating to the medieval period. *Liber Sancti Jacobi* describes stalls selling the scallop shells to pilgrims at Santiago. Today, shops in Santiago still sell scallop-shell *objets d'art*.

The author often receives letters from readers wondering if he is simply inventing the social background and technology of Fidelma's world, and, indeed, one recent reviewer seemed to believe that he was claiming a technology which they felt was beyond Irish capability at that time. It might interest readers to know that the following sources have been drawn on for the background to this particular story:

In this matter of such pilgrimages the author is grateful to 'The Irish Medieval Pilgrimage to Santiago de Compostela' by Dagmar O Riain-Raedal in *History Ireland*, Autumn, 1998.

The author is also grateful to the following for background material: 'Irish Pioneers in Ocean Navigation of the Middle Ages' by G.J. Marcus in *Irish Ecclesiastical Record*, November, 1951, and December, 1951; 'Further Light on Early Irish Navigation' by G.J. Marcus in *Irish Ecclesiastical Record*, 1954, pp. 93–100; 'St Brandan (sic) The Navigator', by Commander Anthony MacDermott RN, KM, in *Mariner's Mirror*, 1944, pp. 73–80; 'The Ships of the Veneti' by Craig Weatherhill in *Cornish Archaeology* No. 24, 1985; 'Irish Travellers in the Norse World' by Rosemary Power in *Aspects of Irish Studies*, Ed. Hill & Barber, 1990; and 'Archaic Navigational Instruments' by John Moorwood in *Atlantic Visions*, 1989.

Principal Characters

Sister Fidelma of Cashel, a *dálaigh* or advocate of the law courts of seventh-century Ireland

At Ardmore (Aird Mhór)

Colla, tavernkeeper and trader
Menma his young assistant

The Pilgrims

Sister Canair of Moville (*Magh Bíle*), leader of the pilgrims
Brother Cian, a former member of the High King's bodyguard, now of the Abbey of Bangor (*Beannchar*)
Sister Muirgel, of the Abbey of Moville
Sister Crella of Moville
Sister Ainder of Moville
Sister Gormán of Moville
Brother Guss of Moville
Brother Bairne of Moville
Brother Dathal of Bangor
Brother Adamrae of Bangor
Brother Tola of Bangor

The Crew of *The Barnacle Goose*

Murchad, the captain
Gurvan, the mate
Wenbrit, cabin boy
Drogan, a crewman
Hoel, a crewman

Others

Toca Nia, a shipwreck survivor
Father Pol of Ushant
Brehon Morann, Fidelma's mentor
Grian, Fidelma's friend at Tara

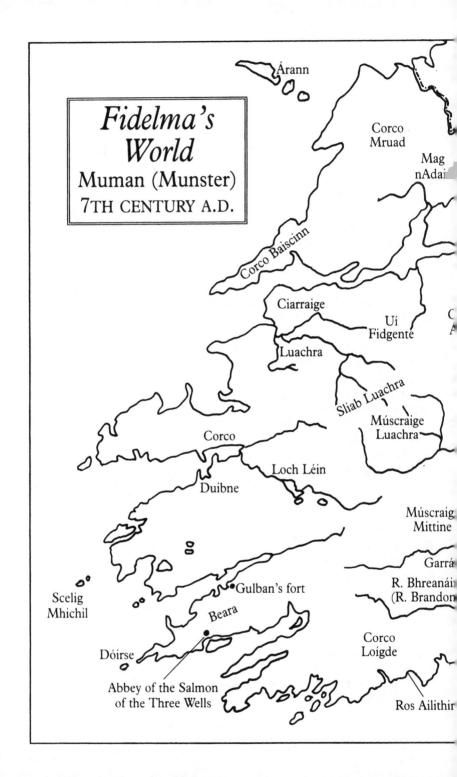

Árann

Corco
Mruad

Mag
nAdai

Fidelma's
World
Muman (Munster)
7TH CENTURY A.D.

Corco Baiscinn

Ciarraige

Uí
Fidgente

C
A

Luachra

Sliab Luachra

Múscraige
Luachra

Corco

Loch Léin

Duibne

Múscraig
Mittine

Garrá

R. Bhreanái
(R. Brandon

Scelig
Mhichil

Gulban's fort

Beara

Corco
Loígde

Dóirse

Abbey of the Salmon
of the Three Wells

Ros Ailithir

ONNACHT

Loch Derg

Biorra (Birr)

Sliab mBladma

LAIGIN

Múscraige Tíre

Cill Dalua (Killaloe)

Arada Cliach

neach erick)

OSRAIGE

Imleach (Emly)

Múscraige Breogain

Cashel

R. Feoir (R. Nore)

aige

R. Siúr (R. Suir)

Lios Mhór (Lismore)

Abhain Mhór (R. Blackwater)

Uí Liatháin

Aird Mhór (Ardmore)

Corcaigh (Cork)

aoí ee)

20 miles

ACT OF MERCY

Chapter One

Colla, the tavernkeeper, tugged on the leather reins to halt the two sturdy donkeys which had been patiently hauling his overladen cart along the track across the precipitous rocky headland. It was a soft autumnal morning and the sun had begun its climb in the eastern sky. The quiet sea below the headland reflected the azure canopy which held only a few white fleecy clouds. There was just a hint of a soft breeze from the north-west, giving impetus to the morning tide. Colla, from this high point on the coast, could see that the sea's long dim level appeared flat and calm. He had lived long enough by its vast expanse to know that this was an illusion, however. From this distance, human eyes were unable to appreciate the swells and currents of the brooding, treacherous waters.

Around him, sea and coastal birds wheeled and darted with their cacophony of morning cries. Guillemots were gathering along the coast in preparation for their departure during the harsh winter months. A few razorbills, who had already left their cliff nests, could still be seen here and there but they, too, would be gone within the next few weeks. The residue of the hardier summer birds was vanishing now, like the cormorants. Now was the time when the gulls began to dominate; these were the abundant flocks of common gulls, smaller and less aggressive than the large, black-backed glaucous gull.

Colla had risen some time before dawn to take his cart up to the Abbey of St Declan, which stood on the top of the steep headland called Ardmore, the high point overlooking the small harbour settlement below. Colla not only kept the local tavern but he traded with the merchants whose ships used the bay as a sheltered haven; merchants sailing to Éireann's shore from as far afield as Britain, Gaul and from even more distant lands.

His trip that morning had been to deliver four great casks of wine and olive oil which had arrived in a Gaulish merchant ship

1

on the previous evening's tide. In return for such wares, the Abbey's industrious Brothers supplied leather goods – shoes, purses and bags – as well as objects made from skins of otter, squirrel and hare. Colla was now returning to the harbour to the Gaulish merchant, who would be sailing on the evening tide. The Abbot had been well pleased with the transaction as, indeed, had Colla; his commission was substantial enough to mould his rugged features into a smile of satisfaction as he set out across the headland.

For a moment, however, he halted his donkeys to view the scene below. It gave him a sense of proprietorship as he gazed down, perhaps of power. He could see the tiny harbour in the bay below and several ships bobbing at their anchorage. For Colla, the view seemed to put things in a perspective from which he felt like a king surveying his kingdom.

A shiver interrupted his thoughts as a fresh wind gusted in from the north-west. He'd discerned a subtle change in the morning breeze and realised that it had become stronger and colder. The sun had been up over an hour now and the tide was on the turn. Any moment now, he expected a movement in the bay below. Colla flicked the reins and eased the cart and its burden forward along the steep track twisting down the hill towards the small sandy bay which stretched before him.

Among the ships below, he caught sight of the black silhouettes of a couple of great sea-going vessels, the *ler-longa*, at anchor in the sheltered harbour. From this vantage point, they looked small and fragile but he knew that, in reality, they were large and sturdy, measuring twenty-five metres from stem to stern – enough to brave the great oceans beyond these shores.

His head jerked as he heard an explosive crack, above the general cries of the birds and the distant hiss of the sea. It was immediately followed by an outraged chorus of cries, as disturbed sea birds rose up above the bay, screaming their displeasure. It was the sound and movement that he had been expecting. His keen eyes saw one of the *ler-longa* moving slowly from its anchorage. The crack had been the great leather sail snapping before the wind as it was hauled into place, straining before the gusts as it was secured. Colla smiled knowingly. The captain would have been in a hurry to utilise the north-western dawn wind combined with the turning tide. What did the sailors call it? A lee-tide running in the same direction as the wind. Good seamanship would soon bring the ship out of the bay and beyond the Ardmore headland southwards to the vast open sea.

Colla strained his eyes to make sure of the identification of the ship, but only one vessel was due to set sail on the morning tide. It was Murchad's *Gé Ghúirainn* – 'The Barnacle Goose'. Murchad had told him that he was due to leave with a collection of pilgrims setting out for some holy shrine beyond the seas. Indeed, as Colla had driven his cart up towards the Abbey, he had passed a band of religieux, men and women, walking down to the harbour to go aboard her. That was not unusual. The Abbey of St Declan was frequented by such bands of pilgrims from every corner of the Five Kingdoms of Éireann. They usually stayed at the Abbey prior to joining their respective ships which would convey them to their various destinations. Some pilgrims, depending on their character, preferred to stay in Colla's tavern. He had a few such staying with him the previous night who must now be on board *The Barnacle Goose*. There was one young female religieuse who had arrived very late and who was anxious to be aboard at dawn. And Colla's nephew, Menma, who helped him run the tavern, had told him that a man and woman had arrived earlier to take a room but they were joining the pilgrim ship as well.

The Barnacle Goose appeared to be making good time through the water, helped onwards by the favourable wind and tide. In some ways, Colla envied Murchad and his handsome ship, heading out across the horizon to adventure and unknown lands. In other ways, the tavernkeeper knew that such a life was not for him. He was no sailor and preferred his days to be more predictable. However, he could have stopped on the headland watching the sea and the ships below all day but he had work to do, a tavern to run. So he turned his attention back to the track, flicking the reins and clucking softly to increase the gait of his donkeys. The animals twitched their ears and obediently strained forward.

It took him all his concentration to negotiate the track because it was always more difficult bringing a cart down a steep hill than hauling it up. He came to a halt in his tavern yard. When he had left, it had been dark, with no one stirring. Now the entire village was a hive of activity as fishermen departed to their boats; sailors, recovering from a drunken night's carousing ashore, stirred and made their way back to their ships, while labourers left for the day's work in the fields.

Menma, Colla's assistant, a dour-faced young man, was sweeping out the tavern's main room when the stocky tavernkeeper entered. Colla glanced around approvingly as he saw that Menma had already cleared the tables where the guests had breakfasted before their departure.

'Have you tidied the guests' chambers yet?' Colla asked, moving to pour himself a mug of sweet mead, to refresh himself from his journey.

His assistant shook his head resentfully.

'I have only just cleared the breakfast things away. Oh, and that Gaulish merchant came by asking for you. He said he would return soon with a couple of men to load the goods on his ship at midday.'

Colla nodded absently as he sipped his drink. Then he put it down with a reluctant sigh.

'I'd better make a start on the rooms then, otherwise we will have more guests arriving before we are ready. Did all the pilgrims get away safely?'

Menma pondered the question before answering.

'The pilgrims? I think so.'

'You only *think* so?' Colla teased. 'You would make a fine host, not to ensure that your guests have departed.'

The young man ignored his master's sarcasm.

'Well, there were a dozen other guests demanding food and only myself in the place to serve them,' he protested sulkily. He thought again. 'The man and woman, the religieux who arrived after the main meal last night – they'd both gone before light. I wasn't even up. I found that they had left money on the table here. You were out and about early. Did you see them leave?'

Colla shook his head.

'I met only one group of religieux on the road and they were coming from the Abbey, heading for the quay. Oh, and a short while after, another religieuse was following. Perhaps they were keen to be on the quay early?' He shrugged indifferently. 'Well, so long as they paid their dues. Out of a dozen guests we had only one other, apart from those two, bound for *The Barnacle Goose* this morning – the young religieuse who arrived so late. Surely you would know if she was up and sailed with the tide or not?'

Menma disclaimed knowledge.

'I cannot remember her. But as she is not here, I presume that she either sailed or went a different way.' He shrugged. 'I have only one pair of eyes and hands.'

Colla pressed his lips together in annoyance. Were Menma not the son of his sister, he would make his ears sting with the back of his hand. He was turning out to be a lazy youth and always complaining. Colla had the impression that Menma seemed to think working in the tavern was a task below his station in life.

'Very well,' Colla replied, biting back his resentment. 'I'll start

4

cleaning the guest rooms. You let me know when the Gaulish merchant returns.'

He turned up the wooden stairs to where the guest chambers were situated. These rooms were well-appointed, with one large room in which a dozen or more could squeeze in at a reduced fee, and with a half-a-dozen rooms for those who could afford to reward their host more generously. The communal room had been filled to capacity last night, mostly with drunken Gaulish sailors who were not able to row back to their own merchant ship due to a surfeit of alcohol and food. Of the rest of the rooms, five had been occupied. Three of the guests had been visiting merchants. Then there had been the religieux who, for one reason or another, had declined the hospitality of the Abbey on the hill. That was not unusual.

Colla had not seen the youthful monk and the young Sister who, so Menma had told him, had arrived without baggage after the main meal had been finished. They had not even asked for food but had taken one of the separate rooms. He did, however, recall the third late arrival, the young religieuse, because she had arrived very late and seemed so nervous and ill-at-ease. She had hung around outside the tavern for some time, as if expecting someone to join her, and had eventually asked Colla if anyone had been enquiring for her. He tried to remember the name she had given but could not. He had wondered whether she would be happier in the cloisters of the Abbey but she had insisted on taking a room and told him that it was too dark to make her way up the steep hill to the protection of the Abbey. She had also told Colla that she had to be up early to meet some fellow religieux and join them aboard a pilgrim ship. As only Murchad's *The Barnacle Goose* was sailing with the morning tide, he had assumed that it could be no other vessel. He should have left Menma with specific instructions to see that the girl was roused in time. The taverner took his duties concerning the welfare of his guests very seriously.

Colla paused on the landing at the top of the stairs for a moment, as if summoning his enthusiasm for the task. He hated cleaning. It was the worst aspect of keeping a tavern. Colla had been hoping that his sister's son would share the burden of work, for he himself had never married, but the boy was turning into a liability.

Taking a broom, he pushed open the door of the communal room, immediately screwing up his face at the stench of stale wine fumes, old sweat and other odours that hung above the jumble and chaos of the discarded sleeping mattresses. Then, deciding to take the easier option, he turned towards the individual rooms. At least they would be easier to clean first and he would return to the general disorder afterwards.

The doors of the rooms all stood ajar, except for one at the end of the row. That was the room in which he himself had installed the young female latecomer. Colla believed himself to be a good judge of human character. He guessed that the young woman was a fastidious person, the type to tidy her room and shut her door when leaving it. He smiled in self-satisfaction at his perspicacity, mentally promising himself a drink if he turned out to be right. It was a game he often played, as if he needed some excuse to take a drink from his own stores. Then, unable to present himself with any further distractions, he forced himself to set to work.

He surprised himself by cleaning each room swiftly but with a thoroughness that belied the quick movements with which he tidied up. He was feeling pleased with his progress by the time he came to the fifth chamber, the one used by the young religieux couple. He entered it. It had been left in almost pristine condition, with the bed neatly made. If only all his guests were so clean and tidy! He was just congratulating himself on not having to do much work in here, when he caught sight of something on the floor. It was a dark stain. It looked as if someone had trodden in something, and yet there was no foul odour of excrement. Cautiously, Colla bent and dabbed at it with his finger. It was still damp yet nothing came off on his hand.

To reassure himself, he glanced around the room. His first impression had been correct: it was tidy enough. He stared back down to the single stain, and frowned in bewilderment.

In retrospect, he did not know why he turned from the room, without cleaning it. As he did so, he saw another stain on the floor outside the entrance to the sixth room. He hesitated a moment, tapped on the door and then lifted the latch, pushing it open.

The room was in shadows for the curtain covering the window had not been drawn back, but it was light enough to see that someone was still lying in the bed.

Colla cleared his throat. 'Sister, you have overslept,' he called nervously. 'Your ship is gone – sailed. Sister, you *must* wake up!'

There was no movement from the form under the blankets.

Colla moved slowly forward, dreading what he would find. He could tell instinctively that something was very wrong. When he reached the window at the head of the bed, he drew back the curtain so that light flooded into the room. At the same time he noticed that the blanket covered the head as well as the body which lay still on the bed. There was a meat-knife on the floor. He recognised it as one from his own kitchen.

6

'Sister?' There was desperation in his voice now. He did not want to believe what his mind was already telling him.

With a trembling hand he took hold of the edge of the blanket. It was sodden to the touch. Even without looking, he knew that it was not with water. Very gently, he pulled the blanket away from the face beneath.

The young woman lay there, eyes wide and glazed, her mouth twisted into a final grimace of pain. Her skin was waxy. She had been dead some time. Deeply shocked, Colla forced his eyes to drop from her pallid stare to her body. The white linen of her shift was ripped and torn and suffused in blood. He had never seen such savagery inflicted with a knife before. The body had been cut – *hacked* – as if a butcher had mistaken the young woman's soft flesh for that of a lamb to be slaughtered.

Colla dropped the blood-soaked blanket back to cover the figure with a curious groaning sound. He turned swiftly away and started to retch.

Chapter Two

Fidelma of Cashel balanced against the taffrail of the ship, watching the coastline bobbing away behind it with surprising speed. She had been the last to board the vessel that morning and had barely stepped aboard when the captain had shouted for the single great square sail to be lifted on its hoistable yard up the central mainmast. At the same time, other sailors were hauling up the heavy anchor. She had not even had time to go below to inspect her cabin before the great vessel strained forward, its thin leather sail cracking and filling with the wind, like a lung filling with breath.

'Set the steering sail!' came the captain's stentorian tone. The crew ran towards a long-angled mast, pointing forward of the main mast. A small sail was pulled into place on a cross yard. Beside the captain, on the raised stern deck, stood two muscular, thickset men. Here, on the larboard side of vessel, a large steering oar was fixed. It was so large that it took the combined efforts of both sailors to control it. At the captain's shouted command, the sailors heaved on the oar. The ship caught the tide and fairly sliced through the wavelets like a scythe through corn.

So fast was the departure of *The Barnacle Goose* from the Bay of Ardmore that Fidelma decided not to go below for the moment but to stay on deck and watch the activity. The only sign of any of her fellow travellers were two youthful religieux standing arm in arm, at the port rail amidships. They were deep in conversation. There were no other passengers in sight, and Fidelma presumed that the rest of the pilgrims were below decks. Half-a-dozen sailors, whose job it was to sail the ship across the stormy seas to Iberia, were going about their various tasks under the watchful eye of the captain. Fidelma wondered why her fellow passengers had chosen to miss one of the most exciting parts of the commencement of a sea voyage, the leaving of harbour. She had made several voyages in her life, but never ceased to be enthralled by the sights and sounds as a vessel left its harbour, feeling the first bounce of the hull against the waves, seeing the rise and dip of the vanishing coastline. She could spend hours simply watching until the distant line of land dipped below the horizon.

Fidelma was a natural-born sailor. She had often been out in a tiny curragh on the wild, windswept west coast, journeying to remote islands, and had not felt any qualms. A few years ago she had journeyed to Iona, the Isle of Saints, off the coast of high-hilled Alba, on her way to the Synod of Whitby in Northumbria, and then she had travelled to Gaul on her way to Rome and back again, and, in all those long voyages, she had never felt the slightest seasickness in spite of the most severe motion of the ship in which she travelled.

Motion. The idea caught at her mind. Perhaps that was the answer? From a child she had been on horseback. Maybe she had become used to the motion of riding horses and therefore did not react to the motion of a ship as someone who had always kept their feet on dry land might do. She promised herself that on this voyage she would try to learn something more about sea lore, navigation and the distances to be run. What was the point of enjoying a voyage if she did not know the practical side of it?

She smiled to herself at the useless wandering of her thoughts and raised herself up against the wooden ship's rail to focus on the vanishing height of Ardmore with its tall, grey-stone Abbey buildings. She had spent the previous night there as guest of the Abbot.

Unexpectedly, as she thought of the Abbey of St Declan, she felt a curious sensation of loneliness.

Eadulf! She identified the cause at once.

Brother Eadulf, the Saxon monk, had been emissary from Theodore, Archbishop of Canterbury, to the court of her brother, Colgú, King of Muman at Cashel. Until a week or so ago, Eadulf had been her constant companion for almost a year, a supportive comrade in several dangerous situations when she was called upon to exercise her skills as a *dálaigh*, an advocate of the law courts of the Five Kingdoms of Éireann. Why was she troubled suddenly by his memory?

It had been her own decision. A few weeks previously, Fidelma had decided to part company with Eadulf to commence this pilgrimage. She had felt that she needed a change of place and space in which to meditate, for she had begun to view her life with dissatisfaction. Afraid of the emotional routine in which she had found herself, Fidelma no longer trusted her own feelings about her purpose in life.

Yet Brother Eadulf of Seaxmund's Ham was the only man of her own age in whose company she felt really at ease and able to express herself. Eadulf had taken a long time to accept her decision to leave Cashel and set out on this pilgrimage. He had raised objections and protested for some time. Finally he had decided to return to Canterbury to rejoin Archbishop Theodore, the newly appointed Greek Bishop whom he had accompanied from Rome and for whom he acted as special envoy. Fidelma was annoyed with herself for missing Eadulf already with the coastline still in sight. The coming months loomed lonely. She would miss their debates; miss the way she could tease Eadulf over their conflicting opinions and philosophies; the way he would always rise good-naturedly to her bait. Their arguments would rage but there was no enmity between them. They had learnt together as they examined their interpretations and debated their ideas.

Eadulf had been like a brother to her. Perhaps that was the trouble. She compressed her lips at the thought. He had always behaved impeccably towards her. She found herself wondering, and not for the first time, whether she wanted him to behave in any other way. Members of the religieux did cohabit, did marry, and most lived in the *conhospitae*, or mixed houses, raising their children to the service of God. Did she want that? She was still a young woman and with a young woman's desires. Eadulf had never given any indication that he felt attracted to her as a man should feel towards a woman. The closest she had come to the subject, to prompt his thoughts upon it, was during a journey when they had spent a cold night on a mountain. She had asked Eadulf if he had heard the old proverb that a blanket was the warmer for being doubled. He had not understood.

There again, she reflected, Eadulf was a firm adherent to the Church of Rome which, while it still allowed its clergy to marry and cohabit, was clearly moving towards the doctrine of celibacy. Fidelma, on the other hand, was an adherent of the Irish Church which disagreed with so many of the rites and rituals of Rome, even to the dating of Easter. She had been raised without any prohibition on her natural feelings. Those differences between her culture and that now espoused by Rome were a major source of the arguments between her and Eadulf. The thought had barely entered her mind when she remembered the *Book of Amos*. 'Can two walk together, except that they be agreed?' Perhaps the philosophy was right and she should dismiss the subject of Eadulf altogether.

She wished her old mentor, the Brehon Morann, were here to consult. Or, indeed, her cousin – the chubby-faced, happy-go-lucky Abbot Laisran of Durrow who had persuaded her, as a young girl, to enter the religious life in the first place. What was she doing here anyway? Running away because she could not find a solution to her problems? If so, she would merely carry those problems into whatever corner of the earth she journeyed. There would be no solution awaiting her at her destination.

She had argued herself into this pilgrimage for the purpose of sorting out her life without any pressure from Eadulf, from her brother, Colgú, or her friends at Cashel, her brother's capital. She wanted to be somewhere that had no connection with her previous life, somewhere she could meditate and attempt to resolve matters. But she was confused. She was not even sure that she wanted to be a religieuse any longer! That thought brought her up with a shock as she realised that she could now ask that very question which she had been suppressing or hiding for this last year or so.

She had entered the life simply because the majority of the intellectual class of her people, all those who wished to pursue the professions, did so, just as their forebears had been members of the Druidic class. Her one abiding interest and passion had been law, not religion in the sense of sublimating herself to a life of devotion within some abbey away from the rest of her fellow beings. She now fell to thinking about the times when the Superior of her abbey had chided her for spending too much time with her law books and not enough time in religious contemplation. Maybe the religious life was no longer for her.

Perhaps this was the real reason for her pilgrimage – to sort out her commitment to God rather than ponder her relationship with Brother Eadulf? Fidelma suddenly felt angry with herself and turned abruptly away from the rail of the ship.

The great leather sail was towering high above her, against the azure sky. The crew were still bent to various tasks, but their movements were less frenetic than they had been when the vessel had initially left the protection of the bay. There was still no sign of the rest of Fidelma's fellow pilgrims. The two young monks were still having their animated dialogue. She wondered who they were and why they were making this voyage. Did they harbour the same conflict of thoughts that she did? She smiled ruefully.

'A fine day, Sister,' called the captain of the ship, moving from his position by the steersmen and coming forward to greet her. He had barely acknowledged her presence when she came aboard, too busy concentrating on the task of getting the ship underway.

She leant with her back against the rail and nodded pleasantly.

'A fine day, indeed.'

'My name is Murchad, Sister,' the man introduced himself. 'I am sorry I did not have time for a proper greeting when you came aboard.'

The captain of *The Barnacle Goose* could not be mistaken for anything other than the sailor he was. A sturdy, thickset man, Murchad had greying hair and weatherbeaten features. Fidelma estimated he was in his late forties; she noted that he had a prominent nose which accentuated the close set of his sea-grey eyes. Their forbidding aspect was offset by a twinkling hidden humour. His mouth was a firm line. When he walked towards her, he moved with the rolling gait she associated with seafarers.

'Have you acquired your sea legs yet?' he asked in his dry, rasping voice; the voice of someone used to shouting commands rather than indulging in social conversation.

Fidelma smiled confidently.

'I think you will find me a pretty good sailor, Captain.'

Murchad chuckled sceptically.

'I'll let you have an opinion when we are out of sight of land in a deep, restless ocean,' he replied.

'I've been on shipboard before,' Fidelma assured him.

'Is that a fact?' His tone was jovial.

'That it is,' she answered gravely. 'I've crossed to the coast of Alba and from the coast of Northumbria to Gaul.'

'Pah!' Murchad screwed up his face in distaste although his eyes did not lose their good humour. 'That is a mere paddle across a pond. We are going on a *real* sea voyage.'

'Is it longer than from Northumbria to Gaul?' Fidelma knew many things but the distances by sea was a knowledge that she had never had to acquire.

'If we are lucky . . . *if*,' emphasised Murchad, 'then we will be ashore within the week. It depends on the weather and the tides.'

Fidelma was surprised.

'Isn't that a long time to be out of sight of land?' she ventured.

Murchad shook his head with a grin.

'Bless you, no. We will sight land a few times on this voyage. We have to keep close to the coast in order to maintain our bearings. Our first landfall should be tomorrow morning; that is, if we find a favourable wind all the way to the south-east.'

'Where does that take us? To the kingdom of the Britons of Cornwall?'

Murchad regarded her with a new appreciation.

'You know your geography, Sister. However, we don't touch the coast of Cornwall. We sail to the west of a group of islands which lie several miles from it – the islands called Sylinancim. We do not stop there but sail on with, I hope, a fair wind and calm seas. If so, we make landfall on another island, called Ushant, that lies off the coast of Gaul. We should be there on the following morning or soon afterwards. That will be our last look at land for several days. Then we sail due south and should touch the coast of Iberia before the week's out, God willing.'

'Iberia, and within the week?'

Murchad verified her question with a nod.

'God willing,' he repeated. 'And we have a good ship to take us.' He slapped at the timber of the rail as he spoke.

Fidelma glanced round. She had taken a special interest in examining the ship when she came aboard.

'She's a Gaulish ship, isn't she?'

Murchad was a little surprised at her knowledge.

'You have a keen eye, Sister.'

'I have seen a ship like her before. I know that the heavy timbers and rigging are peculiar to the ports of Morbihan.'

Murchad looked even more surprised.

'You'll be telling me next that you know who built her,' he said dryly.

'No, that I can't,' she replied seriously. 'But, as I say, I have seen her like before.'

'Well, you are right,' confessed Murchad. 'I bought her in Kerhostin two years ago. My mate . . .' he indicated one of the two men at the steering oar, a man with saturnine features, 'that's my mate, Gurvan, the second-in-command on this vessel. He is a Breton and helped build *The Barnacle Goose*. We also have Cornishmen and Galicians in our crew. They know all the waters between here and Iberia.'

'It is good that you have so knowledgeable a crew,' Fidelma observed with solemn humour.

'Well, as I say, if we have a fair wind and the blessing of our patron, St Brendan the Navigator, this will prove an agreeable voyage.'

Mention of St Brendan turned Fidelma's thoughts to her fellow pilgrims.

'I was wondering why most of my fellow passengers are missing the best part of the voyage?' she queried. 'I always think the most exciting part of a voyage is when one leaves land behind, and heads out on the vast sea.'

'From a traveller's viewpoint, I would have thought that it is more exciting coming into a strange port than leaving a familiar one,' returned Murchad. Then he shrugged. 'Perhaps your travelling companions are not such good sailors as you and those two young Brothers yonder.' He nodded to where the two religieux were still engaged in discussion. 'Though I think those young men are

14

scarcely noticing that they are on shipboard – unlike some of their fellows.'

It took Fidelma a moment before she realised what he was implying.

'Some are seasick already?'

'My cabin boy tells me we have at least a couple suffering. I have had pilgrims actually praying for death to take them even on a calm sea because they were so sick they could not bear it.' He chuckled at the memory. 'I knew one pilgrim who became sick the moment he set foot on shipboard and continued his sickness even while he rode at anchor in the sheltered harbour. Some people can take to the sea while others should remain on land.'

'What are my fellow passengers like?' asked Fidelma.

Murchad pursed his lips and regarded her with some astonishment.

'You do not know them?'

'No. I am not part of their company. I am travelling alone.'

'I thought you were from the Abbey.' Murchad waved his hand in the direction of the distant shoreline behind them as if to indicate St Declan's.

'I am from Cashel – Fidelma of Cashel. I arrived at the Abbey late last night.'

'Well.' Murchad reflected for a moment on her question. 'Your fellow travellers, I suppose, can be described as the usual crowd of religieux. I am sorry, Sister, but it is hard to see beyond the habit to the individual.'

Fidelma was sympathetic to his viewpoint.

'Are they a mixed group, both male and female?'

'Ah, that I *can* tell you. Including yourself, there are four females and six males.'

'Ten in all?' Fidelma was surprised. 'That is a curious total, for surely pilgrims like to travel in bands of twelve or thirteen?'

'So it is in my experience. There were supposed to be six females and six males on this trip. However, I was told that one female did not complete the trip to Ardmore while another of them simply did not turn up on the quay this morning. We waited until the last minute, but a ship cannot dictate wind and tide. We had to sail. Perhaps the missing religieuse had thought better of undertaking this voyage. It is certainly curious, though, to find a woman undertaking a pilgrimage alone,' he added inquisitively.

Fidelma made an imperceptible gesture with her shoulder.

'I arrived at St Declan's Abbey only last evening with the purpose of seeking a ship for Iberia. The Abbot told me that your ship was preparing to sail this morning and he believed that you had room for another passenger. So he entertained me while a messenger came to book my passage. I did not meet my fellow travellers at the Abbey and have no knowledge of any of them.'

Murchad was looking at her speculatively, rubbing a forefinger along the side of his large nose.

'It is true that the Abbot's messenger found me in Colla's tavern last night and booked your passage.' He frowned. 'It strikes me that you are an odd sort of religieuse, Sister. The Abbot entertains you while he sends a messenger to book your passage? Yet you don't appear to be a Superior of your Order.'

There was an implied question in his observation.

'I am not,' she answered, wishing the subject had not been raised.

He was scrutinising her carefully.

'It is unusual to warrant such a privilege.' He paused and his sharp, bright eyes widened in recognition. 'Fidelma of Cashel? Of course!'

Fidelma sighed in resignation as she realised that he had heard of her. However, her identity would have probably been revealed sooner or later in the close confines of this vessel.

'I trust you will keep my identity confidential, Murchad,' she requested. 'Who I am should surely be of no concern to my fellow travellers.'

Murchad let out a long, soft breath.

'The King of Cashel's sister travelling on my ship? It is an honour, lady, and my curiosity is appeased.'

Fidelma shook her head reproachfully.

'*Sister*,' she corrected sharply. 'I am no more than an ordinary religieuse on a pilgrimage.'

'Very well, I will keep your confidence. Yet a princess and a lawyer rolled into the person of a religieuse is an extraordinary combination to encounter. I have heard stories of how you saved the kingdom . . .'

Fidelma drew up her chin a fraction. There was a dangerous sparkle in her eyes as she retorted: 'Wasn't Brendan himself a prince and wasn't Colmcille of the royal dynasty of Uí Néill? Surely it is not so unusual to find people of royal rank serving the Faith? Anyway, this matter remains one that is between us and not to be discussed with my fellow pilgrims.'

'I must surely tell the boy who will serve your needs on the voyage.'

'I would rather you did not. And now, Captain, you were about to tell me about my fellow travellers,' she prompted, interrupting further talk on what she felt was an embarrassing subject.

'I know nothing much about them,' Murchad confessed. 'Although they stayed at the Abbey last night, I do not think they are of its community. Judging by their accents, or those which I have heard, most of them are northerners – from the Kingdom of Ulaidh.'

Fidelma felt a sense of wonder.

'It is surely a long route for pilgrims from Ulaidh to journey to Ardmore to find a ship, rather than sail directly from a northern port?'

'Maybe.' Murchad seemed indifferent. 'As master of this ship, I am pleased to pick up paying passengers whatever their motives. You will have plenty of time to get acquainted with them, lady, and their reasons for coming on this journey.'

He suddenly glanced up at the pennants flying from the central mast, shading his eyes against the sun for a moment.

'Forgive me, lady. I must go to wear the ship – I mean, to change her heading – for the wind is altering course now.' She was about to rebuke him for calling her 'lady' instead of 'Sister' when he continued: 'If you remain on deck, I suggest that you move to leeward out of the wind.' Noticing her perplexity, he indicated the side that would be opposite to the wind direction once he had brought the ship's head around: the wind had changed direction in a surprising fashion as they had cleared the headlands into the open sea.

'I will go below now to find my cabin, if that is all the same to you, Captain,' she replied.

He turned and bellowed so unexpectedly that she was startled for the moment.

'Wenbrit! Pass the word for Wenbrit!' He glanced back to her. 'I must leave you for the time being. The boy will take your dunnage below and show you to your cabin, lady . . .'

He turned away before she could ask him what 'dunnage' meant. She watched him hurry across to the men by the steering oar and then begin to roar: 'Hands to halyards, stand by to wear ship.'

The vessel was bucking and rolling with such a motion that Fidelma was forced to keep changing her balance to remain upright on the deck.

'Bit rough for you, eh, Sister?'

She found herself gazing into the urchin-like features of a young boy of about thirteen or fourteen. He stood legs wide apart, hands on hips, balancing effortlessly as the vessel skewed and rolled while the crew manoeuvred it into its new heading. He had bright, copper-coloured hair and a mass of freckles on his fair skin, and curious elfin eyes of sea green. His face was split by a broad grin and he carried himself with a self-conscious attitude of pride. Though he spoke the language of Éireann effortlessly, she could hear the strange accent which belied the country of his birth. He was a Briton.

'Not so rough,' she assured him, although having to clutch for the nearby rail to steady herself.

The boy screwed up his face in disbelief at her reply.

'Well,' he admitted, 'at least you are standing up to it better than some of your friends below. Sick as dogs, they are.' He wrinkled his nose in disgust. 'And who is it who has to clean out below decks?'

'I presume that you are called Wenbrit?' smiled Fidelma. In spite of the lurching of the vessel, she felt no queasiness. It was a matter of balance only.

'I am,' agreed the boy. 'I suppose you want to go below now?'

'Yes, I should like to see my cabin.'

'Follow me, then, Sister, and hang on tight,' he said as he picked up her bag. 'It is sometimes more dangerous below deck than above it during turbulent water. If I were Captain I would not allow my passengers below until they had a good taste of what it is to be like, at least. Once they found their sea legs, then they could go and hide in the darkness 'tween decks.'

The boy spoke scornfully as he led the way. He moved with sure-footed pride from the stern deck down the steep wooden steps to the main deck. It was as he turned to glance back at her that Fidelma caught a glimpse of a band of white around the boy's neck – the scar of something which had chafed against the flesh. She was momentarily intrigued at its cause. However, it was neither the time nor place to ask such a question. At the foot of the steps, he turned to watch her descent with a critical eye. Fidelma swung herself down and paused to meet the lad's reluctant nod of approval.

'One of your friends slipped and fell on those steps, and that was while we were riding at anchor,' he volunteered airily. 'Land-lubbers!'

'Was he or she hurt?' demanded Fidelma, aghast at the youth's callousness.

'Only their dignity was bruised, if you know what I mean,' he replied lightly. 'This way, Sister.'

He entered a doorway – Fidelma wished she could remember the correct nautical terms – and started down a narrow, dingy set of stairs into the cabin space below. Fidelma came to know that it was called a companionway. A single storm lantern swung and bounced on a chain in the passageway, giving a dim illumination to the darkness.

'You've been placed in a cabin with one of the other Sisters at the far end here.' The boy pointed. 'The other travellers occupy the cabins along here. When I am not on deck then I sleep in the big cabin through there.' He waved his hand for'ard. 'That's where we prepare food and eat. It's called the mess deck. I am always around, if anything is needed.' He threw out his chest in an attitude of pride. 'The captain . . . well, he likes the passengers to deal with me and, if there is anything of an urgent nature, I can pass it on to him. He doesn't like to have much to do with those who take passage on the ship . . .' The boy paused as if waiting for some response.

'Very well, Wenbrit,' Fidelma acknowledged solemnly. 'If there are any problems, I will consult you first.'

'There will be a meal at midday and the captain will attend in order to explain the running of the ship to you all. But he doesn't usually eat with the passengers. He makes an exception on the first day out to ensure everyone knows what's what. And, of course, don't expect hot meals on the voyage. Which reminds me, if you light candles below decks, make sure they are not left unattended. I've heard of ships flaring up like a tinder box.'

Fidelma did her best to hide her humour at the boy's studied self-confident air of a veteran sailor.

'There is a meal at midday, you say?'

'I will ring a bell which will summon the passengers to the meal.'

'Very well.' Fidelma made to turn to the cabin door indicated by the boy.

'Oh, one more thing . . .'

She turned back enquiringly towards him.

'I am required to tell you that these cabins are aft in the vessel. That's the stern. On the deck above is the captain's cabin and other quarters. For'ard lies in that direction. It is also called the bow of the ship. There is a privy at the stern here, through that door there. And there is one up in the bow. Anyone will tell you where it is, should the need arise. If there are any problems, if we need to abandon ship, there are two small boats lashed to the deck athwart ships – that is in the middle of the ship. That is where you should make for if we get in trouble. Don't worry, one of the crew will inform you of what you should do.'

The boy turned abruptly and hurried back on deck.

Fidelma stood, letting a smile spread across her features. It was clear that young Wenbrit did not have a high regard for 'landlubbers' as he called the passengers. She turned back towards the cabin door which he had indicated. As she did so, a door opened on the other side of the passage just behind her. She heard a sharp intake of breath and then a soft masculine voice said: 'Fidelma! What in God's name are *you* doing here?'

She swung round, trying to identify the voice from some long-past memory, a memory that she had almost managed to expunge.

A tall man stood there, irregularly illuminated by the light of the swinging lantern.

Fidelma took an involuntary step backward, reaching out a hand to grasp the wooden wall as if for balance. This was her first bout of dizziness since coming aboard *The Barnacle Goose*, and it had less to do with the sea's swell than with the welling of her emotions.

Chapter Three

'Cian!'

Like a wraith arising from some ghostly past, there stood before her the man who had been her first love; who had awakened her sensuality as a young girl and then brutally discarded her for another.

In one breathless moment, memories came pouring through her mind. Fidelma remembered their first meeting as vividly as if it had been yesterday. Yet it had been ten years ago now; ten long years . . .

Old Brehon Morann had allowed his students time off to attend the great triennial fair of Tara – the *Féis Teamhrach*. Had he not allowed them time off, then they would probably have attended anyway, for the great fair was a major event of the year. The fair had been founded by the High King Ollamh Fódhla some fourteen centuries ago. Its official purpose was to review the laws of the Five Kingdoms. The High King and the provincial Kings were in attendance, together with the most distinguished representatives of all the learned professions from the Five Kingdoms.

Even though it had been a hundred years since the High Kings had abandoned Tara as their principal royal residence, on account of a curse pronounced against it by the Blessed Ruadan of Lorrha in Muman, the great festival itself had not been so abandoned and was held there every third year. No one could devote themselves to study during the seven days of the fair. It started three days before the Feast of Samhain and ended on the third day afterwards.

While learned professors and lawyers, and the Kings and their advisers, discussed affairs of state and the application of the laws, and considered what, if any, new laws should be applied, sports, competitions and feasting were provided for the general public as well as the richer folk who came to see and be seen. Merchants arrived from not only the Five Kingdoms but from many corners of the world – as did entertainers, songsters, jugglers, fools and acrobats. It was a time for relaxing and making merry, for the ancient laws of the fair

21

proclaimed that a sacred armistice was in force during its existence, when all were exempted from arrest or prosecution unless they violated the peace of the fair itself by rowdiness, violence and theft.

Fidelma was barely eighteen years old and had never been to one of the great fairs like Tara. She and her companions from Morann's law school moved eagerly through the good-natured jostling crowds, gazing at the stalls selling all manner of food and drink and also goods from far-flung lands. They paused now and then to look in awe at groups of professional clowns and jugglers, while musicians and songsters created a not-unpleasing cacophony of sound.

Fidelma and her friends halted before one juggler who had nine sharp short swords in his hands which he flung up into the air, one by one, and which he did not let fall to the ground but caught and flung up again quickly and without injury to himself. The whistling sound the swords produced as they passed through the air was like the sound of buzzing bees.

A terrific cheering drew Fidelma and her companions on to the edge of a crowd around a sward of ground where a game of *immán* was in progress. Each player, armed with a wooden *camán*, or stick of ash over a metre in length, carefully shaped and smoothed with the lower end flat and curved, attempted to strike at a ball of leather filled with wool. The name of the game meant urging or driving while the stick took its name from the word *cam* reflecting on its crooked or curve part.

A goal had just been scored by one of the two teams, and as the young students pushed their way to the front of the crowd, the play had commenced again with the ball being thrown up into the middle of the field. The two teams, at opposite ends of the level grassy rectangle, began to run towards it, each trying to drive the ball through their opponents to the narrow goal formed by two poles.

Fidelma's group waited until another goal had been scored, then continued on their good-natured way. It was a happy, carefree day even though Fidelma, at the back of her mind, knew that their mentor, Brehon Morann, had hoped his students would not only indulge themselves at the fair but would also attend the great debates on the laws and thus expand their knowledge of their subject. Fidelma was about to remind her comrades of this when they found themselves pushing through the crowd to where a horse race was about to commence.

Cian had caught her eye immediately.

He was only a year or two older than she was. A young man of striking appearance; tall, chestnut-haired to the point that it was almost red. He was pleasantly featured, well-muscled, and his clothing spoke of some degree of rank. For the race, he was clad lightly in linen trousers and shirt, dyed with several colours, and wearing a short beaver fur-edged cloak of woven wool. He was astride a splendid stallion of magnificent physique which, like his rider, was chestnut in colour but with a white splash on its forehead.

Fidelma had not even noticed the other riders lined up with Cian. She stood staring up at him, strangely attracted by his youth and vitality. Some chemistry must have passed between them for his eyes flickered down, caught her gaze, held it for a second or two and then he smiled. It was a warm, open smile.

There came a yell of warning from the race director and a flag was raised. It fluttered above their heads for a brief moment and fell abruptly. Away thundered the horses to a roar of acclamation from the crowds.

'What a gorgeous man!' whispered Fidelma's companion, Grian. Grian was slightly older than Fidelma and her best friend at the school of the Brehon Morann. She was a capable student but had a frivolous side to her nature and placed enjoyment above serious study every time a choice had to be made.

Fidelma flushed in spite of herself.

'Who do you mean?' she said, trying to sound casual.

'The young man with whom you shared a smile just now,' Grian teased her.

'I don't know what you mean,' protested Fidelma, colouring even more.

Grian turned to a small elderly man, who had been shouting encouragement to one particular rider.

'Do you know who the riders are?' she asked.

The man ceased his exhortations and raised his eyes to her in astonishment.

'Now would I be placing a bet on the outcome of the race if I didn't?' he protested. 'Names of the riders, their horses, and their form are the first things I find out before even setting foot here.'

Grian smiled eagerly. 'Then perhaps you could tell us the name of that chestnut, with the white splash on its forehead, and who it is that rides her?'

'The young man with the red cloak?'

'That's the one.'

'Nothing easier. The chestnut is called Diss . . .'

Fidelma entered the conversation with a frown. 'Diss? But that means "feeble" or "weak"?'

The fellow tapped the side of his nose knowingly. 'That's because the horse is anything *but* feeble or weak.'

Fidelma was bewildered by this logic.

'Who is the rider then?' pressed Grian, not wishing to be sidetracked.

'The man who rides it, owns it,' replied the elderly man. 'He is named Cian.'

'A chief's son, by the look of him,' observed Grian slyly.

The man shook his head. 'Not that I know of. He is a warrior, though. He serves in the bodyguard of the High King.'

Grian turned back to Fidelma with a look of triumph.

The cheers were getting louder and louder and they could hear the thunder of hooves coming closer. The course had nearly been completed, being circular in shape, and the riders were approaching the winning post.

Fidelma leant forward to see the result.

There was the big chestnut just behind the leader, a white mare, its rider leaning close along its neck. The cheers rose up as Cian and his horse, Diss, began to gain but they were just beaten by the white mare and its rider.

Fidelma found herself propelled forward, as the crowd surged to greet the winner. Then she found Grian hanging onto her arm and realised that her companion was pushing her forward as well as the momentum of the crowd. However, Grian was propelling her not towards the winner but towards where Cian was dismounting from his stallion.

'What are you doing?' cried Fidelma in protest.

'You want to meet him, don't you?' replied her friend with self-confidence.

'Not I . . .' But before she could make a further objection she found herself arriving in the midst of a small crowd commiserating with the handsome young rider on being beaten by so fine a margin.

Cian was smiling good-naturedly and accepting their compliments. Catching sight of Fidelma and her companion he turned towards them with a broad smile. Her cheeks crimson, Fidelma dropped her eyes, feeling indignant that she had been manoeuvred into this embarrassing situation.

Cian hooked his reins over his arm and came forward.

'Did you enjoy the race, ladies?' he queried. Fidelma noticed immediately that he had an attractive tenor voice, full of resonance.

'A great race!' Grian spoke for them both. 'But my companion here was wondering why your horse was called Diss. That's why she insisted on coming to meet you,' she added with malicious humour.

The rider laughed tolerantly. 'He is called weak, but he is strong and anything but punny. It is a long story and perhaps you ladies will join me for refreshment after I have taken care of my stallion and have washed myself?'

'I am sorry, but—' Fidelma began, about to reject the suggestion, when her arm was jerked fiercely by her friend.

'We would love to,' Grian replied quickly with a smile which Fidelma found embarrassing.

'Excellent,' returned Cian. 'Meet me in fifteen minutes at that tent yonder, the one with the yellow silk banner flying from it.'

He turned away, leading his horse off with people clapping him on the back as he passed. He seemed very popular.

Fidelma wheeled on her friend with a scowl of annoyance.

'How could you?' she hissed irritably.

Grian stood unabashed.

'Because I know you. Of course you wanted to meet him! Don't deny it. Rather than tell me off, you should be pleased to have a friend like me.'

Deep down, Fidelma knew that Grian was right. She *had* wanted to meet the handsome warrior . . .

The memories of that meeting came and went in an instant of time, hardly more than the blink of an eye, but crystal clear in her mind.

Now, in the darkness of the lower passageway of *The Barnacle Goose*, Fidelma stared at the tall man, lit by the rocking lantern, and felt the conflict of emotions almost overwhelm her. She barely noticed that he was clad in the robes of a religieux. He stood in the cabin doorway, balancing himself with one hand against the doorframe, his handsome face etched in a mass of chasing shadows from the lantern.

She realised that he looked older, more mature, and yet his features had barely altered. The years, if anything, had given more character to his pleasant, handsome looks and – she hated to admit it – giving him a greater attraction.

'Fidelma!' His voice was eager. 'You here? I don't believe it!'

It would be so easy to respond to that glorious smile. She fought the temptation for a moment and finally managed to keep her features expressionless. She was relieved that she had her emotions under control.

'It is a surprise to see you here, Cian,' she replied in measured tone. Then she added: 'What are *you* doing on a pilgrim ship?'

It was as she asked the question that she suddenly realised he was clad in brown woollen homespun, with a bronze crucifix hanging from a leather thong around his neck.

Cian blinked at the cold, measured tone in her voice, starting back a little and then he forced a crooked smile. A bitter expression crossed his features, distorting their handsomeness.

'I am on a pilgrim ship simply because I am a pilgrim.'

Fidelma eyed him cynically. 'A warrior of the High King's bodyguard, a warrior of the Fianna, going on a pilgrimage? That does not seem creditable.'

She did not know whether it was the flickering light but his expression seemed strange.

'That is because I am a warrior no longer.'

Fidelma was puzzled in spite of her hostile reaction at seeing him again.

'Are you telling me that you have left the High King's militia to enter a religious Order? That I cannot believe. You were never comfortable with religion.'

'So you can foretell the course of my entire life? Am I not allowed to change my opinions?' There was an abrupt animosity in his voice. She was not perturbed by it. She had faced his temper many times in her youth.

'I know you too well, Cian. I garnered knowledge the hard way – or don't you remember? *I* remember. I could hardly forget.'

She made to turn into the cabin that Wenbrit had designated for her, when Cian took his hand from the doorframe, by which he had been balancing himself, and made to reach out to her. The ship was tugged a little by the waves, causing him to stumble forward. He caught his balance using his hand again.

'We must talk, Fidelma,' he said urgently. 'There should not be enmity between us now.'

Her attention was caught for a moment by the curious note of desperation in his voice. She hesitated, but only for an instant.

'There will be plenty of time to talk later, Cian. It will be a long voyage . . . perhaps, now, it may be *too* long,' she added with acid in her tone.

She entered the cabin, shutting the door quickly behind her before he could reply. For a moment or two she stood with her back against the door, breathing heavily and wondering why she had broken out into a cold sweat. She would not have suspected that meeting Cian again after all these years would make her feel such a resurgence of the emotions which she had spent many months suppressing after he had deserted her.

She did not deny that she had become infatuated with Cian after that first meeting at the Festival of Tara. No; if she were really honest now, she would admit that she had fallen in love with him. In spite of his arrogance, his vanity, and pride in his martial prowess, she had fallen in love for the first time in her life. He stood for everything that Fidelma disliked but there was no accounting for the chemistry which they shared. They were opposites in character and, inevitably, like magnets, the unlike had attracted. It was surely a recipe for disaster.

Cian was a youth in pursuit of conquests while Fidelma was a young woman bound up in the concept of romantic love. Within a few weeks he had made her life a turmoil of conflicting emotions. Even Grian recognised that Cian's pursuit of Fidelma was merely a superficial one. Her friend was young, attractive and, above all, an *intelligent* woman – and Cian wanted to boast about the conquest. He would not care once the conquest had been made. And Fidelma, intelligent or no, refused to believe that her lover had so base a motive. Her refusal was the cause of many arguments with Grian.

Suddenly, there was a heartrending groan from the gloom of the cabin, causing Fidelma to stiffen and return abruptly to the present, forgetting her tumbling anguished memories. For a second she struggled to recall where she was. She had entered the cabin which Wenbrit had indicated to her; the cabin she was to share. She had entered and stood in the darkness.

The groan was agonised as if someone was in deep pain.

'What's wrong?' Fidelma whispered, trying to focus in the direction of the sound.

There was a fraction of a moment's silence and then a voice cried peevishly: 'I am dying!'

Fidelma glanced swiftly round. It was almost pitch black in the cabin.

'Is there no light in here?'

'Who needs light when one is dying?' retorted the other. 'Who are you, anyway? This is *my* cabin.'

Fidelma re-opened the door to let in some light from the passageway. Just inside the door, she saw a candle stub, which she took to the flickering lantern outside. Thankfully, Cian had disappeared. It took a few moments to light the candle from the lantern and return.

Now Fidelma could see a woman lying on the bottom of the two bunks in the tiny cabin. Her habit appeared dishevelled, her face was deathly pale, though still fairly attractive. She was young, perhaps in her early twenties. By the side of the bunk stood a bucket.

'Are you seasick?' She spoke sympathetically, fully aware that she was asking the obvious.

'I am dying,' insisted the woman. 'I wish to die alone. I did not know it would be as bad as this.'

Fidelma glanced round quickly. She saw that her baggage had been placed on the second bunk.

'I can't let you do that, Sister. I am sharing your cabin for this voyage. My name's Fidelma of Cashel,' she added brightly.

'You are mistaken. You are not one of my company. I have allotted cabins to each and—'

'The captain has put me in here,' Fidelma explained quickly, 'and now let me help you.'

There was a pause. The young, pale-faced Sister groaned loudly.

'Then put that light out. I cannot stand a flickering light. After that, go away and tell the captain that I want to be left alone to die in the dark. I *demand* that you go away!'

Fidelma groaned inwardly. It was all she needed, to be closeted with a moaning hypochondriac.

'I am sure that you would feel better if you were up on deck rather than in this confined space,' she replied. 'What's your name, by the way?'

'Muirgel.' The other's voice was no more than a moan. 'Sister Muirgel from Moville.'

Fidelma had heard of the Abbey founded by St Finnian a century ago on the shores of Loch Cúan in Ulaidh.

'Well, Sister Muirgel, let me see what I can do for you,' Fidelma said determinedly.

'Just let me die in peace, Sister,' whimpered the other. 'Can't you find some other cabin to be cheerful in?'

'You need air, fresh sea air,' Fidelma admonished. 'The darkness and stuffiness of this cabin will only increase your illness.'

The creature on the bunk retched pitifully and did not reply.

'I have heard that if you concentrate your gaze on the horizon then the motion sickness will eventually depart,' volunteered Fidelma.

Sister Muirgel tried to raise her head.

'Just leave me alone, please,' she moaned yet again and added spitefully, 'Go and bother someone else.'

Chapter Four

Fidelma had to admit defeat. It was no use trying to conduct a sensible conversation with the young woman in that condition. She wondered if there was another cabin available. Anywhere would be better than being stuck with someone tormented by largely imaginary fears. Fidelma was sympathetic to anyone who was ill, but not with someone who had the ability to help themselves and chose not to. She decided to find the cabin boy, Wenbrit, and explain the problem.

As she left the cabin, she was surprised to meet Wenbrit himself coming down the stairs. He greeted her with a smile and she noticed that his manner towards her had undergone a slight change. It was less familiar . . . less impudent than before.

'Your pardon, lady.' Fidelma guessed immediately the cause for his changed attitude, and she hid her annoyance that Murchad had revealed her identity. 'I made a mistake,' he said politely. 'You are to have a different cabin as you are not one of the pilgrims from Ulaidh.'

Fidelma knew straight away that it was a lie. Murchad had decided this only *after* he knew who she was. She did not want any special privileges. However, the indisposition of Sister Muirgel and the stifling atmosphere made the thought of a private cabin appear very attractive. It was coincidental that she was being offered the very thing that she was going to seek.

'The Sister with whom I was going to share is rather ill,' Fidelma conceded. 'Perhaps it would be nice to have a cabin to oneself.'

Wenbrit was grinning.

'Seasickness, eh? Well, I suppose the best of people fall prey to it. Yet she looked well enough when she came on board. I would not have thought that she would be the one to fall ill.'

'I tried to tell her that lying down in an enclosed space without light or ventilation was not going to cure her,' Fidelma explained, 'but she would not take advice from me.'

'Nor me, lady. But sickness takes people different ways.' Wenbrit aired his philosophy seriously as if it were born of many years' experience. Then he grinned. 'Wait here, I'll get your dunnage.'

29

'My what?' It was the second time she had heard the unfamiliar word.

Wenbrit assumed the expression of one who is teaching a very backward person.

'Your baggage, lady. Now that you are on shipboard you'll have to get use to sailor's jargon.'

'I see. Dunnage. Very well.'

Wenbrit went to knock on the door of the cabin which Fidelma had just left, and disappeared inside for a few moments, emerging with her bag.

'Come on, lady, I will show you to your cabin.'

He turned and started back up the companionway to the main deck.

'Is the cabin not on this deck?' asked Fidelma as they went up.

'There is a for'ard deck cabin available. It even has a natural light in it. Murchad thought that it would be more fitting for . . .' The boy stopped himself.

'And what has Murchad been saying?' she demanded, knowing full well the answer.

The boy looked uncomfortable.

'I was not supposed to let you know.'

'Murchad has a big mouth.'

'The captain only wants you to be comfortable, lady,' Wenbrit replied, a trifle indignantly.

Fidelma reached out a hand and laid it on the boy's arm. She spoke with firmness.

'I told your captain that I did not want special privileges. I am just another religieuse on this voyage. I would not want others to be treated unfairly. To start with, stop calling me "lady". I am Sister Fidelma.'

The boy said nothing, only blinked a little at her rebuke. Then Fidelma felt guilty for her cold attitude.

'It's not your fault, Wenbrit. I asked Murchad not to tell anyone. Since you know, will you keep my secret?'

The boy nodded.

'Murchad only wanted you to be comfortable on his ship,' he repeated and added defensively: 'It's not his fault, either.'

'You like your captain, don't you?' Fidelma smiled at the protective tone in the boy's voice.

'He is a good captain,' Wenbrit replied shortly. 'This way, lady . . . *Sister*.'

The boy led her across the main deck, beyond the tall oak mast with its single great leather sail, still cracking in the wind. She glanced up and saw that a design had been painted on the front of the sail: it was that of a great red cross, the centre of which was enclosed in a circle.

The boy saw her looking upwards.

'The captain decided to have that painted,' he explained proudly. 'We carry so many pilgrims these days that he thought it would be most appropriate.'

The boy moved off again and Fidelma followed as he led the way to the high prow of the ship across which the long-angled mast cleaved upwards towards the sky, bearing on a cross yard, the steering sail. It was a smaller sail than the mainsail and this helped control the direction of the vessel. The bow of the ship rose so that, as at the stern, it presented an area where there were a number of cabins on the main deck level. Like the stern deck area there were some steps leading up to a deck on top of them. Two square openings covered by grilles looked out on the main deck on either side of an entry which led to the cabins beyond.

Wenbrit opened this door and went in. Fidelma followed and found herself in a small passageway beyond with three doors, one to the right, one left and one straight ahead. The boy opened the door to the right of the entrance, the starboard side of the ship – Fidelma registered the term.

'Here we are, lady,' he announced cheerfully as he opened it and stood back to allow her to go inside.

The cabin was still gloomy, compared with the brightness on deck, but not as gloomy as the stifling cabins below decks. There was a grilled window covered with a linen curtain for privacy which could be drawn aside to allowed more light within. The cabin was furnished with a single bunk and a table and chair. It was frugal but functional and, at least, there was fresh air. Fidelma looked around with approval. It was better than she had been expecting.

'Who usually sleeps here?' she asked.

The boy deposited her bag on the bunk and shrugged.

'We sometimes take special passengers,' he said, as if brushing the subject aside.

'Who sleeps in the cabin across the corridor?'

'On the port side? That's Gurvan's cabin,' replied the boy. 'He is the mate and a Breton.' He pointed towards the bow where she had noticed a third door. 'The privy is in there. We call it the head, because it is at the head of the ship. There is a bucket in there.'

'Does everyone use it?' Fidelma asked, wrinkling her nose a little in distaste and mentally calculating the number of people on the ship.

31

Wenbrit grinned as he realised why she was asking the question.

'We try to restrict the use of this one. I have mentioned that there is another privy at the stern of the ship so you should not be bothered much.'

'What is the position with regard to washing?'

'Washing?' The boy frowned as if it were something he had not considered.

'Does no one wash on board this ship?' she pressed. Fidelma was used, as with most people of her background, to having a full bath in the evening and a brief wash in the morning.

The boy grinned slyly.

'I can always bring a bucket of seawater for a morning wash. But if you are talking of bathing . . . why, when we are in harbour, or if we get a calm sea, we can take a swim over the side. There are no baths aboard *The Barnacle Goose*, lady.'

Fidelma accepted this resignedly. From her previous voyages by sea she had suspected that washing would not be a priority on shipboard.

'Can I tell the captain that you are satisfied with the cabin, lady?'

Fidelma realised that the boy was anxious. She gave him a reassuring smile.

'I will see the captain at midday.'

'But the cabin?' pressed the boy.

'It is very satisfactory, Wenbrit. But do try to call me Sister in front of the others.'

Wenbrit raised his hand to place his knuckles at his forehead in a form of salute and grinned. He turned and scurried off about his duties.

Fidelma shut the cabin door and looked around. So this was to be her home for the next week, provided that they had a fair wind. It was no more than seven feet in length and five feet in width. The table, now that she was able to examine it more closely, was a hinged piece of wood attached to one wall. A three-legged stool stood in one corner. A bucket filled with water stood in another. She presumed that this was for drinking or washing. She tasted the water on her finger. It was freshwater, not seawater – for drinking, she decided. The window, which was at chest-level and which looked onto the main deck, was eighteen inches broad by a foot high, with two struts across it. A lantern hung on a metal hook in one corner; a tinder box and a stump of candle were visible on a small shelf beneath it.

The cabin was well-equipped.

She had a moment of guilt, thinking of her fellow religieux crammed in their airless, lightless cabins below decks. However, the moment passed into thankfulness that she would, at least, be able to breathe fresh air on the voyage and not have to put up with someone else sharing her living-quarters.

She turned to her bag and took out her spare clothes for she saw that there were a number of pegs on which they could be hung. Fidelma did not, like some women, carry treatments for her skin – red berry juice, for instance, to stain her lips – but she did have a *ciorbholg* – a comb bag containing her combs and mirrors. Fidelma usually carried two ornamented bone combs, not through personal vanity but because it was the custom among her people to keep one's hair in good condition and untangled. A fine head of hair was much admired.

Although Fidelma, like most women of her class, kept her finger-nails carefully cut and rounded, for it was considered shameful to have ragged nails, she did not go so far as those who put crimson dye on them. Nor did she use, as some did, the juice of black or blue berries to darken her eyebrows or paint her eyelids. Nor did she heighten the natural colours of her cheeks by using dye extracted from the sprigs and berries of the elder tree to make an artificial blush. She was careful about her personal toiletry without disguising her natural features.

She unpacked her *ciorbholg* and set it on the table. The most bulky part of her baggage was, in fact, two *taigh liubhair*, small satchel books. When the Irish religieux had begun their *peregrinatio pro Christo* during the previous centuries, the learned scribes of Ireland had realised that missionaries and pilgrims would need to take liturgical works and religious tracts to help them spread the word of the new Faith among the pagans, and that such books had to be small enough to carried by them. Fidelma had brought with her a Missal, measuring fourteen by eleven millimetres. Her brother, King Colgú, had given her a second volume of the same size to while away the time on her long journey. It was *A Life of St Ailbe*, the first Christian Bishop of Cashel and patron saint of Muman. She carefully hung these book satchels on the pegs with her clothes.

Then she stood back, surveyed her unpacking, and smiled. There was nothing more to do before the midday meal. She could lie back on the bunk, head resting upon her clasped hands and, for the first time since she had closed Sister Muirgel's door on his pleading features, allow herself a moment to think about the extraordinary coincidence of meeting Cian again.

However, as she stretched out gratefully, there was a high-pitched squeal and something heavy and warm landed on Fidelma's stomach.

She let out a shriek and something black and furry, emitting another strange cry, leapt from her stomach onto the ground.

Shaken, Fidelma sat up. A thin black cat was sitting regarding her with bright green eyes, its sleek fur coat glistening in the rays of the sun which shone through the window. The animal uttered a low 'miaow' as it gazed inquisitively upon her and then calmly proceeded to lick its paw before rhythmically drawing it over its ear and eye.

There was a scrabbling sound outside the cabin door, which opened to reveal Wenbrit, breathless and worried.

'I heard your scream, lady,' he panted. 'What is it?'

Fidelma was chagrined; she pointed at the source of her discomfiture.

'The creature took me unawares. I didn't realise that you had a cat on board.'

Wenbrit relaxed; he smiled broadly.

'That's the ship's cat, lady. On a vessel like this, a cat is needed to keep down the rats and mice.'

Fidelma shivered slightly at the thought of rats.

Wenbrit reassured her. 'Don't worry. They never venture up near people but get below in the bilge or sometimes in the stores. Mouse Lord here keeps them controlled.'

The cat had now jumped back up onto Fidelma's bunk, curled itself into a snug bundle and seemed to be fast asleep.

'She seems at home here,' Fidelma observed.

The boy nodded.

'It's a male cat, lady,' he corrected. 'Yes, Mouse Lord likes to sleep in this cabin. I should have warned you about him. Don't worry, I'll remove him for you.'

He started forward but Fidelma laid a restraining hand on his arm.

'Leave him alone, Wenbrit. He can also occupy the cabin. I don't mind cats. I was just startled when it . . . when *he* jumped on me.'

The boy shrugged.

'You have only to let me know, if he is being a nuisance.'

'What name do you call him?'

'Luchtighern – Mouse Lord.'

Fidelma grinned as she regarded her new travelling companion.

'That was the name of the cat who dwelt in the Cave of Dunmore and defeated all the warriors of the King of Laigin who were sent against him. Only when a female warrior came to fight him did he succumb.'

The boy regarded her in puzzlement.

'I have never heard of such a cat.'

'It's just an ancient story. Who named him Luchtighern?'

'The captain. He knows all the stories although I can't remember him telling me that one.'

'I suppose had it been a she-cat he would have called her Baircne, ship-heroine, after the first cat to arrive in Éireann in the barque of Bresal Bec.' Fidelma mused.

'But it's a male cat,' protested the boy.

'I know,' she assured him. 'Well, we will not disturb Mouse Lord any further.'

After Wenbrit left, Fidelma returned to her bunk and lay carefully back with the cat curled up snugly at her feet. Its warm, purring presence was curiously comforting. She closed her eyes for a moment, and tried to gather her scattered thoughts. What had she been thinking of before the cat arrived? Ah yes – Cian. Her mouth hardened. How could she have been such a fool? Her youth and lack of experience were her only excuses.

She had imagined that Cian had gone out of her life for ever when she was eighteen years old, leaving only painful memories. Now, here he was again, and she was going to have to endure him in the restricted confines of this ship for at least a week. She felt an anxiety about her emotions. Why have this violent reaction if she had recovered from the experience of her youth – if it had not been haunting her ever since her days at Tara? Perhaps it was the fact that she had never dealt properly with the experience, that caused her to feel such anger when she saw him again.

Cian! How could she have been so naive? How *could* she have let him dupe her and tear her soul apart?

She had forgiven him for his behaviour several times, even rejecting the advice of her best friend Grian, who told her to forget Cian and turn him away. But she had not turned him away and each time he erred she was torn apart by unhappiness. As a result, her work as a student suffered until she was called before the aging Brehon Morann.

She could recall the scene vividly, feel those same emotions which had gripped her as she stood before her old mentor.

Brehon Morann gazed at Fidelma with stern but sympathetic eyes.

'You have done yourself little credit this day, Fidelma,' he had begun ominously. 'It seems that you have lost your ability to concentrate on the simplest lessons.'

Fidelma's jaw came up defensively.

'Wait!' The Brehon Morann raised a frail hand as if he anticipated the justifications which rose to her lips. 'Is it not said that the person unable to dance blames the unevenness of the floor?'

Fidelma coloured hotly.

'I know the reason why you have not concentrated on your studies,' the old man went on in a firm, calm tone. 'I am not here to condemn you. I will, however, tell you the truth.'

'What is the truth?' she demanded, still irritated, though she realised that the irritation lay more with herself than anyone else.

Brehon Morann regarded her with unblinking grey eyes.

'The truth is that you must discover what is the truth, and that discovery must be made soon. Otherwise you will not succeed in your studies.'

Fidelma's lips thinned as she pressed them close together for a moment.

'Are you saying that you will fail me?' she demanded. 'That you will fail my work?'

'No. You will fail yourself.'

Fidelma let out a low, angry breath. She stared at the Brehon Morann for a moment before turning to leave.

'Wait!'

She was halted by Brehon Morann's quiet yet commanding voice. Unwillingly, she turned back to him. He had not moved.

'Let me tell you this, Fidelma of Cashel. Once in a while it transpires that an old teacher, such as myself, encounters a student whose ability, whose mental agility, is so outstanding that it seems their life, as a teacher, is suddenly justified. The daily chore of trying to impress knowledge into a thousand reluctant minds is more than compensated for by finding one single mind so eager and able to absorb and understand knowledge – and by using that knowledge to make a contribution to the betterment of mankind. All the years of frustration are suddenly rewarded. I do not say this lightly, when I say that I thought that the choice I had made to become a teacher was going to be justified in *you*.'

Fidelma stood gazing in surprise at the old man. He had never talked this way to her before. For a moment she felt defensive again: her quick mind had reasoned that the old man wanted to extract a payment for his compliment.

'Didn't you once say that to use others as a fulfilment of one's own ambition is a reflection on the weakness of one's own character and abilities?' she demanded hurtfully.

The Brehon Morann did not even blink at her sharp retort. His eyes merely hooded a fraction as he registered her riposte.

'Fidelma of Cashel,' he intoned softly, 'you have such promise and ability. Do not make yourself an enemy to your promise. Recognise your talent and do not squander it.'

Fidelma did not know how she should react to the old Brehon's words, for they were totally out of character. He had never pleaded with any of his pupils before to her knowledge, and now she felt his tone was pleading; pleading with her.

'I must live my own life,' she replied defiantly.

The old man's face became stony and he dismissed her with an abrupt wave of his hand.

'Then go away and live it. Do not come back to my classes until you are willing to learn from them. Until you discover peace within yourself, it is pointless returning.'

Fidelma felt a surge of anger and unable to trust herself, she swung from the room.

Three months passed before she went to see the Brehon Morann again. Three long bitter months full of heartache and loneliness.

Chapter Five

Fidelma started awake, wondering what had disturbed her. It was a bell jangling, high-pitched and querulous. For a moment she wondered where she was. Then, with the movement of the ship below her, she remembered. She had fallen asleep thinking about Cian. No wonder she felt that she had been having some distasteful nightmare! Her mind had been drifting over the unhappy events of her relationship with him; they were still sharp in her memory even though it was nearly a decade ago.

The bell continued its insistent clamour: it must be Wenbrit's summons to the midday meal. Fidelma rose hastily from the bunk. The cat was nowhere in sight. She hurriedly ran a comb through her hair and straightened her clothes.

She left her cabin and made her way along the main deck. The motion of the ship was not unpleasant; the sea appeared fairly calm. She glanced up. Above her, the sun was at its zenith, casting short shadows. There seemed no wind. The sail was hanging limply, billowing only now and again as a faint gust caught it. Yet the ship was moving, albeit slowly, across a flat blue sea. A few sailors, lounging cross-legged on the deck, nodded pleasantly as Fidelma passed and one called a greeting in her own language.

She clambered down the companionway at the stern of the ship, remembering young Wenbrit's directions to what he called the main mess deck. She followed the dim light of the lanterns and the smells of the confined space.

There were half-a-dozen people seated at a long table in the broad cabin which stretched from one side of the ship to another. The table was placed behind the main mast for she could see it, like a tree, cutting through the decks. Murchad was standing at the head of the table, balanced with his legs wide apart. Behind him, young Wenbrit was bent over a side table, cutting bread.

Murchad smiled as she entered and waved her forward, indicating a seat on his right. The seating consisted of two long benches on either side of the long pinewood table. Those already present glanced up at the newcomer in curiosity.

Fidelma moved to her seat and found that she was placed opposite Cian. She hastily turned to her enquiring companions with a brief smile of greeting. Cian rose with a proprietorial smile to introduce her.

'As you do not know anyone here, Fidelma,' he began, ignoring the protocol for it should have been Murchad's place to perform the introductions. He had reckoned without Murchad's strong personality however.

'If you please, Brother Cian,' the captain interrupted irritably. 'Sister Fidelma of Cashel, allow me to introduce you to your fellow travellers. These are Sisters Ainder, Crella and Gormán.' He indicated three religieuses swiftly in turn sitting opposite to her and next to Cian. 'This is Brother Cian, while next to you are Brothers Adamrae, Dathal and Tola.'

Fidelma inclined her head to them, acknowledging them all in one gesture. Their names and faces would come to mean something later. At the moment, the introduction was just a formality. Cian had reseated himself with an expression of annoyance on his face.

One of the women seated directly next to Cian, a religieuse who looked extremely young to be on a pilgrimage, smiled sweetly at her.

'It seems that you already know Brother Cian?'

It was Cian who answered her hurriedly.

'I knew Fidelma many years ago in Tara.'

Fidelma felt their gazes of curiosity on her and she turned towards Murchad to hide her embarrassment.

'I see that this pilgrims' party is only eight in all. I thought there were more?' Then she remembered. 'Ah, there is a Sister Muirgel, isn't there? Is she still confined to her cabin?'

Murchad smiled grimly but it was the elderly, sharp-featured religieuse seated at the end of the table who answered her question.

'I fear Sister Muirgel as well as two others, Brother Guss and Brother Bairne, are still indisposed, being overcome with the fatigues of the voyage, and are unable to join us for the time being. Do you know Sister Muirgel as well?'

Fidelma shook her head. 'I met her when I came aboard although it was not in the best circumstances. I noticed that she was unwell,' she added by way of explanation.

A pale, elderly monk with dirty grey hair sniffed audibly in disapproval.

'Say that they are seasick and have done with it, Sister Ainder.

People should not come on voyages if they have no stomach for it.'

The third religieuse whose name Fidelma had registered as being Sister Crella, a small, young woman with broad features that somehow marred the attractiveness that she would otherwise have possessed, looked disapproving. She appeared to be of a nervous disposition for she kept glancing quickly around as if she expected someone to appear. It was she who made a sound of reproach with her tongue and shook her head.

'A little charity, please, Brother Tola. It is a terrible thing, this sickness of being at sea.'

'There is a sailor's cure for seasickness,' intervened Murchad with grim humour, 'but I would not recommend it. The best way to avoid sickness is to stay on deck and focus your eyes on the horizon. Breathe plenty of fresh sea air. The worst thing you can do in the circumstances is to remain below, confined to your cabin. I would advise you to pass that on to your fellow travellers.'

Fidelma felt a satisfaction that her earlier prescription for sickness had been an accurate one.

'Captain!' It was the sharp-faced Sister Ainder again. 'Must we stir up images of the sick and dead when we are about to eat? Perhaps Brother Cian will say the *gratias* and then we may proceed with our meal.'

Fidelma raised her eyes expectantly. The idea of Cian as a religieux, leading the *gratias*, was something that she had never imagined.

The former warrior flushed, seemingly aware of her inquisitive gaze, and turned to the elderly, austere Brother.

'Let Brother Tola proclaim the *gratias*,' he muttered stiffly, raising his eyes to challenge Fidelma. 'I have little to be thankful for,' he added in a soft whisper meant for her ears only. She did not bother to respond. Murchad, hearing the remark, raised his bushy brows but said nothing.

Brother Tola clasped his hands before him and intoned in a loud baritone: *'Benedictus sit Deus in Donis Suis.'*

They responded automatically: *'Et sanctus in omnis operibus Suis.'*

While the meal was being eaten, Murchad began to explain, as he had previously done to Fidelma, his estimation of the length of their voyage.

'It is to be hoped that we will be graced with fair weather to the port at which you will disembark. The port is not far from the Holy Shrine to which you are bound. It is a journey of just a few miles inland.'

There was a murmur of excitement among the pilgrims. One of the two young Brothers, whom Fidelma had seen up on the main deck earlier, a youth she learnt was called Brother Dathal, leant forward, his face as animated as it had been when he had been speaking to his companion on deck.

'Is the shrine near to the spot where Bregon built his great tower?'

Clearly Brother Dathal was a student of the ancient legends of the Gael because, according to the old bards, the ancestors of the people of Éireann had once lived in Iberia and many centuries ago had spied the country from a great tower, built by their leader Bregon. It was the nephew of Bregon, Golamh, known also as Míke Easpain, who had led his people in the great invasion which secured for them the Five Kingdoms.

Murchad smiled broadly. He had heard the question many times before from other pilgrims.

'So legend has it,' he replied in good humour. 'However, I must warn you that you will find no sign of such a massive construction, apart from a great Roman lighthouse which is called the Tower of Hercules, not of Bregon. Bregon's Tower must have been a very, very high tower indeed, for a man to be able to see the coast of Éireann from Iberia.' He paused but no one seemed to appreciate his humour. His voice became serious. 'Now, since we have a moment together, I need to say a few things to all of you which you must pass on to your fellows who have not been able to join us in this first meal. There are rules which you must observe while on this ship.'

He hesitated before proceeding.

'I have told you that our voyage will take the best part of a week. During that time you may use the main deck as much as you like. Try not to get in the way of my crew while they perform their duties, for your lives depend on the efficient running of this ship and sailing these waters is not an easy task.'

'I have heard stories of great sea monsters.'

It was the youthful Sister Gormán. Fidelma examined her with surreptitious interest, for she felt it would be best to start becoming acquainted with her fellow passengers, to the extent that they would be confined together in the ship for several days. Gormán was, indeed, young; no more than eighteen. She spoke in a nervous, breathless tone, giving the impression of a naive child. In fact, Fidelma had the image of an eager young puppy wishing to please its master. She had one odd feature, in that her eyes seemed never still, but flickering as if in a state of permanent anxiety. Fidelma found herself wondering if she had ever been that young. Eighteen. It suddenly reminded her that she had been eighteen when she had met Cian. She dismissed the thought immediately.

'Shall we be seeing sea monsters?' the girl was asking. 'Will we be in any danger?'

Murchad laughed, but not unkindly.

'There is no danger from sea monsters where we voyage,' he assured her. 'You may observe sea creatures which you have not encountered before, but they pose no threat. Our main danger lies only in inclement weather. Now, if we do encounter storms, it is best, unless I instruct you otherwise, to remain below and make sure that all lamps and candles are extinguished . . .'

'But how can we see down here in the dark without lamps?' wailed Sister Crella.

'All lamps and candles must be extinguished,' insisted Murchad with an emphasis which was his only acknowledgment of her question. 'We do not want to contend with fire on shipboard as well as a storm. Lamps must be extinguished and everything battened down.'

'I do not understand.' The ascetic Brother Tola appeared confused at the term.

'Anything movable, liable to cause damage in the shifting of the vessel, should be securely tied or fastened,' explained the captain patiently. 'In such circumstances, young Wenbrit will be on hand to advise you and ensure that there is nothing you lack.'

'How likely is it that we will encounter a storm?' asked the tall, elderly religieuse, Sister Ainder.

'A fifty-fifty chance,' admitted Murchad. 'But don't worry. I have never lost a pilgrim ship yet, nor even a single pilgrim in a storm.'

There were polite but rather strained smiles among those gathered at the table. Murchad was obviously a good judge of character, for Fidelma noticed that some of her companions were in need of further reassurance and Murchad shared that insight.

'I will be honest with you,' he confided. 'This month is one of frequent storms and rain which can last for many weeks. But why have I chosen to set sail on this particular day? Is it by chance that I insisted we take this morning's tide? Does anyone know the reason?'

The party gazed at one another and there was some shaking of heads.

'Being religious people, you all ought to know what this day is,' the captain chided them good-naturedly. He waited for an anser. They looked bewildered. Fidelma thought she should answer for them.

'Are you talking about the feast day of the Blessed Luke, Beloved Luke the Physician?'

Murchad glanced approvingly at her knowledge.

'Exactly so. The feast day of Luke. Have none of you heard of "St Luke's Little Summer"?'

There was a bewildered shaking of heads.

'We sailors have noticed that there is usually a fine period in the middle of this month which occurs on the feast day of St Luke – a dry period with lots of sunshine. That's why, if we are going to sail during this month, we usually choose to sail at that time.'

'Can you guarantee this fine weather for the voyage?' demanded Sister Ainder.

'I am afraid that nothing can be guaranteed once you set sail on the sea, no matter the time nor the place, whether at high summer or midwinter. I am merely saying that out of the several voyages that I have made at this time of year, only one has failed to be pleasant and calm.'

Murchad paused and, as there were no comments, he continued.

'There is, of course, one other matter that I am sure you have all been told about before you booked passage. The seas are dangerous these days and the waters in which we will be journeying are not excluded from such danger. I no longer refer to risk from the elements – from the tides, winds and storms. I refer to the risk from our fellow men – from pirates and sea-raiders, who attack and rob ships, seize their occupants and sell them into slavery.'

A hush descended on the company.

Fidelma, who had travelled to Rome, knew some of the dangers of which Murchad spoke. She had heard many stories of raiders who sailed against the western ports of Italy from the Balearic Islands, and of the spread of the Corsairs from the Arabian world through the Mediterranean – the great middle sea of the world.

'If we are attacked, what defence shall we have?' asked Cian quietly.

Murchad smiled thinly. 'We are not a warship, Brother Cian. Our defence will lie in our seamanship and the luck of the de—' He suddenly recalled that he was addressing a group of religieux. 'And the protection of the hand of God.'

'What if luck and seamanship are not enough?' queried Brother Tola. 'Are your crew armed and ready to fight in our defence?'

Cian's features broke into a scornful expression.

'What, Brother Tola? Are you asking others to die in your defence while you stand quietly by?' It was clear that Cian had no time for his fellow religieux.

'And are you suggesting that I take up the sword instead of the cross?' Brother Tola leant forward, turning red around his neck.

'Why not?' replied Cian calmly. Fidelma had heard that cold sneering tone before and she shivered slightly. 'Peter did in the Garden of Gethsemane.'

'I am a religieux, not a warrior,' protested Brother Tola.

'Then perhaps you should be content to be defended by the crucifix,' taunted Cian. 'You should not demand that warriors defend you.'

Murchad glanced at Fidelma and she detected a smile of amusement on his features. Then the captain was holding up his hands like a priest bestowing a blessing on the company.

'My friends,' Murchad said pacifyingly. 'There is no need for discord among you. I have no wish to alarm you, but it is my duty to set out the possibilities so that none of you is surprised by any eventuality. If we are so unlucky as to encounter sea raiders, perhaps you will pray so that a power greater than the sword may aid us. After all, that is what you teach, is it not? These raiders tend to keep close to the main ports along the coasts. Our course should take us well away from such dangerous areas . . .'

'Except?' It was Cian who prompted Murchad.

'We will put ashore at an island called Ushant, which lies off the west coast of the land that used to be called Armorica – that which is now known as "Little Britain". It is in those waters that raiders could lie in wait. They could also be found in the approaches to the coast of Iberia. Those might well be the areas where we stand in danger of attack. But I doubt it. The odds make it very unlikely.'

'Have you ever been attacked by pirates, Murchad?' asked Fidelma quietly, for the captain seemed so sure of himself.

He nodded solemnly.

'Twice,' he affirmed. 'Twice in all the years that I have sailed these waters.'

'Yet you seem to have survived,' she pointed out for the benefit of her new companions.

'Indeed.' Murchad shot her a look of gratitude for emphasising the point. 'Two encounters in all the voyages that I have made, and that number is not an inconsiderable one, will show you that such encounters are possible but not probable. We are more likely to encounter storms than pirates. But, if we do have such an encounter, it is my duty as captain to warn you that you must stay clear of my men and allow them to do their work so that we may be able to escape.'

'Perhaps you will tell us what happened during the two times you were attacked?' Brother Tola scowled at Cian while he addressed the captain. 'It could not have been so bad, otherwise, as the Sister,' he inclined his head towards Fidelma, 'points out, you would not be here now.'

Murchad chuckled appreciatively.

'Well, once I outsailed the raider.'

'And the second time?' prompted Sister Crella nervously.

The corners of the captain's mouth turned down in a humorous grimace. 'He caught me.'

There was a bemused silence before Murchad, realising that his passengers did not share his humour, decided to explain.

'Finding an empty ship, without goods and without passengers, for I was on a journey from one port to another to pick up my cargo, the pirate decided to allow me to continue on my way. It was not worth his time to destroy my ship when I might pick up a rich cargo for him later. He told me that he would see me again when I had something to give him. So far, I have not seen him again.'

There was a contemplative silence in the cabin.

'What if there had been pilgrims aboard?' asked Sister Gormán fearfully.

Murchad did not bother to reply. Finally Sister Ainder said: 'God be praised it was not a question that had to be answered.'

There came the sound of a cry from on deck. It made them all start nervously.

'Ah.' Murchad rose abruptly. 'Have no fear. It is only a warning that the wind is changing. You will forgive me – I must return to my duties. If you have any questions about the running of this ship and the rules which you must obey, ask them of young Wenbrit here. The lad has spent most of his life on shipboard and he is my right hand in the care of passengers.'

He clapped the boy on the shoulder and young Wenbrit ventured a slightly self-conscious smile as the captain left to go on deck.

Fidelma, to avoid the inevitable conversation with Cian until she had time to think about matters, turned to the young religieux seated next to her.

'And are you all come from the same abbey?' she opened conversationally.

The one introduced as Brother Dathal, a slim, fair-haired youth, swallowed his cupful of wine before replying.

'Brother Adamrae,' he gestured to his equally young companion, 'and I are from the Abbey of Bangor. But most of our companions are from the Abbey of Moville, which lies not far from Bangor.'

'They are both in the Kingdom of Ulaidh, I believe,' Fidelma observed.

'That is so. In the sub-kingdom of the Dál Fiatach,' replied Brother Adamrae, who had red hair and was covered in freckles. His cold blue eyes sparkled like water on a hot summer's day. He was as quiet as his companion was effervescent in spirit.

'What attracts you to the Holy Shrine of St James?' she continued, fully aware that Cian was awaiting an opportunity to engage her in conversation.

'We are *scriptores*,' explained Brother Adamrae in his mournful voice.

Brother Dathal, who in contrast spoke in a high-pitched, rather squeaky tone, added, 'We are compiling a history of our people in ancient times. That is why we go to Iberia.'

Fidelma was listening distractedly. 'I am not sure that I understand the connection,' she said politely. At that moment she was concentrating on how she was going to deal with Cian and was not giving the matter of what Dathal was saying much thought.

Brother Dathal leaned towards her and waggled his knife before her in mock admonition.

'Surely, Sister Fidelma, you must be aware of the origin of our people?'

Fidelma brought her gaze abruptly back to him and thought hard, suddenly realising what he meant.

'Oh yes – you were talking about Bregon's Tower to the captain. Are you interested in the old legend about the origin of our people?'

'Old legend?' snapped Dathal's ruddy-faced companion. 'It is history!' He raised his mournful voice and intoned:

'Eight sons had Golamh of the Shouts,
Who was also called Míle of Spain . . .'

Fidelma interrupted before he could continue.

'I do know the story, Brother Adamrae. It does not tell me *why* you go to the Holy Shrine of St James. Surely that has nothing to do with Golamh and the origin of the Children of the Gael?'

Brother Dathal was indulgent yet still enthusiastic.

'We go because we are seeking knowledge. It might well be that our ancestors left ancient books in this land called Iberia where the children of Bregon, son of Bratha, grew and prospered and resolved to extend their sway beyond the seas. That is why Bregon built his tower from where he spied Ireland, and it was then that Ith, son of

Bregon, equipped a ship and manned it with thrice fifty warriors; they then put out to sea, sailing north until they reached the shores of the land which became our beloved Éireann.'

'These young men,' interrupted Brother Tola, with disapproval in his dry voice, 'are not interested in the Faith and the Holy Shrine, but go to learn mundane history.'

There was no mistaking the criticism in the elderly man's voice.

'Do you object to your companions' quest?' Fidelma asked.

Brother Tola toyed with the food that was still on his plate.

'I would have thought that much was obvious. Brothers Dathal and Adamrae have no right pretending to go on a religious pilgrimage merely in order to indulge their interest in secular matters.'

Brother Dathal's face whitened and his voice rose considerably.

'Nothing is more sacred than the pursuit of knowledge, Brother Tola.'

'Nothing, except God and His saints,' snapped Brother Tola, suddenly rising from the table. 'Ever since we left Bangor, I have heard only of your precious search for historical truth. I am sick of it. We are here on a pilgrimage to the Holy Shrine of a great saint; one who knew and walked with Christ. That is more important than human vanity.'

'What of Ith, the son of Bregon, who fell in battle in Ireland?' retorted the mournful Brother Adamrae. 'What of Golamh and his sons who were our forefathers? Isn't that of great importance? Without them, you would not even exist to go on your pilgrimage.'

'For one who bears the name of the first man created by God, you care little for your religion,' berated Tola.

Brother Adamrae sat back and began to chuckle. Brother Tola looked shocked at what he mistook for profanity. Even Fidelma hid a smile behind a raised hand. She was surprised by Tola's lack of knowledge.

Brother Dathal was not so diplomatic.

'Your ignorance proves the need for what you describe as our human vanity,' he told Brother Tola bluntly. 'The name Adamrae has nothing to do with the Biblical name of Adam. It is an ancient name of our people, meaning "wonderful". See how much you lack in knowledge if you concentrate on one subject?'

Brother Tola turned with an expression of disgust and left the table.

Sister Ainder who, Fidelma judged from her severity of countenance, was the female counterpart of Brother Tola, made a disapproving noise with her tongue.

'One should not be disrespectful to Brother Tola. He is a man of great learning and piety.'

'Learning?' sneered Brother Dathal.

'He is learned in scripture and philosophy,' replied Sister Ainder.

'He is not learned in our field and he was disrespectful to us,' replied Brother Adamrae defensively. 'We do not disguise our purpose in this voyage. It is our mission to bring back knowledge to our Abbey, already famed for its scholarship. Brother Tola seems to be against scholarship.'

'He is not against that scholarship which we should all be keen to advance – *religious* scholarship,' replied Sister Ainder.

Brother Adamrae was disparaging not only of Brother Tola but his defender, Sister Ainder.

'The pursuit of religious knowledge does not mean that all other arts and sciences have to be ignored. I swear, since this pilgrimage began, there has been nothing but strife in our party. If not from the intolerance of Brother Tola then from the lust of—'

'Enough!'

Sister Crella's voice cut the air like a whip. There was an uncomfortable silence.

'Enough, Brother Adamrae.' Her voice assumed a more gentle tone of rebuke. 'You would not wish our southern companion to think that we northerners are always quarrelling among ourselves, would you?' She turned to Fidelma with a smile. 'I noticed that our captain introduced you as Fidelma of Cashel. Are you from the Abbey there?'

Fidelma thought it better to be noncommittal. In fact, she could make such a claim, and did so.

'But you knew Brother Cian in Tara?' This question came from the young girl, Gormán.

'I was acquainted with him many years ago,' Fidelma replied distantly. She felt their eyes on her but she bent to her meal. She had no desire to get too close to her companion and certainly did not want to be ensnared into whatever friction existed between the various members of the party. There would be enough problems in dealing with Cian.

Brother Dathal broke the awkward silence by quoting from some epic poet:

> 'The leaders of those oversea ships,
> In which the sons of Míle of Spain came to Éireann,
> I shall remember all my life–
> Their names and their individual fates.'

He punctuated the verse with a loud sniff and rose from the table. He was followed a moment later by his dour red-haired companion.

'I hope you will forgive the sharpness of their tempers this morning, Sister . . . Sister Fidelma, is it?' Fidelma realised that Sister Ainder had turned a patronising smile on her. There was no warmth or feeling in it. 'Scholars are notoriously possessed of short tempers, especially when they speak of their own disciplines, which they do loudly and frequently. We have not really had much peace since we set out from Bangor.'

Fidelma inclined her head in acknowledgement.

'I am afraid that it was my question which sparked off their argument.'

Across the table, the broad-faced young Sister Crella grimaced in disagreement.

'If it was not your question, Sister Fidelma, then the clash of temperaments would have been made for some other reason. It is true that Brother Tola has been criticising Dathal and Adamrae ever since we set out.'

Sister Ainder sprang at once to Tola's defence.

'There is no cause to lay the blame on Brother Tola. He is a spiritual man and concerned that this is a pilgrimage in search of spiritual truth.'

'Brother Tola should not have joined this party if he wanted to go in search of some esoteric ideal,' Crella retorted.

If one could flounce on the gently rocking deck of the cabin, Sister Ainder contrived to flounce out. Sister Gormán, the youngest of the party, also rose, mumbled something indistinct and left the table.

Wenbrit, smiling brightly, began clearing up. He seemed to enjoy the conflict between the adult religieux at the table.

Sister Crella picked at her meal in silence for a while, then she raised her eyes to Fidelma.

'I can hear old Ainder saying that the young have no respect these days,' she smirked.

Fidelma did not know whether the comment was a general one or addressed to her. She decided that she should make some reply.

'My mentor, the Brehon Morann, was wont to say that the young always regard their elders as senile. So it is now, but so it was in all our youthful ages.'

'Respect is something that one has to earn, Sister, and not demand because one has survived a few years.'

Wenbrit, standing behind Sister Crella, contrived to wink at Fidelma as he bent to gather the plate.

Chapter Six

Fidelma rose quietly from the table and began to move towards the companionway.

'If you are going on deck, Fidelma, I will join you,' Cian called after her, rising to follow.

'I am going to my cabin,' Fidelma replied shortly, making it clear that she had no wish to speak with him. She knew that it was a silly attitude to take, for sooner or later she would have to confront the situation.

'Then I will walk with you,' Cian responded, unabashed by her obvious rebuke.

Fidelma moved on hurriedly to the companionway and climbed up to the main deck. Cian caught up with her and laid a hand on her arm. She automatically snatched it away, glancing round to ensure that they were unobserved.

Cian let out a low, derisive chuckle.

'You cannot escape me for ever, Fidelma,' he said in the cynical tone she remembered so well.

Fidelma met his eyes a moment and then dropped her gaze. She was still unsure of herself.

'Escape?' she countered defensively. 'I have no idea what you are talking about.'

'Perhaps you are still nursing a resentment at the way our affair ended?'

Fidelma knew that a high colour had come to her cheeks. His mocking barb stung deeply.

'I put the matter out of my mind years ago,' she lied.

Cian's grin of cynicism broadened.

'I can tell by your reactions that you did not. I see hatred in your eyes. There can be no hatred without love. It is the same meal. Anyway, we were young then. Youth makes a lot of mistakes.'

Fidelma now raised her head to meet his gaze, astonished by his calm assurance. She found her anger welling.

'Are you attributing your callous behaviour simply to your youth?' she demanded.

Cian was almost patronising. 'There, now,' he countered. 'And I thought that you had put the matter out of your mind.'

'So I had, but you apparently have a wish to raise it,' she replied. 'If that is so, then do not expect me to agree with any justification which you wish to put forward for your behaviour. I didn't accept it then, I won't accept it now.'

Cian raised an eyebrow. 'Justification? Do I need justification?'

Fidelma felt a hot surge of anger well in her again, along with an overwhelming desire to hit his smiling face as hard as she could. She fought against the impulse. It would have gained her nothing.

'So, you feel that you do not need to justify your behaviour?'

'One doesn't need justification for the follies of one's youth.'

'A youthful folly?' There was a dangerous glint in Fidelma's eyes. 'Is that how you saw our relationship?'

'Not our relationship. Merely the way it ended. What else? Come on, Fidelma; we are adults now and wiser. Let the past be the past. Let us not be enemies. There is no need. We do not want enmity between us on this journey.'

'There is no enmity between us. There is nothing between us,' replied Fidelma coldly.

'Come.' Cian was almost cajoling. 'We can be friends again as we were at first in Tara.'

'Never as we were at Tara!' she shuddered. 'I have no wish to talk with you. You were arrogant and insufferable in your youth, and it seems that you have not altered as you have aged in years.'

She turned swiftly on her heel and walked rapidly away towards her cabin before he had a chance to respond.

Arrogant and insufferable. Yet the words seemed mild compared to the rage that she had felt, the humiliation, the mortification she had suffered during those lonely days waiting for him as she sat in the room she had hired in the small tavern near Tara after she had been expelled from the college of the Brehon Morann. She had moved out of the college hostel after her talk with Brehon Morann. Only Grian knew the truth of the matter, for Fidelma did not even let her family know what had happened. She became a recluse within her tiny room and, apart from Grian, she isolated herself from her family and friends.

Cian came and went as he pleased. Sometimes she did not see him for several days, even as long as a week or more. Other times he appeared and stayed a day or two. One afternoon, they were lying together in her room when Fidelma raised the question of marriage. She had sacrificed her studies for Cian, and knew that the situation into which she had been precipitated could not continue.

She had turned to Cian, as they lay together, and demanded: 'Will you love me for ever?'

Cian smiled down at her. Always that same, slightly cynical smile.

'For ever is a long time. Let us live while we live.'

But Fidelma was serious. 'You really believe that we should think only of the present? That is no way to plan a life of fulfilment and contentment.'

'We exist only in the present.'

It was the first time she had ever heard Cian express something approaching a philosophy of life. She disagreed adamantly.

'We may exist in the present but we have a responsibility to the future. I have completed three years of study and was about to achieve the degree of *Sruth do Aill* this year, which meant that I would be qualified to be a teacher, possibly a minor teacher at my cousin's College of Durrow. Perhaps I could find another college where I could finish that degree. We could get married then.'

Cian rolled over on his side, away from her, and reached out to find the goblet of wine. He took a long draught from it and sighed softly.

'Fidelma, you are always dreaming. Your head is always in your books. For what purpose? You are too intellectual.' He made it sound like a dirty word. 'Get rid of your books. You do not need them.'

'Get rid of . . . ?' She was astonished and words left her.

'Books are not for the likes of you and me. They destroy happiness, they destroy life.'

'You can't mean that,' protested Fidelma.

Cian shrugged indifferently. 'It's what I think. They give false dreams to people, make them have visions of a future which cannot be, or a past that never was. Anyway, soon I shall be returning to Tir Eoghain with my company of warriors, in the service of Cellach the High King. I will not have time to think of such matters as marriage, far less the ability to settle down. I thought you understood that from the outset. I am not a person who can be possessed or tied down.'

Fidelma sat up abruptly in the bed, feeling cold inside.

'I do not want to possess you, Cian. My intention was to go into the future with you. I thought . . . I thought we shared something.'

Cian laughed in amusement.

'Of course we share something. Let us enjoy that which we do share. As for the rest – have you not heard the couplet? Wedlock, Padlock.'

'How can you be so cruel?' She was aghast.

'Is it cruel to be realistic?' he demanded.

'I swear, Cian, I do not know where I stand with you.'

He smiled mockingly.

'Surely, I cannot make it plainer?'

She did not believe his cruelty. She did not believe the words he had spoken. She did not want to believe. It was merely an act he put on, she told herself – an immature act. He *did* love her. They *would* be together. She knew that. She was still possessed of a youthful vanity which refused to admit that her feelings were not based on sound judgement. So their meetings continued as and when Cian felt inclined that they should.

Fidelma found herself leaning on the rail of the ship on the small bow deck, gazing out onto the limitless expanse of the ocean before them. She was not aware of how she came to be there, so immersed in her memories had she been.

She was startled by a hand falling on her shoulder.

'Muirgel?' It was a low, masculine voice.

She turned enquiringly.

A young religieux stood there. He was in his mid-twenties, she estimated quickly. The wind caught at his wispy brown hair. He had a flushed, boyish-looking face, freckled, with dark brown eyes. His eyes widened with consternation as she turned.

'I thought you . . . sorry,' he mumbled awkwardly. 'I was looking for Sister Muirgel. You had your back turned and I thought – well . . .'

Fidelma decided to put the young monk out of his embarrassment.

'It is of no matter, Brother. The last I saw of Sister Muirgel was below. I believe she has seasickness and is indisposed. My name is Fidelma. I have not seen you before, have I?'

The young man jerked his head in an awkward, formal bow.

'I am Brother Bairne of Moville. I am sorry to have disturbed your thoughts, Sister.'

'Perhaps they needed disturbing,' murmured Fidelma.

'What?' Brother Bairne was taken off-guard.

'It is of no significance,' she replied. 'I was just musing. Are you well now?'

A frown crossed his brow. 'Well?' he echoed.

'I understood that you did not join us for the midday meal because you also had a sickness.'

'Oh – oh, yes. I was feeling queasy but I am better now, though I do not think I am recovered enough to eat anything as yet.' He grimaced ruefully.

'Well, you are not alone in that.'

'Is Sister Muirgel still in her cabin?'

'I presume so.'

'Thank you, Sister.' And Brother Bairne scurried along the deck towards the stern, terminating the exchange in a manner bordering on rudeness.

Fidelma gazed after him and gave a mental shrug. She had hoped that her first impressions of her fellow pilgrims would prove wrong. At the moment she felt that she had more in common with Murchad and his crew than with her travelling companions. Had she been able to look into the future and learn that Cian was to be aboard, she would never have set foot on *The Barnacle Goose*.

Fidelma suppressed a shiver; the wind was growing chilly. It had increased its force to that of a strong breeze, cracking the sails like the sound of a stockwhip. She was forced to push her flailing hair from her eyes.

'Breezy, eh?'

She turned towards the young speaker. Wenbrit was passing with a leather bucket in his hand and he greeted her with a grin.

'There is quite a wind getting up,' she replied.

The cabin boy came over to her side.

'I think we are in for a real blow soon,' he confided. 'It will sort out the sailors among the pilgrims.'

'How do you know that we are in for bad weather?' asked Fidelma, hazarding a guess that the term 'blow' meant there was a storm brewing.

Wenbrit merely inclined his head towards the mainsail and, following his glance, she noticed the power of the wind which was filling and cracking it. The boy then touched her lightly on the arm and pointed towards the north-west. Fidelma turned and saw what he was indicating. Across the darkening waters there were black banks of cloud moving rapidly towards them. As she examined them, so it seemed, the clouds were tumbling over each other in a mad rush to be first to reach the ship.

'A storm? Is it dangerous?'

Wenbrit pursed his lips indifferently.

'All storms are dangerous,' he shrugged, as if the darkening sky was of little matter to him.

'What can we do?' Fidelma was awed by the menacing spectacle advancing down upon them. The boy looked at her for a moment and then seemed to relent; he became reassuring.

'Murchad will run before it as it is blowing in the direction we wish to go. However, for comfort's sake you had best go to your cabin, lady. I suppose that I'd better go below to warn the others to keep to their cabins. The wind will have risen to a gale within the hour, I'm thinking. Make sure that you have stowed away anything which is loose and could tumble around the cabin and hurt you.'

In spite of herself, in spite of having journeyed several times by sea, Fidelma felt a quickening of her heart and an increase in the rapidity of her breathing as she went below to her cabin.

It was almost exactly as Wenbrit predicted. The wind continued to rise and the sea's surface turned into a foam. The ship began to rock and heave as if it were an object caught in the maw of some gigantic dog which shook and worried it. Fidelma had, as Wenbrit instructed, made sure that everything was secured in her cabin. Then she sat and waited for the oncoming tempest. Even with Wenbrit's warning, she was unprepared for the violence with which it struck the ship. At one point, she heaved herself across the cabin to the window to look nervously through it onto the main deck. But outside was almost dark, the daylight eclipsed by the black rainclouds.

Above the sound of the howling winds, she heard a knock and her cabin door opened. She swung round, still clinging to the support of the windowframe, to see Wenbrit balancing himself within the doorframe. He looked around, noticed everything was put away and gave her an approving smile.

'I am just checking that all is well with you, lady,' he explained. He seemed very calm in the face of the onslaught of nature. 'Is everything all right with you?'

'As right as it can be,' Fidelma replied, turning and finding herself almost running back to her bunk, precipitated by the incline of the deck.

'The storm is here,' Wenbrit announced unnecessarily. 'It's stronger than the captain anticipated and he is trying to lie head to wind now but there is a heavy sea running. We shall be in for a rough time so please remain here. It is dangerous to move about unless you are used to storms at sea. I'll bring some food later. I don't think anyone will be sitting down for a meal.'

56

'Thank you, Wenbrit. You are very considerate. I have a feeling we will dispense with food while this storm lasts.'

The boy hesitated in her cabin door. 'If there is anything you need, just pass the word for me.'

Fidelma interpreted this quaint phrase as meaning that she should send for him. She shook her head.

'It's all right. If I need anything, I'll just come and find you.'

'*No.*' The boy was vehement. 'Remain in your cabin during the storm. Pass the word to a seaman and do not venture out on deck. Even we seamen wear lifelines on deck during a blow like this.'

'I will remember,' she assured him.

The boy raised his knuckles to his forehead in that curious seaman's salute and disappeared.

She realised how cold and dark it had become yet it was only early evening. There was nothing to do but to sit on her bunk and wrap a blanket over her shoulders. It was too dark even to attempt to read. She wished she had someone to talk to. She found the ship's cat curled up on her bunk and took comfort from his warm black furry body. She reached out a hand and stroked his head. He raised it, blinked sleepily and gazed at her, letting out a soft rumbling purr.

'I guess you are used to this sort of weather, eh, Mouse Lord?' she said.

The cat lowered his head, yawned hugely and returned to his sleep.

'You are not much of a conversationalist,' Fidelma reproached him. And then she lay down with the cat beside her, trying to shut out the sounds of the agonised wailing of the wind through the rigging and sails and the heaving of the sea. She absently scratched the cat behind the ear and his purr intensified. Out of nowhere, the old proverb suddenly came into her mind: Cats, like men, are flatterers.

She was thinking of Cian again.

When Fidelma came awake on her bunk, the wind was still whining and roaring and the ship continued to be tossed this way and that. The cat remained warm and comfortable at her side. If only she had trusted her friend Grian; listened to her warnings about Cian's shallow nature. For years she had been bitter and resentful. Then, out of nowhere, the thought occurred to her that this resentment and bitterness was not, as she had previously thought, directed at Cian. It was directed at herself. Fidelma had been angry with herself, had blamed herself for her stupidity and her silly vanity.

Now she could hear the wind rising, moaning through the rigging and launching itself against the sails. A distant voice was shouting faintly somewhere. She could feel the ship rise as it climbed each wave and then fall as it slid into the heaving waters beneath.

She swung off the bunk leaving Mouse Lord still curled up in a ball, fast asleep, and apparently oblivious to the tempest. By gripping whatever hand-holds she could find, Fidelma manoeuvred herself to the window. Drawing back the sodden linen curtain, she peered out onto the deck. A fine sea spray immediately hit her in the face. She blinked and raised one hand to wipe her eyes, stumbling a little as the deck pitched beneath her. It was dark outside. Evening had passed into night. She looked upwards but there was no sign of moon nor stars. They must be covered by clouds, low and rainladen.

The wind was now a whine through the shrouds and beyond the wooden rail she could just see, by their whiteness, the tops of the waves, being whipped into a froth of white lather by the angry buffets of air. She realised that the bow, where her cabin was situated, must be rising high into the waves as cascades of water pounded on the deck above her.

Dark shadows were heaving on ropes around the main mast. Fidelma was astonished as she watched the silhouettes of men braving the uncontrollable winds, the bucking of the ship and the torrential waters, to lower the big mainsail. A heavy sea suddenly heaved the vessel over almost on its side. Fidelma was flung without warning against one of the walls of the cabin, but she held on and grabbed at the rim of the window, regaining her balance. Another flood of water smashed over the decks and for a moment Fidelma thought the sailors had been washed overboard but, as the spray cleared, she could see them re-emerge from the deluge still hanging onto their ropes.

Once again she had to grasp at the grating of the window to maintain her balance when the ship lurched. She felt an almost overwhelming sense of helplessness. She wanted to run out on deck, help the men or simply do something. She felt so inadequate against the forces of nature of which she knew nothing. However, she realised that there was nothing she could do. The sailors were trained and knew the ways of the sea. She did not. All she could do was return to her bunk and hope the ship would ride out the storm.

As she drew the linen curtain across again and began to haul her way back to her bunk, the cry came clearly: 'All hands! *All hands!*'

It was a fearful call. Panic seized her and she turned for her cabin door and heaved it open.

A dark shadow was outside, as if coming from the opposite cabin.

She did not recognise it but an accented voice shouted at her, raised to carry above the noise of the storm.

'Get back, lady. You are safer in your cabin.'

Reluctantly, she closed the door and returned to her bunk, sprawling rather than sitting on it. The storm continued. She did not know how long she lay in that half-reclining position on the bed. In a curious way, the fury of the storm became soporific. With nothing to do but to think, the constant jerking, the crash of the seas, the whine of the wind all combined, after a while, into a single sound and gradually Fidelma found herself hypnotised by it. Her languorous thoughts wandered back to Cian. And while she was thinking of Cian, sleep sneaked up on her without her even knowing.

Chapter Seven

Fidelma was up, washed and dressed and just putting the final touches to her hair when there was a knock on the cabin door.

It was the Breton mate, Gurvan.

'I beg your pardon, lady.' With an inward sigh, Fidelma noted the form of address. Doubtless it was all around the ship that her brother was King of Muman. Gurvan did not notice her irritated expression and continued, 'I was checking that you were recovered from the storm and that there were no problems?'

'Thank you, I am fine,' Fidelma acknowledged. Then she hesitated. She vaguely remembered being disturbed just about dawn when the storm had died away. She had the impression that someone had opened the door of her cabin, looked in and then closed it. She had been too tired to open her eyes and had fallen back to sleep immediately. 'Did you attempt to call me earlier?'

'Not I, lady,' the mate assured her. 'The others will be breaking their fast shortly if you would join them.' He made to go, then turned back. 'I hope that I was not lacking manners when I ordered you back into your cabin during the storm.'

So it had been Gurvan outside her door when she had a momentary panicky desire to go on deck.

'Not at all. I should not have attempted to go out on deck but I was worried.'

Gurvan smiled shyly and touched a hand to his forehead.

'The breakfast will be served in a moment, lady,' he repeated.

Fidelma realised that she had probably overslept a little.

'Very well. I am coming now.'

The mate withdrew. She heard him go into the cabin opposite and close the door.

When she left her cabin, she was amazed at the sight that met her eyes. It was as if they had entered a cloud, for a thick white mist enveloped *The Barnacle Goose*. Fidelma could barely see the top of the mast, let alone the stern of the vessel. She had encountered such conditions before, often high up in the mountains when such mists

61

came down suddenly. It was always best to halt and wait for them to disperse, unless one knew the safest mountain route by which to descend.

There was a strange, echoing silence, with the soft breath of the sea lapping all around the ship. The mist swirled and eddied like smoke from a fire. It was not being dispelled, however, and Fidelma found that strange. She felt an uncontrollable urge to attempt to blow the mist away, so easily did it move as she waved her hand at it.

Gurvan suddenly re-emerged from his cabin.

'It's a sea mist,' he explained unnecessarily. 'It rolled up on us in the wake of the storm. I think it is something to do with the warmth of the seas in this area and the coldness of the storm. There is nothing to be afraid of.'

'I'm not afraid,' Fidelma assured him. 'I've seen such mists before. It was just unexpected after the storm last night.'

'The sun will chase it away as soon as it climbs higher and warms the skies.'

He turned to speak with a couple of sailors, who were hardly discernible in the shroudlike atmosphere. Sitting cross-legged on the deck, they were apparently engaged in sewing some pieces of canvas.

Fidelma made her way along the misty deck towards the stern of the ship. She was surprised, after the stormy weather of the previous night, to feel the soft air on her cheek which caused the mainsail to flap languidly, a birdlike fluttering in that echoing silence. The ship was steady, indicating that under the blanket of mist, the sea was flat and calm. She could see no sign of storm damage amidst the shadows. Everything appeared shipshape.

Barely able to see a few feet in front of her, and walking too rapidly, Fidelma bumped into a figure shrouded in a robe with the hood over his or her head. The figure grunted as Fidelma collided with it.

'I am so sorry, Sister,' Fidelma apologised, realising that it was one of the religieuses. There was something familiar about her.

But to her surprise, the figure kept her face turned away, muttered something indistinguishable and hurried off to be absorbed into the mist. Fidelma gaped at this lack of courtesy, and wondered who it was who would not exchange a civil greeting.

Then Captain Murchad himself materialised in front of her. He was descending the wooden steps from the stern deck to the main deck. Recognising her, the captain raised his hand in greeting.

'A curious morning, lady,' he said as he joined her. She could see that he was looking irritated. 'Have you ever seen the like of this before?'

'Up in the mountains occasionally,' she nodded.

'So you would,' agreed Murchad. 'Yet it should clear away soon. The sun should rise and its warmth ought to dispel the mist.' He was making no move to continue on below decks. 'How did you fare during the blow?' he asked suddenly.

'Blow?' Then Fidelma remembered that this was the sailors' term for the storm. 'I eventually fell asleep but more from exhaustion than anything.'

Murchad let out a long sigh.

'It was a bad blow. The storm has driven me a half-day or more off my course. We've been pushed south-east – far more easterly than I was intending.' He seemed preoccupied and far from happy.

'Is that a problem?' Fidelma queried. 'Surely no one is worried about an extra day or so on this voyage.'

'It's not that . . .' He hesitated.

Fidelma was bewildered by his hesitancy and his seeming reluctance to join the others below.

'What's wrong then, Murchad?' she pressed.

'I am afraid . . . we have lost a passenger.'

Fidelma stared at him in incomprehension. 'Lost a passenger? You mean one of the pilgrims? How, lost?'

'Overboard,' he elaborated laconically.

Fidelma was shocked.

After a pause, Murchad added: 'You did the right thing by remaining in your cabin during the blow, lady. Passengers have no right to be on deck when such a sea is running. I will have to lay down a rule that this is so. I have never lost anyone overboard before.'

'Who was it?' Fidelma asked breathlessly. 'How did it happen?'

Murchad raised his shoulders and let them fall in an eloquent shrug, disclaiming knowledge.

'How? That I don't know. No one saw anything.'

'Then how do you know that they were lost overboard?'

'Brother Cian suggested it.'

Fidelma drew her brows together.

'What does *he* have to do with it?'

'He came to see me just after dawn. Apparently he feels that he should be in charge of all the pilgrims on board this ship – be their spokesman.'

Fidelma sniffed disparagingly.

'You may rest assured that he has no authority to speak for *me*,' she said tightly.

Murchad did not take any notice. He went on, 'After the storm, he took it upon himself to go round and see if everyone was all right. He even went to your cabin.'

'He did not check on me.'

'Begging your pardon, lady,' Murchad contradicted. 'He said he looked into your cabin but saw that you were still asleep.'

So that was what had awoken her! The soft sound of a door shutting. She felt anger and a sense of violation that Cian, of all people, had entered her cabin and looked on her while she slept.

'Go on, then.' She decided that she would make very sure that, in future, Cian did not have such easy access to her cabin again.

'Well, he found that one of the party was nowhere to be seen. Their cabin was deserted. When he came to me and told me his fears, I ordered Gurvan to conduct a thorough search of the ship. He found nothing. I have how sent him to double-check.'

So that explained Gurvan's curious visit to her cabin a few moments ago. As if thinking of him had caused him to be drawn to them, Gurvan came swinging along the deck.

Murchad gazed anxiously at him. The first mate shook his head at the captain's unasked question.

'Stem to stern, skipper. No sign.' Gurvan was not a man who believed in wasting words.

Murchad turned back to Fidelma with a mournful look.

'That was our last chance. I had hoped that she might have become so scared of the storm that she had found some hole on board ship to hide in.'

Fidelma felt somewhat deflated. It was not an auspicious beginning to the pilgrimage. The first night out from Ardmore and a pilgrim lost overboard.

'Who was it?' she asked. 'Who is the missing person?'

'It is Sister Muirgel. We'd better get below, for the others are breaking their fast. I'd best give them this sad news of their companion. I do not want to lose any more passengers on this voyage.'

He dismissed Gurvan to look after the running of the ship while he went below. Fidelma was feeling shocked as she followed him down the companionway.

Yesterday, Sister Muirgel could barely raise her head from her bunk; she had been so sick and ill. The idea that, in the middle of such a terrifying storm, the pale-faced young woman had been able to leave her cabin, climb up on deck unnoticed and then get swept overboard was startling in the extreme.

In the mess-deck cabin, young Wenbrit was serving a meal of bread, cold meats and fruit to the pilgrims who had gathered there. Fidelma immediately noticed that Brother Bairne had now joined the company. There was a muttered greeting, not hearty in the circumstances, as Fidelma took her seat and Murchad went to the head of the table. Everyone had obviously been told about the missing Sister Muirgel. Cian was the first to ask the news from Murchad. The captain addressed the entire assembly.

'I am afraid that I have some very bad news for you,' the captain began. 'I can confirm that Sister Muirgel is no longer on board. A thorough search has been made of the vessel. No other explanation remains except that she was washed overboard in the night during the storm.'

There was a grim silence among those at the table. Then one of the religieuses, Fidelma thought it was the broad-faced Sister Crella, made a sound like a suppressed sob.

'I have never lost a passenger before,' Murchad continued, in a heavy tone. 'I do not intend to lose another. Therefore, I am forced to tell you again that you must remain in your cabins, or below decks, should any further bad weather strike. Then you will only come on deck at my specific orders. In calm weather, of course, you may come on deck but only when one of my men is there to keep a watchful eye on you.'

The red-haired Brother Adamrae was frowning.

'We are adults, Captain, not children,' he protested. 'We paid for our passage, we did not expect to be confined as if we were . . . criminals.' He had paused a moment to search out a suitable word.

Cian was nodding in agreement.

'Brother Adamrae does have a point, Captain.'

'You are not trained sailors,' Murchad countered brusquely. 'The deck of a ship can be treacherous in bad weather unless you know what you are doing.'

Cian flushed with annoyance.

'Not all of us have spent our lives closeted within abbey walls. I was a warrior and—'

The grim-faced Brother Tola raised his voice in interruption to add to the debate.

'Because a silly woman who, by all accounts, was too sick to know what she was doing, went on deck when she should not and was lost overboard, surely there is no need to make us all suffer?'

There was an angry exclamation from Sister Crella. She sprang up, leaning across the table.

'Apologise for those words, Brother Tola! Muirgel was the daughter of nobility before whom, if you did not wear that brown homespun robe, you would have to fall on your knees as they walked by you. Muirgel was my cousin and my friend. How *dare* you insult her?' Her voice had risen hysterically.

Sister Ainder, tall and commanding, rose and, without any apparent effort, drew Crella from the table and led her away to the cabins, making strange noises like a mother comforting her child.

Brother Tola sat looking uncomfortable at the reaction he had provoked.

'What I meant to say was that we paid our passage money, as Brother Adamrae has said. What if we refuse to obey this order?'

'Then the captain has the right to imprison you.' Fidelma spoke quietly and yet her voice penetrated the muttering which greeted Tola's words so that a deathly hush fell as everyone turned towards her.

Brother Tola was frowning at her, clearly disapproving of what he considered to be her impertinence.

'Oh – and by what right?' he demanded. 'And how do you know?'

Fidelma glanced at Murchad as if ignoring his questions.

'Do you own this vessel, Murchad?'

The captain replied with a curt nod, although he seemed puzzled by her question.

'And where is your home port?'

'Ardmore.'

'The ship, then, is to all intent and purposes, subject to the laws of Éireann.'

'I suppose so,' agreed Murchad reluctantly, not understanding what she was getting at.

'Then that is the answer to Brother Tola's question,' she explained, not bothering to turn to him.

Brother Tola was not appeased.

'It is not.'

Only now did Fidelma look towards him and without humour.

'Yes, it is. The *Muirbretha*, the sea-laws, apply in this matter.'

Brother Tola looked astonished, and then his features formed in a patronising smile.

'And what would *you* know of such laws?'

Fidelma sighed and started to open her mouth but Cian cut in.

'Because she is a *dálaigh*, an advocate of the courts. Because she is holder of the degree of *anruth*.' There was a scathing tone to his voice.

Everyone knew that the level of *anruth* was only one degree below the highest qualification that the ecclesiastic and secular colleges could bestow.

In the moment of silence which followed Cian's announcement, Sister Ainder returned to the cabin.

'Crella is resting,' she announced, unaware of the new tension. 'We must remember that she was Sister Muirgel's close friend and relative. Her death has been a great shock to her. It does not need thoughtless remarks to be made in such circumstances, Brother Tola.'

Brother Tola scowled and turned to Cian.

'What were you saying about this woman?'

'Fidelma of Cashel is an advocate of the law courts; one with a reputation that has extended to Tara and the court of the High King.'

'Is that true?' demanded Tola, not convinced.

'That is true,' confirmed Murchad, intervening. 'She is also the sister of the King of Muman.'

There was a crimson splash on Tola's cheeks and he lowered his head to hide his confusion by examining the table before him.

Fidelma would have preferred that her rank had been left out of the matter. She glanced uncomfortably at them.

'All I am saying is that under the *Muirbretha*, the sea-laws, Murchad as captain of this vessel stands in the same position as a king. In fact, he has more power for, as well as a king, he also has the authority of a Chief Brehon. In other words, he is the ruler of everyone on this vessel. *Everyone.* I think I have explained the position clearly. Or do you have another question, Brother Tola?'

The tall religieux glanced up in irritation at her.

'No other question,' he replied frostily.

Fidelma turned to Murchad.

'You may be assured that your rules will be strictly obeyed and that everyone here is aware that disobedience invokes punishment.'

Murchad smiled in nervous appreciation.

'My purpose is only to safeguard your lives. This . . . accident with Sister Muirgel should never have happened.'

He was about to leave them when the youthful Sister Gormán stayed him.

'Can we . . . may we at least hold a small service for the repose of Sister Muirgel's soul, Captain?'

Murchad looked uncomfortable for a moment.

'It is our Christian duty to do so,' pressed Sister Ainder, coming to her support.

'Of course,' muttered Murchad. 'You may hold your service at midday when I hope the mist will have cleared.'

'Thank you, Captain.'

Murchad left them as Wenbrit began to pass round the mead and water. The meal was taken in total silence and Fidelma was thankful to escape back onto the deck. The mist was still thick and swirling and it had not cleared by midday.

The service was, indeed, simple. Everyone gathered on the main deck apart from Gurvan and another sailor who controlled the steering oar, plus a lookout perched out of sight atop the mist-shrouded mainmast, whose duty it was to see when there might be a clearing of the skies. It had been some time ago when Murchad had lowered his sails and thrown out sea anchors in case the ship drifted into danger. But Fidelma could feel that the vessel was drifting despite the anchors and Murchad's anxious eyes were darting around, attuned for trouble.

It was a strange group that stood there, surrounded by the wispy mist, like wraiths in an Otherworld setting. Surprisingly, Brother Tola led the prayers for the repose of the soul of Sister Muirgel. His voice echoed as if he were speaking in a sepulchre. He ended his prayer and then, without preamble, began to intone lines which Fidelma recognised from the Book of Jeremiah. Lines she found a strange choice:

'We have left our lands, our houses have been pulled down,
Listen, you women, to the words of the Lord,
That your ears may catch what He says.
Teach your daughters the lament,
Let them teach one another this dirge;
Death has climbed in through our windows,
It has entered our palaces,
It sweeps off the children in the open air . . .'

Fidelma gazed at the forbidding monk in some bewilderment, for she thought his harsh cadences were not suited to a service for the repose of a soul. She glanced round at her fellow mourners and found, even through the swirling mist, that Sister Gormán's eyes were bright and that she was nodding in time to the rhythm of the recitation. Next to her, Cian stood looking absolutely bored. The others appeared to be standing impassively, perhaps mesmerised by the tenor of Brother Tola's religious declamations.

'The corpses of men shall fall and lie like dung in the fields,
Like swathes behind the reaper . . .'

Brother Bairne suddenly cleared his throat noisily. It was meant to interrupt and it did.

'I, too, would offer a word from the Holy Book for the soul of our departed sister,' he announced, as Brother Tola fell silent. 'I believe I knew her just as well as everyone else who is gathered here.'

No one seemed to contradict him.

He began to recite and Fidelma realised that he was doing so with raised eyes and a grim expression on his face as if he were addressing the words at someone. He was focusing his gaze across the gathered circle. From her position, and with the mist still thick, she could not quite tell who he was looking at. Was it Sister Crella, standing with downcast eyes; or was it Cian, gazing upward in his boredom? And there was the naive young Sister Gormán by Cian's side. It was difficult to follow the line of his eyes.

'I will not punish your daughters for playing the wanton
Nor your sons' brides for their adultery,
Because your men resort to wanton women
And sacrifice with temple prostitutes.
A people without understanding comes to grief . . .'

Sister Crella raised her head abruptly.

'What have these words to do with Sister Muirgel?' she demanded threateningly. 'You did not know her at all! You were just jealous!' She turned to Sister Ainder, who was looking shocked at the interruption. 'Make an end of this farce. Proclaim a blessing and let's have done.'

Already, in embarrassment, those members of the crew who had attended were drifting quietly away. Fidelma wondered what hidden passions were being enacted in this little memorial.

Sister Ainder, flushing, intoned a quick blessing and the group of religieux broke up. Only Brother Bairne stood with his head bowed at the spot as if in silent prayer.

When Fidelma turned away she encountered Murchad. He was looking perplexed.

'A strange group of religieux, lady,' he muttered.

Fidelma felt inclined to agree.

'What was that last piece about temple prostitutes?' went on Murchad. 'Was it truly from the Christian Holy Book?'

'Hosea,' affirmed Fidelma. She pulled a doleful face. 'I think Brother Bairne was quoting from the verses of that fourth chapter.

'The more priests there are, the more they sin against me;
Their dignity I will turn into dishonour.
They feed on the sin of my people
And batten on their iniquity,
But people and priest shall be treated alike.'

Murchad gazed at her in admiration.

'I have often felt like saying that about some of the religieux I have met.'

'It seems that God said it first, Captain,' she rejoined solemnly.

'How do you remember such things, lady?'

'How do you remember how to sail this ship, knowing the winds and tides and the signs that keep *The Barnacle Goose* from danger? There is no secret to it, Murchad. We all have a memory and can memorise things. The more important thing is how we act on that which we know.'

She turned down the companionway back to the mess deck in search of some water. At the doorway, she found Wenbrit. He had not come up on deck during the service but had excused himself on the grounds of his duties. Now she noticed for the first time how pale his face was, and how strained he looked. He seemed relieved to see her.

'Lady, I need—' He stopped abruptly and his eyes focused on something above and beyond Fidelma's head.

She frowned at the young boy.

'What is it, Wenbrit?'

'Er . . .' He looked distracted for a moment. 'I just wanted to remind you that the midday meal will be served soon.'

The boy pushed past her towards the cabins, lowering his voice so that she hardly caught his words.

'Meet me in the cabin which the dead sister used. As soon as you can.'

There was a cough slightly above her head; she looked up and saw that Cian had followed her down the companionway. He stood, leaning down, a few steps above her.

'I must talk properly with you, Fidelma.' He still had that confident smile. 'We didn't really finish our discussion yesterday.'

Fidelma swung round to hide her anger. It seemed obvious to her that Wenbrit had wanted to speak urgently with her but not in the presence of Cian.

'I am busy,' she replied in a cutting tone.

Cian did not seem perturbed by her attitude.

'Surely you are not afraid to speak with me?'

She gazed at him with open dislike. There was no escaping his presence. She could make no further excuse. She had known that sooner or later they would have to talk with one another. Perhaps it was better sooner rather than later. There were many days of the voyage yet to come. She hoped that Wenbrit's news could wait awhile. She was busy remembering.

Chapter Eight

It had been left to Grian to bring her the news. Grian had arrived at the tavern where she was staying and entered into her room without knocking. Fidelma was lying on her bed staring up at the ceiling. Her brows drew together in annoyance as she saw Grian.

'I hope you haven't come to lecture me again,' she said belligerently, before her friend could speak.

Grian sat down on the bed.

'We all miss you, Fidelma. We don't want to see you like this.'

Fidelma grimaced, her annoyance spreading.

'It is not my fault that I am not at the school,' she countered. 'It was Morann who interfered in my life. It was he who expelled me.'

'He did it for the best.'

'It was none of his business.'

'He thinks it is.'

'I don't interfere with his private life. Nor should he interfere in mine.'

Grian was clearly unhappy.

'Fidelma, I feel a responsibility for all that has happened. It was my foolishness . . .'

'You need not claim that you have any rights over me because you introduced me to Cian,' Fidelma retorted sharply.

'I do not. I said I feel responsibility. My action may have destroyed your life. I cannot bear that.'

'Morann destroyed my studies, not you.'

'But Cian—'

'No more stories about Cian. I know he is immature at times but he has good intentions. He will change.'

Grian was quiet for a moment and then she said slowly, 'You are fond of quoting from Publilius Syrus. Didn't he say that an angry lover tells himself many lies? The same may be said in the feminine case. Lovers know what they want, but not what they need. You do not need Cian and he does not want you.'

Fidelma tried to start up angrily from the bed, but Grian reached

73

forward and pushed her back against the pillow. Fidelma never knew that her friend possessed such strength.

'You will listen to me, even if this is the last time we ever speak. I am doing this for your good, Fidelma. This morning Cian married Una, the daughter of the High King's steward, and they have gone to live at Aileach, among the Cenel Eoghain.'

The words came out in a rush so that Fidelma did not have time to silence her.

Fidelma stared at Grian for several long moments. There was a deathly hush as she slowly took in the meaning of Grian's words. Then her face assumed a graven look as though she had turned to stone.

Grian waited for her friend to speak, to react, and when she did not, she pressed: 'I did try to warn you before. Surely you must have known, surely you realised . . . ?'

Fidelma felt divorced from reality. It was like being immersed in cold water. She was left stunned; incapable of speech. Grian had warned her and she, if the truth were known, suspected – even feared – that it was true. She had tried to fool herself and deny it. Finally, she managed to articulate one of the many thoughts whirling around in her mind.

'Go away and leave me alone,' she cried, emotion cracking her voice.

Grian gazed at her in anxiety. 'Fidelma, you must understand . . .'

The next moment, Fidelma had thrown herself at her friend, screaming, beating with her hands, scratching. Had Grian not been a practitioner of the art of the *troid-sciathaigid* – battle through defence – she might have been badly hurt. As it was, Grian was adept at the technique, which had been developed centuries before when the learned ones of the Five Kingdoms had to defend themselves from attack by thieves and bandits. As they believed that it was wrong to carry weapons of defence, they had been forced to develop another method of defending themselves. Now, many of the missionaries who journeyed abroad had become adepts of the art.

Grian found it easy to constrain Fidelma's uncontrolled fury, for physical intent without control will recoil on itself. Grian soon had her powerless in one of the holds, face down on the bed.

At this point the innkeeper came bursting into the room, demanding to know the reason for the noise which disturbed his guests, his shocked eyes immediately alighting on the broken pots and chair that had been the casualties before Fidelma had been pinioned by her friend.

Grian merely shouted at him to get out and that any damage would be paid for.

For a long, long time, she held on to her friend until the fight and frenzy left her body, until the tension was evaporated and the muscles had become relaxed.

Finally Fidelma said in a quiet and reasonable tone: 'I am all right now, Grian. You may let go.'

Reluctantly, Grian pulled away and Fidelma sat up.

'I would prefer it if you let me alone for a while.'

Grian gave her a searching look.

'Don't worry,' Fidelma said softly. 'I shall not do anything silly again. You can go back to the college.'

Still Grian hesitated to leave her alone.

'Go on,' insisted Fidelma, scarcely keeping back her sobs. 'I have promised you – isn't that enough?'

Grian decided that the moment of madness had passed and she rose.

'Remember, Fidelma, that you have friends nearby,' she said.

It was over a month before Fidelma returned to Brehon Morann's school. The old man immediately noticed the tight little lines at the corner of her eyes and mouth. A brittleness that had not been there before.

'Do you know your Aeschylus, Fidelma?' the Brehon greeted her without preamble as she was shown into his room.

She gazed blankly at him and did not reply.

'"Who, except the gods, can live time through for ever without any pain?"'

She was silent for a moment. Then, not responding to his words, she said: 'I would like to return to my studies.'

'I, for one, would be happy to see you do so.'

'*May* I return to my studies?' she asked him quietly.

'Is there anything to prevent you, Fidelma?'

Fidelma raised her chin in her old gesture of defiance. She waited for several seconds before replying decisively: 'Nothing.'

The old man sighed sadly, an almost imperceptible sigh of breath.

'If there is bitterness in your heart, study is no sugar to dilute it.'

'Don't the ancient bards say that we learn by suffering?' she replied.

'Truly said, but in my experience the sufferer reflects on their pain either too much or too little. I fear you are reflecting too much, Fidelma. If you return, you must give your mind to study and not to the wrong which you feel that you have suffered.'

The corners of her mouth tightened.

75

'Have no worry for me, Brehon Morann. I shall now apply myself to my studies.'

So she did. The years had fled by. She had gained her degree, completing eight years of study and becoming the best pupil that the Brehon Morann had produced. The old man himself admitted as much and he was someone who did not readily praise his pupils. Yet the innocent young girl who had arrived at his school was gone. Innocence and youth could certainly not last for ever, but it was the slight change of character that saddened old Morann. A bitterness had entered where there should have been joy.

Fidelma had never really retrieved her unaffected nature. Cian's rejection had left her feeling disillusioned and violated, although the years gradually tempered her attitude. But she had never forgotten her experience, nor really recovered from it. Bitterness left a deep scar and a sense of mistrust. Perhaps that was what had made her a good *dálaigh*; that sense of suspicion, of questioning motives. She could penetrate deception as a diviner might unerringly find water.

Fidelma came back to the present in an angry mood.

'All right, Cian,' she said flatly. 'We will speak, if you wish it.'

She made no effort to move nor make him feel at ease. Cian tried to take command of the situation by moving down the stairs as if to push her towards the mess deck so that they could sit down, but she stood still, blocking the movement. They were positioned in the small passageway between the cabins with Fidelma obstructing the doorway.

'It has been many years since last we met, Fidelma,' Cian opened.

'Ten years precisely,' she cut in tightly.

'Ten years? And your name is now spoken of as one who has garnered a reputation. I understand that you went back and continued your studies with the Brehon Morann.'

'Obviously. I was lucky that he accepted me back into his school after I nearly threw away my chances.'

'I thought that you wanted to go into teaching rather than law.'

'There was a lot I wanted when I was young. My plans changed and I found that I had a talent for discovering the truth from those who wished to hide it. It was a talent which I developed from harsh experience.'

Cian did not rise to her acerbic tone. He simply smiled as if absent-minded, pretending that he did not understand her innuendo.

'I am glad that you made a success of your life, Fidelma. It is more than I have made of mine.'

She waited a moment, expecting some expansion, and then she said sourly: 'I am surprised that you have forsaken your profession to take up the religious life. Surely, of all the professions in the land, the calling of a religieux would be the least suited to your temperament?'

Cian laughed; there was an unpleasantly morose tone in that laughter.

'You have hit the nail on the head immediately, Fidelma. My change of calling was none of my choosing.'

She waited quietly for an explanation.

Then Cian took his left hand and reached across to his right and lifted it up as if it had no power to raise itself. He held it up and let go. It fell limply by his side. He laughed again.

'What demand is there for a one-armed warrior in the High King's bodyguard?'

For the first time since she had seen Cian again, Fidelma realised that his right hand had always hung loosely at his side and that he did everything with his left hand. How could she have been so blind not to notice that fact before? Here she was, priding herself on her observational ability when only now she realised that Cian had the full use of just one arm. A fine *dálaigh* she was! She had been so filled with hatred for him that she was looking on him as he had been ten years ago at Tara. She had not seen him as he was *now*. She recalled that Cian always seemed to keep his right arm hidden within his robes. In a surge of instinctive sympathy she found herself reaching out to touch him lightly on the arm.

'I am—'

'Sorry?' he interrupted her almost with a snarl. 'I do not want anyone's sorrow!'

She remained quiet, her eyes downcast. Her attitude seemed to irritate Cian.

'Aren't you going to tell me that a warrior should expect to be wounded? That it is one of the hazards of his profession?' he sneered.

She was surprised to hear the self-pitying whine creep into his voice. She found it repulsive and her initial sympathy was gone as swiftly as it came.

'Why? Is that what you want to hear?' she countered.

Her tone drew more anger from Cian.

'I have heard it many times from people who are prepared to let the likes of me do their dirty work and then disown me afterwards.'

'Were you wounded in combat?' She ignored his accusation.

'An arrow in the right upper arm, piercing the muscles and making the arm useless.'

'When did it happen?'

'About five years ago. It was during the border wars between the High King and the King of Laigin. I was taken by my comrades and nursed in the House of Sorrow at Armagh. It was soon realised that I would no longer be any use as a warrior and so, when I was well enough, I was forced to enter the Abbey at Bangor.' It was clear that Cian felt himself ill-done by.

'Forced?' queried Fidelma.

'Where else would I go? A one-armed man – what work could I do?'

'The wound is irreversible? There are some very good physicians at Tuam Brecain.'

Cian shook his head sullenly.

'Not good enough, then or now. I spent a few years in the Abbey doing such menial tasks as much as my one good arm allowed.'

'Have you consulted any other physicians?'

'That is the purpose of my journey now,' he admitted. 'I was told about a physician in Iberia, a man named Mormohec who lives near the Shrine of St James.'

'And you intend to see this Mormohec?'

'There are enough shrines and tombs of saintly men in the Five Kingdoms for me not to be inspired to journey across the sea simply to see another. Yes, I am going to see this Mormohec. It is my last chance to get back to a real life.'

Fidelma raised her eyebrows slightly. 'A real life? Apparently you do not consider your current religious calling a real life then?'

Cian gave a bark of cynical laughter.

'You know me, Fidelma. You know me well enough. Can you see me settled as some fat *frater*, stuck behind the walls of an abbey all my life, or what is left of it, singing pious Psalms?'

'What does your wife say?'

Cian looked disconcerted.

'My wife?'

'As I recall, you married the daughter of the steward of the King at Aileach. Her name was Una. Wasn't that why you left me at Tara without a word?'

'Una?' Cian pulled a face as if he had tasted something disagreeable. 'Una divorced me the moment the physicians pronounced my wound would never be cured and that I would be crippled for the rest of my life.'

Fidelma struggled to stop an expression of sheer malicious pleasure moulding her features. Mentally, she rebuked herself that her personal feelings intruded into another's misfortune and yet she was still governed by what had happened to her ten years before.

'That must have been a great shock to you . . . receiving a taste of your own medicine.' The words were out before she could stop them.

Cian was lost in his thoughts and missed the last part of the sentence which Fidelma had uttered with such satisfaction.

'Shock. Yes, it was! That mercenary little cow!'

Fidelma disapproved of his vehemence.

'Had you not been divorced already, Cian, you have uttered one of the fundamental grounds for a wife to divorce her husband, according to the laws of the *Cáin Lánamna,*' she pointed out diffidently.

Cian would not be constrained.

'I would say worse about her, if it were worth my while.'

'Did you have any children?'

'No!' The word cracked out. 'She claimed it was my fault and laid that as the grounds for the divorce, rather than admitting the truth of it, that she did not want to live with a man who could no longer provide luxury for her.'

'She accused you of sterility?'

Fidelma knew well that sexual failings on the part of a husband provided grounds for divorce. A man who was claimed to be sterile was given as one of the grounds for divorce under the law. Fidelma hardly believed that Cian, so much the archetypal virile and lusty male, always intent to prove his masculinity, could be accused of that. Nevertheless, it seemed ironic to her that he, of all people, had been divorced for that reason.

'I was not sterile. It was she who refused to have children,' Cian protested with resentment in his voice.

'But the court surely demanded and examined evidence in proof of what she accused you of?'

Fidelma knew that the law adopted a very severe line towards women who left their husbands without just cause, as it did towards men who left their wives without a legal reason. A woman who could not show evidence of just cause was proclaimed 'an absconder from the law of marriage' and lost her rights in society until she had made amends.

Cian made a noise, blowing air through his clenched teeth. His eyes dropped momentarily and in that gesture Fidelma knew that the courts would not have made their decision without that evidence. It sounded as if natural justice had caught up with Cian at long last. What was it her mentor, Brehon Morann, used to say? 'Of injustice and justice, the guilty find justice the harder to bear.'

'Anyway,' Cian went on, shaking himself as if to rid himself of past ghosts, 'I am glad the Fates have thrown us together again, Fidelma.'

She pursed her lips cynically.

'Why would that be, Cian? Do you want to attempt to make amends for the anguish you put a naive young girl through?'

He broke into that old smile of charm that she had come to resent so deeply.

'Anguish? You know that I was always attracted to you and I admired you, Fidelma. Let's forget the past. I believed that I was doing the best for you. We have a long voyage ahead and . . .'

Fidelma felt a sudden icy tingle at his attempt to disarm her. She took a step backwards.

'Enough has been said between us, Cian,' she responded coldly.

She made to push by him but he caught her arm with his left hand. She was surprised at the strength of his grip.

'Come, Fidelma,' he said urgently. 'I know that you still care for me, otherwise you would not respond with such passion. I can see your feeling in your eyes . . .'

He made an attempt to draw her towards him with his one good arm. Balancing on one foot, she kicked him sharply in the shins. He winced and let go with a curse.

Her features were filled with loathing.

'You are pathetic, Cian. I could report your action to the captain of this vessel, but instead I will give you the chance to remain out of my way for the rest of the time we are forced to spend on this ship. Take your miserable little existence from my sight.'

Without waiting for him to do as she instructed, she pushed roughly by him in search of Wenbrit. There was no one in the short corridor between the stern cabins. She paused outside the one that had been used by Sister Muirgel, for she had noticed that the door was slightly ajar. There was a sound of movement from beyond. She pushed the door open a fraction and called softly into the darkness.

'Wenbrit? Are you in here?'

There was another movement in the shadows.

'Is that you?' hissed Fidelma.

There was a scraping noise and a flickering light illuminated the cabin. Wenbrit had adjusted the wick of a lantern to light the scene. Fidelma heaved a sigh of relief and entered the cabin, closing the door behind her.

'What are you doing in the dark?' she demanded.

'Waiting for you.'

'I don't understand.'

'At breakfast, I heard them speaking of you as one who has a reputation for solving mysteries. Is it really true that you are a *dálaigh* of the law courts of your country?'

'It is true.'

'There is a mystery here that needs a solution, lady.' The boy's voice was full of suppressed excitement and something else – a curious tension, almost fear.

'You'd better explain to me what this is all about, Wenbrit.'

'Well, it is about the Sister who used this cabin – Sister Muirgel.'

'Go on.'

'She was sick, as you know.'

Fidelma waited patiently.

'They say that she went up on deck in the storm and fell overboard.'

'It sounds as though you do not believe that, Wenbrit,' Fidelma observed, judging the tone of his voice.

Wenbrit suddenly reached forward and, from under the nearby bunk, he pulled out a dark robe.

'I was sent down to tidy the cabin after breakfast and to gather her things. This was her robe.'

Fidelma glanced at it.

'I don't understand.'

Wenbrit grasped her hand and pressed it against the robe. It was moist.

'Look closely at your hand, Sister. You will find that there is blood on it.'

Fidelma held out her fingers to the flickering light; she could just see a dark stain on her fingertips.

She stared at Wenbrit for a moment. Then she took the robe and held it up; there was a jagged tear in the front of it.

'Where did you find this robe?'

'Hidden under the bunk here.'

'If this is blood . . .' Fidelma paused thoughtfully, looking at the boy. Now she could understand the combination of fear and excitement on his face.

'I am saying that Sister Muirgel was ill. Before I turned in last night, I came to see her, to find out if there was anything she wanted. She was still poorly and told me to leave her alone.'

'And you did so?'

'Of course. I went to my bunk. But something worried me.'

'Such as?'

'I think that Sister Muirgel was frightened.'

'What, you mean frightened of the storm?'

'No not the storm. You see, when I went to find out if she needed anything, she had her cabin door locked. I had to call out and reassure her who I was before she would open it for me.'

Fidelma turned to the door-latch.

'I did not think these doors could be secured,' she said.

The boy took the lantern and raised it so that she could see.

'Look at the scratchmarks. All it needs is a piece of wood, even the end of one of those crucifixes that you religieux wear, lodged here so that the latch cannot be raised, and there you have a lock.'

Fidelma stood back.

'And Sister Muirgel had secured her door in this manner?'

'She had. She was ill and she was frightened. It is impossible that she would have gone wandering out on deck in such a terrible storm in that state.'

'Did you see her afterwards?'

'No. I went to my bunk and fell asleep. I never stirred again until dawn.'

'You were not on deck during the storm?'

'It was not my duty to be, unless the captain specifically sent for me.'

'So you did not see any more of Sister Muirgel after you left her?'

'No. I was awakened by one of the religieux searching the ship just after dawn. I heard him talking to the others, saying that Sister Muirgel was missing. It was the man with whom you were speaking just now. Then I heard Murchad saying that if she was not on the ship she must have gone over the side during the night. The captain thought it was the only possible explanation.'

'So, Wenbrit,' Fidelma asked reflectively, 'what do you make of it? Do you have another explanation?'

'I say that Sister Muirgel was in no condition to go up on deck, especially not with the sea running as it was during the night.'

'Desperation makes people do desperate things,' observed Fidelma.

'Not that one,' pointed out Wenbrit.

'So what do you say?'

'I say that she was too sick to move on her own. The robe she was wearing has a jagged hole in it and bloodstains all over it. If she went overboard, it was not by accident.'

'So what do you think happened?'

'I think she was killed and then thrown overboard!'

Chapter Nine

A short silence fell between them as Fidelma considered the implications of the discovery.

'Have you told the captain about this yet?' she finally asked.

Wenbrit shook his head.

'After I heard that you knew about the law, I thought that I should speak with you first. I have not said a word to anyone else.'

'Then I shall speak to Murchad. It might be a wise thing not to say anything to the others. Let everyone continue to think that Sister Muirgel was swept overboard.' Fidelma picked up the robe and examined it again. 'I will take this,' she decided.

There was one immediate aspect which puzzled her. The tattered state of the robe suggested that Sister Muirgel had been violently attacked and killed with a knife. Yet there was comparatively little blood on it. There was some – but not the quantity she would have expected to see from the grievous wounds suggested by the cuts in the material. And, if the killer had then thrown Sister Muirgel's body overboard, why bother to remove the robe from the body before doing so? Why place it under the bunk where it must surely be discovered?

Fidelma found Murchad in his own cabin. She quickly told him of Wenbrit's discovery.

'What do you suggest we do, lady?' Murchad was anxious. 'Nothing like this has ever happened on board my ship before.'

'As I explained earlier, you are the captain and under the *Muirbretha* you have the rights of a King and Chief Brehon while the ship is sailing the seas.'

Murchad gave a lopsided grin.

'Me? King and Chief Brehon? Hardly. But even though this ship is mine to control, I wouldn't know how to set about finding who is responsible for this deed.'

'You are the representative of law and order on this vessel,' she insisted.

Murchad spread his hands.

83

'What could I do? Demand that the guilty person come forward from the passengers?'

'Are we even sure that the guilty one would be found among the passengers?'

Murchad raised his eyebrows.

'My crew,' he boomed indignantly, 'have been with me for years. No, this evil came aboard with those pilgrims, I'll guarantee it. You must advise me, lady.'

He appeared so bewildered and undecided that Fidelma felt sympathy for the captain in his predicament.

'You could request me to make some enquiries; give me authority to do so on your behalf.'

'But if, as you say, someone killed this woman and threw her overboard during the storm, it will surely be impossible to discover the truth.'

'We don't know that until we start making those enquiries.'

'You may put your own life in jeopardy, lady. A ship is a confined space where it is hard to hide. And once the killer knows you are on their track . . .'

'It might act two ways. The ship is equally confined and impossible for a murderer to hide in.'

'I would not like my King's sister to be placed in such peril.'

Fidelma was reassuring.

'I have been at risk several times before, Murchad. So, do I have your authority?'

He rubbed his jaw reflectively.

'If you are certain that this is the right way to proceed, then, of course, you have my authority.'

'Excellent. I will start an investigation but we will keep our suspicion of murder secret for the time being. We will not tell anyone about the discovery of the robe. You understand? I shall merely say that I am conducting an enquiry on your behalf because, under the laws of the *Muirbretha*, you must make a report to the legal authorities as to why a passenger has been lost overboard.'

The idea that he should do so had not even occurred to Murchad.

'Is that true? Is that what I must do?'

'The family or kin of a passenger lost at sea can claim negligence against you and demand compensation unless it can be shown that it was an accident. That is the situation under law,' she explained.

Murchad looked dismayed.

'I had not thought of that.'

'To be honest, that is the least of your problems. The more

serious situation would be if she *was* murdered and the culprit is not discovered. The family could demand you pay her full honour price – and didn't Sister Crella claim that she was of a noble family of the North? Ah, I wish I had my textbooks with me. I have not had many dealings with the *Muirbretha*. I recall the basic laws but I wish my knowledge were more exact. I will do my best to safeguard for any eventuality, Murchad.'

The captain was despondent as he reflected on the enormity of the task.

'May the saints grant you success in your enquiries,' he said fervently.

Fidelma thought for a moment and then gave a little sardonic grimace.

'How shall we judge success? To discover that Muirgel has been murdered? Or that she simply fell overboard?'

Murchad seemed so forlorn and Fidelma felt sorry for her cynicism.

'We will take it that success merely means discovering the truth,' she said solemnly. 'I'll start immediately.'

As she went out onto the main deck she spied the shadowy but unmistakable figure of Sister Ainder leaning against the wooden rail gazing into the menacing sea mist which still enveloped the ship. She decided she would start with the sharp-faced Sister.

Sister Ainder straightened as Fidelma greeted her. Fidelma, who was by no means short in stature, found herself having to look up at the tall woman. Sister Ainder was a woman of mature years, and still impressively handsome, although a smile did not sit easily on her immobile, mask-like features. Her striking eyes were set deep in a sallow symmetrical face. They were dark eyes which seldom blinked, focusing on Fidelma's own in a searching gaze which gave the younger woman the uncomfortable feeling that they were seeing beyond the tangible and into the very depths of her soul. Sister Ainder exuded a calm, lofty demeanour, almost not of this world. Her voice was strong, smoothly modulated and controlled.

'I must apologise for the embarrassing end to our service, Sister Fidelma,' she intoned rather than spoke, like a reciter engaged at a reading while her co-religionists were at their meal. Fidelma had never noticed her curious manner of speaking before. Perhaps it was because previously she had been distracted in the company of others. 'I do not understand the passions of the young.'

'You refer to the exchange between Sister Crella and Brother

Bairne? I did find Bairne's choice of text from the Holy Book somewhat bizarre!'

'There are some things better left unsaid,' Sister Ainder remarked, as if agreeing with her.

Fidelma asked, 'Do you know what Bairne was accusing Crella of, or what Crella was accusing Bairne of? It seemed that something was going on between them.'

'Whatever it was, it is doubtless no affair of ours.'

'I would prefer your comments, Sister, and I would especially like to know more about Sister Muirgel.'

'Is there not an old saying which exhorts people not to enquire what goes into a neighbour's cooking pot? I see no reason for such questions.' Sister Ainder exuded disapproval.

When Fidelma explained her purpose more fully, using the excuse she had agreed with Murchad, it made little difference to Sister Ainder.

'The matter is perfectly straightforward and best forgotten. Sister Muirgel was silly enough to go on deck during the storm. She paid for her mistake with tragic consequences.'

Fidelma pretended to agree, concluding, 'Yet there is wisdom in the request of Murchad for me to make an official report to ensure that he is not liable for the . . . accident, if compensation is claimed by the deceased's family.'

Sister Ainder made a slight movement of her shoulders as if to dismiss the matter.

'I know nothing of her family, but surely the captain cannot be blamed if one of his passengers is silly enough to put their own life at risk?'

'True,' agreed Fidelma, 'but I have to be assured that this was, indeed, the situation. The testimony of witnesses is important.'

The voice of the tall religieuse grew cold. 'I am certainly no witness.'

'I did not mean witness to the actual tragedy. However, you could give me some background detail. I presume that you knew Sister Muirgel?'

'Of course.'

Fidelma suppressed a growing feeling of irritation. Extracting information from Ainder was like trying to draw teeth.

'Where did you first meet her?'

'At the Abbey of Moville.'

'So you knew her well?'

'No.'

Fidelma decided to attempt a different path.

'When did you decide to come on this pilgrimage?'

'A few weeks ago.'

'And did you travel with Sister Muirgel from Moville to Ardmore?'

'I did.'

'Can you give me any impression about what sort of person she was?'

'I really could not say.'

'Yet you must have spent some time in her company on the journey?'

'No.'

'No?' pressed Fidelma, exasperated.

'No.' Sister Ainder suddenly relented and finally volunteered some extra information. 'There were twelve of us who started out from Moville. One of us died before we had gone twenty miles. She was an elderly Sister and should not have even started out on the journey. Our party was large enough for me not to take a particular interest in Sister Muirgel.'

'Isn't that strange for a group of pilgrims from the same Abbey, setting off on a pilgrimage to a distant land? Strange that they would not share a friendship or at least a knowledge of one another's background?'

Sister Ainder sniffed deprecatingly.

'Why so? A pilgrimage has nothing to do with being friends with one's fellow religieux or not. Sometimes we did not even stay in the same hostel on our journey to the seaport. Besides, while the Abbeys of Moville and Bangor are situated not far from one another, they are separate institutions.'

Fidelma decided to make a final attempt.

'Let me put it another way then. Was there any enmity among your group?'

'I could not say. Nor do I see the relevance of any of these questions in connection with the accident which claimed Sister Muirgel's life during the storm.'

'It is my way of doing things.' Fidelma was surprised that she responded so defensively to the haughty attitude of Sister Ainder. In other circumstances, she might have rebuked the inflexible religieuse sharply.

'It seems a waste of time to me,' replied Sister Ainder, unimpressed. 'And now I am going to my cabin for my devotions and meditation.' She made a move as if to leave.

'One moment, Sister.' Fidelma refused to be intimidated.

'Well?' The penetrating dark eyes bore down at her.

'When did you last see Sister Muirgel?'

The tall woman frowned. For a moment Fidelma believed that she was going to refuse to answer.

'I suppose it was when we came aboard. Why?'

'You *suppose*?' Fidelma ignored her question.

'I have said so.'

Fidelma observed the eyes darken with anger; there was a moment of quiet in which it seemed that Sister Ainder was making up her mind whether to add something to her negative response.

'You saw her when you came aboard but not afterwards?'

'You already know that afterwards she was confined to her cabin with sickness.'

'You did not go to her cabin to enquire after her?'

'I had no interest in doing so.'

'You were not disturbed during the night, by the storm?'

'I would imagine that everyone was disturbed by the storm.'

'But you did not leave your cabin?'

'Where do these questions lead?' countered Sister Ainder scathingly.

'I merely want to ascertain whether anyone saw Sister Muirgel leave her cabin and go up on deck from where we presume she was swept overboard.'

Sister Ainder's face was set firmly.

'I did not leave my cabin.'

'When did you learn that Sister Muirgel was missing?'

'When Sister Gormán awoke me with the news or, rather, the sound of her conversation with Brother Cian awoke me.'

'Sister Gormán?'

'We share a cabin. She had apparently been woken by Brother Cian conducting some search for Muirgel. I am usually a sound sleeper. Their voices woke me up. A stupid fuss about nothing.'

'A fuss about nothing. But Muirgel, as it turned out, *had* fallen overboard. That is not a charitable remark.'

'I meant their argument,' snapped Sister Ainder. 'Now . . .'

'Argument?'

But Sister Ainder would not amplify. Fidelma tried again.

'What was the argument about?'

'I could not say.'

'Presumably, as you were sharing a cabin, you know Sister Gormán well?' Fidelma wanted to move to the matter in another way.

'Know? Hardly. A silly young girl.'

'As a matter of interest, who among your party did you know?' asked Fidelma caustically.

The eyes narrowed and darkened again.

'It depends on what degree of knowledge you mean when you use the word "know"?'

'What meaning would you give to it?' Fidelma shot back in frustration.

'I would give various meanings. And now I think that we have wasted enough time on this matter.'

She turned and left. Fidelma remembered a game that she used to play as a child. A number of apples were floated on top of a barrel filled with water. The intention was to pick up as many apples as possible without using one's hands. This game of extracting information from Sister Ainder was like that game. It seemed to be based on the same principle.

Fidelma was left feeling utterly confounded. She could not remember anyone getting the better of her questioning before, or answering in such a way that she learned absolutely nothing. She stood breathing deeply for a moment or two, feeling rather like a young student who had been soundly trounced by in a debate with Brehon Morann. Well, if there was one thing Morann had taught her, it was not to give up at the first blank wall she encountered.

She made her way below deck again and went into the mess-deck in search of the other pilgrims. At first she thought the big cabin was deserted but then she saw a shadow in the corner bending over something. Fidelma cleared her throat noisily.

The hooded figure sprang up, swinging round, with cat-like agility. The cowled hood fell away from the face and revealed Sister Crella. The broad-faced young woman looked red-eyed, as if she had been crying.

'I am sorry that I frightened you, Sister.' Fidelma smiled reassuringly.

'I thought . . . I did not hear you come in.'

'With the creaks and groans of this vessel, you would have to possess good hearing to isolate the sound of footsteps,' Fidelma observed. 'I should have made my presence known but I thought this place was deserted.'

'I had dropped something in the corner here and was searching for it.'

'Can I help you?' Fidelma looked towards the dim lamp that still spluttered on the table.

'No,' Sister Crella replied quickly, apparently having recovered

89

from her fright. 'I thought I dropped it here but I must have left it back in my cabin. It is of no consequence.'

Fidelma regarded her slightly antagonistic expression thoughtfully.

'Very well,' she said. 'Do you have time to talk with me for a moment?'

Crella's eyes narrowed with suspicion.

'Talk about what?'

'About Sister Muirgel.'

'I suppose you mean about the matter of the service? I shall not apologise. Brother Bairne was always jealous and stupid.'

'Why would he quote from the Book of Hosea? It seemed a strange thing to do at such a ceremony.'

Crella sniffed in annoyance.

'. . . "For a spirit of wantonness has led them astray and in their lusts they are unfaithful to their God",' she recited. 'I know the passage well. Brother Bairne was jealous that Muirgel and I were found attractive by men as we were attracted to certain men. That is all. He disapproved of it.'

'I gather that he was not one of the men to whom you were attracted?'

Crella actually laughed sharply.

'Decidedly not.'

'Did the same dislike of Bairne apply for Sister Muirgel?'

'Of course. We both considered Bairne a boor. And now, if that is all . . . ?'

'Not exactly. The main subject I wanted to talk to you about is the tragic loss of Sister Muirgel.'

Crella sat down abruptly at the table. Fidelma lowered herself to the bench opposite her. Clearly now, in the light of the lamp, Fidelma could see that the young woman had, indeed, been crying.

'I think you mentioned at breakfast that Sister Muirgel was your cousin,' she prompted gently.

'*And* my closest companion,' affirmed the girl vehemently, as if it was a matter being disputed.

Fidelma reached forward and laid a sympathetic hand on Crella's arm.

'I have been asked by the captain to make some enquiries. You see, under law, he has to present a report about Sister Muirgel's death to the legal authorities at his home port, otherwise her family may take action against him for negligence.'

Crella's eyes widened innocently.

'But I am of her family and I know that Murchad was not to blame for her death.'

'Well, Murchad has to show that in law. Otherwise, no matter the good intentions of yourself, one of her closer family might claim her honour price. Her father, for example, or her brother. As I am a lawyer, he has requested me to ask a few questions and make up the report for him.'

Crella made a sound halfway between a sniff and a sigh.

'I do not know anything. I was in my bunk all night, scared to death to even move during the storm.'

'Of course. Rather, I wanted to ask for some background details. You say that you were Sister Muirgel's cousin and closest companion? Then you will be able to tell me something of her family.'

Crella seemed reluctant. She regarded Fidelma somewhat warily.

'We are from the Abbey of Moville. It stands at the head of Loch Cúan. It was founded a hundred years ago by the Blessed Finnian. Colmcille trained there and it is now one of the most celebrated ecclesiastical colleges in the country.'

'I know of it,' Fidelma acknowledged. 'So, you were both members of the community of Moville.'

'We were cousins. Our fathers were of the chiefly family Dál Fiatach.'

Fidelma looked at her sharply.

'The Dál Fiatach whose lands include Moville?'

'And the great Abbey of Bangor,' Crella added almost proudly. 'The Dál Fiatach territory is one of the largest sub-kingdoms of Ulaidh.'

'I see. So Sister Muirgel . . .'

'. . . would have a high honour price.' Sister Crella anticipated the question. 'Seven cumals.'

Fidelma was surprised by the girl's knowledge.

'You clearly know your honour prices.' The sum was equivalent to the value of twenty-one milch cows.

'Muirgel's father was chief of the territory and my father was his tanist or heir-apparent. We were raised knowing such things,' the girl explained.

'So what made you enter the religious life?'

Sister Crella hesitated only for a moment and then spread her arms in an encompassing gesture.

'Muirgel. It was Muirgel who suggested it. We had brothers and sisters at home and Muirgel thought it would be good to leave home to study.'

'How old was Muirgel?'

'The same as I. Twenty years old.'

'When did you enter the Abbey of Moville?'

'When we were sixteen.'

'Why did you come on this pilgrimage?'

Sister Crella began: 'It was . . .' Then she stopped as if a thought struck her.

Fidelma smiled encouragingly.

'It was also Muirgel's idea?' she guessed.

Sister Crella nodded.

'Did you always follow Muirgel?'

Crella was on the defensive again.

'We were always very close. She was more like a sister than a cousin. We were always together.'

Fidelma leant back, fingers drumming unconsciously on the table.

'Why weren't you sharing a cabin with Muirgel on this voyage?'

Crella was confused.

'I don't know what you mean.'

'I was just wondering. If you and Muirgel were so close, and you came on this voyage because it was her idea, I would have expected you to be sharing a cabin when the need arose for people to share cabins. When I came on board I was initially asked to share a cabin with her.'

'Oh, I see. I had promised Sister Canair to share with her because she was frightened. She had never been on a sea voyage before.'

'I see. But Sister Canair did not come aboard, did she? She missed the sailing time.'

Sister Crella looked troubled.

'She was the leader of our band of pilgrims. She was from Moville as well and a good friend of ours.'

'Any idea why she would have led you to Ardmore and then missed the sailing time?'

'None. I was still fully expecting her to be on board when we sailed, that was why I was in one cabin and Muirgel was in another.'

'How many of you were from Moville?'

'Dathal, Adamrae, Cian and Tola were all from Bangor. The rest of us were from Moville.'

'I gather that there was a Sister who died almost as soon as you set out?'

'Old Sister Sibán? She was very aged. We had not even left the territory of Dál Fiatach when she collapsed and died. She was from Moville.'

'So twelve of you set out on this journey?'

'Now there are nine of us left.'

'Why do you think that Sister Canair did not join you? If she had travelled from Moville all the way to Ardmore with you, why would she stop there?'

Crella gave a quick, nervous shrug.

'Who knows? Perhaps she was afraid of the sea or perhaps she grew tired of our company.'

Fidelma knew instinctively that Sister Crella did not believe the reasons she was putting forward. She decided not to press the matter but to return to the subject of Muirgel's disappearance.

'When did you last see your cousin?'

'Soon after the storm started – I am not sure of the hour. The sky had grown quite dark. I looked in to see if I could bring her something to comfort her. Or, as now we knew that Canair was not on board, whether she wanted me to move into her cabin with her. She had been confined to the cabin as soon as we came on board.'

'And did she?'

'Did she what?' Sister Crella did not follow what Fidelma meant for the moment.

'Did Muirgel want you to move into the cabin with her?'

The girl hesitated for a moment and then shook her head.

'She did not. She said she wanted to be left alone.'

'Were you surprised by that?' Fidelma asked quickly.

Sister Crella flushed and thought a moment as if wanting to frame the reply carefully.

'We are young women. Sometimes it is . . . inconvenient to share a room or cabin.'

Fidelma considered the reply and decided not to follow it through at that moment. She would soon find out if Crella's obvious suspicion was correct or not. But if Muirgel was expecting the company of a male companion during the storm, it certainly did not fit with her being sick.

'How was Sister Muirgel when you saw her?' she asked next.

'She was still weak and ill. I have never known her go down with seasickness before.'

'Has she travelled by sea before?'

'We have made several journeys to Iona but Muirgel was never sick once.'

'You were in the next cabin to her, weren't you?'

'I was.'

'But you did not go to see how she was when the storm broke.'

'I was too scared.'

'Imagine how she felt, sick as she was.'

'I was feeling ill myself,' Crella protested. 'Are you saying that I should have risen from my bunk and tried to go to her cabin? That I might have been able to have prevented her going on deck, stopped her from being washed overboard?' Her voice rose querulously.

'I would not suggest that. And I think what you are saying to me is that you suspected that Muirgel was not so ill as she claimed and, indeed, was expecting someone.'

Crella's chin rose as if she were about to utter a denial. Then she let her head drop. She did not say anything.

'Do you know who Muirgel's boyfriends were? Are you sure it was not Brother Bairne?'

'Bairne?' Crella replied with an awkward laugh. 'I told you that he would be the last person that Muirgel would be interested in. There was . . .' She hesitated.

'Yes?' Fidelma encouraged.

'Well, Brother Cian is a friend of yours . . .'

It was Fidelma's turn to flush.

'He is not! I knew him ten years ago at Tara and have not seen him since, until I set foot on this ship. Anyway, what about Cian?'

'Cian had a reputation at Moville. There is hardly a young female there who has not been persuaded to share his bed, from silly young things like Gormán to more mature women such as my cousin. But I had an impression that Muirgel wanted to end her relationship with Cian even before we left the Abbey. She started to become secretive, which was unusual.'

The revelation of Cian's shortcomings did not surprise Fidelma.

'Was there anyone Muirgel was afraid of?' she asked.

Sister Crella shook her head and then glanced curiously at Fidelma.

'What have such questions to do with enquiring as to how Muirgel came to be washed overboard? I don't understand.'

Fidelma knew that she had overstepped the mark and begun to create suspicion in the young woman's mind. She hurriedly changed the direction of her questions.

'I was just seeking some background, that is all. So far as you are concerned, you remained in your cabin until the next morning.'

'I was going to see her the next morning but just after dawn Brother Cian came into our cabin saying that he was making a check on everyone. That arrogant—' Crella caught herself. 'He has

94

now taken upon himself the leadership of our party and thinks it is up to him to shepherd us like his own lost sheep.'

Fidelma leaned forward slightly.

'So Cian came in, making a check? And this was just about dawn. What then?'

'He had not been gone long when he came back and told me that Muirgel was not in her cabin and that he was going to raise the alarm with the captain.'

'What sort of character was Muirgel?'

'Is that relevant?'

'I just want to get an idea of what made her leave her cabin, being so ill, and go up on deck.'

'Panic, I suppose.' Crella replied. 'I certainly thought the ship was going to founder at times, the way it was tossed hither and thither. Not even in our journeys to Iona have the seas been so rough.'

'How many times did you cross the strait to Iona?'

'Muirgel and I took messages from the Abbot of Moville to Iona several times.'

'And she was never seasick then? It is a storm-tossed strait, isn't it? I have made the journey only once but I could understand if people found it fearful, for the seas can be frightening.'

'I can't recall her ever being sick.'

'Yet last night you think she panicked and ran up on deck in the middle of a storm?'

'It is the only conclusion one can come to. Maybe she simply wanted to get some air for the cabin was stifling and odorous.'

Fidelma paused for a moment and then added softly: 'You did not say what sort of character Muirgel was.'

Crella's reply was immediate and enthusiastic.

'Decisive. Possessed of a quick wit. She knew what she wanted. Maybe that is why I followed her lead. She was the one who had all the ideas.'

'I see.' Fidelma rose abruptly. 'You have been very helpful, Crella. Oh, one thing more – when did Cian decide to join your party?'

Crella made a gesture of annoyance. 'Him? Oh, he joined as soon as Sister Canair announced her plan to lead a party to the Holy Shrine.'

'Ah! So it was Canair's idea to go to the Shrine of St James?'

'She was to be our leader. Cian was from Bangor, although he often came to Moville. We knew him well. He served the Abbot of Bangor as his messenger to Moville. When Canair announced the pilgrimage, he attached himself to our party from the first.'

There was a sudden shouting from the deck above and Wenbrit came scampering through.

'What is it?' demanded Fidelma, as he rushed past.

'The mist is clearing,' cried the boy, 'but I think there is trouble.'

Chapter Ten

Fidelma found that several of her fellow travellers were gathered on deck to discover what all the excitement was about, generated by the crew of *The Barnacle Goose*. It was close to midday and the sun had dispelled most of the sea mist, sending it whirling away like smoke from a fire.

As Fidelma had come onto the main deck, there had been another cry from the masthead – a shout filled with alarm. She turned to the stern deck where Murchad, standing by his helmsmen, was looking to port and followed his gaze. Through the rapidly disappearing mist she saw the swell breaking white over a group of rocks on which cormorants stood like glowering sentinels. It was then that Fidelma realised that the sea all around was speckled with such reefs and protruding islets.

Gurvan, the mate, came hurrying along the deck to join the captain.

'What is this place?' Fidelma called.

'Sylinancim,' grunted the Breton. He did not look happy. 'The storm has pushed us too far east and south.'

So Murchad had been right, she thought, when he had told her that the storm had driven them eastward off their course.

Neither Gurvan nor Murchad objected when she followed the Breton onto the stern deck to stand near the grim-faced captain.

'I did not think that the Sylinancim Islands were as gaunt and harsh as this,' she said, gazing a little in awe on the jagged rocks which surrounded them.

'The main islands are inhabited and have gentle landing places,' replied Gurvan. 'We would usually avoid this area by standing out to westward. I think we've missed the Broad Sound, which would be a safe channel, and now the winds and tide are driving us through Crebawethan Neck.'

These latter sentences were addressed to Murchad, who nodded in agreement of his mate's assessment. Fidelma knew nothing of these places. However, she picked up the anxious note in the Breton's usually phlegmatic voice.

'Is that a bad place?' she asked.

'It is certainly not a good place to be,' Gurvan replied. 'If we can get through the Neck we might be able to slip south of the Retarrier Ledges – more rocks. Once clear of them we could make a straight run to the Island of Ushant. We'll be a full day off our course, providing . . .' He suddenly realised that he was speaking to a passenger and glanced guiltily at his companion. Murchad was too preoccupied to notice.

'Providing we manage to get through this Crebawethan Neck?' Fidelma finished for him.

'Exactly so, lady.'

The captain had been watching the wind-filled sail with a careful eye and now signalled one of the men on the steering oar to exchange his position with Murchad himself. Some of the sailors had crowded in the bows ready to cry out warnings in case the ship came too close to the rocks.

'Secure the bowline!' Murchad cried.

Two of the hands rushed to the weather side of the ship and hauled on a rope which was attached to the square sail. They pulled on it, swinging the sail more to the starboard side so that the wind strained against the great leather expanse.

Murchard turned towards Fidelma.

'Lady, I would rather all the pilgrims were on deck during this passage,' he called. 'Would you mind asking the rest of them to come up?' Then he had to return his attention to the steering oar and left it to Gurvan to explain.

'If . . .' Gurvan hesitated and shrugged. 'If we strike the reefs, well . . . It's just that the pilgrims might stand a better chance if they are on deck.'

'Is it that dangerous?' she asked and then saw the affirmative in the man's eyes. Without a further word, Fidelma hurried across to the companionway. Wenbrit was standing there.

'The captain wants everyone on deck,' she explained.

Wenbrit turned and disappeared. Within seconds she could hear him urging the pilgrims from their cabins to join their fellows on deck. They came reluctantly for the most part. Wenbrit took charge, telling them where to stand. Most of them did not seem aware of the dangers, and even when Fidelma joined her entreaties to those of the young cabin boy, they moved with agonising slowness, grumbling all the while. Then, as some of them saw the closeness of the rocks and reefs, a quiet descended as they finally understood the peril they were in.

The pilgrims huddled on the main deck, leaning against the rail and watching the black rocks, drenched with yellow-white foam, speeding by so dangerously near the sides of the vessel.

The wind was blowing quite fresh, but ugly little white caps were beginning to form on the swell. There was a great deal of hissing white water on all sides and Fidelma realised that it portended something more dangerous to the vessel than the taller, black granite outcrops. It indicated submerged rocks which could tear the bottom out of the ship in a second.

Fidelma shivered. The sunshine had taken on something of a brittle cold quality. White clouds, like long pieces of fleece, were stretching over the blue canopy. A curious glare hung on the waters, reflecting with such intensity that Fidelma had to rub her eyes. She could feel the salt deposits from the fine spray irritating them. The wind was dying away. She saw the strength beginning to go out of the sail; it flapped forlornly and almost limply.

Murchad looked up and mouthed something; perhaps it was a curse. She could forgive him for that. Then Gurvan rushed forward and shouted an order. Two men were left at the bow but the others came scurrying amidships and stood ready as if waiting for an order.

The rocks were still gliding by as the momentum of the ship's motion continued, helped by the tide.

Looking around, Fidelma had a tremendous sense of isolation. Here, in the middle of the sea, with the pounding noise of the waves on the rocks, she felt terribly vulnerable and alone. She had a sense of being chilled, was weighed down by foreboding.

She found herself muttering something.

'Deus misereatur . . .'

She surprised herself when she realised that she was reciting one of the Psalms.

> '"God be gracious and bless us,
> God make His face shine upon us,
> That His way may be known on earth
> And His saving power among all the nations."'

She stood, hands white on the ship's rail, as the bowsprit plunged into the spray and rose again, like a horse, bowing and throwing its head back, eager to be into the race. Fidelma could hear a creaking sound; startled, she looked up to see the main mast bending at the top like a whip; the yards were groaning as the winds threatened to burst the straining sails asunder. Murchad was standing feet apart, both hands holding the steering oar, his face an expressionless mask as he concentrated on his task.

Fidelma realised that if anyone fell into that turbulent water they would not last five seconds. There would be no hope. They all had to trust to Murchad's seamanship. Fidelma was someone who felt unhappy unless she had some degree of control over events. Here she could do nothing and it frustrated her.

Murchad remained impassive, hair streaming in the wind, eyes screwed tight. His only orders were to his companion as they both held tightly to the steering oar.

Now they were entering a narrow passage between what looked like a great island of rock to the starboard side and a scattering of hidden rocks and reefs to the portside. The water was frothing and roaring around them and the ship seemed to be moving uncontrollably with the flood of waters that propelled it towards its doom. Fidelma prayed that Murchad and his companion had an iron grip on the steering oar.

The wind was literally screaming through the spars and cordage of the rigging, and the vessel seemed totally out of control as it swung and bounced perilously close to the jagged granite teeth that rose around them. Yet Murchad and his companion held on.

There was cry from the bows, taken up by two or three of the crew. Fidelma went to the rails and strained forward to see what was amiss.

They seemed to be heading for a great black rock, standing immediately in their path, rising among the streams of yellow-white froth which poured down the sides as the seas broke over it. Great waves thundered as they burst over what must be a line of hidden reefs. It was like a boiling cauldron. For a moment, Fidelma closed her eyes as she imagined the ship being torn to pieces in that maelstrom. She was almost jerked off her feet as the deck tilted. She thought they had impacted on the rocks. She felt an arm round her and Gurvan's voice hissed: 'Do not let go of the rail!'

As she opened her eyes, she saw the rocks dashing by along the side of the ship in the hollow of the waves. She could have reached forward and touched them. The tall black rock swept past and then, with an abruptness which she found astonishing, they seemed to have entered calm waters.

There was a triumphant cry from those at the bow.

Fidelma saw the saturnine face of Gurvan break into a lopsided grin of relief.

'Have we escaped?' she asked.

'We passed through the Neck,' replied Gurvan solemnly. 'We can turn south into calmer waters from here.'

He turned then, shouting an order to Wenbrit to allow the passengers to go below if they chose.

Fidelma was still standing, gripping the rail and gazing at the black seas sliding by, when Cian approached her.

'How long are you going to keep up your antagonism?' he began, slightly belligerently. 'I am just trying to be friendly. After all, we shall be in one another's company for a long time yet.'

Fidelma came back to the reality of her situation with a sharp exhalation of breath. She was about to respond when she changed her mind.

'As a matter of fact, Cian,' she said tightly, turning towards him, 'I do need to talk with you.'

It was obvious that Cian was not prepared for her acquiescence. He looked at her in blank astonishment for a moment and then a triumphant look came into his eyes.

'There, I knew you would see sense eventually.'

Fidelma hated that knowing look of one who had won some victory. She would dispel that notion immediately. Her voice was cold.

'Murchad has asked me to make an official enquiry into the disappearance of Sister Muirgel in order to protect him from any action her kin might take against him for negligence. I need to ask you some questions.'

Cian's face fell. It was clearly not the reply he had been expecting.

'I hear that you have taken it upon yourself to lead this company.'

Cian's mouth tightened and his jaw tilted upwards.

'Is there anyone better qualified?'

'It is not my place to challenge your competence, Cian. I am not one of your company. I merely asked to get the matter clear in my report.'

'There needs to be a leader. I have said as much ever since we left the Abbey.'

'I thought Sister Canair was the leader of this pilgrimage?' she asked.

'Canair was . . .' He paused and shrugged. 'Canair is not here.'

'What made you become concerned for the safety of your company last night? What made you start checking if everyone was all right and at dawn? Surely it was not your place to do so? Were you disturbed by the storm?'

'I was not disturbed.'

101

The blunt denial caused Fidelma to raise an eyebrow slightly.

'I thought we were all disturbed by the violence of the storm,' she commented.

'You know that I am . . . *was* . . . a warrior. I am used to being in situations where—'

'So you slept through the storm?' Fidelma cut him short.

'Not exactly, but—'

'So you *were* disturbed along with the rest of us?' Fidelma took a vindictive pleasure in pressing the point. 'But you have not answered my question. Why did you feel that you needed to check on the members of your company?'

'As I have said, someone needed to be in charge. Sister Muirgel was clearly not in control.'

'So it was merely to show your claim to authority?'

Cian glowered.

'I just wanted to make sure no one had any problems.'

'So you appointed yourself as guardian to check on everyone?'

'As it turned out it was a good thing I did so.'

'So everyone was safe in their cabin, with the exception of Sister Muirgel?'

'Since you are being so specific,' he sneered, 'no, not everyone was in their cabin.'

'Can you explain?'

'When I awoke, Brother Bairne, with whom I share, was not in his bunk. I later found that he had been to what these sailors call the head.'

'I see. Anyone else apart from Muirgel not in their cabin?'

'No.'

'When did you discover Muirgel was missing?'

'Almost at once. As you will recall, her cabin is opposite mine. When I entered, she was not there.'

'Was her door locked?'

'Why should it be?' He frowned.

'No matter. Go on. What did you do?'

'I turned from the cabin and that was when I saw Brother Bairne returning from the head. He went back into our cabin.'

'Where did you go then?'

'I checked Sister Crella's cabin. She was asleep. Then I checked with Sister Ainder and Sister Gormán. Sister Gormán was already awake and dressed.'

'Did you have an argument with Gormán?'

His features became guarded.

'Why would I have an argument with her?'

'Sister Ainder says she was awakened by the sound of it.'

'Rubbish! Ainder was angry that our voices disturbed her sleep. I then checked the other cabins and everyone was where they should have been, with the exception of Sister Muirgel.'

'And so?'

'Then I came to check that you were all right. You were still asleep. Having realised that Sister Muirgel was the only person not in her cabin, I checked the head and the large cabin where we eat. Then I saw the captain, Murchad, and informed him that I could not locate Sister Muirgel. He said that he would search the ship for me and asked the Breton, Gurvan, to do so. When the ship had been searched and Muirgel was found not to be on board, Murchad concluded that she had been swept overboard during the storm. He then asked Gurvan to make a double-check which, as you know, confirmed our worst fears.'

'And you heard nothing during the night, saw nothing which might provide an explanation of what happened?'

'It is as I have said, Fidelma.'

She paused thoughtfully.

'How well did you know Sister Muirgel?'

Cian frowned suspiciously.

'If you want to know about Sister Muirgel, ask Sister Crella. She was her close friend and they were related.'

'It is what *you* know that I am keen to discover. You told me that you entered the Abbey of Bangor. I understand that you went to Moville frequently. You would surely have met Muirgel there.'

Cian's mouth tightened.

'I ran messages for the Abbot of Bangor and helped in the fruit garden.'

'Was that how you first met Sister Muirgel, running messages?'

'As I recall, it was Sister Crella who introduced me.'

'Did Crella also introduce you to Sister Canair?'

'Muirgel did. Why?'

'I merely want to know how you came to be part of this company of pilgrims.'

'I have already told you.'

'Tell me again.'

'I came because I had heard of Mormohec the healer at the Shrine of St James.'

'So you said. You therefore persuaded Sister Canair to accept you into the pilgrimage which she had organised?'

'It was hardly organised. This band lacks discipline.'

'They are pilgrims, Cian, not militia. Yet one thing puzzles me. If Sister Canair was the organiser, why did she fail to come aboard the ship when it set sail?'

'It is not for me to say. Some people have a habit of lateness. Isn't there an old proverb that a late man brings trouble on himself? So with women. Perhaps she thought the tides and winds would stop for her.'

'Are you saying that Sister Canair had a reputation for dilatoriness?'

'I am not saying that. It is just an observation to explain why she might have missed the sailing.'

'It is strange, though, that the leader of this party could not even sail with the ship, having led the group all the way from Ulaidh south to Muman.' Fidelma pressed the point once again.

'Life is made up of strange occurrences.'

'Such as poor Sister Muirgel's untimely demise?' observed Fidelma softly.

'I do not see that as strange. Sister Muirgel was a very self-willed woman. Once she had made up her mind to do something, nothing would change it. It was the same when she decided to come on this voyage.'

'How do you know anyone wanted to change her mind about this voyage?' Fidelma was interested by his innuendo.

'After I spoke to her about it and told her that I was going to join Sister Canair's party,' replied Cian, unabashed, 'Sister Muirgel went to see Sister Canair immediately. She persuaded Canair to reject two other Sisters whom she had approved of in order to allow Muirgel and Crella to take their places. Sister Muirgel was very strong in her influence with others.'

Fidelma grew thoughtful.

'You seem to imply that Sister Muirgel decided to come on this journey only when she knew that *you* were to be part of the company.'

Cian shook his head.

'I would not say that.'

'I am now under the impression that Sister Muirgel had more influence in the formation of this pilgrimage than had Sister Canair.'

'The journey was several weeks in the planning. I suppose Sister Muirgel did attempt to take over the leadership from Sister Canair. She was backed by Sister Crella who always supported her in everything. But Sister Canair was strong also. She was more than a match for the dictates of our missing friend.'

'You seem to know Sister Muirgel's faults well.'

'You learn many things when . . .' Cian sought for the right phrase. 'When travelling with people. You learn about their faults.'

'You were saying that you did not find her death strange because she was self-willed?'

'What I meant by that was that she was pig-headed enough to have gone up on deck no matter what advice she had from anyone. Once she made up her mind to do something, she did it.'

Fidelma's eyes flickered with interest.

'Did anyone advise her not to go up on deck in the storm?' she asked quickly.

Cian shook his head.

'I used that merely as an example. It was what she was like. Now, I have told you all I know on the matter.'

Cian made to turn back along the deck, but Fidelma called him back sharply.

'One more thing . . .'

He turned, expectantly.

'I would like to know more about the circumstances in which your party became separated from Sister Canair. I still can't quite see how she missed the sailing time and why she did not come on board with the rest of you.'

Cian regarded her uncertainly for a moment.

'Why are you so interested in Sister Canair when you are investigating how Sister Muirgel came to be swept overboard?' he countered.

'Call it my natural curiosity, Cian. You will doubtless remember that, when I was younger, I lacked curiosity until it was awakened in me that I should be more interested in the reasons and motives for people's behaviour.'

An aggressive expression crossed Cian's features but it was gone in a second.

'As I recall, we were separated from Sister Canair before we reached Ardmore,' he said.

'Why was that?'

'We were going to spend the night at St Declan's Abbey, but Sister Canair left our company about a mile or so from the Abbey.'

'Why did she leave you?'

'She told us that she wanted to meet with a friend or relative who lived in that part of the country. She promised that she would join us in the Abbey, where we were to spend the night. She did not join us at the Abbey, however, and when she did not turn up to meet us on the quay at the time appointed for the ship to sail, it was Sister Muirgel who took charge. She finally achieved what she wanted – control of the group.'

'Her control did not last long,' observed Fidelma dryly. 'Two of your leaders have not enjoyed that office for long. Are you sure that you still want to aspire to such office?' There was a cynical smile on her lips.

Cian's features tightened.

'I don't know what you mean.'

Fidelma's smile broadened.

'Just an observation, that's all. Thank you for your time and for answering my questions.'

Cian turned to leave again and then hesitated. He raised his good arm in a curiously helpless gesture.

'Fidelma, we should not be enemies. This bitterness . . .'

She regarded him disdainfully.

'I have told you before, Cian, we are not enemies. To be enemies means some feeling remains between us. There is nothing between us now. Not even bitterness.'

Even as she spoke, Fidelma realised that she was lying. Her present contempt for Cian meant that there *was* a feeling there – and she did not like it one bit. If she really had recovered from the hurt he had done to her then, indeed, she would have no feeling at all. That fact worried her more than she cared to admit.

Chapter Eleven

The next person she should question, Fidelma decided, was the Breton mate, Gurvan, who had conducted a thorough search of the ship. She asked Murchad where he might be found, and the captain told her that he was below, 'caulking'. She did not know what that meant, but Murchad had signalled Wenbrit and instructed the boy to take Fidelma down to where Gurvan was working.

Gurvan was in a forward area of the ship where, it seemed, some stores were kept. It was well forward of the area where the men who formed the crew of *The Barnacle Goose* slung their hammocks, hanging beds of fibre netting suspended by cords at both ends attached to the beams of the ship so that they swung with the motion of the ship. Some of the crew were sleeping, exhausted from having been up most of the night during the storm. Wenbrit wound his way between the hammocks, holding a lantern, and moving into a cabin space filled with boxes and barrels.

Gurvan had shifted some of the boxes in order to get to the side of the ship. He had balanced a lantern on the boxes and was bent with a bucket pushing what looked like mud between the planking. Wenbrit left them, having been assured that Fidelma could find her own way back to the main deck.

Gurvan did not pause in his work and Fidelma crouched down beside him. She noticed that little rivulets of water were streaming here and there through the planking of the vessel and suddenly realised that the sea was on the other side of those planks of wood.

'Is it dangerous?' she whispered. 'Will the sea flood in?'

Gurvan grinned.

'Bless you, no, lady. Seepage happens to the best of ships, especially after the rough passage we have had. First the storm and then sailing through the Neck back there. It's a wonder we did not get some of our planks stove in. But this is a good, sturdy vessel. Our planks are fitted carvel style; they'll hold back most seas.'

'So what are you doing?' She did not feel entirely reassured and did not want to admit that she had no clue as to what 'carvel style' meant.

'It's called caulking, lady.' He indicated the bucket. 'Those are hazel leaves. I press them into the joints of the planking and it serves to make the cracks watertight.'

'It seems so . . . so flimsy against such turbulent seas.'

'It's a tried and trusted method,' Gurvan assured her. 'The great ships of our Veneti ancestors went into battle against Julius Caesar similarly caulked. But you did not come down here to ask me about caulking, did you?'

Fidelma reluctantly nodded agreement.

'No. I just wanted to ask you about your search for Sister Muirgel.'

'The religieuse who went overboard?' Gurvan paused and seemed to be examining his work. Then he said: 'The captain asked me to conduct a search. In a ship twenty-four metres in length there are not too many places where a person can hide, either by accident or intentionally. It soon became apparent that the woman was not on board.'

'You searched everywhere?'

Gurvan smiled patiently.

'Everywhere that a person could possibly conceal themselves if they wanted to. I presumed, however, that the woman would not want to, so I did not look in the bilge – that is, the bottom of the ship's hull, which is usually where the rats, mice and sediments of refuse congregate.'

Fidelma gave an involuntary shiver. Gurvan smiled a little sadistically at her reaction.

'No, lady, apart from the passenger cabins which had already been searched, I looked everywhere. The only conclusion is that the poor woman went overboard.'

'Thank you, Gurvan.' Fidelma rose and made her way back through the ship.

Fidelma had not thought to question Sister Gormán next, but found herself passing the cabin door. She knocked and looked in. Sister Gormán was sitting on her bunk, looking pale and unhappy.

'Am I disturbing you?' Fidelma asked as she entered in response to Gormán's invitation.

'Sister Fidelma.' The young girl looked up nervously. 'I do not mind being disturbed. This voyage is not as I expected it to be.'

'What did you expect?' asked Fidelma, taking a seat.

'Oh.' The girl paused as if to give the question some thought. 'I don't suppose anything is ever as one would expect, but a pilgrimage, a voyage to a shrine wherein lies the body of one who knew the living Christ . . . surely that should be a momentous journey filled with excitement?'

'Is this not a journey filled with excitement? I would have thought so, filled as it is with incident.' Fidelma kept her tone light.

Sister Gormán pursed her lips. Fidelma waited and when there was no response, she altered her tone to one of seriousness, sitting down on a chair near the girl.

'Obviously, the loss of Sister Muirgel is a sad blow for your party.'

The girl wrinkled her nose distastefully.

'*Her!*' she said, summoning in that word an expression of dislike.

Fidelma picked up her tone immediately.

'I gather that you were not a friend of Sister Muirgel?'

'I regret that she is dead,' Sister Gormán responded defensively.

'But you did not like her?'

'I do not feel guilty about not liking her.'

'Has anyone suggested that you should feel guilty?'

'If someone dies one always feels guilty for harbouring bad thoughts about them.'

'And have you harboured bad thoughts?'

'Didn't everyone?'

'I do not know as I am a stranger. I thought you were all pilgrims travelling together.'

'That is so. It does not mean we all liked one another. I have nothing in common with the others in this party except . . .' She paused and continued quickly: 'However, Sister Muirgel was a bully and I – I *hated her!*'

The expression was given emphasis by the way that Sister Gormán almost spat it out. Fidelma examined the girl with gravity.

'So now you believe you should experience guilt for feeling that hate?'

'But I do not.'

'What exactly made you hate her, Sister Gormán?'

The young girl sat, considering carefully.

'She always picked on me because I am young and came from a poor family. My father was not some chieftain but an hostler. I learned to read a little and went into the Abbey at Moville to continue to study. Muirgel and Crella forced me to become their servant.'

'*Forced* you?' Fidelma was not naive enough to think that bullying did not go on behind the walls of abbeys and religious foundations, just as it went on in any other institution. 'Both Sisters Muirgel and Crella bullied you?'

'Sister Muirgel led and Sister Crella followed. Muirgel was always the leader in these things.'

'So you do not feel sorrow for her death?'

'Doesn't it say in Paul's epistle to Romans: "Bless those who persecute you; bless and do not curse them"? If that is so then my soul is doomed. But I do not care.'

Fidelma smiled thinly.

'Well, in the circumstances, I am sure that you will be forgiven such feelings. One of the hardest things to feel is love for our enemies.'

'But isn't forgiveness of our enemies one of the primary acts of Grace which mark us as blessed of God?' queried the young girl stubbornly.

'The theme of forgiveness is central to the Gospels,' agreed Fidelma. 'The Gospels tell us that Christ's willingness to forgive us is conditional on *our* willingness to forgive our enemies. The old self has to be reborn in the new loving person if it is to be accepted into the eternal Kingdom of God.'

Sister Gormán looked pained.

'Then my doom hangs heavy over my head.'

'Surely now that Sister Muirgel is dead . . .' Fidelma began.

'I still cannot forgive Sister Muirgel for the suffering she caused me.'

Fidelma sat back thoughtfully.

'If you hated her, as you say, why did you come on this pilgrimage?'

'It was Sister Canair who was to be in charge of the pilgrimage. But Canair was a bad person.'

'In what way?' Fidelma was surprised. 'Are you saying that Sister Canair also bullied you?'

'Oh no.' The girl shook her head. 'Sister Canair just ignored me. She did not even know of my existence. How I hated them all! How I wished—' The girl suddenly paled and looked anxiously at Fidelma. 'I did not wish Sister Muirgel dead in this manner. I just wanted to punish her.'

'Punish her? What are you saying?'

Sister Gormán looked anxious.

'I swear, I did not mean it.'

'Mean what?' frowned Fidelma. 'What did you not mean, Sister? Are you saying that you are involved in Muirgel's disappearance?'

Wide-eyed, the young girl stared at Fidelma as if horrified by the thoughts that had come to her mind.

'I ill-wished her. I stood outside her cabin last night at midnight and cursed her.'

Fidelma did not know whether to feel amused by the dramatic revelation or to be shocked by it.

'You say that you were outside her cabin last night at midnight, during the storm – and that you cursed her? Is that what you are saying?'

Sister Gormán nodded slowly.

'I was there during the storm.'

'Did you go into her cabin to see her?'

'I did not. I stood and I cursed her with the words of the Psalms.' She began to chant in a wailing voice:

> 'May her eyes be darkened so that she does not see,
> Let continual agues shake her loins.
> Pour out Thine indignation upon her
> And let Thy burning anger overtake her
> . . . multiply her torments.
> Give her the punishment her sin deserves.
> Exclude her from Thy righteous mercy.
> Let her be blotted from the Book of Life
> And not be enrolled among the righteous!'

Fidelma blinked at the vehemence in the young girl's voice and then tried to make light of the matter.

'That is hardly an exact translation of Psalm 69,' she observed.

'But it worked, it worked! My curse worked!' The girl's voice had an hysterical edge to it. 'She must have gone up on deck soon afterwards and been swept away by God's vengeful hand.'

'I think not,' replied Fidelma dryly. 'If there was any hand in it, it was a human hand.'

Sister Gormán regarded her for a moment and then had an abrupt change of emotion. There was suspicion in her eyes.

'What do you mean? I thought everyone said that she was swept overboard.'

Fidelma realised that she had let slip more than she had intended.

'I merely meant that your curse and invocation were not responsible.'

Sister Gormán considered that for a moment.

'But a curse is a terrible thing and I must atone for my sin. Yet I cannot do so by forgiving Sister Muirgel, nor by feeling guilt myself.'

'Just tell me this, Sister Gormán,' Fidelma said, beginning to feel irritable at the self-centred attitude of the girl and her attachment to a

111

belief that one was responsible for Sister Muirgel's death. 'You say that you left your cabin about midnight?'

The girl inclined her head in agreement.

'You share your cabin with Sister Ainder, don't you?'

'I do.'

'Did she see you leave the cabin?'

'She was fast asleep. She is a heavy sleeper. She did not see me leave.'

'The storm was in progress?'

'It was.'

'Your cabin is by the stairs or whatever they are called. So, you are telling me that you went down that passage to her cabin and neither met nor saw anyone?'

Sister Gormán shook her head.

'There was no one about at that hour,' she confirmed, 'and the storm was very bad.'

'And, again, from what you tell me, you stood outside her door, did not go in, but just stood there cursing her. No one heard this?'

'The storm was rising then. I doubt that anyone would have heard me even if they had been standing next to me.'

Fidelma looked at her and found herself struggling to believe her. It seemed so bizarre but then it was often that the incredible was the truth and the plausible was the lie.

'How long did you stand by her cabin door with your so-called cursing?' she demanded.

'I am not sure. A few moments. A quarter of an hour. I don't know.'

'What did you do after pronouncing your curse?'

'I returned to my cabin. Sister Ainder was still asleep and the storm still raging. I lay on my bed but did not sleep until the storm abated.'

'You heard nothing from outside your cabin?'

'I think I heard the cabin door opposite bang shut. I was just dozing off when it woke me momentarily.'

'How could you have heard that in the noise of the storm? You just said that no one would have heard *you*. How, then, could you hear such a thing as a cabin door shutting?'

Sister Gormán's jaw jutted out pugnaciously.

'I heard it because it was *after* the storm began to die down.'

'Very well,' Fidelma said. 'I just want to make sure that I have the facts clearly in my mind. And this cabin door, the one you heard banging shut, you say it was the door opposite your cabin.'

112

'It is the one shared by Cian and Bairne.'

'I see. Then you went back to sleep and were not disturbed again?'

Sister Gormán looked troubled. 'My curse killed her, you know. I suppose I will have to be punished.'

Fidelma rose and stood looking down with pity at the young girl. Sister Gormán was definitely unstable. She badly needed help from her soul-friend, the companion who was responsible for hearing problems and discussing them. Each person in the churches of the Five Kingdoms chose an *anam-chara*, a soul friend.

'Perhaps you are unaware of the ancient proverb,' she tried to reassure the girl. 'A thousand curses never tore a shirt.'

The girl glanced up at her.

'I have cursed Sister Muirgel and caused her death. Now I must curse myself.'

She began to rock back and forth, arms wrapped around her shoulders, crooning softly.

'Perish the day when I was born
And the night which said, "A child is conceived"!
May that day turn to darkness; may God above not look for it,
Nor the light of dawn shine on it.
May blackness sully it, and murk and gloom,
Cloud smother that day, swift darkness eclipse its sun.
Blind darkness swallow up that night:
Count it not among the days of the year,
Reckon it not in the cycle of the months.
That night, may it be barren for ever,
No cry of joy be heard in it.
Cursèd be it . . .'

Fidelma left the irrational young girl chanting to herself and walked away with a slight feeling of disgust. Who, among the unlikely female religieuses, should she turn to, and ask to take Sister Gormán in hand? The young girl needed some counsel, and Fidelma herself could not take on such a responsibility now. And yet there seemed no one else. Sister Ainder was not sympathetic enough and Crella was too young herself. Fidelma would have to deal with the matter later. There was still Dathal, Adamrae, Bairne and Tola left to question.

Fidelma suddenly realised that there was one member of the pilgrim group whom she had not yet seen at all. His name was Brother Guss. He had not stirred from his cabin since he had come on board, nor

113

had he emerged even when Murchad ordered everyone on deck during the dangerous passage through the rocks. He was sharing a cabin with Brother Tola. She had seen Brother Tola sitting by a water-butt at the main mast, reading, and felt that now might be a good opportunity to tackle this elusive religieux.

She knocked at the cabin door and waited.

There was the sound of someone moving behind the door and then a long pause. She knocked again. A voice called faintly from within and she entered, blinking in the darkness of the cabin and waiting until her eyes adjusted sufficiently to see. The shadowy figure of a man was seated on one of the bunks.

'Brother Guss, I presume?'

She saw the dark head of the religieux turn in her direction as she paused on the threshold.

'I am Guss,' a tremulous voice replied.

'May we have some light in here?' suggested Fidelma and, without waiting for an answer, she took the lantern which was hanging outside in the passage, and set it in the cabin.

The light revealed the religieux to be young. She noticed several things about him, from his reddish tousled hair to the splash of freckles on his pale skin, to his frightened, large blue eyes, and his tall but wiry frame. He dropped his eyes like a guilty child as she met his gaze.

'We have not seen you on deck or at mealtimes,' she opened, seating herself on the bunk beside him. 'Are you still unwell?'

Brother Guss regarded her with suspicion. 'I have been sick – the sea motion, you understand. Who are you?'

'My name is Fidelma. Fidelma of Cashel.'

'Brother Tola mentioned you. I have been ill,' he added, repeating himself.

'So I understand. But you are feeling better now?'

He did not reply.

'The sea is much calmer now and it is unwise to confine yourself to a cabin for so long a period. You need to be on deck getting some fresh air. In fact, I did not see you on deck when everyone was ordered there.'

'I did not realise that the order applied to me.'

'Did you not know of the dangers?'

The young man did not reply. Instead he continued to regard her with distrust.

'Guss is an unusual name,' Fidelma began again. 'It is a very old name, is it not?' The best way to get him to drop his defensive attitude towards her was to encourage him to speak.

The young man inclined his head slightly.

'It means, as I recall, vigour or fierceness. I suppose people call you Gusán?' she added, using the diminutive. A comment on his youthfulness might provoke him.

Indeed, this caused a scowl to cross the young man's face.

'I am called Guss,' he replied in annoyance.

'And you are from the Abbey of Moville?'

'I am a student at the Abbey,' confirmed the youth. He was scarcely more than twenty years old.

'What are you studying?'

'I am studying the star-lore under the Venerable Cummian, and helping keep the records of the phenomena of the skies.' There was a note of pride in the boy's voice in spite of his woebegone attitude.

'Cummian? Is he still alive then?' Fidelma said with genuine wonder.

The youth frowned.

'Do you know the Venerable Cummian?'

'I know of his reputation. He studied under the great Abbot of Bangor, Mo Sinu maccu Min, and has written many works on astronomical computus. But he must be very old. You say that you are his student?'

'One of them,' admitted Guss proudly. 'But I have already obtained to the degree of the fifth order of wisdom.'

'Excellent. It is good to know that there is someone who can recognise the map of the heavens and chart our way safely home in the middle of these tempestuous seas.'

Thus Fidelma encouraged him, gently leading the youth on and trying to break down his initial hostility to her intrusion. She noticed that his right hand kept going to his left arm to massage it. There was a dark stain on the sleeve.

'You seem to have hurt your arm,' she commented sympathetically. 'Have you cut it? Shall I examine it for you?'

He flushed and a scowl spread over his features again. 'It is nothing. I scratched it, that is all.' Then he relapsed into silence.

Fidelma pressed on. 'What made you decide to come on this pilgrimage, Brother Guss?'

'Cummian.'

'I don't understand. Cummian told you to come on this voyage?'

'Cummian had been on a pilgrimage to the Holy Shrine of St James and advised me that I should also take the voyage for my own education.'

'To see foreign worlds?' hazarded Fidelma.

The young man shook his head patronisingly.

'No; to see the stars.'

Fidelma thought for a moment before suddenly understanding what he meant.

'The Holy Shrine of St James at the Field of Stars?'

'Cummian says that when you stand at the Holy Shrine you can look up into a clear night sky and trace the Way of the White Cow, curving directly to the kingdoms of Éireann. It is said that our ancestors over a thousand years ago followed the Way of the White Cow and thus they came to the shores of the lands in which they settled.' For a moment, the youth's tone rose in enthusiasm.

Fidelma knew that the Way of the White Cow was described by many names; in Latin it was called the Circulus Lacteus, the Milky Way.

'That is why the spot is called the Field of the Stars because the stars are laid out so clearly,' added the youth.

'So Cummian suggested you come on this pilgrimage?'

'When Sister Canair announced that she was organising the pilgrimage, Cummian arranged for me to accompany her.'

'You knew Sister Canair, of course?'

He shook his head.

'Not before the Venerable Cummian introduced me. We students of star lore did not mix with other sections of the community.'

'So you knew none of the party on this pilgrimage?'

Brother Guss frowned.

'I did not know Brother Cian, Dathal nor Adamrae, nor even Brother Tola. They were all from Bangor. I knew some of the others by sight.'

'Sister Crella, for example?'

A spasm of dislike crossed his face.

'I know Crella.'

Fidelma leaned forward quickly.

'You do not like her?'

Guss suddenly looked guarded.

'It is not my position to like or dislike.'

'But you do not like her,' repeated Fidelma. 'Was there any particular reason for that?'

Guss shrugged but said nothing.

Fidelma decided to try another tack.

'Did you know Sister Muirgel well?'

116

Brother Guss blinked rapidly, and that guarded look crossed his features once more.

'I met her several times at the Abbey before the pilgrimage was announced.' There was a tightness in his voice. Fidelma decided to hazard an interpretation.

'Did you like Muirgel?'

'I do not deny it,' he said quietly.

'More than like?' she guessed.

The youth's jaw clamped shut. His eyes met Fidelma's and it seemed that he hesitated as if to make up his mind what he should say.

'I said . . . I liked her!' The words came out like a protest.

Fidelma sat back for a moment trying to gauge what was going on in his mind.

'Well, there is nothing wrong in that,' she pointed out. 'How did she feel about you?'

'She returned my feelings,' he said quietly.

'I am sorry,' Fidelma said, automatically laying a land on his arm. 'I have been too impertinent. The captain requested me to enquire into the circumstances of her death. So I must ask these questions. You understand that, don't you?'

'The circumstances of her death?' The youth actually laughed – a harsh, unmusical bark. '*I* will tell you the circumstances of her death. She was murdered!'

Fidelma stared into the angry face of the youth, and then she said quietly: 'You do not accept that she was merely swept overboard then? So what *do* you believe happened to her, Brother Guss?'

'I do not know!' Was his reply a little too hurried?

'And why would someone have killed her?'

'Jealousy, perhaps.'

'Who was jealous? Who would murder her?' demanded Fidelma. She suddenly remembered Sister Crella's accusation against Brother Bairne at the memorial ceremony. 'You were just jealous.' Those were the words she had used. Fidelma leaned forward. 'Was it Brother Bairne who was jealous?'

Brother Guss looked bewildered.

'Bairne? He was jealous, right enough. But it was Crella who killed her.'

Fidelma did not expect the reply and it made her quiet for a moment or so.

'Do you have evidence for what you say?' she asked softly.

The youth hesitated and then shook his head firmly.

'I know that Crella is responsible, that is all.'

'You'd better tell me the whole story. When did you meet Sister Muirgel? What exactly was your relationship with her?'

'I fell in love with her when she came to the Abbey. At first, she barely noticed me. She preferred more mature men. You know, men like Brother Cian. He was mature. He had been a warrior. She certainly liked *him*.'

'And did he like her?'

'At first she was in his company a lot.'

'Did they have an affair?'

Brother Gus flushed and his lower lip trembled for a moment. Then he nodded.

'Why was Crella jealous?'

'She was jealous of anyone who took Sister Muirgel away from her. But in this case . . .' He paused, as if reflecting.

Fidelma prompted him to continue: 'In this case . . . what?'

'It had been Sister Muirgel who had taken Cian away from Crella.'

Fidelma had to control her features. Brother Guss was full of surprises.

'Are you saying that Cian was having an affair with Crella and then turned from her to Muirgel?'

'Sister Muirgel admitted it was all a mistake. It lasted a few days, that is all.'

'Did you have a relationship with Sister Muirgel?' Fidelma was abrupt.

The youth nodded.

'When did this relationship start?'

'It was just before we began this pilgrimage. When I told Muirgel that I was joining the pilgrimage because my tutor had instructed me to do so, she forced Canair into allowing her to come. Of course, Crella had to come as well.'

'She must have liked you a lot to have followed you on this journey.'

'Well, to be honest, I thought that I never stood a chance of being noticed by her in that way, if you know what I mean. However, she sought me out and told me outright that she had become attracted to me. I had never said anything to her before because I thought she would never have looked at me. When she told me . . . well, we grew together and we were in love.'

'Did Crella know about this relationship? She thinks Muirgel was still having an affair with Cian.'

Guss's eyes grew dark.

'I believe she knew. I think she knew and was jealous of Muirgel's happiness. Muirgel told me that she was being threatened.'

'What – Muirgel told you that Crella was threatening her? Did you hear some argument between them?'

'They argued – yes. It was a few days before we reached Ardmore. We had stopped at a tavern for a meal and Muirgel had gone to a nearby stream to wash. I had fetched ale and was taking it down to where Muirgel was washing when I heard Crella's voice raised in argument with her.'

'And can you recall what was being said? The precise words?'

'I don't know whether I can recall the precise words, but Crella was accusing Muirgel of . . .' he hesitated and coloured, '. . . of playing with my affections – those were the words she used. Of playing with my affections as she had played with others. Crella believed that Muirgel still loved Cian.'

'Playing with your affections?' echoed Fidelma. 'You are sure that Muirgel had ended her relationship with Cian, then? She was not using you in some way to hit back at Cian for ending the affair?'

Guss looked angry.

'Of that I am very sure. We expressed our love in the way any normal healthy people would.'

It was clear what the youth meant.

'You found the time and space on a journey among your co-religionists?' Fidelma tried to keep the scepticism out of her voice.

'I do not lie,' Guss replied indignantly.

'Of course not.' Fidelma's reply was solemn.

'I do not!' He seemed irritated at her tone. 'Don't listen to Crella's jealousy.'

'Very well. Let us come to the morning that the ship sailed. Did you and Muirgel come aboard together?'

'Everyone came aboard at the same time, with the exception of Sister Canair.'

'How did you all come aboard together?'

'We left the Abbey after breakfast and went down to the quay. There was no sign of Sister Canair and so Muirgel took charge. Murchad came up and told us that we must be on board or we would miss the tide, in which case our passage-money would be forfeit. So we all went on board.'

'Did anyone raise a protest at leaving without Sister Canair?'

'Everyone agreed that if Sister Canair had been serious in her intention to accompany us, then she would have kept to the arrangement to join us on the quay at dawn. It was Sister Crella who pointed out that Canair had not even sent a message.'

'Why had Sister Muirgel taken charge?'

'She was next in seniority from the Abbey.'

'Surely Brother Tola or Sister Ainder were senior.'

'Tola was from the Abbey of Bangor. Sister Ainder was senior only in age.'

'Yet Brother Cian seems to have taken charge now. *He* is from Bangor.'

'He has no right to take charge. Sister Muirgel did not allow him to do so. She was very conscious of her rank. It would have taken a powerful person to wrest her status from her.'

'So she took charge of the party and you came on board. What then?'

'We all went straight to our cabins.'

'Who organised the accommodation arrangements?'

'Muirgel did so.'

'When?'

'As soon as we came aboard.'

'Why didn't Muirgel and Crella share a cabin, if they were such good friends?'

'Muirgel did not want to, for the reason I have told you. Muirgel and Crella argued about me.'

'Crella told me that she had promised to share her cabin with Canair.'

'It is the first I've heard of that.' Brother Guss was dismissive of the idea. 'Besides, Sister Canair was not there.'

'So Sister Muirgel was not immediately so sick as to neglect that duty as the new leader of your party then?'

'She was aware of her responsibilities,' replied Guss. 'But she did not realise that you were coming on board. She arranged it so that she could have a cabin on her own. We planned later . . .' He shuddered and raised his hands to his face.

'It must have been an irritation when I came into her cabin, an unannounced passenger,' Fidelma suggested.

'It was,' agreed Guss.

'How do you know that?' Fidelma asked quickly.

Guss was unabashed.

'I went to see her,' he said.

'Yet she had become so unwell that she said she didn't want to see anyone.'

'She wanted to see *me*.'

'Very well. When was the last time that you saw her?'

'I suppose it was sometime after midnight. The storm was really bad by then.'

'Tell me what happened.'

'I took her some food and drink and we talked a while. That is all. Oh, at one stage we heard someone outside the cabin. We heard their voice in spite of the terrible storm, but I don't think they were speaking to anyone. It sounded more like someone reciting loudly against the wind and the roar of the sea.'

'Who was it?'

'I do not know. It was a woman's voice. Whoever it was, they did not come in nor did they knock. They just stood outside muttering. When the muttering stopped, I went to the door and looked out. They had vanished, though I think I heard a cabin door close.'

'What did you do then?'

'Muirgel said that she wanted to rest that night and told me to go back to my cabin. We would find more opportunities later. I did so. Then, in the morning, Cian came with the news that she had been lost overboard. I did not believe it.'

'So the shock of it is why you have remained in your cabin ever since?'

Brother Guss shrugged.

'I could not face the others, especially Crella.'

Fidelma rose and went to the cabin door.

'Thank you, Brother Guss. You have been most helpful.'

The youth looked up at her.

'Sister Muirgel was not swept overboard,' he said fiercely.

Fidelma did not reply. Silently, however, she agreed completely. But there was one thing troubling her. For someone who had just lost the woman they claimed to have loved, Brother Guss did not seem to be displaying any of the signs of grief one would normally expect at such a time.

Chapter Twelve

It was late afternoon. The skies had cleared and the sun, though not warm, was bathing the sea with dazzling pinpricks of dancing lights. Fidelma was standing, leaning against the rail by the bow reflecting on what she had been told so far about the strange disappearance of Sister Muirgel. A curious picture was emerging. Some of the pilgrims seemed to have strong opinions about Sister Muirgel. Brother Guss claimed to have been in love with her and yet, strangely, he was not overly upset at her death. Guss was undoubtedly lying about something – but what? About his relationship with Muirgel? Or was it something else?

A cry from the masthead interrupted her thoughts. There seemed some unusual activity at the stern of the ship where Murchad was standing in his usual position by the steering oar. Fidelma made her way along the main deck and found the captain and some of his men looking intently towards the north-east. She followed their collective gaze but could discern nothing except sparkling grey seas.

'What is it? she asked Murchad. 'Is something wrong?'

The captain appeared preoccupied. 'The masthead lookout has sighted a ship,' he replied.

'I can't see anything.' Fidelma peared again in the direction on which they were all intent.

'It is hull down to the north-east but under full sail.'

Fidelma was unsure what these nautical terms meant and said so.

'She is hidden from us by the sea,' explained Murchad. 'Usually on a day like this, we can see three to four miles to the horizon. Whoever she is, she is just below our range of vision but her sail can be sighted from the masthead because of its higher elevation.'

'Is it a matter of concern?' Fidelma wondered.

'Until I know who she is, a strange ship is always a matter of concern,' Murchad replied.

Gurvan, who was at the steering oar with another sailor whose name Fidelma now knew as Drogan, called across to Murchad.

'She'll have the wind behind her whoever she is, Captain. She should be in full sight within another hour.'

Murchad's response was thoughtful.

'We ought to remain to windward of her until we know who she is. Who has the sharpest eyes?'

'Hoel, Captain.'

Murchad turned and bellowed towards the well of the ship.

'Hoel!'

A thickset man with long, muscular forearms came forward in the rolling gait Fidelma had long associated with sailors.

'Up to the masthead, Hoel, and keep us informed on the progress of that ship.'

The man acknowledged the order and then sprang into the rigging with an agility that Fidelma would not have deemed possible. Within a few seconds he had swarmed up the ropes and replaced the man at the masthead who had first sighted the ship.

Fidelma could sense the curious tension on the ship.

'Surely the ocean is not so large as to find the sight of another ship so alarming?' she asked.

The captain smiled tautly.

'As I said, until you know the identity of the other ship, you must be cautious. Remember what I warned of the other day? These northern waters are full of Saxon slave ships; if not Saxons then they are Franks or even Goths. They are all frequent raiders in these waters.'

Fidelma stared towards the horizon which hid the ship that seemed to hold such menace.

'You think that it is a pirate ship?'

Murchad shrugged.

'It is better to be cautious than credulous. It will not be for an hour or so that we shall know enough to answer the question.'

Fidelma was disappointed.

It seemed to her that seamanship was nothing but long, boring periods of inactivity, interspersed by frenetic outbursts of action and turmoil. It was a curious way of life. As much as she was fascinated by the sea, she decided that she preferred a life on land. There was nothing to do now about this particular problem but wait, in which case she could best occupy the time continuing her quest for information about Sister Muirgel.

She saw the tall, austere-looking Brother Tola sitting on the deck with his back against one of the water butts by the main mast. He was reading a small satchel book of the kind most pilgrims carried these days and appeared oblivious to the tensions from the sailors.

She walked over to him. As her shadow fell across him, Brother Tola looked up and an expression of irritation crossed his long, graven features.

'Ah, the *dálaigh*.' There was a tone of disrespect in his voice. Then he carefully closed his book and replaced it in the book satchel which lay beside him. 'I know what you want, Sister. I have been warned by Sister Ainder.'

'Did she need to warn you?' Fidelma's riposte came automatically to her lips.

Brother Tola smiled thinly.

'A matter of expression, that is all. There is nothing to be read in words, I assure you.'

'Often a great deal can be read in the choice of words we use, Brother Tola.'

'But not in this case.' He gestured to the deck planking beside him. 'Perhaps you would care to take a seat, if you intend to ask me questions?'

Fidelma lowered herself to the deck beside him and assumed a cross-legged position. It was actually pleasant sitting in the sun, with a faint breeze cooling her face and rustling her red hair.

Brother Tola folded his arms across his chest and gazed out across the now calm seas.

'A pleasant enough day now,' he sighed. 'In other circumstances this voyage could be stimulating and rewarding.'

Fidelma looked at him questioningly.

'Why is it not so?'

Brother Tola leant his head back against the mast and closed his eyes.

'My fellow pilgrims leave much to be desired in a company supposedly pledged to the religious pursuit. I swear there is not a truly committed servant of God among them.'

'You think not?'

The monk's face was severe.

'I think not. Not even you, Fidelma of Cashel. Would you claim to be first and foremost a servant of the Christ?' His eyes came open and Fidelma found his bright, dark orbs examining her unblinkingly. She shivered slightly.

'I would hope that I am a servant of the Faith,' she countered defensively.

He surprised her by shaking his head negatively.

'I do not think so. You are a servant of the law, not of religion.'

Fidelma considered his accusation carefully.

125

'Are the two things incompatible?' she asked.

'They can be,' replied Brother Tola. 'In many cases, the old saying is correct, that one's religion is whatever one is most interested in.'

'I do not agree.'

Brother Tola smiled cynically.

'I think that you are more interested in your law than in your religion.'

Fidelma hesitated, for Tola's words struck home like an arrow. Wasn't that the very reason she was on this pilgrimage, to sort out her thoughts on this matter? Tola saw the confusion on her face and smiled in satisfaction before resuming his posture, leaning back and closing his eyes.

'Do not be confused, Fidelma of Cashel. You are merely one of many thousands in the same position. Before the Faith was brought to the Five Kingdoms, you would have been a *dálaigh* or Brehon without having to wear the garb of a religieuse. Our society confused learning with religion and inexorably the two were bound as though they were one.'

'There are still bardic colleges,' Fidelma pointed out. 'I attended that of Brehon Morann at Tara. I only entered the religious life after I obtained my degree.'

'Morann of Tara? He was a good man; a good judge and professor of law.' Brother Tola was approving. 'But when he died, what happened to his college?'

Fidelma realised that she did not know and admitted as much.

'It was absorbed into the Church on the order of the Comarb of Patrick.' The Comarb was the successor of Patrick who was Bishop at Armagh, one of the two senior religious figures of the Five Kingdoms. The other was the Comarb of Ailbe who was the Bishop of Emly in Fidelma's own kingdom. 'Morann's college should have remained outside the Church. Secular and ecclesiastic learning are often conflicting paths.'

'I don't agree,' she countered stiffly, rebuking herself that she had not known that her old college had been closed down.

'I am a religieux,' Brother Tola went on. 'There is certainly room for learning within the Church but not to the exclusion of religion itself.'

Fidelma felt annoyed at his implied criticism of her role as a *dálaigh*.

'I have not excluded religion from my life. I have studied and—'

'Studied?' Brother Tola made a noise which took Fidelma a few moments to realise was meant as a sardonic chuckle. 'Those who

126

claim to achieve things from book learning might do much more by merely listening to God.'

'The sky and the trees and the rivers tell me little about the world of man,' Fidelma replied. 'My instruction comes from the experiences of men and women.'

'Ah, therein is the difference between the pursuit of a religious life and the pursuit of learning.'

'Truth is the goal of our lives,' returned Fidelma. 'You do not find truth without knowledge and, as Brehon Morann used to say, "love of learning is to come close to knowledge".'

'Whose knowledge? Man's knowledge. Man's law. You speak eloquently, Fidelma. But remember the words of James: "The kind of religion which is without stain or fault in the sight of God our Father is this: to keep oneself untarnished by the world".'

'You have left out an important part of that sentence, the piece about going to the help of orphans and widows in distress,' she said waspishly. 'I believe I do help those in distress.'

'But you tarnish yourself by maintaining man's law in preference to God's Commandments.'

'I see nothing contradictory between the Commandments and man's law. Since you are fond of quoting the epistle of James, you should remember the lines – "the man who looks closely into the perfect law, the law that makes us free, and who lives in its company, does not forget what he hears, but acts upon it; and that is the man who by acting will find happiness". I have heard and have not forgotten and act upon the law, and this is why I have come to speak with you, Brother Tola. Not to engage in a discussion on our differences of theology.'

Her voice was sharp now. Yet she felt uncomfortable for she knew that Tola must have spotted her weakness; her pride in being a *dálaigh* and not simply a religieuse.

'I hear you, Sister Fidelma,' he replied. His face was still serious but Fidelma could not help feeling that he was secretly laughing at her discomfiture. Then he intoned softly:

'. . . do not think lightly of the Lord's discipline,
Nor lose heart when He corrects you;
For the Lord disciplines those whom He loves.
He lays the rod on every son and daughter whom He
 acknowledges.'

Fidelma suppressed her annoyance.

127

'Hebrews, twelve,' she stated with a tight smile meant to demonstrate that he was not going to impress her with his knowledge of Scripture. 'But now, I have some questions that I must ask you on behalf of Murchad, the captain.'

'I know, as I have already said. Sister Ainder has spoken about your enquiries.'

'Good. You are older than most of your party, Brother. Why did you come on this pilgrimage?'

'Need I make an answer?'

'I have no compulsion to make you do so.'

'That is not what I meant. I meant that it should be obvious.'

'I take it that you are saying that your pilgrimage was made because of religious conviction? Surely that *is* obvious. But why did you choose to join Sister Canair's group? They are quite young, with the exception of Sister Ainder. And according to your view, your fellow travellers are not truly concerned with religion.'

'Sister Canair's group was the only party journeying to the Holy Shrine of St James. Had I not travelled with them, I might not have found group for another year at least. There was a place for me and so I joined them.'

'Did you know Sister Canair and the others before you joined them?'

'I knew none of them except those from my own Abbey of Bangor.'

'Being Brothers Cian, Dathal and Adamrae?'

'Just so.'

'You have indicated that you found them an ill-assorted group.'

'Most certainly.'

'Does that opinion include Sister Muirgel?'

Brother Tola opened his eyes wide and a spasm contorted his features.

'A most distasteful young woman! I disliked *her* most of all!'

Fidelma was surprised at the vehemence in his voice.

'Why so?'

'I remember when she first tried to dominate our company of travellers on the basis that her father had been chieftain of the Dál Fiatach. He was nothing to boast about – an evil rascal out for power and self-aggrandisement. Sister Muirgel was the daughter of her father.'

'With your views, surely that would make you hesitate before joining Sister Canair's group?'

'I did not know that Sister Muirgel was part of the group until we set out. I decided that I could avoid her immediate company on the journey.'

'Did you know her personally, or only by the fact that she was the daughter of a chieftain whom you disliked?'

'I knew her from the stories that circulated within our abbey.'

'What stories?' Fidelma was curious.

'Of her promiscuity, of her unchaste relations with other Brothers. Of the way she used people for her own ends, and the fact that she was the opposite to a truly religious person.'

'That is a harsh judgement of a Sister,' observed Fidelma.

'One greater than I will be her judge. "Look eagerly for the coming of the Day of Judgement and work to hasten it on; that day will set the heavens ablaze until they fall apart, and will melt the elements in flames. But we have His promise, and look forward to new heavens and a new earth which is the home of justice".'

Fidelma was not impressed with his quotation from the Holy Book and ignored it.

'How is it that such stories came to circulate in your Abbey of Bangor when Muirgel was a religieuse at Moville?'

'There was plenty of intercourse between our two communities. Our Abbot often had cause to send to his Brother the Abbot of Moville. Once he had to inform him that he had heard such tales and that he must not let his community descend into a sink of iniquity.'

'How did the Abbot of Moville respond?'

'He did not.'

'Perhaps he thought that it was not the place of the Abbot of Bangor to tell him how to lead his community?' Fidelma smiled without humour. 'Anyway, you formed a harsh judgement of Sister Muirgel.

Brother Tola nodded and intoned:

> 'A prostitute is a deep pit,
> A loose woman, a narrow well;
> She lies in wait like a robber . . .'

Fidelma interrupted him sharply.

'Apart from the fact that I seem to recall that Christ said harlots would enter heaven before some religious leaders, are you now saying that Sister Muirgel was a *harlot*?'

Tola merely continued his quotation from the Book of Proverbs.

> 'I glanced out of the window of my house,

I looked down through the lattice, and I saw among simple
   youths,
There amongst the boys I noticed
A lad, a foolish lad,
Passing along the street, at the corner,
Creeping out in the direction of her house
At twilight, as the day faded,
At dusk as the night grew dark;
Suddenly a woman came to meet him,
Dressed like a prostitute, full of wiles,
Flighty and inconstant,
A woman never content to stay at home,
Lying in wait at every corner,
Now in the street, now in the public squares.
She caught hold of him and kissed him;
Brazenly she accosted him and said,
"I have had a sacrifice, an offering to make, and I have paid my
   vows today" . . .'

Fidelma held up a hand to quell his sonorous recital and finally had
to cut in sharply.

'I think I can also recall the words of Proverbs, seven. What are you
saying by reciting that passage? You disapproved of Sister Muirgel
because she had relationships with men, or that she was selling her
body to whoever paid? Let us be precise about it. What is your
definition of a harlot?'

'You are the lawyer, you may interpret as you please. All I say
is let the simple fools follow her like oxen on their way to the
slaughterhouse.'

She had heard the same narrow views preached before by several
religieux who argued for the reform of the Irish Church in favour of
the concepts of Rome. She decided to clarify his attitude.

'Tell me, Brother Tola, are you one of those who believe that
the religieux should be celibate? I have often heard the argument
at Rome.'

'Does not Matthew say that our Lord Christ ordained celibacy for
His followers?'

It was a favourite argument of those who wished all religieux to
take an oath of celibacy. Fidelma had heard it many times and had
no problem about the answer.

'When the disciple asked Christ whether it was better not to marry,
He replied that celibacy was not something everyone could accept; it

was only meant for those for whom God had appointed celibacy. His words were that while some are incapable of marriage because they were born so, or were made so by men, there were, indeed, others who had themselves renounced marriage for the sake of the Kingdom of Heaven. He left it as the choice of the individual. Let those accept it who can. So far the churches of Christ have adhered to that free choice . . .'

Tola's features expressed irritation. He obviously did not like being out-quoted from the Scriptures.

'I accept the teachings of Paul on this matter. Celibacy is the ideal of a Christian victory over the evil of the world and must become the main basis of religious life.'

'There is a lobby in Rome who believe in this celibacy,' agreed Fidelma, her tone indicating that she did not think much of the argument. 'But if Rome accepts it as a dogma of the Faith, they say that the Faith stands against that which God created. Had God wanted us to be celibate, he would have made us so. However, instead of theology, I would prefer to return to the matter in hand. You clearly did not like Sister Muirgel.'

'I make no effort to disguise it.'

'Very well. Apart from her being, in your eyes, prone to indiscriminate sexual liaisons, I am at a loss to understand the depth of your dislike.'

'She seduced and perverted young men.'

'Can you give me an example?'

'Brother Guss, for example.'

'So you knew that Brother Guss claims to have been in love with Sister Muirgel?'

'She ensnared him with her wiles, as I have been trying to tell you.'

'A harsh thing to say. Had Brother Guss no free will?'

'I warned the boy,' went on Brother Tola. He screwed up his eyes as he sought to recite another passage from memory.

> '. . . My son, listen to me,
> Attend to what I say.
> Do not let your heart entice you into her ways,
> Do not stray down her paths;
> Many has she pierced and laid low,
> And her victims are without number.
> Her house is the entrance to Sheol,
> Which leads down to the halls of death.'

'You seem attracted by Proverbs, seven,' remarked Fidelma mockingly. 'Do you often quote it?'

'I did my best to warn poor Brother Guss.' Tola ignored her tone. 'I praise the Hand of God which swept the harlot overboard.'

Fidelma did not say anything for a moment or two. It had become clear to her that Brother Tola was a man of strong religious conviction, to the point of extreme intolerance. She had known men to kill for religious intolerance before.

'When did you learn that Sister Muirgel had been swept overboard?' Fidelma queried.

'At the same time that everyone else did,' he replied. 'This morning.'

'When did you last see Sister Muirgel?'

'When we came aboard. I think she was ill almost from the time we rowed out to the ship. No, that is not so. She was all right until after we came aboard. In the absence of Sister Canair, another one who was loose with her sexual favours, Muirgel took charge and allocated the cabins. We all went to these cabins and most of us remained below until after we had set sail. I never saw her afterwards and word came she was suffering from the motion sickness. Perhaps that was a warning of God's punishment to come.'

'Did you sleep during the storm?'

'Last night? How would one sleep? It was not the best of experiences. I did manage to get some sleep after a while, though. A sleep of exhaustion.'

'I presume Brother Guss was also disturbed?'

'I suppose he was. But you can ask him.'

'Were you awake when he left the cabin?'

Brother Tola frowned as he reflected on her question.

'*Did* he leave the cabin?' he countered.

'So he says.'

'Then it must be so. Ah, now I recall, he went out. But not for long.'

'Do you know where he went?'

'I presume he went to the privy. Where else would one vanish to on board this ship?'

Fidelma stared at him for a moment, knowing full well that Brother Tola must be aware that Guss had gone to see Sister Muirgel before midnight. Was Tola simply trying to protect Guss, or was there some other reason why he should attempt to cover up for the young man?

Inwardly she sighed, for she knew that she was not going to get anything further out of Brother Tola. She rose carefully to her feet.

'One point I would like clarification on,' she said. 'You obviously have strong feelings on female religieuses who fall in love or have affairs. Harlots and prostitutes, I hear you call them. I have heard no condemnation of any male religieux who often seduce these same young women. Do you not consider your judgement flawed?'

Brother Tola was in no way abashed.

'Was it not a woman who first succumbed to temptation, eating of the forbidden fruit and seducing man, for which we were all driven from the Garden of Eden? Women are responsible for all our suffering. Remember what Paul wrote to the Corinthians – "I am jealous for you, with a divine jealousy; for I betrothed you to Christ, thinking to present you as a chaste virgin to her true and only husband. But as the serpent in his cunning seduced Eve, I am afraid that your thoughts may be corrupted and you may lose your single-hearted devotion to Christ".'

'I know the passage,' replied Fidelma. 'But as the serpent in *his* cunning seduced Eve, it seems that the sex of the serpent was male. I will leave you to your contemplations then, Brother Tola. I thank you for taking the time to answer my questions. You have been most helpful.'

Brother Tola's eyes narrowed in suspicion as Fidelma deliberately added her last sentence. She had some uncanny feeling that the last thing Brother Tola wanted to be was helpful in the matter of Sister Muirgel's disappearance.

She was turning away from him when a further cry from the masthead above caused her to look up.

There it was, the mysterious vessel, clearly visible now! She had been so engrossed with Brother Tola that she had not noticed how close it had approached.

In the afternoon sunlight she could make out several details on the approaching ship: the low, square sail with some design on it, like a lightning flash; a bank of oars that rose and fell rhythmically; and the sun sparkling on objects on the side of the vessel that was turned towards her.

She hurried back to Murchad who was observing the vessel with a grim face.

'I'd get yourself and the pilgrim below decks, lady,' he greeted her as she came up.

'What is it?'

'A Saxon, by the cut of her. See the lightning flash design on her mainsail?'

Fidelma nodded briefly.

133

'Pagans, no doubt,' continued Murchad. 'That's the symbol of their god of thunder, Thunor.'

'Do they mean us harm?' Fidelma asked.

'They mean us no good,' replied Murchad grimly. 'See the bank of shields above the oars, and the sun glinting on their weapons? I believe that they mean to take us as a prize and those they don't kill will be sold as slaves.'

Fidelma felt her mouth suddenly go dry.

She knew that some of the Saxon kingdoms were still pagan in spite of the efforts of missionaries both from the Five Kingdoms of Éireann and from Rome. The South Saxons particularly were clinging to their ancient gods and goddesses even against missionaries from their fellow Saxons of the Eastern and Northern kingdoms. She swallowed hard in an attempt to dispel the sandy texture of her mouth.

'Go below, lady,' Murchad insisted again. 'You'll be safer there if they board us.'

'I'll stay and watch,' she replied firmly. She could think of nothing worse than being in darkness below and not knowing what was taking place.

Murchad was about to protest but he saw the resolution around her mouth, the slightly jutting jaw.

'Very well, but stay out of harm's way and if that ship closes on us, get below without me telling you again. When they first attack, the bloodlust obscures their vision. Man or woman, it is all the same.'

He turned to Gurvan, without wasting his time in further pleading, and glanced up at the sail.

'We'll hold our course until I say.'

Gurvan acknowledged this with only a slight forward jerk of his head.

Fidelma backed to the far corner of the stern deck and watched the unfolding drama.

'Deck there!' came the cry from the masthead. 'She's beginning to close.'

The approaching ship was turning bow towards them. The bow was high and cleaving through the waters which seemed to spray out on either side of it. The oars were rising and dipping, the water sparkling like silver as it dripped from them. She could hear the beat of something that sounded like a drum. She knew, from her previous experience of travelling to Rome, that galleys sometimes employed a man to beat time to keep the rowers synchronised.

'How many do you make it, Gurvan?' Murchad was squinting forward. 'Twenty-five oars each side?'

'So it seems.'

'Oars. They give the Saxons an advantage over us . . .' Murchad seemed to be thinking aloud. 'However, I think their use of oars might mean that they are not relying on sailing skill at close quarters. Maybe that's where we have some advantage.'

He glanced up at the mainsail.

'Tighten the starboard halyards,' he roared. 'Too much slack there.'

The tighter the sail, the more speed through the water, but with the wind blowing it might lay the ship over and expose her to any contrary sea. It would also put a strain on the mainmast.

'Captain, if the wind moderates then we'll be helpless without oars,' Gurvan pointed out nervously.

At that moment, Fidelma found Wenbrit beside her.

'Aren't you going below, lady?' he asked anxiously. 'The others are all below and I've told them to stay there. It will be dangerous here.'

Fidelma shook her head swiftly.

'I would die below not knowing what was happening.'

'Let's hope that none of us die,' muttered the boy, staring at the oncoming ship. 'Pray God may send a strong wind.'

'Loose the port sheets! More slack to the port halyards!' shouted Murchad.

Sailors jumped to do his bidding and the large square mainsail swung round at an angle.

Murchad had judged the wind's change of direction with such accuracy that almost at once the sail filled and Fidelma could feel the speed of the vessel as it suddenly accelerated over the waves.

Wenbrit pointed excitedly at the Saxon ship as the distance between the two vessels began to increase. The sail on the other ship had fallen slack. Murchad was right: the captain of the other vessel had been relying on his oarsmen and neglected to watch the wind and his sail. For several valuable moments, the Saxon lay becalmed in the water.

Even against the sibilant hiss of the sea and the whispering sound of the wind in the sail and among the rigging, Fidelma caught a faint shouting drifting over the waters.

'What was that?' she wondered.

Wenbrit pulled a face.

'They call on their god of war to help them. Hear the cry? "Woden! Woden!" I have heard such roars from Saxon throats before.'

Fidelma glanced at him with a silent question.

'The land of my people has an eastern border with the country of the West Saxons,' he explained. 'They were always raiding into our territory, and continually cried to Woden for help. They believe that the greatest thing that can happen to them is to die, sword in hand, and with the name of their god Woden on their lips. Then it is said that this god will carry them into some great hall of heroes where they will dwell for ever.'

Wenbrit turned and spat across the railing into the sea to show his disgust.

'Not all Saxons are like that,' Fidelma protested as the image of Eadulf suddenly came into her mind. 'Most of them are Christian now.'

'Not those in that ship,' Wenbrit corrected with a cynical expression.

The other vessel had eased into the wind now; its oars had been withdrawn and the sail was filling. Now Fidelma could see the great lightning flash on the sail. Wenbrit saw her narrowing her eyes as she focused on it.

'They have another god called Thunor who wields a great hammer. When he strikes with it, thunder is caused and the sparks that fly are the lightning,' he informed her solemnly. 'They even have one weekday sacred to that god called Thunor's day. It is the day we Christians called Dies Jovis.'

Fidelma refrained from telling the boy that the Latin name was merely that of another ancient pagan god, but this time of Rome. It was a pointless piece of pedantry now. But she had heard of Thunor from her long talks with Brother Eadulf concerning the ancient beliefs of his people. She found it hard to believe that there were still Saxons who believed in the old gods after two centuries of contact with the Christian Britons and the Irish missionaries who had converted the northern kingdoms from their wild superstitions founded on war and bloodlust. She continued to keep watching the Saxon ship as it began to overhaul them once again.

'He's using the wind now, Captain,' she heard Gurvan call. 'She seems a fast ship and her captain knows how to sail her with the wind behind him.'

It was an understatement. Even Fidelma could see that the approaching vessel was faster in the water than *The Barnacle Goose*. After all, the attacking ship was built for war and not, like Murchad's ship, for peaceful trade.

Murchad kept glancing at the sails and then at the oncoming craft. He swore. It was an oath such as Fidelma had never heard before; a full savoured seaman's oath.

'At this rate, she'll be on us in no time. She's smaller and faster, and what's more she's weathering on us.'

Fidelma wished she understood the terms. Wenbrit saw her frustration.

'The direction of the wind, Sister,' he explained. 'Not only is the wind causing the Saxon to overhaul us but, because of the angle we are at in position to the wind, we are being pushed towards the Saxon's course. In other words, we are drifting on to the Saxon's course and cannot maintain any parallel distance from her.'

A feeling of apprehension went through her.

'Is the Saxon going to overtake us then?'

Wenbrit gave her a reassuring grin.

'Her captain made a mistake before; perhaps he will make another mistake. It will take a good seaman to outsail Murchad. He lives up to his name.'

And Fidelma recalled that the name Murchad meant 'sea battler'.

At this moment, the captain was pacing up and down, thumping his balled fist into the palm of his other hand, his brows drawn together as if working out a problem.

'Bring her into the wind!' he shouted abruptly.

Gurvan looked startled for a second and then he and his companion leaved on the steering oar.

The Barnacle Goose swung around. Fidelma stumbled and grabbed for the rail. For a few moments the great ship seemed becalmed and then Murchad shouted another order to tack.

Caught up in the sudden change of tactic by Murchad, Fidelma took a few moments to look around for the Saxon ship.

So confident had the opposing captain been of overhauling this prey and coming alongside, that it had taken him several precious moments to realise what Murchad was about. The lightly-built Saxon warship had gone speeding by under full sail with the wind right behind it. It had sped on for almost a mile before the sails were shortened and the craft had come about to follow the new path of *The Barnacle Goose*.

'A good manoeuvre,' Fidelma said to Wenbrit. 'But aren't we pushing against the wind now? Won't the Saxon be able to catch up with us?'

Wenbrit smiled, and pointed up at the sky.

'We might have to sail against the wind, but so does the Saxon. Look at the sun on the horizon. The Saxon will not catch up before nightfall. I think that Murchad plans to slip past her in the darkness, provided those clouds remain and there is no moon.'

'I don't understand.'

'With the wind behind our sails, the Saxon, being lighter and therefore faster, had the advantage of speed. We were heavy and more cumbersome. When we come into the wind, it's a different matter. The waves that impede our progress also hinder the progress of the Saxon . . . but even more so. Whereas we can ride the heavy seas, the contrary waves will push their lighter craft farther to the leeward, and they will have more work to do to catch up with us.'

Murchad had overheard the boy's explanation; he now came over to them with a broad grin. He seemed pleased with his seamanship and more relaxed now that the Saxon ship was struggling behind them.

'The boy's right, lady. Also, the keel of our ship reaches down farther under the surface than theirs will. A light vessel is beholden to the choppiness of the slightest wave, whereas we can maintain a better hold because we can reach below superficial turbulence. We can outsail the Saxon against the wind.'

Murchad was back in a jovial mood.

'The Saxon will be struggling awhile, by which time I hope night will come down, heavy and cloudy. Then we'll turn south-south-west again and with luck, slip by her under cover of darkness.'

Fidelma stared at the sturdy sailor with some admiration. How well Murchad knew his ship! Something made her start thinking of a horse and its rider. For a moment she did not know why such an image had come into her mind, and then she understood. Murchad felt for his ship and the elements in which it sailed, the sea and the wind, as a good rider felt for his horse. He was at one with it, as if he were but an extension of it.

She peered behind to the distant square-sailed vessel.

'Are we safe then?'

Murchad did not want to commit himself to absolutes.

'Depends if her captain shows more forethought than before. He could guess that we will change course under cover of darkness and do the same, hoping to meet us at dawn. My guess, however, is that he will think we are turning tail and running for the safety of a Cornish port. That is the direction in which we are heading now.'

'Then the excitement is over for the time being?'

Murchad made a humorous grimace.

'The excitement is over,' he confirmed. 'Until daylight!'

Chapter Thirteen

That evening, after the meal, Fidelma decided to complete her enquiries. She found Brother Dathal and Brother Adamrae in their cabin. Like the other cabins below deck, it was stuffy and airless there and the lantern which illuminated it also gave off a degree of heat as well as light. She found it stifling after the cool breezes of the deck.

'What is it you want, Sister?' demanded Brother Adamrae gruffly as she entered in answer to his sharp invitation when she had knocked upon the door.

'A brief word – the answers to a few questions,' she said politely.

'I suppose this concerns Sister Muirgel,' Brother Dathal muttered. 'I heard from Sister Crella that you were following it up.'

Brother Adamrae looked at her with disfavour.

'What business is it of yours to ask questions?'

Fidelma was not perturbed.

'I do so at the request of the captain,' she replied. 'I am a—'

'I know. You are an advocate,' snapped Brother Adamrae. 'This matter is no concern of ours. We did not come from the same Abbey. Anyway, ask your questions and be gone.'

Brother Dathal looked apologetically at her.

'What Adamrae means to say is that time is precious to us. We are engaged in scholarship, you see, trying to translate some material.'

'Time is precious to everyone,' Fidelma agreed solemnly. 'It is especially precious for those who have run *out* of time – like Sister Muirgel.'

She picked up the parchment that lay on the table before Brother Dathal. It was written in the ancient Ogham script, the earliest form of calligraphy of the language of Éireann.

'*Ceathracha is cheithre chéad . . .*' She began to read the ancient lettering.

Brother Dathal looked surprised.

'Can you read the ancient Ogham letters?'

She grimaced.

'Did not the pagan god Ogma, god of literacy and learning in primeval times, give the knowledge of such letters to the people of Muman first?' she countered. 'Who is able to construe the ancient letters if not a woman of Muman?'

Brother Adamrae scowled.

'Anyone might be able to pronounce the letters, but what of the meaning of the text? Construe the words, if you are so clever.'

Fidelma pursed her lips and glanced over the ancient words. It was clearly a rhyme.

> 'Forty and four hundred
> Years, it is not a falsehood
> From the going of the people of God,
> I assure you,
> Over the surface of the sea of Romhar
> Till they sped across the sea of Meann,
> Thus came the sons of Míle to the land of Éireann.'

Dathal and Adamrae stared at the effortless way she read the ancient poem.

Then Brother Adamrae grunted in disgust as if to belittle her effort.

'So you know the ancient language of the texts, but do you understand them? Where, for example, is the sea of Romhar? Where is the sea of Meann?'

'Easy enough,' replied Fidelma. 'Romhar is known today as Rua Mhuir, the Red Sea; and Meann must obviously be a form of the great Middle Earth Sea which the Latins call the Mediterranean.'

Brother Dathal was smiling at the discomfort of his companion.

'Well done, Sister. Well done, indeed,' he said approvingly.

Brother Adamrae finally relaxed and even forced a smile.

'It is not everyone who knows the mysteries of the ancient texts,' he conceded. 'We are dedicated to retrieving their secrets, Sister.'

'As I am dedicated to pursuing the truth in law,' Fidelma replied. 'As you are aware, the captain has asked me to make a report because, in law, he may be liable to pay compensation if there is a fault to be found, should it be claimed that he was negligent.'

'We understand. What is it that you want from us?' replied Brother Dathal.

'Firstly, when did you last see Sister Muirgel?'

Brother Dathal frowned and glanced at his companion. He shrugged.

'I don't remember.'

Brother Adamrae said: 'Wasn't it when we came aboard?'

Brother Dathal thought a moment.

'I think that you are right. She allotted us the accommodation. After that we did not see her again. We were told she had fallen prey to the motion sickness and remained in her cabin.'

'And neither of you saw her after that?'

They shook their heads in unison.

'Can I ask where you were during the storm last night? I just want to be sure that no one saw Sister Muirgel making her way to the deck during the storm.'

'We were here during the whole time of the storm,' Brother Dathal confirmed. 'It was a bad storm and we could scarcely stand, let alone go wandering about the ship.'

Brother Adamrae nodded agreement.

'We were comparing it to the great storm which came among the Children of the Gael on their voyage to Gothia. That was when Eber, son of Tat, and Lamhghlas, son of Aghnon, died and soon after the mermaids rose from the sea playing such sad music that the Children of the Gael were lulled to sleep, and only Caicher the Druid was immune; he managed to save them all by pouring melted wax into their ears. When they came to the extremity of Sliabh Ribhe, Caicher prophesied that they would not find a resting place until they reached the land called Éireann, but added that they themselves would not reach it; their descendants would.'

Fidelma stared at the enthusiastic young man in his breathless discourse. His whole being had become animated by his subject.

'You are much concerned with these ancient times,' she commented. 'You must enjoy your subject.'

'It is our purpose to write a volume on the history of the Children of the Gael before they reached the Five Kingdoms,' Brother Dathal beamed.

'Then I wish you luck in your endeavours. I would be fascinated to read such a work. However, I must finish my enquiry. You say that you both remained all the time in your cabin and never saw Sister Muirgel after you came aboard?'

Brother Adamrae nodded.

'That is an accurate summary, Sister.'

Fidelma suppressed a sigh of frustration.

Someone was lying among the pilgrims. Someone must have gone into Sister Muirgel's cabin and stabbed her, dragged her on deck and thrown her overboard. Fidelma was sure of it. Then her earlier question came back to her. Why throw the body overboard and leave her bloodstained robe, clearly showing the stab wounds? That *was* odd.

'I am sorry?' She became aware that Brother Dathal was speaking.

'I was saying that it is a sad business if one dismissed the value of human life. But in honesty, there are probably few who will grieve for Sister Muirgel for any length of time.'

'I realise that some people disliked her.'

'Some even hated her. Brother Tola, for example. Then there is Sister Gormán. Oh yes, there are several who will not grieve too much.'

'Including yourselves?' Fidelma asked quickly.

Brother Dathal glanced at his companion.

'We did not hate her. But she was not someone we would say that we liked,' he admitted.

'Why did *you* dislike her?'

Brother Adamrae shrugged.

'She despised us. She was a highly-sexed young woman. I do not think we need tell you why she looked down on Dathal and me. Anyway, one cannot greet everyone in love and charity. Look at Brother Tola. I would not be saddened if we had lost *him* from our company.'

Remembering Brother Tola's views on scholarship, Fidelma gave a quick smile.

'I take your point. But was there anything particular about Sister Muirgel which created dislike?'

'Particular?' Brother Dathal actually giggled. 'I would say everything about her caused us irritation. She liked people to know that she was a chieftain's daughter and that she should be in charge of things because of her social rank.'

'Why did you agree to come on this pilgrimage . . . ?' Fidelma knew the answer as soon as she let the question slip.

'Because it was Sister Canair who was the leader when we set out. Muirgel was just one of the party. Sister Canair was able to keep her under control, even though Muirgel tried to assert her authority.'

'She was a different personality to Sister Canair?'

'Absolutely. Sister Muirgel was mean-minded, riddled with jealousy, haughty and ambitious!' Brother Dathal snapped out the words with venom. Fidelma examined him in surprise. Brother Adamrae came to his companion's rescue.

'I think Dathal may be forgiven for his unchristian thoughts.' He smiled softly. 'Telling the truth can also be considered as being unkind and harsh.'

'What was she ambitious for?'

The two men exchanged a glance. It was Brother Dathal who responded.

'Power, I suppose. Power over people; power over men.'

'I understand she bullied little Sister Gormán.'

'It's the first that we have heard of it,' replied Adamrae. 'But Gormán always kept herself to herself.'

'And you said that Muirgel was jealous. Of whom was she jealous?' she asked, turning to Dathal.

'Of Sister Canair obviously. Ask among her companions from Moville. We never met her until we started our journey although we heard many things on the excursion to Ardmore. You do not journey with a small group for several days without picking up the things that others try to hide. Muirgel was jealous of Sister Canair, with an intensity that alarmed us.'

'What was the cause of her jealousy?'

'I think that there was a hate embedded in Sister Muirgel that could have developed into violence.'

'It was said that Muirgel was jealous of Canair because of . . . of Brother Cian.'

'Who told you this?'

'Brother Bairne,' replied Dathal.

'Were you concerned then when Sister Canair did not join you on the morning the ship sailed, and Sister Muirgel took charge?'

Brother Adamrae gave a shake of his head and answered.

'It might have been a cause for concern but for two things. Firstly, Sister Canair had not accompanied us to Ardmore. She went to visit someone before we reached the Abbey. It was logical to assume she did not even come to Ardmore. Secondly, Sister Muirgel stayed at the Abbey with us until we came to the quay and found there was no Canair and that we had to get aboard or miss the sailing. Dathal and I would have come aboard anyway, Canair or no Canair, because we would not have considered forgoing our chance to travel to Iberia and finish our task of tracing the ancient history of our people.'

Fidelma was thinking carefully.

'I still have a question.'

Brother Dathal smiled.

'Questions always provoke more questions.'

'Are you *sure* that Muirgel was jealous of Sister Canair and Cian? I have been told that Muirgel wanted to end the affair with Cian.'

'Well, Bairne has his problems. He was moonstruck on Muirgel.

143

But Muirgel did dislike Canair. She might well have been hungry for power and for the little brief authority that Canair had.'

Brother Adamrae nodded decisively.

'I think we have helped you all we can, Sister. I don't believe you will find the answers you want among our gossip. You have doubtless talked about this to Brother Bairne or will do so?' He rose and opened the cabin door, and Fidelma left, in a greater state of confusion than before.

Cian looked up in surprise as Fidelma knocked on his cabin door and entered.

'What can I do for you?' he asked. 'Have you come to bemoan the past again?'

Fidelma answered him coldly. 'I was looking for Brother Bairne, who shares your cabin.'

'As you can see, he is not here.'

'As I can see,' confirmed Fidelma. 'Where would I find him?'

'Am I my brother's keeper?' quipped Cian sarcastically.

Fidelma stared at him with distaste.

'You should remember in what context that question was asked before making it into a joke,' she replied, withdrawing before he could respond.

She found Brother Bairne seated at the meal table on the mess deck, looking dolefully at a mug of mead. His eyes were red-rimmed and there was little need to ask about his emotional state.

He looked up as she entered and sat down near him.

'I know,' he said, 'a few questions. I have heard all about your investigation. Yes, I was in love with Muirgel. No, I did not see her after last evening when the storm rose.'

Fidelma took in his statement without apparent surprise.

'You told me that you were from Moville, didn't you?'

'I was training there in order to preach the Word among the heathen,' he confirmed.

'Did you know Sister Muirgel well there?'

'I told you that I was in love . . .'

'With respect, that is not the same thing as knowing someone.'

'I knew her for several months.'

'And, of course, you knew Sister Crella?'

'Of course. They were more or less inseparable. Muirgel and Crella seemed to share everything.'

'Including boyfriends?'

Brother Bairne flushed but said nothing.

'Did Muirgel return your feelings for her?'

'You have no doubt asked Sister Crella for her opinion?'

'I'll take that as a negative answer. Unrequited love is hard to bear, Bairne. Did you hate Muirgel for rejecting you?'

'Of course not. I loved her.'

'It's just that I wondered why you chose to quote from the Book of Hosea this morning.'

'I was upset. I did not think. I wished to hit out . . .'

'You wished to hurt Muirgel?'

'I . . . I don't think so. Had Muirgel turned to me I would have loved and protected her. But she rejected my love and turned to people who could and *did* hurt her. Even that one-armed bastard that I am forced to share my cabin with was able to have his way with her . . .'

'Brother Cian?' queried Fidelma.

'Cian! If only I had trained as a warrior I would have taught him a lesson.'

'You told Dathal and Adamrae that he had had an affair with Muirgel? That Muirgel still felt for him and that she was jealous of Canair because of the fact that Cian was now having an affair with her.'

'I knew that he had dropped her for Sister Canair; for the same reason he finishes with all his women. Canair had more to offer him for the time being.'

'And Muirgel was jealous?'

'What does anyone feel when they have been rejected?'

Fidelma found herself blushing. She wondered if Bairne knew about her past but the young man was staring at the drink on the table.

'When was the last time you saw Muirgel?'

'Saw her? Last evening, I suppose. I spoke to her through her cabin door just before midnight.'

'*Through* the door? What do you mean exactly?'

'She did not open it when I knocked. I asked if she was better and whether I could fetch her anything. She called through the door that all she wanted was to be left alone. Then I went to bed.'

'Did you get up during the night?'

He shook his head.

'When did you get up then?'

'It was just about dawn, I think. I needed to find the *defectora*.' He used the Latin term out of politeness rather than the colloquial one.

'Ah yes. I am told you did not use the *defectora* by the stern cabins but apparently made your way to the one in the bow of the ship. That was a long way to go. Why was that?'

Brother Bairne looked at her in surprise.

145

'I suppose that I had forgotten about the *defectora* at the stern. I am not sure.'

'And when you returned, was anyone about?'

'I saw that bastard Cian at the door of Muirgel's cabin. He said something about checking that everyone was all right after the storm. I waited, for I wondered if he was trying to get back with Muirgel. But a few seconds later he re-emerged and said he could not find her.'

'And then you learnt that there was no sign of her on board?'

Brother Bairne leant across the table and stared at her closely.

'If you want to know the truth, Sister, then I'll tell you. I don't believe that Muirgel fell overboard. I believe that she was pushed. And I'll tell you who did it.'

He paused dramatically so that she finally had to prompt him: 'Who did it?'

'Sister Crella.'

Fidelma tried to make her face inscrutable.

'You have told me who; now tell me why.'

'Jealousy!'

Fidelma examined Bairne's intent expression cautiously.

'What would she be jealous of?'

'Of Muirgel, of course! Ask her. It's all to do with that self-opinionated bast—'

Fidelma interrupted: 'Who are you talking about?'

'That one-armed bastard, Cian. He is at the root of all this! Mark my words!'

Fidelma awoke early. It was still dark when she swung from the warmth of her bunk and heard the angry hiss of protest from Mouse Lord as he uncurled himself from the bottom of the bed, disturbed by her sudden movement.

She washed swiftly and dressed, wishing that she was able to have a more thorough bath for she felt sweaty and uncomfortable. She put on her heavy cloak and went out on deck.

A faint line of light along the eastern horizon showed that it was close to dawn. There was a strange eerie silence on the ship, and yet she could see the dark figures of men standing here and there, as if waiting for something. Like her, they were waiting for dawn.

Fidelma made her way cautiously aft and, as she had expected, she found Murchad and Gurvan standing together on deck. Two other shadowy figures stood ready by the steering oar. The only sound was the wind in the rigging and the soft movement of the leather sails.

Darkness had fallen the previous evening with the Saxon ship still

146

clawing into the wind behind them. As soon as it was dark, Murchad ordered that no light was to be shown to give away their position. He tacked north for another hour before turning and running before the wind at an angle which would take them south-west away from the last known position of the Saxon ship.

With the coming of the dawn, it was time to see whether the ruse had worked.

It was cold in the grey dawn and the winds were not strong. The weather was certainly clearing and the thin strip of grey light was even now broadening.

No one had exchanged a greeting. All were standing as still as statues watching the eastern sky.

'Red,' muttered Gurvan, breaking the silence.

Nothing else was said. Everyone knew what he meant. A red sky in the morning foretold bad weather ahead. However, there was a more important consideration now that the daylight was spreading across the waters. Everyone was peering into the vanishing half-light as it grew brighter.

'Masthead there! Hoel! What do you see?'

There was a pause. Then a faint cry came back.

'The horizon's clear. Not a sail in sight.'

Murchad was the first to visibly relax.

'No sign,' he muttered. 'No sail nor even a spar.'

'I think it worked, Captain,' Gurvan agreed.

Murchad clapped his hands together in glee. His smile was one of sheer pleasure.

'Give me a sail against oars any day,' he grinned. 'Ah, there it is . . .' He held his head to one side and nodded in satisfaction.

Fidelma wondered what he meant.

'The dawn breeze . . . yes, the wind's veering. We'll be at Ushant later today. Maybe by midday, and if the wind increases,' he turned his head towards the dissipating red sky, 'we can shelter there if the weather gets really bad. I don't want to run across the Biscain sea in bad weather, if I can help it.'

Murchad appeared to be back to his jovial mood now that the evasion of the Saxon sea raiders had proved successful.

'Keep her on course, Gurvan. I shall be at breakfast. Sister Fidelma, will you join me in my cabin for the meal?'

Fidelma acknowledged the unusual invitation and Murchad called for Wenbrit to bring food to his cabin for the two of them.

It was much more comfortable to breakfast with Murchad than with her fellow pilgrims, Fidelma decided, especially after the tensions of the last twenty-four hours. It was Murchad who came to the point that had been uppermost in both their minds.

'Well, what information have you gathered about the death of this woman – Muirgel?'

Fidelma lowered herself into one of the two chairs squeezed each side of a small wooden table in Murchad's cabin. The captain took a bottle from a cupboard and two clay cups.

'*Corma*,' he announced, as he poured the liquid. 'It will keep out the morning chill.'

Ordinarily, the idea of drinking such strong spirits just after dawn would have seemed repulsive to Fidelma. But the day was chill and she was cold. She took the cup and sipped at the fiery liquid, letting it trickle over her tongue and then spreading it across her lips with the tip of her tongue. She coughed slightly.

'I have spoken to all those in her party, Murchad,' she replied. 'I have told no one that we suspect that she was not simply swept overboard. It is of interest, however, that at least two of the party suspect that she was murdered.'

'And?' prompted Murchad with interest.

'There are no easy answers to the matter . . .'

There was a knock on the cabin door and Wenbrit entered carrying a tray of cooked meet, cheeses and fruit, together with hard-baked bread.

Wenbrit grinned at Fidelma.

'Brother Cian has been asking where you were. I said you were breakfasting with the captain. He looked very resentful.'

Fidelma did not bother to reply. It was of no concern to her that Cian was asking after her.

'Have you told them that we have eluded the sea raider, boy?' asked Murchad.

Wenbrit made an affirmative nod.

'Few of them seemed interested,' he replied. 'They would soon have been interested had the Saxons caught up with us, that's for sure.'

He turned to the door and then hesitated.

'There is something you wish to say?' grunted Murchad. He was obviously sensitive to the boy's actions.

Wenbrit turned back with a frown.

'It's nothing. After all, the pilgrims have paid their passage and . . .'

'What is it? Come on!' Murchad was a little impatient at his hesitation.

'I noticed that someone has been helping themselves to food. Some

148

meat, bread and fruit was missing. Not much. In fact, I noticed some missing yesterday morning, and now this morning . . .'

'Missing food?'

'And a meat-knife. I thought I was mistaken, but now I am sure. I did not think that I was being frugal with the food. If they want extra, they have only to ask. But knives are valuable.'

'Wenbrit,' Fidelma leant forward with sudden interest, 'what makes you so sure that it is one of the passengers who is helping themselves? The meals that you have provided are surely more than enough. Could a member of the crew be responsible?'

Wenbrit shook his head.

'The crew's food is stored separately. This ship is used to taking passengers and so we have to cost and store independently for them. No one in our crew would steal from the passengers' stores.'

Murchad cleared his throat irritably.

'I will make an announcement to the pilgrims that they have only to ask if they want extra rations. Just to be even-handed, I will also mention the matter to my crew.'

The boy acknowledged his captain and left.

Fidelma examined Murchad thoughtfully.

'You are fond of the boy, aren't you?'

Murchad looked uncomfortable for a moment.

'He is an orphan. I took him from the sea. My wife and I were never blessed with children. He has become the son that I never had. He is a bright lad.'

'I think he has just provided me with an idea. I might want Gurvan to accompany me an another search of the ship later,' Fidelma said.

Murchad frowned. 'I don't understand.'

'I'll explain when I have given more thought to the problem.'

Murchad reached forward and raised the jug of *corma* but Fidelma declined a second drink of the fiery liquid.

'One is more than enough for me, Murchad.'

He poured another liberal cup for himself and sat back. He regarded her with speculation.

'This Brother Cian seems to take more than a passing interest in you, lady,' he observed.

Fidelma felt herself blush.

'As I said, I knew him ten years ago, when I was a student.'

'I see. The little I had to do with him, I would say he was a bitter man. The useless arm, I suppose?'

'The useless arm,' agreed Fidelma.

'Now, we were discussing Sister Muirgel.' Murchad changed the subject when he saw that Fidelma was uncomfortable. 'You said that the answers were not easy; I did not expect that they would be. But is there any indication at all of what happened?'

Fidelma uttered a short sigh of exasperation.

'I think it is obvious that murder was done aboard this ship. But I cannot say with certainty who is the culprit.'

'But you have an idea, some suspicion?'

'Sister Muirgel seems to have been someone who was intensely disliked by several of those aboard and, when she was not disliked, she was the object of a jealousy that might have no bounds. One thing I *am* certain of is that the person who plunged the knife into her habit is still aboard. But whether I shall have time to find them before this ship reaches Iberia, I am not all that certain.'

'But you are going to try to discover the murderer?'

'That is my intention. However, it will take time,' Fidelma agreed gravely.

'We still have several days' sailing before we reach Iberia,' Murchad reflected sombrely. 'I don't like to think that we shall be sailing without knowing the identity of the murderer. We could all be in danger.'

Fidelma shook her head.

'I don't think so. I believe that the killer selected Sister Muirgel because she was the object of a particular hatred which overwhelmed them. I doubt if anyone else is in immediate danger.'

Murchad looked at her in apprehension.

'But you do have a suspicion as to who this killer is, Fidelma?' She detected the hidden tension in his voice as if he were pleading for reassurance.

'I never speak until I am sure,' she replied. 'But don't worry; as soon as I am sure I will inform you.'

She had finished nibbling at some selected morsels of the food which Wenbrit had served. Fidelma was never one to eat a large breakfast and some fruit usually sufficed. Now she rose to her feet.

'What is your next move?' enquired Murchad.

'I am going to have a thorough search of Muirgel's cabin and belongings.'

Murchad accepted her departure reluctantly.

'Well, do keep me informed. And be careful. A person who has killed once usually has no compunction about killing again, especially if they believe that you are getting close to them. I do not share your belief that there is no further danger here.'

She smiled briefly from the cabin door.

150

'Don't worry on my behalf, Murchad,' she said. 'I am sure that this is a crime of some passion and involves only Sister Muirgel.'

Outside, it was fully light now. The morning was clear and blue but the wind had risen fresh and chilly. The reddening sky had vanished but while it usually heralded a period of stillness, it also meant that bad weather would soon follow. Indeed, no changeable weather arrives without warning. Fidelma, from her childhood, had been taught that the signs were usually to be seen in the sky. It was a matter of observation and interpreting the evidence correctly. It might look bright now, with the hope that the pale sun would grow warmer, but she doubted it. There was bad weather coming. She wondered what had happened to the captain's faith in 'St Luke's Little Summer'.

She made her way below decks to the cabin area and paused to hear the sounds of voices from the mess deck. The pilgrim band were still at their breakfast. It was an ideal time to search Sister Muirgel's cabin and belongings without being disturbed. Later she would have to tell the company of her suspicions, but she wished she could do so at the same time as revealing who might have pushed her overboard.

The problem was that there were several people who could easily have killed Sister Muirgel; several on whom an obvious suspicion fell. In her experience, it was never the obvious that counted. But what happened when you had many obvious suspects? She hated to admit it, even to herself, but she wished Brother Eadulf was with her so that she could discuss her ideas with him. Often his comments put things into a sharp focus for her.

She entered the dark, odorous cabin and paused on the threshold to light a lamp from the lantern that swung on its hook in the passageway. Glancing round to ensure that she had not been observed, she entered and closed the door.

A couple of blankets were heaped carelessly on the bunk which Sister Muirgel had used. Fidelma held the lamp high and peered round. There was hardly anything of interest in the cabin at all. No baggage, papers or books that might furnish her with clues.

She frowned and made a more careful examination, standing still but turning to search the corners of the room for any cupboards or hooks. There was no obvious sign of Sister Muirgel's baggage nor any other belongings. Someone must have placed the baggage beneath the lumpy heap of blankets on the bunk. She did not remember it being so untidy when she had last been in the cabin with Wenbrit to examine Muirgel's robe, which she had given to the charge of Murchad, as captain of *The Barnacle Goose*, in case it was needed as evidence.

Setting the lamp down beside the bed, she bent forward. It was only then that a cold feeling of anticipation gripped her. The blankets, she now saw, were concealing the shape of a body. Hesitating barely a fraction of a second, she reached forth a hand and drew back a fold of cloth.

There, on her back, lay the form of a woman, clad in bloodstained undergarments. Her eyes were still open and blood was pumping in little spurts from a jagged knife-wound across her throat, where it had penetrated the jugular vein. Even as Fidelma gazed down, the dark glazing eyes turned to her, silent and pleading. The lips twitched, a gurgling sound came forth and blood began to form on them.

Fidelma bent forward quickly.

There was a gulping breath, but no words came. The dying woman seemed to he pushing a clenched hand towards Fidelma.

Then her head flopped uselessly to one side and blood fountained out of the halt-opened mouth. Something fell with a clatter from the dead woman's fist as her fingers relaxed and unfurled. Automatically, Fidelma bent down and picked it up. It was a small silver crucifix on a broken chain.

Fidelma rose slowly, holding her lamp high, in order to examine the woman's face. She stood looking down in bewilderment for a few moments, trying to reconcile what she was seeing with the events of the last twenty-four hours.

The body of the woman who lay sprawled on the bunk before her, with her throat just recently cut, was Sister Muirgel.

Chapter Fourteen

'I don't understand it,' Murchad announced, not for the first time, as he scratched the back of his head and stared down at the body. Fidelma had called him down to the cabin without informing anyone else. He looked utterly bewildered. 'Are you sure that this is Sister Muirgel? I only saw her for a few moments on the day when they all came aboard. Maybe it is another of the Sisters?'

Fidelma shook her head firmly.

'I saw her only for a few minutes as well when I went into her cabin, but I am certain that this is the same woman. It is certainly none of the other three.'

Murchad heaved a frustrated sigh.

'It seems, then, that this Sister Muirgel has been murdered twice,' he observed dryly. 'Once during the first night out when her bloodstained robe was found but not her body, and once just now when someone stabbed her and cut her throat. What can it mean?'

'It means that Sister Muirgel initially wanted us to *believe* that she was dead . . . whereas in reality she was still aboard, hiding somewhere . . . or being hidden by someone. Remember what Wenbrit said about the missing food? I suspected immediately. That was why I wanted another search. Muirgel was faking it. Yet there is no sign of the knife.'

'But why did Muirgel want us to believe that she had been stabbed or swept overboard in the storm?' asked Murchad. 'Why was the robe planted so that we would then immediately suspect that she had been murdered?'

Fidelma glanced down at the crucifix she was holding in her hand. It was the one which Muirgel had been holding. Fidelma had almost forgotten it during the last few minutes while she tried to seek an explanation for the mystery.

'What's that?' enquired the captain, noticing Fidelma studying it.

'Her crucifix. It must have comforted her during the last few minutes of her life. She was holding it in her hand when she died.'

153

'A pious woman,' Murchad observed, indicating a larger and more ostentatious crucifix still around the dead woman's neck.

Fidelma gazed down at the crucifix in her hand. It was of an entirely different style to that worn by Muirgel. Albeit smaller, it was of a more tasteful workmanship, and she suddenly realised that this crucifix did not belong to Muirgel. She turned it over in her hand thoughtfully. It was only on the second time of turning it over that she suddenly realised that a name was scratched on it.

'Hold the lamp nearer,' she instructed Murchad.

He did so.

The lines of the marks were faint but the name was easily discernible. *Canair.*

Fidelma pursed her lips thoughtfully.

'Did you ever meet this Sister Canair?' she asked Murchad.

'I never saw her. The passage money, like your own, was negotiated by the Abbey of St Declan before the pilgrims arrived. I knew the names of the pilgrims only and they had to tally with the number booked for the passage. Eleven passage fares were paid, but only ten people came on board plus yourself. I was told that this Sister Canair, who was leading the pilgrims, had not arrived at Ardmore and, as we had to sail with the tide . . .' He made a dismissive gesture with a shrug of his shoulders. 'What can we do now?'

Fidelma hesitated a moment or so before making up her mind.

'I will continue as before, but now we have a body to prove the crime. Initially it seems that some things might begin to make sense. For example, it explains why Brother Guss, who claimed to be in love with Muirgel, was not distraught with grief when we all thought she had been swept overboard. He obviously knew that she was still alive. However, my suspicions as to who the culprit is have to be altered. I am afraid that I am no nearer solving this mystery than I was before. There are still many more questions to be asked.'

Fidelma looked at the captain.

'Everyone is still at breakfast, I suppose? Will you fetch Brother Tola and Brother Guss here? Do not allow them to come into the cabin until I ask them. Oh, and can you spare one of your sailors to come down here? I think we shall need to put a guard on this cabin.'

Murchad went off without further comment. After a short while, there was a tap on the door. A ruddy-faced sailor put his head around it. 'My name is Drogon, lady. The captain says you want someone down here.'

'I do. Stand outside and make sure no one comes into this cabin unless I say.'

Drogon raised his fist to his brow in salute and withdrew. A moment or two later, she heard Brother Tola's querulous tones outside demanding to know why he had been summoned. Fidelma went to the door.

'Come in, Brother Tola,' she ordered curtly. Then, seeing Brother Guss behind him, she added: 'Wait there. I will speak with you in a moment.'

Brother Tola came in with a frown.

'Well, what now?' he demanded, looking around him in distaste.

Fidelma went to the bunk and raised the lantern over the dead body.

Brother Tola let out a gasp and took a step nearer.

'Who is this, Brother Tola?' Fidelma asked, her eyes not leaving his face.

An expression of utter amazement crossed it and he bent forward shaking his head.

'It is Sister Muirgel,' he whispered. 'What does this mean? I thought she had been swept overboard.'

There was no questioning the genuineness of his surprise.

'Return to the others, Tola,' Fidelma instructed quietly, 'and do not say anything about this until I come along, which will be shortly. Tell Brother Guss to come in as you leave.'

Shaking his head a little, the shocked religieux left. Fidelma was disappointed. She had been almost counting on some sign that Tola was not exactly astonished to see the body of Muirgel. She was certain that he was not that good an actor. He was as bewildered at the reappearance of Muirgel as she was. There was a cough and the young monk entered.

Again, Fidelma simply held the lantern high and watched his face.

'Who is this, Brother Guss?'

The young man's face went white, drained of blood and he staggered back. Fidelma thought he was going to faint for a moment. His hands went to his face and he emitted a heartrending groan.

'Muirgel! Oh my God, Muirgel!' He started to rock back and forth on his heels.

Fidelma hung up the lantern and pushed him gently into a chair.

'You have some explaining to do, Brother Guss. You knew that Sister Muirgel was still alive when I questioned you yesterday. You did not show this grief when we all presumed her to be washed overboard. Where has she been hiding and why?'

'I loved Muirgel,' the youth sobbed quietly.

'And you knew that she was still alive?'

155

'Yes, I knew,' he confirmed between sobs.

'Why did she go to such an elaborate charade, pretending that she had been swept overboard?'

'She feared that she was going to be killed,' he wept.

Fidelma examined him curiously.

'Are you saying that she hid herself somewhere on board this ship because she felt in danger of her life?'

The young man nodded, trying to control his grief-stricken sobs.

'Why did she come aboard ship in the first place if she believed that? Isn't a ship the last place to find refuge in?'

'She did not realise that she would be the next victim until after she came aboard. Then it was too late, for we had set sail. So she arranged to hide and I helped her.'

'The *next* victim?' Fidelma asked abruptly, picking up on the word.

'Sister Canair had been killed before we came aboard.'

'Canair?' Fidelma's eyebrows shot up. 'Are you telling me that when Sister Muirgel and yourself came aboard this ship, you both knew that Sister Canair was dead?'

'It is a long story, Sister,' Brother Guss gulped, having managed to get his emotions under control.

'Then let us begin it. What was the purpose of Sister Muirgel hiding in the ship and not remaining in her cabin?'

'The idea was to hide from the murderer, and then I would smuggle her off at our first landing-place. That was to be the island of Ushant. We hoped to land there under the cover of darkness and remain in hiding there until after the ship sailed again, taking the murderer with it.'

'A curious plan. Why not simply take your story to the captain? If you knew that a murderer was on board and attempting to kill . . .'

'It was Muirgel's idea. She felt that no one would believe her. They will have to now.' The young Brother shuddered in deep distress.

'So the murderer was on board. Did you know their identity?'

Guss shook his head sadly.

'I did not know, not for sure. Muirgel knew but refused to tell me. She wanted to protect me. However, I can guess who it was.'

The youth was still suffering from deep emotional shock for he spoke as if he were a somnambulist, slowly and deliberately, his eyes unfocused.

In other circumstances Fidelma would have tended to him, given him a strong drink, but she needed information and she needed it quickly. Reaching into her habit, she pulled out the small silver cross which Sister Muirgel had been clutching in her hand and held it up before his eyes.

'Do you recognise this?' she demanded.

Guss gave an hysterical laugh.

'It belonged to Sister Canair.'

'How do you know that Canair is dead? Or is that something else that only Muirgel knew for certain?'

'I saw her body. We saw it together.'

'Are you sure that it was Canair?'

'I am not likely to forget the sight of that corpse.'

'When was this?'

'It was the night before we came on board ship.'

'At the Abbey of Ardmore?'

'Not at the abbey. Muirgel and I did not stay there all that night.'

Fidelma was almost beyond being surprised by the contrary turns to the story.

'I thought that your entire party stayed at the Abbey.'

'Our company arrived at the Abbey during the late afternoon. Prior to our arrival, Sister Canair had told us that she was going to visit someone nearby and left us before we reached the Abbey. She said that she would join us later. If she arrived too late, she said that she would simply meet us on the quay at dawn. The Abbot had already booked our passage on *The Barnacle Goose* so there was nothing to be done but meet and go on board.'

'I see. But Sister Canair did not turn up on the quay the next morning, did she?'

'No. She was dead by then.'

'So when did you know that she was dead?'

'We had arrived at the Abbey, as I say. Most of our company was exhausted and retired to their beds. Muirgel whispered to me that she was going for a walk before retiring. She told me to meet her outside the Abbey gates and come without being seen. Crella was dogging her the whole time, getting on her nerves. She said she wanted to be alone with me. I told you – we were in love.'

'Go on,' prompted Fidelma when he paused. 'Did you meet her outside?'

'I did. She was in good humour and . . . and a very wicked humour, too. She told me that there was a tavern at the bottom of the hill and we could spend the night there without anyone finding us or interfering.'

'Did you agree to that?'

'Of course.'

'And you spent the night at this inn?'

'Some of it.'

'And Sister Canair? Where does she come into this story?'

Brother Guss took in a deep breath and expelled it as a long sigh.

'We . . . after we . . . sometime after we were in bed – in the tavern, that is – we heard the sound of scuffling in the next room. We did not think anything of it. Then there was a sort of cry and we heard someone hurrying down the corridor. We would not have taken any notice except we heard moaning coming from the next room.'

'What did you do?'

'Out of curiosity Muirgel went to the door and listened for a moment. Then she looked out into the corridor. The door of the next room was slightly ajar and a candle was flickering inside. She went in to see if she could help, for someone was obviously in pain.'

The young man came to a halt. His mouth appeared to have gone dry and Fidelma helped him to some water from a jug. After a pause he continued.

'Muirgel came hurrying back to me. She was shocked and upset. She whispered: "It's Sister Canair!" I went into the room and saw Canair lying on the bed; she had been stabbed several times in the chest, around the heart. Then it seemed her throat had been cut.'

Fidelma's eyes narrowed.

'That was surely indicative of a frenzied attack,' she commented.

Brother Guss did not respond.

Fidelma prompted him again.

'Yet you say that she was still alive? You said you heard her moaning?'

'Her dying breaths, so it turned out,' the young man replied. 'She was dead by the time I went into the room. I covered her body with the blanket from the bed and blew out the candle. Then I went back to Muirgel.'

'Was she dead when Muirgel entered the room? Did Canair say anything before she died?'

Brother Guss shook his head.

'Muirgel saw the wounds and panicked. She did not check and even if she had, the woman was already beyond uttering any intelligible sound.'

'Was there a sign of the weapon that inflicted the wounds?'

'I did not see a weapon, but then I was too shaken to investigate. We sat a long time discussing what we should do. It was Muirgel's idea that we simply leave the tavern and return to the Abbey, and pretend that we had been there all night.'

'But the tavernkeeper would have given evidence that you had been there.'

'We didn't think of that.'

'Why didn't you raise the alarm? Perhaps the murderer could have been discovered.'

'Because it would have meant revealing that we had been in the next room. Our presence would have been made known to the murderer, our journey would have had to be cancelled. There were all manner of complications.'

He looked shamefaced.

'It seems silly and selfish now, I agree, but it did not seem so to us at the time; not when we sat in the room next to that awful corpse. You will no doubt judge us harshly, for it is easy to be logical in the day and far away from the event.'

'Time to judge when the facts are clear. Go on.'

'We were back at the Abbey before dawn.'

'You were not worried that the tavernkeeper would raise the alarm and, because you had fled, you might be implicated in the murder?'

'We left money for our lodgings. We ensured that the door of Canair's room was shut and hoped it would be well after dawn when her body was discovered. We believed everyone was still asleep but, as we were leaving, we saw the tavernkeeper loading his cart by torchlight outside. He did not see us. We hurried back to the Abbey, and took our seats in the refectory, so that when other members of our party appeared, they did not question that we had spent the night there.'

Fidelma stroked the side of her nose with her forefinger, pondering matters. It was such a strange story that she had no doubt that the young man spoke the truth.

'And was everyone else at the Abbey, everyone in your party?'

'Yes, they were.'

'No one suspected that you had not spent the night there?'

Brother Guss shook his head but added, 'I think Crella was suspicious. She kept giving us dirty looks.'

'So Canair did not turn up and the two of you told no one your story and then you all came on board.'

Brother Guss made an affirmative gesture.

'I thought everything was all right. Muirgel had taken charge and allotted the cabins as I told you before. She took one for herself in the hope that we might get together later. But even before we sailed, Muirgel called me into her cabin. She was pale and trembling, almost out of her mind with fear.'

'And she told you why?'

'She said that she knew Canair's murderer was on board.' He pointed to the cross Fidelma still held in her hand. 'She saw someone wearing that cross. It was Canair's cross and she was never without it. She once told Muirgel it was a gift from her mother. Muirgel swore that Canair was wearing it when she left us all to visit her friends. It could only have been taken afterwards from her body by the person who killed her.'

'But that was surely not enough to frighten Sister Muirgel. She obviously recognised the person with the crucifix. She could have gone to the captain and told him everything.'

'No! I told you – she was very frightened. She said she knew why Canair had been killed, and that she would be the next victim.'

'Did you seek further explanation from her?'

'I tried. When I asked her how she knew, she quoted a verse from the Bible.'

'What verse?' Fidelma asked quickly. 'Can you remember?'

'The words were something like this:

> 'Wear me as a seal upon your heart,
> As a seal upon your arm;
> For love is strong as death,
> Jealousy cruel as the grave;
> It blazes up like blazing fire,
> Fiercer than any flame.'

Fidelma was reflective.

'Did she explain what she meant by it?'

Brother Guss flushed.

'Muirgel had . . . had known men before me; I'll not deny it. She told me that she and Canair had once been in love with the same man. Then she would say no more.'

'In love with the same man? "Jealousy cruel as the grave"?' Fidelma sighed. 'There is a glimmer of sense here but not much. Are you sure that she told you nothing further?'

'Just that she knew that the person who killed Canair would kill her before the voyage was done.'

'The motive being jealousy?'

'That's right. She told me that she was going to lock herself in her cabin all day, pretending to be seasick.'

'Then I came on board and young Wenbrit thought I should share her cabin,' said Fidelma.

'Yes – she protested at your presence, but even though you were removed she still felt vulnerable. That was when she evolved this plan to hide and leave her bloodstained robe in her cabin. She wanted people to think that murder had already taken place so that they would not search for her.'

'She was going to pretend to be swept overboard in the storm?'

'No. We did not know a storm would descend on us. She was simply going to leave a bloodstained robe to make it look as though she had been stabbed. The idea was to get people to think that she had been killed and thrown overboard during the night. The storm merely confused matters. People thought she had been washed overboard during the night. We then cursed ourselves for leaving the robe because it complicated matters.'

'Indeed; had you *not* left the robe to be found, we would have accepted that Muirgel had been the victim of an accident.' Fidelma smiled grimly. 'And you, obviously, supplied the blood for the robe.'

Brother Guss's right hand went automatically to his left arm and then he shrugged.

'I cut my arm to supply the blood for the robe,' he confirmed. 'I did not know you had already seen the robe. I wondered why you were so interested in the fact that my arm was hurt. I had to improvise.'

'That certainly made me suspicious of your involvement in her so-called death. Where did she hide? The mate scoured the ship without a trace being found.'

'Simple enough. She hid under my bunk. Brother Tola is a sound sleeper. Not even the trumpets announcing the Second Coming would awake him. She had to get out now and then for obvious reasons, but did so during the night or just at dawn before anyone stirred. It was very simple. Who would think of looking under my bunk?'

'And this morning?'

'She rose early and felt that it would be safe to go back to her own cabin. No one, she told me, would think of looking there now that she was officially dead. I was going to join her after breakfast.'

'What do you think happened then?'

'She was seen and murdered by the same person who killed Sister Canair.'

'Very well. You implied you knew who killed her, or rather, whom you suspected of killing her. Are you referring to the same person on whom you put the blame during our talk yesterday?'

'Crella? Yes, I believe that it was she who came and muttered outside Muirgel's door that night. It was Crella who was spying on us. She was jealous of Canair and she was jealous of Muirgel, although she pretended to love Muirgel as her friend.'

'But you did say that Muirgel did not reveal the name of the person whom she suspected? She did not tell you the name of the person she had seen with Canair's cross? It is only your suspicion that it was Sister Crella?'

'I told you, I think—'

'I want facts,' Fidelma cut in sharply, 'not your suspicions. *Did* Muirgel say who she was afraid of?'

The youth shook his head.

'She did not,' he admitted.

Fidelma rubbed her chin thoughtfully.

'We cannot act on suspicion, Guss. Unless you can give me something more substantial, then . . .' She let the sentence hang in the air.

'Then you are going to let Crella escape?' Brother Guss accused angrily.

'My concern is to discover the truth.'

The youth stared belligerently at her for a moment and then his features dissolved into a mask of misery.

'I loved her! I would have done anything for her. Now I am afraid for my own life, for Crella must know now that I was her lover and tried to hide Muirgel. How far does her jealousy spread?'

Fidelma eyed the young man sympathetically.

'We shall be wary, Brother Guss. In the meantime, take comfort from the thought that you loved Muirgel and if, as you say, she loved you in return, then you were twice blessed. Remember the Song of Solomon, for that is the verse which Muirgel was quoting to you. The next verse is:

> 'Many waters cannot quench love;
> No flood can sweep it away.'

Brother Guss could not bring himself to rejoin his companions but had returned to his own cabin to grieve alone. Fidelma joined Murchad outside the door where he was standing with the sailor named Drogon.

'Remain on watch here, Drogon, and do not let anyone in without my permission or that of Murchad,' she instructed him. She turned to the captain. 'Is everyone still gathered at breakfast?'

He nodded affirmatively.

'What will you say to them?' he asked.

'I shall tell them the truth. Our murderer knows the truth, so why not the others? The sooner all is revealed, the sooner the murderer may make a slip.'

Murchad followed Fidelma into the mess deck where Wenbrit was clearing the breakfast remains. The pilgrims sat in silence. Brother Tola had rejoined them and though he refused to tell them what was amiss, they all realised that something had happened. When Fidelma entered and strode to the head of the table, only Cian attempted to acknowledge her. She did not respond. Everyone fixed their eyes on her, trying to guess what news she was bringing them.

Even young Wenbrit realised something was afoot and halted, hands still filled with dirty plates.

'We have found the body of Sister Muirgel,' announced Fidelma.

There were several reactions as they digested the statement.

Sister Crella half-rose and then sat down again with a low moan of anguish. Sister Gormán sniggered agitatedly.

It was Brother Tola, now able to speak having had to contain himself until she arrived, who asked the first question.

'Are you telling us that she was on board all this time? That she had not fallen overboard?'

'I am.'

'I don't understand. How could she have drowned without falling overboard?' demanded Sister Ainder.

Fidelma fixed her with a cold smile.

'That is simple: she did not drown. She had her throat cut within the last half an hour.'

Sister Crella's moan rose to a sharp wail.

Fidelma quickly glanced round the table. Sister Crella seemed to be the one most visibly shaken, although everyone else seemed to register some emotion.

'Are you sure?' It was Cian who asked the question.

'Sure about what?' she demanded.

Cian shifted uneasily under her sharp gaze.

'Sure that it is Sister Muirgel of whom we speak,' he explained lamely. 'First we are told she is dead, then alive and now dead. Is it she or not?'

Fidelma looked across the cabin to Brother Tola.

'It is Sister Muirgel,' Tola confirmed quietly. 'I identified the body. So did Brother Guss . . .' He glanced round, realising for the first time that Guss had not returned.

Fidelma guessed the question he was about to form.

'Brother Guss has gone to his cabin to lie down,' she told them all. 'He was very shocked as well.'

There was no sound from those at the table except Sister Crella's sobbing.

'Sister Muirgel met her killer within the last hour,' Fidelma resumed. 'Can you all account for your movements during that time?'

'What?' Sister Gormán was all a-flutter.

'Are you claiming it is one of us?'

Fidelma looked at them each in turn.

'It is certainly not one of the crew!' She smiled thinly. 'Sister Muirgel knew her killer. In fact, she had engineered her disappearance in order to *avoid* her killer. She hid during the day and emerged to eat and exercise during the night or early morning.' As she spoke, Fidelma suddenly remembered something. 'In fact, the morning after she was supposed to have been swept overboard, when that thick mist enveloped the ship, I encountered her on deck and did not recognise her. We may assume, Wenbrit, that your missing food was consumed by her.'

The boy was looking at her in amazement.

'You are saying that Sister Muirgel arranged for us to think that she had fallen overboard?' Sister Ainder was still having problems coming to terms with what she had been told. 'Why?'

'She wanted to mislead her killer.'

Brother Tola made a sardonic barking laugh, expressing his disbelief.

'Where, in God's name, could she have hidden on this ship? There is nowhere.'

'You'll forgive me if I disagree with you.' Fidelma felt tempted to tell him that Muirgel had spent the first night within a yard or so of him while he slept. 'The more important matter is that Sister Muirgel's murderer is a member of your company. Where were each of you during this last hour?'

They looked at each other suspiciously.

Brother Tola acted as their spokesman.

'We sat down to breakfast all at the same time. That was about an hour ago.'

It turned out that everyone claimed to be in their cabins before that, with the exception of Sister Ainder, who accounted for her absence by stating she was in the *defectora*, and Cian, who said he was exercising on deck.

'Were you in your cabin, Brother Bairne?' enquired Fidelma.

'I was.'

'It is next to Muirgel's cabin. Did you hear anything?'

'Are you accusing me?' stormed the young man, his face reddening. 'You might have to prove such an accusation.'

'If I made such an accusation I would do so when I am sure of proving it,' replied Fidelma confidently. 'I shall want to speak with each of you individually again.'

'By what right?' snapped Sister Ainder indignantly. 'This matter is ridiculous. People being washed overboard when they are not. Accidents that turn to murders. Corpses that are not corpses!'

'You already know my right and authority for this investigation,' Fidelma interrupted her tirade.

Brother Tola glanced at Murchad.

'I presume that Fidelma still acts with your approval, Captain?'

'I have appointed Fidelma of Cashel in full charge of the matter,' Murchad said heavily. 'That is final.'

Chapter Fifteen

They had sighted the western coast of Armorica – that land which was now being called 'Little Britain'.

Murchad announced, 'Within a few hours we shall be sighting the island of Ushant, which is at its western extremity.'

Fidelma had never been to Armorica but knew that within the last two centuries, tens of thousands of Britons had been driven out of their lands by the expansion of the Angles and Saxons, and most had found a new home among the Armoricans. Many others had found refuge in the north-west of Iberia which had come to be named Galicia, the land to which they were sailing; others still had settled in the Five Kingdoms of Éireann, although not in such large numbers as elsewhere. But it was in Armorica, among people who shared a similar language and culture, that the refugees from Britain had begun to change the political map of the country so that the land was renamed 'Little Britain'.

'We'll take on water at Ushant and some fresh food,' continued Murchad. 'We are under the halfway mark on our journey but, after this, there will be no other opportunity for you to stretch your legs on firm ground and to have a hot meal and a bath.'

Fidelma had acknowledged the information absently. She was watching her fellow pilgrims taking their ease on the main deck. She felt confused. One of them was a murderer and she had no idea which one she should even start suspecting! She had not revealed Brother Guss's secret, that Sister Canair was also dead. She hoped, by withholding the information, that someone would eventually reveal knowledge which might indicate that they also knew – and that knowledge would identify them as the murderer. The accusation against Sister Crella certainly could not be substantiated as yet.

Brother Tola had taken up his usual position on deck, seated with his back against the water butt near the main mast reading his Missal. Brothers Dathal and Adamrae were arm in arm, strolling along the deck incongruously, or so it seemed to Fidelma, laughing together at a shared joke. The tall figure of Sister Ainder was seated on the starboard side lecturing Brother Bairne. Sister Crella was pacing the deck, arms folded around her, still agitated and muttering to herself. Fidelma looked round for Brother Guss but he was nowhere to be seen. Nor was Sister Gormán.

'Well, Fidelma?' Cian appeared at her side, interrupting her thoughts. His voice was mocking. 'From the reputation you have gathered to yourself these last few years, I would have thought that the mystery of Sister Muirgel would have been solved by now.'

She found it hard to believe that she had once been so immature as to be in love with this man. Resisting the impulse to utter a sharp rebuke, she recalled that she still needed information from him – and here was an opportunity to obtain it. Instead of reacting, she asked coolly, 'How long did your affair with Sister Muirgel last?'

Cian blinked rapidly. His supercilious smile broadened.

'Are you checking up on my affairs now? Why do you want to know about Muirgel?'

'I am simply pursuing my enquiries into her death.'

Cian studied her phlegmatic expression, then shrugged slightly.

'If you must know, not very long. Are you sure that you have no personal interest in asking?'

Fidelma chuckled.

'You flatter yourself, Cian – but then, you always did. Sister Muirgel was murdered by someone she knew. I told you at breakfast.'

'Are you trying to implicate me?' demanded Cian. 'Has your hurt pride, after all these years, turned your mind so that you accuse me? That is utterly ridiculous!'

'Why should it be ridiculous? Don't lovers kill each other?' she asked innocently.

'My affair with Muirgel was over long before we set out on this journey.'

'Long is an abstract term.'

'Well, a week or so prior to the journey.'

'Did you walk out on her without a word, or this time did you have sufficient courage to tell her face to face?' she added brutally.

Cian coloured hotly.

'As a matter of fact, it was she who walked out on *me* – and, yes, she did tell me. Incredible as it may seem, she told me that she was in love with someone else – that young idiot, Brother Guss.'

Here was confirmation that some of Guss's story was truthful, in spite of Crella's denial that her friend was having an affair with him.

'Knowing you, it was not something you would meekly accept, Cian. You have too much vanity. You would have protested.'

Cian's hearty chuckle took Fidelma by surprise.

'If you must know, I was very relieved by her confession, because I was about to end the relationship myself.'

She did not believe him. 'I find it hard to credit that you would let a young boy like Guss take over from you without your pride being wounded.'

'If you want the gory details, Canair and I had been lovers for a short while. I was trying to ditch Muirgel. Thankfully, she made it easy for me.' It was plain by his boastful attitude that Cian was not lying.

'When did you become Canair's lover?'

'Oh, so you want details of that as well! Really, Fidelma, when did you become a voyeur?'

She had to restrain herself from slapping his sneering face.

'Let me remind you,' she said icily, 'that I am a *dálaigh* investigating a murder.'

'A *dálaigh* miles from our homeland, on board a pilgrim ship,' Cian said mockingly. 'You have no rights to pry into my life, *dálaigh*.'

'I have every right. So you had affairs with Muirgel *and* Canair? I suppose, knowing your character, you dallied with most of the young women at Moville.'

'Jealous, are we?' Cian sneered. 'You were always possessive and jealous, Fidelma of Cashel. Don't disguise your prying as being part of your duty. I had enough of your sulky ways when you were younger.'

'I am not interested in your foolish pride, Cian. I am only interested in knowledge. I need to find Muirgel's killer.'

She had become aware that their voices were raised and they had been shouting at each other. Luckily the sound of the wind and sea seemed to have disguised their words, although Murchad, standing nearby at the steering oar, looked studiously out to sea as if embarrassed. He must have heard their exchange.

Fidelma suddenly noticed that the young, naive Sister Gormán had come unnoticed on deck and was standing nearby, watching them with an expression of intense curiosity. She was picking at a shawl that she had draped over her shoulders to protect her from the chilly winds. When Fidelma caught her eye, she giggled and began to chant.

> 'My beloved is fair and ruddy
> A paragon among ten thousand.
> His head is gold, finest gold,
> His locks are like palm fronds.
> His eyes are like doves beside brooks of water,

Splashed by the milky water
As they sit where it is drawn . . .'

Cian uttered a suppressed exclamation of disgust and turned down the companionway, brushing by the girl as he left Fidelma. Sister Gormán uttered a shrill laugh.

Gormán was a strange little thing, Fidelma thought. She seemed able to quote entire sections of Holy Scripture effortlessly. What was it that she had been quoting just then, something from the Song of Solomon? Sister Gormán glanced up and her eyes met Fidelma's once more. She smiled again – a curious smile that had no humour to it, only a movement of the facial muscles. Then she turned and moved away.

'Sister Gormán!' Fidelma had promised herself to spend some time with the young girl for she was clearly highly-strung and no one seemed to be concerned for her. The girl watched suspiciously as Fidelma came up. 'I hope you are not still blaming yourself for what has happened to Sister Muirgel?'

The girl's apprehensive expression deepened.

'What do you mean?'

'Well, you did tell me, when we thought she had fallen overboard, that you felt guilty because you cursed her.'

'That!' Gormán pouted in a gesture of dismissal. 'I was just being silly. Of course my curse did not kill her. That's been proved by her death now. If my curse *had* killed her, she would not have been alive these past two days.'

Fidelma raised her eyes a little at the apparent callousness of the girl's tone. But then Gormán displayed curious swings of temperament.

'As you know,' Fidelma passed on hurriedly, 'I was asking where everyone was immediately before sitting down to breakfast. I think you said you were in your cabin?'

'I was.' The reply came curtly.

'And you were there with Sister Ainder who shares that cabin?'

'She went out for a while.'

'Ah yes; so she said.'

'Muirgel is dead. You are wasting your time asking these questions,' snapped Gormán.

Fidelma blinked at her rude tone.

'It is my duty to do so,' she ventured, and then tried to change the conversation to put the young girl at her ease. 'I notice you like chanting songs from the Scriptures.'

'Everything is contained in the holy words,' replied Gormán, almost arrogantly. 'Everything.' She suddenly stared unblinkingly into Fidelma's eyes and her features formed once more into that eerie smile.

> 'There can be no remedy for your sore,
> The new skin cannot grow.
> All your lovers have forgotten you;
> They look for you no longer.
> I have struck you down.'

Fidelma shivered in spite of herself.

'I don't understand . . .'

Gormán actually stamped a foot.

'Jeremiah. Surely you know the Scriptures? It is a suitable epitaph for Muirgel.'

At that, she turned away and hurried past the tall figure of Sister Ainder. The latter moved towards her as if to speak with her, but the girl pushed by her, causing the sharp-faced woman to give an exclamation of annoyance as the girl almost made her lose her balance.

'Is there anything wrong with Sister Gormán?' she called to Fidelma.

'I think she is in need of a friend to counsel her,' replied Fidelma.

Sister Ainder actually smiled.

'You do not have to tell me that. She has always kept to herself, even talking to herself at times as though she needs no other companion. But then, they say that true saints see and speak to angels. I would not condemn her for she might have more of the Faith then the rest of us put together.'

Fidelma was sceptical.

'I think she is just a troubled soul.'

'Yet madness can be a gift from God, so perhaps she is to be blessed.'

'Do you think that she is mad?'

'If not mad, then a little eccentric, eh? Look, there she is again, muttering her imprecations and curses.'

Sister Ainder pursed her lips and apparently did not wish to pursue the topic of conversation, for she changed the subject, remarking: 'It seems that for a pilgrimage of religieux on our way to a Holy Shrine there is one thing missing on this voyage.'

'Which is?' asked Fidelma cautiously.

'Religion itself. I fear that apart from a few exceptions, God is not with those on this voyage.'

171

'How do you judge that?'

Sister Ainder's bright eyes bore into Fidelma.

'There was certainly no religion in the hand that killed Sister Muirgel and she, in turn, was certainly no religieuse. That young woman would have been better off in a bawdy house.'

'So you disliked Muirgel?'

'As I have told you before, I really did not know her enough to dislike her. I only disapproved of her loose ways with men. But, as I say, she does not appear to be outrageous company among our band of so-called pilgrims.'

'I presume you don't include yourself in the "outrageous company"? Are there any other exceptions?'

'Brother Tola, of course.'

'But not me?' Fidelma smiled.

Sister Ainder looked at her pityingly.

'You are not a religieuse. Your concern is the law and you are simply a Sister of the Faith by accident.'

Fidelma fought to keep her face impassive. She had not thought it was so obvious. First Brother Tola, and now Sister Ainder felt able to take her to task on her religiosity. Fidelma decided to move the conversation onwards.

'What of the others of your party then? You don't consider they should be in religious Orders?'

'Certainly not. Cian, for instance, is a womaniser, a man without morals or thought for others. There is no caring in him. With his vanity, it would not occur to him that he was hurting anyone. As a warrior he was probably in the right occupation. Fate caused him to seek security in a religious house. It was the wrong decision.'

Then Sister Ainder gestured across the deck of the ship to Dathal and Adamrae.

'Those young men should be . . . well!' Her face was twisted in disapproval.

'You would condemn them?' asked Fidelma.

'Our religion condemns them. Remember the words of Paul to Romans: "Their men in turn, giving up natural relations with women, burnt with lust for one another; males behave indecently with males, and are paid in their own persons the fitting wage of such perversion . . . Thus, because they have not seen fit to acknowledge God, He has given them up to their own depraved reason".'

Fidelma pulled a face.

'We all know that Paul of Tarsus was an ascetic who believed in austerity and rigidity in morals.'

Sister Ainder shook her head in irritation.

'It is very clear, Sister, that you take no thought to the words God spoke to Moses. Leviticus, eighteen, verse twenty-two: "You shall not lie with a man as with a woman; that is an abomination." *An abomination!*' she repeated in an angry voice.

Fidelma waited a moment or two and then said, 'Isn't the basis of our Faith salvation for everyone? Surely we are all sinners and we *all* need salvation? God did not judge the world, therefore we have no right to judge it. I give you back the words of John's Gospel: "It was not to judge the world that God sent His Son into the world, but that through Him the world might be saved".'

Sister Ainder actually chuckled, though sourly.

'You are indeed a *dálaigh*, quoting sentences here and there to support your arguments. You are ever a woman of law and yet you can speak about not judging the world?'

'I don't judge. I seek the truth – and in truth is accountability.'

Sister Ainder sniffed and made to end the conversation. But she paused and turned back.

'Brother Bairne is probably the only other person I would save from this ship of fools,' she added. 'He has some religious potential but the others, Sister Crella, for example – well, she seems no better than her friend Muirgel. I swear that, in this tiny ship, traversing the waters, we have all seven of the deadly sins that are cursed by the Living God. There is anger, covetousness, there is envy and gluttony, there is lust and pride and sloth.'

Fidelma looked at the strict religieuse with unconcealed amusement.

'Have you identified all these sins among us?'

Sister Ainder's features did not soften.

'You will find that lust features prominently on this ship. Lust is the one sin that seems to be shared among many of our company.'

'Oh?' Fidelma smiled softly. 'Am I supposed to be part of this sin of lust?'

Sister Ainder shook her head.

'Oh no, Fidelma of Cashel. You are guilty of the worst sin of the seven . . . for pride is your sin. And pride is the mask of one's own faults.'

Fidelma found her features hardening slightly. She would have been prepared to chuckle in earnest if any of the other six had been levelled at her by Sister Ainder, but she was not expecting pride. The barb hurt because it was something which had worried Fidelma for a long time. She *did* have a pride in her abilities, but not a vanity. There was a difference. Yet she was never sure what the difference was. To her, false humility was worse than pride in one's achievements.

Sister Ainder was smiling complacently, watching the conflict on Fidelma's features.

'Proverbs, Sister Fidelma,' she intoned. 'Proverbs sixteen, verse eighteen: "Pride comes before disaster and arrogance before a fall".'

Fidelma flushed with annoyance.

'And which of the sins do you own up to, Ainder of Moville?' she demanded testily.

Sister Ainder smiled thinly.

'I keep all the Lord's covenants,' she replied with self-assurance.

Fidelma's eyebrows arched a little.

'A person with snot on their nose rejoices to see snot on the nose of another,' she said brutally.

It was an old rural proverb which Fidelma had once heard a farmer use. It was coarse and strong, but Fidelma felt a sudden anger at the conceit of the woman and she uttered it without a thought.

Sister Ainder gasped in fury at the vulgarity.

Fidelma heard Murchad, who was still standing nearby, snort in mirth. It was a humour he could appreciate.

Yet the moment she had uttered the saying, Fidelma felt contrite and turned to express her regret that she had let anger get the better of her. However, Sister Ainder had already stalked away.

Fidelma paused for a moment and then met Murchad's eye guiltily. The captain was still grinning; he suppressed a chuckle.

'I'm sorry, lady, but you were in the right. That creature is the epitome of the very pride which she accused you of.'

Fidelma appreciated his support but continued to feel contrite.

'Words uttered in anger, whether true or not, are not likely to have an effect, and—'

A cry cut her short. It was not the cry of the lookout, but a shout of alarm. Someone on the main deck, she thought it was Brother Bairne, had shouted some warning. He was pointing forward.

On the for'ard deck of the vessel were two figures. Sister Crella was standing there. A short distance in front of her stood Brother Guss. He was backing away from her, almost in a cringing attitude. The shouted warning from Brother Bairne was because Guss was backing dangerously near the ship's rail.

The warning cry came too late.

Brother Guss teetered on the edge of the starboard side of the vessel and then fell backwards into the sea with a cry of fear.

Sister Crella stood, apparently reaching forward with both hands outstretched towards the spot where he had fallen overboard.

Murchad bellowed: 'Man overboard!'

Many of those on deck, including Fidelma, ran to the starboard side. The ship was moving fast and they saw Brother Guss's head bobbing past at an alarming rate and disappearing aft.

'Stand by to wear the ship!' came Murchad's cry.

The ship's crew materialised as if by magic and started to haul down the sail while Gurvan and another crew member threw their weight against the oar, turning the ship with what seemed incredible slowness in a wide arc.

Fidelma had run forward, along the main deck to the small for'ard deck.

Sister Crella was still standing there. She was bent forward now, her arms wrapped around her shoulders. She saw Fidelma scrambling towards her. Her features were white, her eyes wide. The shock on her face was plain.

'He . . . he fell . . .' she began helplessly.

'What did you say to him?' Fidelma demanded sharply. 'What did you say?'

The girl stared at her as if unable to speak.

'He was backing away from you,' Fidelma pressed, speaking roughly to shock her into speech. 'Were you threatening him?'

'Threatening?' Sister Crella returned her gaze in bewilderment. 'I don't know what you mean.'

'Then what made him back away from you in such fear that he fell overboard?'

'How do I know?'

'What did you say to him?'

'I told him that I knew about the seventh union, that's all.'

'What?' Fidelma was in the dark.

'You should know,' retorted Sister Crella, pulling herself together. Her face took on a defiant look. 'Now leave me alone. They'll pick him up in a moment and you can ask him yourself.'

Sister Crella pushed her way by Fidelma and went running along the deck.

Fidelma hurried back to Murchad. The crew and the other passengers were still lining the sides of the ship, staring across the water attempting to catch sight of Guss.

'Can we reach him?' Fidelma asked breathlessly as she came up to Murchad.

The captain was sombre.

'I'm afraid we can't even see him yet.'

'What? But he passed us by so closely.'

Murchad's attitude was morose.

'Even shortening sail and beginning our turn at once, we would have gone on for a long distance from the spot where he went in. I've turned and come back on my wake but I can see no sign of him.'

He glanced up to the mast head where a lookout had been posted.

'Any sign, Hoel?' he bellowed up.

The voice came back with a negative.

'We'll search as much as we can. The only chance is if he is a strong swimmer.'

Fidelma glanced across to where Brother Bairne was standing surveying the waters anxiously.

'Do you know if Guss swims well?' she demanded.

Brother Bairne shook his head.

'Even a good swimmer in these waters would surely not last long.'

'I'll try my best,' Murchad was saying. 'The best is all that I can try.'

Fidelma moved to Brother Bairne's side.

'When you cried the warning, what was it that you saw?' she asked softly so that the others would not hear her question.

'Saw? I shouted a warning because Guss was stumbling too near the edge.'

'But did you see why he was backing himself into that dangerous position?'

'I do not think he realised he was.'

Fidelma was impatient.

'Did you see Sister Crella threatening him?'

Brother Bairne looked shocked.

'Sister Crella threatening him? Are you serious?'

'You did notice Sister Crella on the for'ard deck with him?'

'Of course. They were speaking together and then Brother Guss began to move backwards, a little rapidly, or so I thought. I cried the warning but he stumbled and fell.' Brother Bairne was examining her with some perplexity.

'Thank you,' Fidelma said. 'I just wanted to make sure of what you had seen, that's all.'

She walked slowly back to the stern deck, her head bent slightly forward in thought. As the minutes went by, a feeling of depression descended on everyone. It was a full hour later before Murchad called off the search.

176

'I am afraid there is nothing that we can do for the poor boy,' he told Cian, who had again asserted his leadership of the party. 'I think he went under almost immediately. There is no hope now. I am so sorry.'

Fidelma went below and made her way to Sister Crella's cabin.

Sister Crella was lying on her back staring up at the deck above. As Fidelma entered, she sat up with a hopeful expression, saw Fidelma's grim features and her own hardened.

'Murchad has called off the search for Brother Guss,' announced Fidelma. 'There is no hope of finding him alive.'

Sister Crella's face was immobile.

'Now perhaps you will tell me what you meant?' went on Fidelma.

Sister Crella's voice was tight.

'It should be easy for a *dálaigh* such as you to know what the seventh union means.'

'The seventh union?' Fidelma's eyes cleared. 'Do you mean the seventh form of union between man and woman? The law term that means secret sexual relations?'

Sister Crella closed her eyes without replying.

'Yes, I know the law on the seventh union,' Fidelma agreed, 'but there is nothing about it that makes sense in these circumstances. Why did Brother Guss react in the way he did?'

'I merely told him that I knew how he had been pestering Muirgel.' Her eyes were bright, her gaze defiant. 'You see, I think Guss killed her because she would not respond to his advances.'

Fidelma lowered herself on to the chair in the cabin.

'Pestering? That is an interesting word.'

'What else would you call it when one person tries to enforce their attentions on another?' demanded Sister Crella.

'So you believe that Brother Guss forced his attentions on Sister Muirgel, and that she did not respond to him?'

'Of course. He was a moonstruck youth – just like Brother Bairne. Muirgel did not want to have anything to do with him. Of that I am sure.'

'How can you be so sure?'

'Because Muirgel was my friend. I told you before – there were no secrets between us.'

'Yet Muirgel did not tell you that she feared for her life and had gone into hiding on this ship, did she? If there was no relationship, why did Muirgel ask Guss to help her to hide . . . even from you?'

Crella stared angrily at Fidelma.

'Guss has been telling lies about Muirgel.'

'How do you explain, then, that it was Guss to whom Muirgel turned when she felt threatened?' insisted Fidelma. 'That it was Guss who helped to hide her during the last two days?'

'That spotty-faced youth was saying that he was Muirgel's lover. That is why I challenged him on the seventh union.'

She suddenly bent down and reached under the bunk, drawing out a long slim knife in one continuous motion, then she stood up and brandished it before her. Fidelma rose quickly to her feet, her mind reacting swiftly, thinking that she would have to defend herself from attack. However, Sister Crella simply stood staring down at the knife for a moment. Then she held it out, hilt towards Fidelma.

'Here, take it.'

Fidelma was startled.

'Go on!' snapped Sister Crella. 'Take it! You'll see it has dried blood on it still.'

'What is it?'

'The knife that probably killed my poor friend, what else?'

Fidelma took the knife carefully from her grasp. It was true that there were signs of dried blood on the blade. Whether it was, indeed, the murder weapon she did not know. Nor could she prove it was *not* the weapon. It was a knife usually used to cut meat.

'Why do you suspect that this is the weapon?' She phrased her question carefully. 'How did you come by it?'

'Brother Guss planted it in my cabin.' Crella gulped 'I had gone along to have breakfast. Then you came in and told us of Muirgel's death. I was returning when I bumped into Guss in the corridor. I did not like the way he was staring at me. He brushed by me and went up on deck. I continued into my cabin. It was then I found the knife.'

Fidelma's eyes dropped to the bunk; she could not see under it from where she stood.

'Where was it hidden?' she asked.

'Under the bunk.'

'How did you spot it?'

'By luck, I suppose.'

'Luck does not make one's vision see through solid objects! It could not be seen from any point in this room unless you were down on your knees peering under the bunk.'

Crella was not flustered.

'I came back with an apple in my hand. When I opened the door, I dropped my apple. It was as I was bending down to pick it up that I saw the knife.'

'You did not actually see Guss put it there, did you? Your account does not explain why you think he was responsible.'

'Because we were all at breakfast – with one exception. Brother Guss was not there. You claimed that he was in his cabin, but I saw him *coming* from his cabin. Guss has been trying to implicate me in Muirgel's killing. He told everyone that I was the murderer.' She frowned. 'He must have told you.'

'Where did you hear that he had told everyone that you were the murderer?' demanded Fidelma.

Crella hesitated. 'It was from Brother Cian. Guss had told him; Cian told me.'

'What did you do? You had found the knife and Cian told you that Guss was accusing you. What then?'

'I was so furious I went charging up on deck to confront Guss.'

'But you left the knife here in your cabin.'

'How did you know?'

'Because you did not have it in your hand when you were on deck. A moment ago you reached under your bunk and took it out.'

'I suppose I did leave it here.'

'Strange, therefore, that you did not confront him with the weapon. Wouldn't that be the normal thing to do?'

'I don't know. I just wanted him to know that I was wise to his little tale about secret sexual relations with Muirgel. I just meant to warn him that he would not get away with his claims!'

'And he did not, did he? He was so fearful of you that he backed away from you and fell overboard.' Sister Crella began to protest but Fidelma went on sternly, 'A fine ruthless killer was this Brother Guss, who not only killed but planted evidence – and yet, when faced by a woman in full view of everyone, he was so scared that he allowed himself to be literally *driven overboard*.'

Sister Crella listened to the sarcasm in her voice.

'He planted the knife and accused me!'

'Sadly, we cannot now question Brother Guss,' observed Fidelma dryly. 'It seems that everything is so conveniently tied up with this death.'

Crella regarded her suspiciously.

'I don't know what you mean.'

'Tell me, why are you so sure that Muirgel was not having an affair with Guss? That is something that I still do not understand.'

Crella raised her jaw defensively.

'You do not believe me?'

'Did Muirgel have many affairs?'

179

'We were both normal young women. We each had our amours.'

'So she always told you with whom she was having affairs?'

Crella sniffed defensively.

'Of course.'

'When was the last time she told you about an affair?'

'I mentioned it before. She was having an affair with Cian. In fact, I had a brief affair with Cian before I tired of him.'

'Isn't the truth rather that Cian dropped you for Muirgel?'

Crella coloured hotly.

'No one drops me.'

'Didn't that make you jealous and angry?'

'Not enough to kill her! Don't be ridiculous. We often swapped lovers. We were close friends and cousins, don't forget.'

'And you believe that she was still having an affair with Cian and not with Guss?'

'Not with Guss, but I think she and Cian had some sort of row just before we set out from Moville.'

'Why are you so sure that she was not having an affair with Guss? In spite of Muirgel's frankly libertine views?'

'Because she would have told me,' Crella said doggedly. 'Guss is the last person she would have an affair with. He was too serious. It is obvious to me that when Guss became moonstruck on her and she rejected him, he plotted her death and then killed her.'

'What's your explanation as to why and how Muirgel hid herself on this ship for a couple of days, trying to lead people into thinking she had been swept overboard?'

'Maybe it was to escape from Guss's unwanted attentions.'

'Then why didn't she let you in on the secret? I am sorry, Crella, but I have to tell you that the evidence points to the fact that Guss, indeed, *was* her lover. There is one other matter. How do you explain about Sister Canair?'

Fidelma looked deeply into Crella's eyes to judge her reaction.

A slight expression of bewilderment could be discerned there.

'Sister Canair? What about her?'

'Are you claiming that Guss killed her as well?'

The bewilderment grew and was unfeigned.

'What makes you think Sister Canair has been killed?' the girl demanded. 'You didn't even meet our company until after we set sail. How do you know anything about Sister Canair?'

Fidelma stood examining the girl for a moment or two and then she smiled briefly.

'No reason,' she said, dismissing the subject. 'No reason at all.'

180

She turned and left the cabin holding the knife.

Either Sister Crella was telling the truth, or . . . Fidelma shook her head. This was the most frustrating case that she had ever been involved in. If Sister Crella was telling the truth, then Guss must have been an exceptional liar. If Brother Guss was telling the truth, then Crella must be the liar. Who was telling the truth? And who was telling the lies? She had always been taught that truth was great and would prevail. But with this matter she could not begin to recognise the truth.

It would serve no purpose to lay the complete story as told by Guss before Crella. She would merely deny it, if she was guilty, and without any further evidence, it would lead nowhere. Fidelma, it seemed, had reached a dead end.

Chapter Sixteen

Murchad pointed to the black coastline emerging from the haze on the sea.

'That is the island of Ushant.'

'It looks a large island,' Fidelma observed, from her position at his side. During the last few hours she had been considering the story that Guss had told her about Sister Canair's death and the involvement of Muirgel and himself. Had Muirgel been killed because she was a witness? Or had Guss been right that there was another motive? And if he were, and that motive was jealousy, could Crella have been the killer? Had Guss met his own death because of it? Fidelma knew that Crella's truth was certainly not the truth of Brother Guss but she had no firm evidence to solve the riddle.

An hour or so previously, they had held a service for Sister Muirgel and committed her body to the deep; it was the second service they had held for her, more subdued and restrained than the first. At the same time, they held a remembrance for poor young Guss and commended his soul to God's keeping. It was odd knowing that one among them did not share the sentiments that had been uttered during the service. Now, it was late afternoon with the sun lowering in the cloudy western sky which was streaked with darkening billows. It was growing chilly and slowly, above the horizon, the dark coastline had emerged and drawn closer. The gloomy coast to which Murchad was pointing must have been a few miles in length.

'It is a large island,' the captain replied to Fidelma's question. 'And a dangerous one. I think we shall be lucky, though.'

Fidelma glanced at him in surprise.

'Lucky? In what way?'

'This haze . . . it could easily develop into a sudden fog, which is frequent around Ushant, and there are strong currents here and innumerable reefs, added to which, if the wind is harsh one stands in danger of being hurled, if not onto the reefs, then onto the rocky, broken shore. A blow here can last a week or ten days without letting up.'

Even in the haze there seemed something sinister about the low black outline they were approaching. There was no sign of any hills. Fidelma estimated that the highest point of the island could not be more than two hundred feet, but there was still something very threatening about the distant crash and hiss of the waves breaking on the rocks along the shoreline. It seemed an island full of menace.

'How do you know where to land?' she asked. 'I can see only an impenetrable wall of rocks.'

Murchad grimaced.

'We certainly won't attempt to land on this coast. This is the northern coast. We must sail south, around a point into a broad bay where the main settlement is situated. There is a church there which was set up a century ago by the Blessed Paul Aurelian, the Briton.'

He pointed.

'We have to round that headland over there – do you see? Where that ship is standing out towards us.'

Fidelma followed his outstretched arm and saw that a distant ship had appeared from behind the dark headland and was beating around towards them. A voice cried from the masthead.

Murchad took a step forward and shouted back in annoyance: 'We already see it. You should have let us have a holler ten minutes ago!'

Gurvan appeared from the bow of the ship.

'She's a square-rigged ship out of Montroulez.'

'That's the type of ship. It doesn't tell us who is sailing her,' replied Murchad. 'A lookout is useless unless he keeps the deck informed.'

Fidelma could make out the square-sail rig, similar to some extent to *The Barnacle Goose* with its high prow.

Gurvan, who had joined Drogon at the steering oar, was peering forward, straining to take in the details of the approaching vessel.

'I think there is something wrong with her, Captain,' he called.

Murchad swung round frowning to examine the other vessel.

'Her sail is badly set and pulling her too close to the wind,' he muttered. 'That's bad seamanship for you.'

For her part, Fidelma could see nothing wrong with the ship itself but accepted that the trained eyes of Murchad and Gurvan could pick out the faults of their fellow seamen.

Then Murchad let out an uncharacteristic exclamation which caused Fidelma to start.

'The fool! He should be wearing the ship now. That onshore wind is going to turn the vessel towards the rocks.'

The two vessels were drawing closer together, except that *The*

Barnacle Goose was standing well out to the west of the grim line of rocks, with plenty of sea room to manoeuvre. The other vessel was straining under the wind towards the shore.

'Why doesn't he wear the ship? Can't he see the danger?' Gurvan cried. No one answered him.

Some members of the crew were lining the port rail and watching the other ship, making critical comments on the other's seamanship.

'Belay that!' bellowed Murchad. 'Stand by the halyards.'

The sailors broke off and made towards the ropes which raised and lowered the sail. Fidelma was mentally noting down this strange seaman's jargon for she was interested in learning what was happening. She felt a sudden shift in wind. It was curious how she had now grown accustomed to noticing wind changes since she had observed how essential it was on shipboard.

'I knew it!' cried Murchad, almost stamping his foot. 'Damn that fool of a captain!'

His cry caused her to look towards the other vessel which stood quite some way away. If she understood Murchad correctly, the other captain should have reset his sail and tacked or zigzagged his ship against the wind. Whatever the technicality was, she could see the result.

The wind had hit the sail of the ship with such force that it lurched forward like an arrow from a bow, pushing it directly into the low line of rocks ahead. Then a contrary wind heeled the vessel over, so far that, for a moment, Fidelma though it would turn right over on its side. It balanced precariously for a moment and then swung upright again. The wind caught once more at the sail and, even above the sound of the sea and the wind, Fidelma could hear a terrible rending sound as the sail tore across.

'Say a prayer for them, lady!' cried Gurvan. 'They have no hope in hell now.'

'What do you mean?' gasped Fidelma, and then realised it was a silly question to ask.

For a moment or two the other ship seemed strangely becalmed and then the hanging shreds of the mainsail, and the still intact steering sail, caught in the wind and the vessel lurched forward yet again.

There was a sound the like of which Fidelma had never heard before. It was like a gigantic animal tearing through the undergrowth, splintering wood and uprooting bushes and trees in its wake. That sound was magnified a thousand times across the water.

The other vessel seemed to be hurled forward and, as Fidelma looked on in horror, it began to disintegrate.

185

'Smashed on the rocks, by the living God!' cried Murchad. 'Heaven help the poor souls.'

She watched with a cold fascination as the distant mast suddenly splintered and crashed over like a tall tree falling, bringing the rigging and remains of the tattered sail with it. Then it seemed as if the planks were breaking up. She could see small dark figures leaping from the ship into the white frothy waters. She imagined she could hear cries and screams, although the wind and the sound of the water smashing against the rocks would have drowned out such sounds.

Within a few moments the other vessel had disappeared and around the dark jagged teeth of the rocks there seemed little but flotsam and jetsam bobbing on the water – bits of wreckage, mainly shattered wooden planks. A barrel. A wicker basket. And here and there, face downwards, a few bodies.

Murchad stood looking on as if he had turned to stone. Then, as a man rousing himself from a sleep, he first shook his head and coughed to clear the emotion from his voice.

'Lower the mainsail!' he cracked out.

The hands, already at the halyards, began hauling.

Cian and some of the other members of the pilgrim party had come up on deck, aware that something was happening, and demanding to know what had taken place.

Murchad stared at Cian for a moment and then roared angrily: 'Get your party below! *Now!*'

Fidelma went forward, feeling embarrassed, and began to push her fellow religieux towards the hatchway.

'A ship has just struck the rocks over there,' she replied in answer to their protests. 'There does not seem much hope for the poor souls on board.'

'Can't we do something?' asked Sister Ainder. 'Surely it is our duty to be of assistance?'

Fidelma glanced back to where Murchad was shouting instructions and compressed her lips for a moment.

'The captain is doing all he can,' she assured the tall religieuse. 'You may best help him by obeying his commands.'

'Bring her head to the wind, Gurvan! Sea anchors! Hold her steady. Stand by to launch the skiff!'

From the jumble of orders, Fidelma realised that Murchad was going to attempt to pick up any survivors.

Seeing her companions going reluctantly below, she turned back to Murchad. 'Is there anything we can do to help?' She asked.

Murchad grimaced and shook his head.

'Leave it to us for the moment, lady,' he replied gruffly.

Fidelma did not really want to go below nor return to her cabin, so she moved to a corner where she thought she would be out of the way and could observe what was taking place.

Gurvan had relinquished his position on the steering oar to someone else and had taken a couple of men to lower the longboat – the skiff as Murchad called it – into the choppy seas. Fidelma marvelled at how each man seemed to know his position and what he must do. *The Barnacle Goose* was now hove-to, sails down and sea anchors dragging to keep the vessel in a fairly steady position. Nevertheless, Fidelma realised that no ship could hold a stationary position for long in these waters; it was just a matter of time before Murchad would have to hoist sail and get out of harm's way. The rocks looked so dangerously near.

The small craft had hit the waters with a smack and with Gurvan in the bow to direct them and two sailors hauling on the oars, it went slicing across the chopping waters in the direction of the rocks and the bobbing wreckage.

Fidelma bent forwards watching them.

'I doubt there'll be any survivors from that lot,' said a small voice at her side.

She glanced down to find Wenbrit beside her. The lad looked very white and he held his hand to his throat, against the scar which she had noticed when she had first come on board. She had never seen such an expression of fear on his face before. She presumed that he was shocked by what had happened.

'Do such things often happen at sea?'

The boy blinked, his voice was tight.

'Ships going on the rocks like that, do you mean?'

Fidelma nodded.

'Frequently. Too frequently,' answered the boy, still not relaxed. 'Only a few go on the rocks due to bad seamanship, due to people who have no knowledge nor respect for the sea and who should never set foot on shipboard, let alone be in charge of a vessel responsible for other people's lives. Many more go on the rocks due to the weather which cannot be controlled, with the winds, tides and storms. A few other ships founder because the crew or their captain have taken too much liquor.'

Fidelma was intrigued at the suppressed vehemence in the boy's tone.

'I can see that it is a matter that you have pondered on at length, Wenbrit.'

187

The boy gave a bark of laughter which surprised her by its angry note.

'Have I said something wrong?' she wondered.

Wenbrit was at once apologetic.

'Nothing wrong, lady. Sorry, it's not your fault. I don't mind telling you now. Murchad saved my life. He pulled me from the seas, from such a wreck as that.' He gestured with his head towards the floating debris across the water.

She was surprised. After a pause she prompted him, 'When was that, Wenbrit?'

'A few years ago now. I was on a ship that ran onto some rocks due to bad seamanship. I can't remember much about it, except that the captain was drunk and gave the wrong orders. The ship went to pieces. Murchad picked me out of the sea several days later. I was tied to a piece of wooden grating, otherwise I would have slid into the sea and drowned. One of the ropes that lashed me to it had slipped around my throat. I know you have noticed my scar.'

Fidelma began to understand now why the boy almost hero-worshipped Murchad.

'So you were a cabin boy when you were very young, then?'

Wenbrit smiled without humour.

'Didn't your parents mind?' she asked gently.

Wenbrit gazed up at her. She could see the deep anguish in his dark eyes.

'My father was the captain.'

Fidelma tried not to register her shock.

'Your father was a sea captain?'

'He was a drunk. He was often drunk.'

'And your mother?'

'I don't remember her. He told me that she had died soon after I was born.'

'Was anyone else saved from the ship?'

'Not that I know of. I do not recall anything from the time it struck to the time I came to on board *The Barnacle*. Murchad told me that I must have been in the sea several days and was near dead when he fished me out of the water.'

'Did you make any attempt to trace any survivors? Your father might have lived.'

Wenbrit shrugged indifferently.

'Murchad put into the port in Cornwall which was the home port of my father's vessel. There was no word there. All the crew had been given up for lost.'

'Apart from Murchad, who else knows your story?'

'Most of the men on this ship, lady. This is my home now. Thanks be to God that Murchad came along when he did. Now I have a new family and a better one than I ever knew.'

Fidelma smiled and laid a hand on his shoulder.

'Thanks be to God, indeed, Wenbrit.' Then the thought struck her. 'And thanks be to whoever it was who lashed your unconscious body to that grating, so that you at least stood a chance of rescue.'

There was a cry across the waters as the skiff reached the patch of floating wreckage. Gurvan was standing up, precariously, examining the waters. Then he pointed and sat down. They could see the oars stroking the water.

'Have they found a survivor?' Fidelma asked.

Wenbrit shook his head.

'I think it's a dead body. They are letting it back into the water.'

'Can't we pick up the bodies?' Fidelma protested, thinking that some funeral ceremony should be performed.

'At sea, lady, the concern must always be for the living before the dead,' Wenbrit told her.

They heard another shout across the water and could see a second figure being hauled into the skiff. Then they saw a splashing nearby. Someone was trying to swim to the rescue vessel.

'Two souls saved at least,' muttered Wenbrit.

It was fifteen minutes later when the skiff returned. In all, only three people had been found alive and now Murchad was in a hurry to get his ship underway, for even Fidelma could see that the winds and tides were steadily pushing *The Barnacle Goose* towards the rocks in spite of the lowering of the sail and the sea anchors. Fidelma had wondered what exactly sea anchors were. She knew what a normal anchor was. She found, thanks to Wenbrit's explanation, that the ship carried four great leather bags which were dropped into the water and acted as drags to prevent the vessel moving without any resistance.

The three rescued seamen were hoisted onto the main deck and then Murchad was barking a series of orders.

'Hoist the mainsail! Weigh sea anchors. Stand by to wear the ship. Gurvan to the steering oar.'

Fidelma took it upon herself to move across to the three rescued men. Most of the crew were already busy trying to take the ship out of danger.

One of them was already sitting up and coughing a little. The other two lay senseless.

Fidelma registered several things immediately. The two men who lay senseless were dressed in the usual sailors' clothing – ordinary seamen, by their appearance. The man sitting up and recovering was well dressed, and even though his clothes were sodden and he wore no weapons, Fidelma saw that he was a man of some rank.

He was well built, which might have accounted for his surviving relatively unscathed in the water, and fair-haired with a long moustache, which dangled on either side of his mouth in Gaulish fashion. Salt crusted his features. His eyes were light blue, and his features were clean-cut. In spite of his sea-soaked appearance, his clothing was of excellent quality. He seemed to be a man used to outdoor life. She noted he wore some rich pieces of jewellery.

'*Ouomodo vales*?' she asked him in Latin, judging that if he be of rank he would have some knowledge of Latin no matter his nationality.

To her astonishment he replied in her own tongue and with an accent she judged to be that of the Kingdom of Laigin.

'I shall be all right.' He indicated his unconscious companions. 'But they look in poorer shape.'

Fidelma bent down and felt for the pulse of the first man. It was present, but very faint.

'He has swallowed much water, I think,' added the Irishman.

Wenbrit came forward.

'I know something about reviving him, lady,' he offered.

Fidelma moved back and watched the boy roll the man over on his back and then sit astride him.

'We must get the water out of him. Go to his head and stretch his arms back and when I say, push them forward to me. Like a pumping action.'

Another member of the crew was doing likewise with the other sailor.

Fidelma placed herself under the instruction of the young boy and saw that the movement raised and lowered the man's chest. Between each movement, the boy blew deeply into the man's mouth. It was just when Fidelma was saying that the manipulation seemed not to be succeeding that the man gave a croaking sound; water spurted from his mouth and he started coughing. Wenbrit rolled the man onto his side and the sailor started to retch and vomit on the deck.

Fidelma stood back. The other sailor had a gash on his forehead and was clearly unconscious but, apparently, he was breathing normally. Two sailors were carrying him to the crew's quarters. Fidelma found the Laigin man was already standing up and appeared none the worse for his experience. He was staring about him ruefully.

Wenbrit helped the resuscitated sailor sit up. The man was muttering something to which Wenbrit replied in the same language.

'He is not Irish, then?' Fidelma addressed her remark to the Irishman.

'It was a Breton trading ship, Sister. A Breton crew. I had purchased passage on her as far as the mouth of the Sléine.'

Fidelma regarded him thoughtfully.

'You are obviously from Laigin.'

'I am. Is this an Irish ship?'

'Out of Ardmore,' confirmed Fidelma. 'But with a mixed crew. Murchad is the captain.'

'Out of the Kingdom of Muman?' The man looked about him and smiled. 'A pilgrim ship, no doubt. Whither bound?'

'For the Holy Shrine of St James in Iberia.'

The man let out a soft curse.

'That will be little use to me. Who did you say is the master of this ship? I must speak with him right away.'

Fidelma glanced to where Murchad was busy on the quarter deck.

'I would advise that unless you want to renew your acquaintance with the rocky waters, you should wait awhile,' she smiled. 'Anyway, we shall be putting into Ushant for fresh water shortly.'

The corner of the man's mouth turned down.

'Ushant is where we just came from.'

Wenbrit had helped one of the crew move the survivors and was now swabbing down the deck.

'Will the sailors be all right?' Fidelma called to him.

The boy grinned.

'They are lucky, those two, I'm thinking. I shall find some spirits in a moment that will put warmth into that gentleman there.'

'Good thinking, boy,' approved the new arrival.

'What is your name?' Fidelma asked the man pleasantly.

'I tell that to the captain,' the man said dismissively.

Fidelma swung round to rebuke him for his ill manners and, in doing so, the emblem of the Golden Chain slid from her loosed habit. The ancient dynastic order of the Eóghanacht had been bestowed on her by her brother, Colgú, the King of Cashel. The sun glinted on the golden cross. Afterwards, Fidelma was uncertain whether she had subconsciously made the movement on purpose so that it would be revealed. It certainly had a sharp effect on the man.

He stared at it, eyes widening in recognition. The emblem of the Niadh Nasc, the order of the Golden Chain or Collar, was a venerable Muman nobiliary fraternity which had sprung out of the ancient élite warrior guards of the Kings of Cashel. The honour was in the personal presentation of the Eóghanacht King of Cashel, and each recipient observed personal allegiance to him, being given, in turn, a cross to wear which had originated from an ancient solar symbol – for it was said that the origins of the honour were shrouded in the mists of time. Some scribes claimed that the Order had been founded almost a thousand years before the birth of Christ.

The man from Laigin knew that no ordinary religieuse would be wearing such a symbol. He had apparently remembered that the boy had addressed her as 'lady'. Now he cleared his throat nervously and moved his head forward in a bow.

'I am forgetting my manners, lady. I am Toca Nia of Clan Baoiscne. I was once commander of the bodyguard of Fáelán, the late King of Laigin. Whom am I addressing?'

'I am Fidelma of Cashel.'

The man's astonishment was evident.

'The sister of Colgú of Cashel? The *dálaigh* who appeared in the dispute between Muman and Laigin and . . . ?'

'Colgú is my brother,' she interrupted.

'I know your reputation, lady.'

'I am only an advocate and a religieuse bound on a pilgrimage to Iberia.

'*Only*?' Toca Nia laughed disarmingly. 'I realise now that I have seen you before, but I did not recognise you until you spoke your name.'

It was now Fidelma's turn to be surprised.

'I do not recall our meeting.'

'No reason why you should, for we did not actually meet,' he explained. 'I merely saw you from across a crowded abbey hall. It was in the Abbey of Ros Ailithir, well over a year ago. After Fáelán, my king, had died, I continued on for a while in the service of the young King of Laigin, Fianamail. I accompanied him, the Abbot Noé of Fearna and the Brehon Fornassach, to the Abbey, where you revealed the plot to set Laigin and Muman at war with each other.'

It seemed a lifetime ago, reflected Fidelma. Could it only have been a year or so ago?

'A strange place to meet again,' she remarked courteously. 'How *is* Fianamail, the Laigin King? A fiery and tempestuous young man, as I recall.'

Toca Nia smiled and nodded.

'I left his service after Ros Ailithir. I think that I had had enough of war and being a professional warrior. I had heard that the Prince of

Montroulez sought a man to train his horses. I have been successful in that field. I spent a year at his court and was returning to Laigin when . . .'

He gestured eloquently with his hand towards the sea. The gesture drew Fidelma back to the situation. She turned and saw, to her surprise, that the line of jagged rocks were receding in the distance. Once again Murchad had displayed his seamanship by manoeuvring his ship out of harm's way.

Indeed, Murchad was coming from the stern deck towards them with a purposeful step.

Toca Nia turned to greet him.

'Have you suffered injury?' Murchad demanded, his keen eyes gliding swiftly over the broad-framed warrior.

'None, thanks to the timely intervention of you and your crew, Captain.'

'And your companions?'

Wenbrit came forward and answered for him.

'Two sailors from the crew. One will be a little the worse for the ordeal, but the other may take a few days to recover. His head was badly gashed by the rocks when he went in.'

'What ship were you on?' Murchad asked the survivor.

'The ship was called the *Morvaout* – we would call that *The Cormorant*, I think.'

Murchad examined the man keenly.

'Was she a pilgrim ship?'

Toca Nia smiled. 'A trading ship, taking wines and olive oil to Laigin, and me along with it.'

Fidelma decided to intervene.

'This is Toca Nia, one time commander of the King of Laigin's bodyguard and more lately a trainer of horses for the Prince of . . . of where?'

'Montroulez is a small mainland princedom on the north coast of Little Britain.'

'What was your captain thinking of, by steering his ship in such dangerous waters?' was Murchad's next question.

The former warrior shrugged.

'The captain died two days ago. That is why the ship came south to Ushant instead of sailing directly north for Laigin. The mate took over and, I fear, he was not a competent seaman nor could he handle some of the crew who refused to obey his orders. He was too fond of cider.'

'Are you saying that the crew were in mutiny?' asked Fidelma.

'Something like that, lady.'

'Were either of the survivors involved?' demanded Murchad. 'I don't want mutineers on my ship.'

'I could not say. There was a lot of chaos after the captain died.'

'What did he die of? Was he killed in the mutiny?'

'He simply dropped dead at the wheel. His heart stopped beating. I have seen a few such deaths, inexplicable deaths before and even after a battle. Death not from wounds but because the heart stopped beating.'

'And the captain was the only competent sailor?' pressed Murchad. 'That is strange.'

'Strange or not, you saw the result. Thankfully you were there to see it or else I would not be alive. Captain, I need a passage to Laigin.'

Murchad shook his head.

'We are on a pilgrim voyage to the Holy Shrine of St James. I doubt that we will see Ardmore again for a full three weeks or more. But we are putting in to Ushant. You will soon pick up a ship sailing home from there.'

The former warrior smiled ruefully.

'I'll have to sell a few of these baubles.' He indicated his bejewelled hand. 'A year's earnings have sunk to the bottom of the sea there.' He jerked his hand back towards the rocks. 'I own only what you see. Ah well, perhaps I can persuade a ship to take me on as crew.'

Murchad examined him doubtfully.

'Do you have experience as a sailor?'

The man laughed uproariously.

'By the gods of battle, not at all. I am a good warrior. I know battle strategy and the art of weaponry. I love horses and have an ability to train them. I know three languages. I can read and write and even cut some Ogham. But as for sailing a ship, no experience at all.'

Murchad pursed his lips.

'Well, it will be up to you to find a passage at Ushant. You will excuse me?' He turned back to his duties.

Wenbrit had come up with the spirits and handed the cup to the warrior.

'You should change out of those wet clothes,' he advised. 'I think I can find some spare garments that will fit you.'

'Good for you, youngster . . .' The man paused in mid-sentence.

Fidelma noticed that the former warrior had frozen, the cup of spirits halfway to his mouth. His mouth was open as if to swallow the liquid, but his eyes were wide and staring. An expression of disbelief crossed his features; a nerve began to twitch in the side of his face.

Fidelma turned to see what had caused his abrupt change of attitude.

On to the deck had come Cian, looking around as if to see what had taken place since the pilgrims had been sent below by Murchad. He saw Fidelma and started to come towards them.

A curious animal sound came from the back of Toca Nia's throat. The cup dropped from his hands, spilling its contents onto the deck.

Before Fidelma realised what he was going to do, the man launched himself across the deck towards an astonished Cian.

'Bastard! Murderer!'

The two words cracked twice like a whip into the air.

Almost at the same time, he reached Brother Cian and his fist impacted straight into the dumbfounded man's face. For a moment, Cian stood there, his nose a red, bloody pulp; his eyes wide with incredulity above it. Then he fell backwards, slowly, as if his fall was in defiance of gravity.

Chapter Seventeen

Fidelma was rooted to the spot in stupefaction. It was Wenbrit who reacted first, giving a cry of alarm. Two of Murchad's crew managed to reached Toca Nia as he was raising his foot to stamp on Cian's unprotected head while he lay on the deck. The sailors dragged him, struggling, away from Cian's prone form. Murchad came running back across the deck.

'What the devil . . . ?' he began.

'Devil is right!' snarled Toca Nia, wrestling in the grip of the sailors, his face contorted with hatred.

Fidelma came forward and bent down to the unconscious Cian to check his pulse. She raised her head to Murchad.

'Would someone mind carrying Brother Cian below to his cabin and attending him? I don't think the blow is serious, but he is unconscious.'

Murchad signalled to two crewmen and without a word, they lifted Cian's body and carried it below deck.

Fidelma had risen and faced Toca Nia. He stood still in the firm grip of the sailors. She folded her arms and regarded his agitated features with a frown.

'What does this mean?' she demanded.

Toca Nia did not reply.

'You have been asked for an explanation, my friend,' Murchad said. 'I did not pluck you from the sea to watch you murder one of my passengers; a holy Brother on a pilgrimage, at that. What possessed you?'

Toca Nia gazed at the stern features of Murchad and then turned to address Fidelma.

'He is no holy Brother!'

'Explain yourself,' insisted Murchad. 'Brother Cian is one of a band of pilgrims taking passage on my ship.'

'Cian! That certainly is his name: I have cause to remember it. But he is a warrior, like me. One of the warriors of Ailech. He is the "Butcher of Rath Bíle"!'

Fidelma stared at Toca Nia, trying to understand his accusation.

'The "Butcher of Rath Bíle"?' she repeated, bemused.

'A whole village and fortress destroyed, the buildings burnt, men, women and children annihilated at the orders of Cian of Ailech. One hundred and forty souls, dispatched to heaven by that most monstrous evil . . .' Toca Nia's voice rose in agitation.

Fidelma held up a hand to silence him.

'Calm yourself, Toca Nia. What makes you certain that Brother Cian was the man responsible for such an outrage?'

The Irishman's face was a mask of fury and his eyes were blazing in torment.

'Because my mother, sisters and young brother were butchered there; because I was there and stand as witness.'

Fidelma sat on the bunk in Murchad's cabin while the captain sprawled in a chair. Toca Nia had been placed in Gurvan's cabin with Drogon standing guard outside. Fidelma was looking anxious. There seemed an unreality about the new situation.

'I have never seen such a change in a person's character before,' she observed to Murchad. 'This Toca Nia seemed a pleasant, friendly person at first but the moment he saw Cian he became a raging maniac, totally out of control.'

Murchad shrugged.

'If his claims are correct, his frenzy is understandable. Surely, as you knew Cian in the past, you must have heard something of the claim Toca Nia is making?'

Fidelma stirred uncomfortably.

'I knew Cian ten years ago,' she admitted. 'He was a warrior in the King of Ailech's bodyguard. But beyond that I know nothing. I have never heard of this Rath Bíle.'

There was a long silence while it seemed that Murchad was trying to dredge up a memory.

'I recall something of it,' he said at last.

'When did it happen?'

'Several years ago now. Maybe five years ago. Rath Bíle is in the country of the Uí Feilmeda, in the Kingdom of Laigin.'

'That is south of the Abbey Kildare,' frowned Fidelma. 'I was some years in the Abbey, but I do not recall hearing the story.' She considered for a moment. 'Five years ago? It may well have happened when I was sent to the west for a while. What do you know of this massacre?'

Murchad shrugged.

'Precious little. There was some conflict between the High King Blathmac and Faelán of Laigin – some dispute about whether the Uí Chéithig should pay tribute to Blathmac at Tara or to Faelán at Fearna.

'I know a treaty was agreed. But it seemed that Blathmac wanted to teach Faelán a lesson for his defiance and sent a band of his élite warriors by ship down the coast to the country of the Uí Enechglais. They marched on the fortress of Faelán's brother at Rath Bíle and there was a great slaughter. It is true that many old men, women and children died as well as the handful of Laigin warriors who were defending the place.'

Fidelma was troubled.

'This is a complication which we did not want on this voyage.'

Murchad shared her anxiety.

'And you are no nearer solving the murder of Sister Muirgel? There is a whisper that Sister Crella is responsible. Is that true?'

'I am not satisfied yet. There is more here than meets the eye. How long before we reach harbour in Ushant?'

'With this wind, we will be there within the hour. You will have to advise me what to do about Toca Nia and Cian, lady.'

Fidelma shook her head. 'If I remember the laws appertaining to crimes committed in war in the *Críth Gablach*, it states that once the *cairde,* the peace treaty, is agreed, only a month is allowed for anyone to pursue claims under its condition. Those wishing to exact retribution under law for any unlawful deaths that might have occurred have to make claim by that time. This massacre you speak of took place several years ago.'

Murchad looked morose.

'Murder and now war crimes! Never in all my sailing days have I encountered the like. What must we do? Toca Nia is quoting the Holy Book at me and demanding vengeance.'

'Vengeance is not law,' replied Fidelma. 'This matter needs to be heard before a senior Brehon, for I am not competent to advise what should be done.'

'Well, *I* certainly am not, lady.'

'I will speak with Cian,' Fidelma decided, rising. 'The first thing to do is see what he has to say on this matter.'

Cian was lying back on his bunk, though in a semi-sitting position with a bloodstained rag at his nose. The cabin he shared with Brother Bairne was in gloom. A lantern swung from a hook in the ceiling, casting flickering lights which chased one another about. No one, as yet, had apparently told him of Toca Nia's accusation. He removed the rag and gave Fidelma a lopsided smile as she entered the cabin.

'Our shipwrecked mariner has a curious way of expressing gratitude to his rescuers,' he greeted her wryly.

Fidelma remained impassive.

'I presume that you did not recognise the man?'

Cian shrugged and then winced painfully.

'Should I have recognised him?'

'His name is Toca Nia.'

'Never heard of him.'

'He was not a mariner but a passenger on the ship that went down. In fact, he was a warrior of the Faelán of Laigin.'

Cian was dismissive.

'Well, I do not know all the warriors of the Five Kingdoms. What is his quarrel with me?'

'I thought you might know him, as he knows you.'

'What was his name again?' frowned Cian.

'Toca Nia.'

Cian thought for a moment and then shook his head.

'Toca Nia of Rath Bíle,' added Fidelma coldly.

There was no doubting that the addition of Rath Bíle meant something to Cian.

'Do you want to tell me about it?' Fidelma went on.

'About what, precisely?'

'About what happened at Rath Bíle.'

'It was at Rath Bíle that I lost the use of my arm.' There was bitterness in his voice.

'What were you doing at Rath Bíle?'

'I was in the service of the High King.'

'I think I need a little more information than that, Cian.'

'I was commanding a troop of the High King's bodyguard. We fought a battle there and I received an arrow in my upper arm.'

Fidelma heaved a deep breath, indicating her frustration.

'I do not want to fight for every detail.'

Cian's mouth tightened.

'What exactly is it that this Toca Nia accuses me of?'

'He is claiming that you are the "Butcher of Rath Bíle". That it was on your orders that some one hundred and forty men, women and children were slaughtered and the village and fortress put to the torch. Is there truth in that?'

'Did Toca Nia tell you how many warriors of the High King were slain there?' Cian countered in anger.

'That is no defence. If those warriors were attacking the village and fortress, then it was their choice to put themselves in harm's way. The death of women and children is no compensation for their deaths. There is no just cause that exonerates mass slaughter.'

'How can you say that?' challenged Cian. 'Just cause enough if the High King wills it!'

'That is a precious morality, Cian. It is no justification at all. I would urge you to tell me what happened, otherwise it might be argued that Toca Nia's charges must be true and that you are answerable for them.'

'Not true! Not at all true!' cried Cian in frustrated anger.

'Then tell me your version of events. There was some border dispute between the High King and the King of Laigin, wasn't there?'

Cian reluctantly agreed.

'The High King believed that the Uí Chéithig who dwelt around Cloncurry should pay tribute directly to him. The King of Laigin argued that he was lord over them. The High King said that their tribute stood in place of the *bóramha*.' Cian used an old word meaning cattle-computation.

'I do not understand this,' Fidelma told him.

'It goes back to the time when the High King Tuathal the Legitimate sat in judgement at Tara. Tuathal had two daughters. The story goes that the King of Laigin was then called Eochaidh Mac Eachach and that he married the first daughter of Tuathal but found he did not like her as much as he liked the second daughter. So he returned to the court of Tuathal and pretended that his first wife had died and thus he was able to marry the second daughter.'

Cian paused and grinned despite the seriousness of his position.

'He was a sly old goat, that King Eochaidh.'

Fidelma made no comment. There was no humour in the deception.

'Well, naturally,' continued Cian, 'the two daughters eventually discovered the truth. The second daughter learned that she was married illegitimately, for her sister was still alive. When they found out that they had a husband in common, it is said that they died of shame.' He interrupted his narrative and smirked. 'What stupidity! Anyway, the story came to the ears of their father, the High King, and as revenge he marched his army into Laigin and met Eochaidh in battle. He slew him and ravaged the kingdom.

'The men of Laigin came forward and sued for peace and agreed to pay an annual tribute – predominantly in cattle. From that time onwards the Uí Néill successors of Tuathal demanded this *bóramha* or cattle tribute, but often they had to use force to obtain it. That was why Blathmac ordered us to go south and raze Rath Bíle as a demonstration to show he was determined to extract the tribute from the Laigin King.'

'But hadn't a treaty already been agreed?' Fidelma pointed out. 'Didn't you go south after both kings agreed the treaty?'

Cian replied with a gesture of impatience.

'It is not for a warrior to question his orders, Fidelma. I was ordered to go south. South I went.'

'You admit that you were in command?'

'Of course I was. I do not deny it! But I was acting under the legitimate orders of the High King. I went to extract the tribute.'

'Even the High King himself is not above the law, Cian. What do you say happened?'

'We sailed in four ships, four fifties of warriors of the High King's Fianna. We were the best warriors of the élite bodyguard itself. We landed at the port of the Uí Enechglais and marched west across the River Sléine until we came on Rath Bíle. The brother of Laigin's King refused to surrender the fort and village.'

'So you attacked it?'

'We attacked it,' confirmed Cian. 'It was the High King's orders that we did so.'

'Do you admit that you and your warriors slaughtered women and children?'

'When our men went in, we could not stop to enquire who was our enemy and who not. People were fighting us, shooting arrows at us, whether they were warriors or old men, or indeed women or children. Our job was to fulfil our objective and obey our lawful orders.'

Fidelma considered his story for a few moments. The situation on *The Barnacle Goose* was getting more than complicated. The mystery of Sister Muirgel's murder had been bad enough, and then Brother Guss's claim that Sister Canair had also been murdered before the ship even sailed. Now she was faced with the added complication of Toca Nia's accusation against Cian.

'This matter, Cian, is serious. It needs to be brought before the Chief Brehon and the High King's court. I know little of the law on warfare. A more competent judge is needed to see what must be done. I know there are circumstances in which the killing of people is justified and entails no penalties. It is not against the law to kill in battle – or, indeed, to kill a thief caught in the act of stealing . . . But the decision is up to a court.'

Cian's face mirrored his resentment.

'Are you telling me that you believe the word of Toca Nia against mine?' he demanded.

'It is not my place to judge who is telling the truth. Toca Nia makes an accusation and you must answer it. It is an accusation of gravity. It is for your own good, Cian, for Toca Nia knows well that a violator of the law can be killed by anyone and with impunity. He could kill you and claim immunity.'

'The law does not reach outside of the Five Kingdoms,' protested Cian.

'It does not matter. You are on an Irish ship and come under the laws of the Fénechus here just as much as if you stood on the soil of Éireann. You must return to Laigin to make your plea.'

Cian stared at her in disbelief.

'You cannot do this to me, Fidelma.'

She met his gaze; her eyes were hard.

'I can,' she said softly. '*Dura lex sed lex.* The law is hard, but it is the law.'

'And if I were not on this ship, it would not be the law?'

Fidelma answered him with a shrug and turned to leave. She paused at the cabin door.

'It is up to Murchad as captain to fulfil his obligations under the law. I am afraid that he must judge what is to be done with both Toca Nia and you, whether to let you go or return you both to Éireann for trial. My recommendation will be that he must return you to a Brehon in Laigin.'

'I was acting on the High King's orders,' Cian protested again.

Fidelma stood at the cabin door.

'That may not be an exoneration. You have a moral responsibility.'

Later, when she explained matters to Murchad, the sturdy captain pursed his lips in a soundless whistle.

'You mean that I must take Cian and Toca Nia back to Éireann?'

'Or hand them over to another ship to take them back,' she pointed out.

'Then let's hope there is such a ship at Ushant,' muttered Murchad.

'In the meantime, Captain, I would suggest that you confine both Cian and Toca Nia to their cabins. We don't want any more bloodshed on this ship.'

'That I will do, lady,' agreed the captain. 'Let us pray that Father Pol, at Ushant, will have some means of helping me in this matter.'

* * *

The Barnacle Goose rounded the headland of Ponte de Pern, standing well out to sea, for the rocks and islets were dangerous there. Murchad hardly needed to indicate the dangers for the headland showed the black, jagged pieces of granite poking from the sea like bad teeth, surrounded by yellowing foamy waters. Under Murchad's guidance they drifted slowly into the long U-shaped bay of Porspaul and headed towards the sheltered anchorage at the far end.

'It will be good to be on terra firma for a while,' Fidelma commented thankfully to Murchad.

Murchad pointed to the shore.

'There are no other ships in the harbour,' he stated the obvious. 'The main village and church of Lampaul are above the little quay you see there. I was planning to spend only a day here to take on fresh food and water. The next stage of our journey is going to be the longest, depending on the wind. We'll be sailing almost straight south, out of sight of land.'

'But we must consider the matter of Toca Nia,' Fidelma reminded him.

Murchad looked troubled.

'I am all for putting Toca Nia and Cian ashore here and leaving them to sort it out between them.'

'An easy solution . . . for *us*. But I can foresee complications in that proposal,' she replied.

The Barnacle Goose tacked its way along the three-kilometre stretch of water to the far end of the inlet, where Fidelma could see a path leading upwards to the settlement of Lampaul. Their approach into the bay had been observed by some local people and several of them had come down to the harbour to greet them.

Murchad shouted for the mainsail to be dropped and then the steering sail. An anchor was heaved from the bow and the ship swung gently at her mooring in calm waters for the first time in the last few days.

'I shall be going ashore,' Murchad told Fidelma. 'Would you like to come with me and meet Father Pol? He is not only the priest here but is more or less the chieftain of the island. It might be best to discuss the matter of Brother Cian and Toca Nia with him.'

Fidelma had indicated her willingness to do so. They were launching the skiff when Brother Tola and the other pilgrims began to emerge on deck. Tola immediately demanded to know if they could go ashore and his companions joined in a chorus of claims.

Murchad silenced them by raising his hands.

'I must go first and arrange matters. You will be able to go ashore later and, if you wish, spend a night on shore to get exercise while we gather our stores for the rest of the voyage. But until I have made arrangements, it is best that you all stay aboard.'

It was clear that the arrangement did not make them happy, especially when they saw Fidelma joining the captain to go ashore.

Murchad and Gurvan rowed the small light craft, with Fidelma in the stern, across the short distance from *The Barnacle Goose* to the rock-built quay.

A tall man, dark and sharp-faced, whose clothes and crucifix, hanging from a chain around his neck, proclaimed his profession, greeted Murchad as the captain climbed out of the craft.

'It is good to see you again, Murchad!' The man spoke in an accent that showed that the language of the children of the Gael was not his first tongue.

Gurvan had tied up the skiff and helped Fidelma out.

'It is good to be on your island again, Father Pol,' Murchad was replying. He motioned to Fidelma who had joined him. 'Father, this is Fidelma of Cashel, sister to our King, Colgú . . .'

'I am Sister Fidelma,' interrupted Fidelma firmly with a grave smile. 'I have no other title.'

Father Pol turned and took her hand with a quick scrutiny of her features.

'Welcome, then, Sister. Welcome,' he smiled and then turned towards the mate. 'And you are welcome, too, Gurvan, you rascal. It is good to see you again.'

Gurvan grinned, looking sheepish. It appeared that the entire crew of *The Barnacle Goose* were known on the island for it was a frequent port of call.

'Come, join me in refreshment at Lampaul,' the priest continued, waving his hand towards the pathway. 'Do you bring me any interesting news?'

They began to follow him up the path.

'Bad news, I am afraid, Father. News of the *Morvaout*.'

Father Pol halted and turned sharply.

'The *Morvaout*? She set sail from here only this morning. What news do you bring?'

'She went to pieces on the rocks north of the island.'

The priest crossed himself.

'Were there any survivors?' he asked.

'Only three men. Two sailors and a passenger who was bound for Laigin. I'll land the sailors shortly.'

Father Pol appeared sorrowful for a moment.

'Ah well, this is often the fate of those who sail these seas. The crew were all from the mainland. We will light some candles for the homecoming of their souls.' He caught sight of Fidelma's puzzled expression. 'We are an island people here, Sister,' he explained. 'When our people are lost at sea, we set up a little cross and light a candle, and sit up in a vigil all night, praying for the repose of the souls of those lost. The next day, the cross is deposited in a reliquary in the church and then in a mausoleum among the crosses of all who have disappeared at sea. There they will await the homecoming of the souls from the sea.'

They reached the village, a typical seaport settlement spreading around the central structure of a grey, stone-built chapel.

'There is my little chapel.' Father Pol indicated the building. 'Come, we will join in a prayer of thanks for your safe arrival.'

Murchad coughed discreetly.

'There is something we need to talk to you about most urgently,' he began.

Father Pol smiled and laid a hand on his arm.

'Nothing is ever so urgent that a prayer of thanks need not take precedence,' he observed firmly.

Murchad glanced at Fidelma and then shrugged.

They went into the little chapel and knelt before an altar which surprised Fidelma by its opulence. She had thought that the island was poor but there was gold and silver displayed on the silk-covered altar table.

'You appear to have a rich community here, Father,' she whispered.

'Poor in goods but rich in heart,' replied the priest indulgently. 'They donate what they have to God's house to praise His splendour. *Dominus optimo maximo . . .*'

He failed to notice the corners of her mouth turning down in disapproval. She did not approve of idle opulence when people lived in poverty.

Father Pol bent his head and intoned a prayer of in Latin while they echoed the 'amens'.

Finally he led them to his small house next to the church and offered them pottery cups of cider while Murchad explained the situation about Toca Nia and Cian.

Father Pol rubbed the side of his nose reflectively. It seemed a habit of his.

'*Quid faciendum?*' he asked when Murchad had finished. 'What is to be done?'

'We were hoping that you might have some suggestions,' Murchad replied. 'I cannot keep Toca Nia and Cian on board my ship all the way to Iberia and then back again to Laigin. I am advised that these charges must be heard before a competent judge in Éireann but I cannot take these men directly there, nor can I afford to wait until a ship bound there puts into Ushant.'

'Why should you do either?'

'Because,' intervened Fidelma carefully, 'Toca Nia has to make his accusations before the courts of Éireann. I think Murchad was hoping that you might keep them both securely here until the next ship for Éireann puts in.'

Father Pol considered the matter for a moment and then made a dismissive gesture.

'Who knows when that might be? Anyway, surely you cannot dictate to a Brother of the Faith that he must leave a pilgrimage to answer these charges? What do you know of law, Sister?'

'Sister Fidelma is a lawyer of our courts,' explained Murchad hastily.

Father Pol turned to her with interest.

'Are you an ecclesiastical lawyer?'

'I know the Penitentials but I am an advocate of our ancient secular laws.'

Father Pol seemed disappointed.

'Surely ecclesiastical law has precedence over secular laws? In which case, you do not need even consider these claims.'

Fidelma shook her head.

'That is not how the law works in our country, Father. Toca Nia has made one of the most serious charges possible. Cian must answer them.'

Father Pol pondered for a moment or two before shaking his head negatively.

'I have to say, as leader of the community here, and as representative of the Church, that your law does not run on this island. I can do nothing. If, out of their free will, this Brother Cian or Toca Nia, or both of them, wish to leave your ship and stay here until a ship bound for Éireann arrives, then they are free to do so. Or if they want to go anywhere else, they are free to do so. But I am not able to dictate or restrain them unless they break the laws that govern this island. You must decide what is best.'

Murchad was clearly unhappy.

'It seems,' Fidelma said, turning to him, 'there is now only one choice. Your ship is your kingdom, Murchad, which you rule as chief according to the laws of the Fénechus. It is your obligation to keep Cian and Toca Nia on your ship and eventually take them back to Éireann.'

Murchad started to raise objections but Fidelma raised a hand and silenced him.

'I said, it is your obligation. I did not say it was your commitment. You are the arbiter of what must be. I can only advise you as to how the law might view the matter.'

The captain shook his head despondently.

'It is a hard decision. Where do I get recompense for all this? Cian will certainly refuse to pay me for his return passage, with his journey made under duress, and Toca Nia's jewellery will provide insufficient compensation. I have to think not only of my own welfare, you understand, but that of my crew, who need to be fed and who also have families to support.'

'If Toca Nia's charges are proved, then the King of Laigin should compensate you. If not, then you can issue a distraint claim on Toca Nia.'

Murchad was reluctant to make a decision.

'I doubt if he has money or property. I must think about this.'

Father Pol clapped his hands as if to dismiss the subject.

'And while you do, friend Murchad, your passengers may come ashore here to relax from the toils of the sea and to join in the feast of the great martyr of my country, Justus.'

'You are kind, Father Pol,' muttered Murchad, although he was still clearly preoccupied with the problem.

'I would also thank you, Father,' Fidelma added. 'It is good of you to take this trouble over our internal matters.' She paused. 'The Feast of Justus? I know several great churchmen of that name but I cannot place a Justus from this part of the world.'

'He was killed when he was a young boy,' Father Pol explained. 'It happened during the persecutions of the Emperor Diocletian. It is said that he hid two other Christians from the Roman soldiers and was killed for it.'

Father Pol rose slowly and Murchad and Fidelma followed his example, together with Gurvan who had taken no part in the discussion.

'I presume that you wish to take on fresh water, bread and other stores?'

The captain agreed that was his intention.

'Gurvan will see to it, Father, and I will have my passengers land to stretch their legs.'

'Our service of Justus will begin at sundown and will be followed by the feast.'

They bade a temporary farewell to the priest and walked slowly back towards the quay. Murchad was gloomy at the prospect of keeping Cian and Toca Nia on board his ship until his return to Ardmore, but said in resignation that it seemed the only thing he could do in the circumstances.

'I think you have made a wise decision, Murchad,' Fidelma replied warmly. 'What worries me more is the matter of Sister Muirgel, for I have never had a problem set before me where I have not even seen one likely path to start down in search of a solution.'

Chapter Eighteen

Fidelma awoke abruptly with her heart beating fast. It was dark and she was not sure what had made her wake with such a start. She was feeling exhausted: it had been a long day. Everyone had gone ashore with the exception of Cian and Toca Nia, who had been confined under guard in their cabins. The shipwrecked sailors had been sent ashore while the pilgrims and members of the crew had attended the service and Feast of Justus. It was midnight before everyone had returned on board; no one stayed overnight in Lampaul, for Murchad had announced that he intended to sail on the morning tide, having already loaded his provisions. The sooner he reached Iberia, he told Fidelma, the sooner he could take his two troublesome passengers back to Ardmore.

As Fidelma lay wondering what had awoken her, she heard a curious scrabbling sound: it seemed to come from the deck planking under her cabin. She raised herself on her bunk, frowning. Then she remembered what Wenbrit had said. Rats and mice inhabited the lower quarters of the ship.

Reaching out to the heavy warm bundle at the foot of her bunk, she stroked the black cat's fur.

'Come on, Mouse Lord,' she whispered. 'Aren't you rather neglecting your duty?'

The cat stirred, uncoiled itself and stretched to the full length of its body. It always surprised Fidelma to see the length most cats could stretch their body to. The animal then gave a curious cheeping noise, more like a bird than a cat, and jumped from the bunk. Fidelma saw it stalk across the room, leap for the window and then it was gone.

The scrabbling noise soon ceased and Fidelma shivered slightly, thinking about the rats in the darkness below her, separated from her only by some planking. She listened intently. There was no sound now. Perhaps they were gone. Mouse Lord must be carrying out his nocturnal task very efficiently.

Yawning, she lay back on her pillow and was immediately asleep again. Only a moment later, it seemed, Fidelma found herself being shaken awake by Gurvan. The mate was clearly worried.

211

'Please come into the next cabin, lady,' he urged, his voice barely above a whisper.

Draping her robe around her shoulders, Fidelma swung out of her bunk. The expression on Gurvan's face was enough for her not to waste time with pointless questions. She recalled that it was in Gurvan's cabin that Toca Nia was confined.

Gurvan stood in the passage holding the door of his cabin open. A lantern was alight in its small confines, for it was still not quite dawn. Fidelma glanced in.

Toca Nia was lying on his back, eyes wide open, his chest a bloody mess.

'Stabbed several times around the heart, I would say,' Gurvan muttered behind her, as if she needed an explanation.

Fidelma stood for a moment, allowing the feeling of shock to ebb away.

'Has Murchad been told?' she asked.

'I have sent word to him,' replied Gurvan. 'Careful, lady, there is much blood on the floor.'

She looked down and saw that the severed arteries had pumped blood all over the floor. It had been trodden about, presumably by Gurvan but a thought occurred to her.

'Stand still,' she requested. Then she moved to the door, her eyes following the sticky marks on the floor. There were no distinct footprints, and it was obvious that Gurvan had walked over the initial prints which could only have been made by the killer. The prints went to her cabin door and halted. This puzzled Fidelma. She would have expected them to go to the exit to the main deck. She moved across to her cabin door and opened it. Some fainter traces showed where Gurvan had entered her cabin. The only solution to the mystery was if the killer had noticed the trail they were leaving and had managed to wipe the blood from their feet before they departed from the area.

Some instinct made her check her bag where she had put the knife which Crella had given her. It was gone. She turned back to Gurvan.

'You'd better send someone to Cian's cabin,' she suggested. It was the obvious thing to do in the circumstances.

Just then, Murchad came along the passage; anxiety was etched all over his features. He overheard Fidelma's directive.

'I have already sent for Cian, lady. As soon as I heard the news, I knew that you would want to see him. However, he is no longer on board.'

'What?' Fidelma had never seriously thought that Cian would do

212

anything stupid. Then she realised that she did not really know the depths of Cian's mind, nor had ever understood the workings of his mind.

'Drogon went to check his cabin. The man I placed on guard there was asleep. Bairne, who shares the cabin, says he did not hear him leave. I don't think we can blame my crewman. We are not used to guarding prisoners.'

Fidelma was not interested in excuses.

'We need to double-check,' she said decisively. 'Will you do that immediately, Gurvan?'

The mate moved off.

'It seems pretty obvious what happened,' Murchad muttered, glancing at Toca Nia's body. 'Cian killed his accuser and has fled ashore.'

It seemed the only logical explanation. Fidelma uttered a sigh of resignation.

'It does look that way,' she admitted. 'Yet he must know that the island is not large enough for him to hide in. It is still an island. We will find him eventually. I'll get dressed. We must go ashore and find Cian immediately.'

Murchad, Gurvan and Fidelma landed at the quay in the ship's skiff. There was no one stirring in the grey, early morning light. They walked directly up the pathway towards the church, and were surprised when a figure left the shadows of the doorway and came forward to greet them. It was Father Pol. His expression was grave.

'I know who you have come for,' he greeted them.

Fidelma matched his solemnity.

'Has he told you why he has fled here?' she asked.

'I know what he is accused of,' replied the priest.

'Do you know where he is? It would be helpful if you could tell us, rather than us spending time in searching the island for him.'

'You do not have to, Sister. Nor would I permit such a search. Brother Cian is within the church.'

She was puzzled by the priest's harsh tone, which was unlike that of the day before.

'Then we shall take him back to *The Barnacle Goose* so that he may offer his defence.'

The priest frowned and held up his hand to stop them as they started forward.

'I cannot allow it.'

Fidelma gazed with some surprise at Father Pol.

'You cannot allow it?' she echoed in amusement. 'Yesterday, you said the situation with Cian was no business of yours. Now you say that you cannot allow us to take Cian back to the ship. What manner of logic is this?'

'I have the right to stop you removing Cian.'

'The crime was committed on board Murchad's ship, not on your island. The jurisdiction is surely Murchad's?'

The priest seemed puzzled for a moment and then folded his arms in an attitude of immovability.

'In the first place, Brother Cian has sought the sanctuary of this place,' he announced. 'In the second place, this so-called crime of which he is accused took place five years ago and hundreds of miles away. You have no authority to hear such accusations on board your ship. You said as much yesterday.'

Murchad was scratching the back of his head and gazing at Fidelma as though to seek her guidance.

'Sanctuary?' he said, looking baffled. 'I am not sure I understand . . .'

Father Pol interrupted.

'Sister Fidelma will tell you that it is written in the Book of Numbers that the Lord God said, "You shall designate certain cities to be places of refuge, in which the homicide who has killed a man by accident may take sanctuary. These cities shall be places of refuge from the vengeance of the dead man's next of kin . . .".'

'We know what is written in Numbers, Father Pol,' Fidelma agreed in a quiet tone. She turned to Murchad in explanation. 'This ecclesiastical sanctuary is compared with our own law of the *Nemed Termann* in which a person who is accused of an act of violence, even if he is guilty of it, can seek sanctuary for a time until his case is heard in a proper manner – but our law, Father,' she turned to Father Pol, 'also states that the guilty one in seeking sanctuary is *not* thereby enabled to finally escape from justice.'

Father Pol bowed his head in acknowledgment.

'I understand this, Sister. However, we are not governed here by your laws of Éireann. The law is God's law as given in His Holy Writ. Exodus says, "The slayer may flee to a place which I shall appoint for you". He is allowed asylum in that place until such time as he can prepare a proper defence against those who would seek vengeance on him.'

'Father Pol, we do not seek vengeance. But Brother Cian must come forward to defend himself against this crime.'

'He has asked for asylum in the proper manner and been granted it.'

Fidelma thought quickly.

'In a proper manner?' she echoed.

She was trying to behave as a *dálaigh* should, acting without emotion and only with regard to the facts, but this was Cian they were talking about, not some stranger fleeing from the law. Cian! Whether she hated him now, she had been enamoured of him once. She had to ignore her emotional involvement, for she did not trust her feelings any more. She must think only of the law. The law was all that mattered now.

'He asked for sanctuary in a proper manner?' She repeated her question.

Father Pol chose not to reply, sensing she was about to make a point.

'You quoted the law from Exodus just now, but you did not finish that quotation. The verse ends, "But if a man has the presumption to kill another by treachery, you shall take him even from My altar to be put to death". Is that not so?'

'Certainly. But what treachery was there in war? In war, killing may be done. A warrior may have a battle fever and lose his mind. If he did so, Cian will certainly answer for the consequences. But I doubt if you can claim that treachery was part of his act.'

'We are not speaking of the crimes of which Toca Nia accused Brother Cian when he was a warrior,' she replied slowly. 'We are referring to the fact that Toca Nia was murdered in his bunk on board Murchad's ship this morning at the same time that Brother Cian fled from it to seek sanctuary with you.'

Father Pol looked startled and dropped his hands to his side.

'He did not say anything about that.'

Fidelma leaned forward like a hunter whose prey is in sight.

'Then let me remind you of the law as given in Joshua. "When a man takes sanctuary . . . he shall halt at the entrance and state his case in the hearing of the elders . . ." *Did* he halt and state his case relating to the murder of Toca Nia?'

Father Pol was clearly troubled.

'He did not speak of that. He sought sanctuary only for the crime of which Toca Nia accused him.'

'Then, under the ecclesiastical code which you quote, he did not properly state his case, and cannot now claim asylum.'

Father Pol was in conflict. Finally he made up his mind and stood back with a gesture for them to precede him.

'We shall put the matter to Brother Cian,' he said quietly.

Cian was sitting in the shaded garden at the back of the church when

Father Pol led Murchad and Fidelma to him. He stood up, looking nervously from Fidelma to Murchad.

'I have been granted sanctuary,' he announced. 'You can tell that to Toca Nia. I shall remain here. You and your laws cannot touch me.'

Murchad frowned and opened his mouth but Fidelma silenced him with a gesture.

'What makes you think that Toca Nia will listen?' she asked innocently.

'You have a way with words, Fidelma. You can tell him about the law of sanctuary.'

'I do not think Toca Nia is interested in the law any more.'

Brother Cian blinked rapidly.

'Do you mean that he is withdrawing his charges?'

Fidelma gazed deeply into Cian's eyes. She saw suspicion, she saw hope even, but there was no guile nor cunning there.

'I mean that Toca Nia is dead.'

There was no mistaking the surprise in Cian's reaction.

'Dead? How can that be?'

'Toca Nia was murdered about the same time as you fled from the ship.'

Cian took an involuntary step backwards. His shock was genuine; he could not be acting.

Father Pol shrugged helplessly.

'This puts me in an awkward situation, Brother. Under our ecclesiastical law, I granted you asylum within this church, but only in respect to the charge you claimed that you stood accused of. Now this . . .'

Cian looked from the priest to Fidelma in bewilderment.

'But I know nothing about Toca Nia's death. What is he saying?' he demanded of her.

'Do you deny that your hand struck those blows that deprived Toca Nia of life?'

Cian's eyes widened even more in confusion.

'Are you serious? Do you mean that . . . that I am accused of his killing?'

Fidelma was unsympathetic.

'So you do deny it?'

'Of course I deny it. It is not true,' cried Cian in outrage.

Fidelma's face assumed a cynical expression.

'Are you claiming that his murder was a coincidence? That you know nothing about it?'

'Call it what you like, I did not kill him.'

Fidelma took a seat on the bench from which Cian had risen.

'You have to admit that if this is a coincidence, then it is an extremely convenient one. Perhaps you will tell me why you fled from the ship?'

Cian sat down opposite her, leaning forward towards her. His whole attitude was one of someone pleading.

'I did not do this thing, Fidelma,' he said with a quiet intensity. 'You know me. I admit that I have killed in war, but I have never killed in cold blood. Never! You must know that I would not—'

'I am a *dálaigh*, Cian,' she interrupted sharply. 'Tell me the facts as you know them. I need no other appeal.'

'But I know nothing. I have no facts to tell you.'

'Then what made you flee from *The Barnacle Goose* and come seeking sanctuary here?'

'That should be obvious,' Cian responded.

'Unless you killed Toca Nia, I would say that it is far from obvious.'

Cian flushed angrily.

'I did not . . .' he began and then stopped. 'I came here for sanctuary because I needed time to think. When you interrogated me after Toca Nia's accusation, I realised that you were in earnest. That you and Murchad were going to restrain me and send me back to face trial in Laigin. It is certain that I would be found guilty of the slaughter at Rath Bíle.'

'As I recalled, you admitted to the slaughter.'

'To the action, not to a crime. It was war and I was simply doing what I was told to do.'

'Then you should be prepared to answer to the accusation. If you were not guilty of murder then you should put your trust in the law.'

'I needed time to think. It was so sudden, being accused like that.'

Murchad interrupted harshly.

'More pressing is the fact that you now have to answer to the charge of killing Toca Nia.'

Fidelma found herself in agreement.

'In fact, unless another witness comes forward to accuse you, Toca Nia's accusations have died with him. We cannot restrain you nor make you answerable to those accusations, for he made no legal record of them.'

Cian was totally astonished.

'You mean that the accusation about Rath Bíle is dropped?'

'Toca Nia made no official charge; no charge was written down nor witnessed. A dead man's oral accusation, unless it is his dying testimony, and witnessed as such, cannot be adjudged as evidence against you.'

'Then I am free of that charge?'

'Unless there are other witnesses from Rath Bíle who appear to testify against you. As there are none here, you are free of that charge.'

Brother Cian's features broadened into a smile and then, as he realised the implications, he grew serious again.

'I swear by the Holy Trinity that I did not kill Toca Nia.'

Fidelma heard the ring of truth in his voice, but her personal scepticism made her doubt his protestations of innocence. What was it that Horace had said? *Naturam expelles furca tamen usque recurret* – you may drive out nature with a pitchfork, but it always returns. Cian was a natural deceiver and his truth was always to be doubted. Then she realised, with a sudden pang of guilt, that she was once again letting her personal feelings condemn him.

She was about to speak when there came a fierce shouting from nearby.

Father Pol looked up with a frown as one of the islanders, a thin, wispy fellow in the garb of a fisherman, came running around the corner of the church building. He drew up sharply at the sight of them and stood gasping for breath.

'What is it, Tibatto?' demanded Father Pol disapprovingly. 'You know better than to come to the House of God in such turmoil.'

'Saxons!' grunted the man, breathlessly. 'Saxon raiders!'

'Where?' demanded the priest, as Murchad jerked around in consternation, his hand going to the knife in his belt.

'I was on the point above Rochers . . .'

'It is our northern coast,' explained Father Pol in a swift aside to them.

'And I saw a Saxon ship beating southward around into the bay. It is a warrior ship with a lightning symbol on its mainsail.'

Murchad exchanged a quick glance with Fidelma, who had risen to her feet with Cian.

'How soon will they be in the bay?' the priest demanded, his face grim.

'Within the hour, Father.'

'Sound the alarm. Let's get the people into the interior,' he said decisively. 'Come, Murchad, you'd better get your crew and the pilgrims ashore. There are caves where we can hide or, at worst, defend ourselves.'

Murchad shook his head firmly.

'I'll not abandon my ship to pirates, Saxon, Frank or Goth! The tide is only just on the turn. I am sailing out of the bay. If any of my passengers want to come ashore, then it will be up to them.'

Father Pol stared at him aghast for a moment.

'You will never have time to get underway before they close off the mouth of the bay. If they are off the Rochers they will be around the headland within half an hour.'

'Better to be on the ship than sitting on this island waiting for them to land and slaughter everyone,' Murchad replied. He turned to Gurvan. 'Is anyone else ashore apart from ourselves?'

'No one else except us, Captain.'

'Will you come, lady?' he demanded of Fidelma.

She did not hesitate.

'If you are going to make a run for it, then I am with you, Murchad.'

'Let's go!'

Cian had been standing by while they discussed the position. Now he took a step forward.

'Wait! Let me come with you.'

Murchad stared at him in surprise.

'I thought you were seeking sanctuary,' he sneered.

'I told you, I only sought sanctuary to give me time to prepare to defend myself against the accusations of Toca Nia.'

'But now you may have to defend yourself against an accusation of his murder,' Fidelma reminded him.

'I'll chance that. But I don't want to be caught here without defence by these raiders. Let me come with you.'

Murchad shrugged. 'We have no time to waste. Come or stay. We go now.'

There came the sound of a horn being blown. An angry warning note. As they left the church, they saw people running in all directions, women holding screaming children, men grabbing what weapons they could.

Murchad grasped the priest's hand and shook it.

'The best of luck, Father Pol. I think you will find that these particular Saxons are looking for us, rather than raiding your island. We escaped them once; perhaps we will do so again.'

Murchad speedily led the way along the path to the cove below.

Fidelma glanced behind and saw Father Pol's arm raised in a

blessing and then he was gone. His duty now was to ensure that his people were taken to a place of safety.

No word was spoken as the four hurried down the winding path to the quay where they had left their skiff. Only when they were in the boat, with Gurvan and Murchad pulling strongly towards *The Barnacle Goose*, did Cian meet Fidelma's quizzical green eyes. He held their gaze and did not flinch.

'I did not kill Toca Nia, Fidelma,' he affirmed quietly. 'I did not know he was dead until you came to Father Pol's house to tell me. I swear it.'

Fidelma found herself almost believing him but she wanted to be sure. She could never trust Cian: she had learnt that lesson a long time ago.

'There'll be plenty of time to make your pleas of innocence later,' she replied brusquely.

They were alongside the ship. Fidelma was almost the last on deck, for Murchad had already leapt on board and was bellowing orders. Gurvan followed her, bringing up the rear to secure the skiff.

'Is everything squared away?' demanded Murchad, as Gurvan joined him on the stern deck. The crew had already been roused by Murchad's hail as they approached the ship.

'Aye, Captain,' called the mate, taking charge of the steering oar with the sailor called Drogon.

Fidelma went to take a stand by Murchad's side. It seemed natural that she should.

'What can we do, Murchad?' she demanded, glancing towards the entrance of the bay.

His face was an emotionless mask, his sea-grey eyes narrowed as he gazed along the deep inlet. They could see the dark outline of the Saxon shipping coming around the southern headland, determined to block off their escape from the inlet. From their anchorage it was three kilometres to the mouth of the bay which was hardly more than a kilometre at its widest point. The sea raider had plenty of time to cut off any attempt they might make to escape.

'They are tenacious, these Saxon devils,' Murchad muttered. 'I'll say that for them. Their captain must have had some good sea sense to realise that we had doubled back past him the other night. That he was able to follow us here says much for him.'

'There is no darkness now to hide us,' Fidelma pointed out.

Murchad paused to shout orders that the pilgrims should remain below as he noticed that Cian, left to his own devices, had gone below to rouse his fellows with news of the arrival of the raider. Now he glanced ruefully up at the hazy blue sky with its tiny individual beads of white cloud, rippling along in high lines.

'That's for sure,' he answered Fidelma. 'That's a mackerel sky up there – clear but unsettled. It's not going to swallow us up either in darkness or in fog. If there was a mist, I might try to run out past him. Ha! That's the first time you will find a sailor praying for a fog!'

Fidelma felt that he was talking merely to prevent her from panicking.

'Don't worry about me, Murchad. If we are to be attacked, let's not go down without a fight of it.'

He regarded her with approval.

'That's not a religieuse speaking, lady.'

Fidelma returned his fierce grin.

'It's an Eóghanacht princess who speaks. Maybe it's my fate to end my life as I began it, as a daughter of King Failbe Fland and sister to King Colgú. If we must go down fighting, we'll make sure that we extract a high price from our foes.'

Gurvan left his position to join them. His face was without humour.

'I, for one, am *not* going to go down fighting,' he said. 'A good retreat is better than a poor defence.'

Murchad knew Gurvan well and caught something in his mate's voice.

'Are you saying that you have something in mind?'

'It'll depend on the wind and sail again,' Gurvan replied with a brief nod. 'The Saxon is sure he has the better of us. He is hauled to by the Pointe de Pern to the north, ready to close with us should we make a run for it. Like a cat waiting to jump on a mouse, eh?'

'It doesn't need a sailor's eye to see that,' agreed Fidelma.

'Has your eye taken in the islet which stands in front of us?' Gurvan pointed along the bay.

'I see it, about a kilometre distant from us,' Murchad observed.

'Now look at the Saxon ship,' Gurvan said.

They did as he bid them.

The big oblong sail was being hauled down.

'He plans to rely on his oars again to close with us. That didn't work last time, as I recall,' muttered Gurvan.

Murchad smiled approvingly for he had suddenly caught on to what his mate was suggesting.

'I see what you mean. We'll make for the islet first and pass along the south side out of his sight. He won't know which exit we'll use. It might give us a head start.'

Fidelma was frowning.

'I am not sure that I am following this plan, Murchad.'

A wind rustled the furled sail and shook the rigging. The crew was waiting expectantly.

'No time to explain,' Murchad cried. 'Let's get underway!' He turned and began to shout. 'All hands! All hands to the sails!'

His crew sprang into action.

Fidelma stood back, watching the sailors hoisting the sail to catch the wind. Gurvan seized the steering oar, once more with Drogon. There was the usual exhilarating crack as the leather sail caught the breeze. The anchor was raised with some alacrity. Then *The Barnacle Goose* seemed to leap forward.

Across the waters of the bay they could hear a great shout go up from the sea raider. A cry of, *'Woden!'* The blades of the oars were raised, the water sparkling in the sunlight, and the high prow of the ship seemed to cleave towards them.

As Gurvan had suspected, the Saxon was rowing to intercept them, keeping in the broad northern channel. The wind blew to the south-west and soon an arc of foam was feathering back from the bow of *The Barnacle Goose* as it strove to make the southern channel behind the shelter of the islet.

'It'll be dangerous,' she heard Murchad cry.

'True enough,' replied his mate. 'But I know these waters.'

'I'll get to the bow and signal you through the channel,' replied Murchad.

Confused, Fidelma watched the captain go forward. Midships he paused and gave his men some orders. Half a dozen of them went below decks to return after a short while with some traditional longbows five feet in length and quivers of arrows. Murchad was taking no chances. If fight he had to, fight he would. By this time *The Barnacle Goose* had come behind the shelter of the islet. It seemed to speed by them, and as they emerged, she saw that the captain of the Saxon ship had hesitated, suspecting that his prey might attempt to take down its sails and put out the sea anchors to hide behind the island in a game of hide and go seek. Alternatively, *The Barnacle Goose* could attempt to double back and use the northern channel after all. The Saxon captain's hesitation allowed *The Barnacle Goose* a fraction of time to gain a head start on its enemies by sailing straight through the southern channel behind the island. Once they realised what was happening, the Saxon ship clumsily turned around to go after them, its oars splashing frantically with the sailors' endeavous.

Gurvan grinned at Fidelma and held up his thumb.

'All we have to pray, lady, is that her captain decides to cram on his sail and come racing after us.'

Fidelma was still confused.

'I thought the Saxon ship was faster under sail with the wind behind it.'

'Well remembered – but let's hope he has not heard the old saying, one glance in front is worth two behind.'

There was an expression of amusement on Gurvan's face which told Fidelma nothing.

The Barnacle Goose was almost heeled over before the wind, cleaving through the waters within yards of the rocky granite coastline of the southern side of the bay. Fidelma realised that Gurvan was going to steer the *Goose* around the southern headland. After that, she could not understand what he meant to do, for they would surely be into the open sea and on a fairly calm open sea at that. The Saxon ship would be able to overhaul them with ease.

Did the answer lie with the longbows that the crew had brought to the deck? Did Murchad and Gurvan simply mean to fight it out once on the open sea?

It was then she caught sight of what lay ahead of them: a maze of granite islets and rocks through which strong currents were roaring in a cascade of white water. There were innumerable reefs as far as she could see. It was far more threatening to her gaze than their passage through the rocks off the Sylinancim islands.

Gurvan saw the sudden tautness of her body.

'Trust me, lady,' he shouted, his eyes straight ahead. 'What you are seeing is why ships never sail out around the southern headland of this island. Here, the wind and tide are the masters and will hurl a ship against the broken and rocky shores to be splintered into a thousand pieces. This is why we are taking this passage. I've sailed through here once; I hope I may do so again. If not, well . . . better to die free than to be a slave or die tasting Saxon steel.'

'What if the Saxon comes after us?'

'Then he should pray to his god Woden that he is a good sailor. I doubt he is and if he takes the wider channel, away from the rocks, we will have a good many miles' start on him.'

She looked for'ard to where Murchad was balanced on the prow of the ship. His hands were waving in signals which obviously meant something to Gurvan and his companion on the steering oar, for they seemed to move in response to each signal. Fidelma could feel the currents catching at *The Barnacle Goose*, sweeping it along at an

223

increasing speed. Once a rock scraped along the ship's side with a strange groaning sound.

She closed her eyes and uttered a short prayer.

Then the rock had sped by and they were still in one piece.

'Can you see behind us, lady?' called Gurvan. 'Do you see any sign of the Saxon?'

Fidelma went to grip the stern rail and peer aft.

She shivered as she saw the frothing white water of their wake, the reefs and rocks rushing behind them. Then she raised her eyes to look beyond.

'I can see the sail of the Saxon,' she called excitedly. She could just make out that same lightning flash on the sail which Murchad had pointed out to her before.

'I see them,' she cried again. 'They are following us through the channel.' Her voice rose in excitement.

'Let their god Woden help them now,' replied Gurvan with a fierce grin.

'Let God help *us*,' whispered Fidelma to herself.

The Barnacle Goose was bouncing down so that the horizon moved violently and she kept losing sight of the sail of the pursuing vessel.

The ship plunged and bucked at an alarming speed. Gurvan and Drogan had thrown their full weight on the steering oar and now called for assistance from another of the crew as the pressure grew too much for them to handle by themselves.

With Murchad frantically signalling from the bow, *The Barnacle Goose* made a dizzy ride through the foam-swept rocks and islets until it seemed to be tossed out into calmer waters. Almost before they had settled, Murchad was running back towards the stern deck, his face filled with anxiety.

'Where are they?' he grunted.

'I lost sight of them,' Fidelma called. 'They were following us through the rocky passage.'

Murchad squinted back in the direction in which they had come, back towards the rocky coastline which, at this distance, seemed covered in a faint mist.

'Sea spray from the rocks,' he explained without being asked. 'It makes it difficult to see.'

He looked towards the black jagged teeth which protruded through the white foam.

Fidelma shivered a little, not for the first time. It did not seem possible that they had come out safely from that dangerous maw.

'There!' Murchad cried suddenly. 'I see them!'

Fidelma strained forward but could see nothing.

There was a pause for a moment or two and then Murchad sighed.

'I thought I saw their top mast for a moment, but it is gone.'

'We have a good head start on them, Captain,' Gurvan cried. 'They'll have to do some fast sailing to keep up with us.'

Murchad turned and slowly shook his head.

'I don't think we will need to worry about them, my friend,' he said quietly.

Fidelma glanced back to the fast-vanishing coastline of the island. There was no sign of any pursuing ship.

'Do you think that they've struck the rocks?' she ventured to ask.

'Had they come through the passage, we would see them by now,' replied Murchad heavily. 'It was us or them, lady. Thank God it was them. They've gone to their pagan hall of heroes.'

'It is a terrible death,' Fidelma said soberly.

'Dead men don't bite,' was Murchad's only comment.

Fidelma muttered a quick prayer for the dead. She was thinking that it was a Saxon ship, whether pagan or not, and she was remembering Brother Eadulf.

Chapter Nineteen

'It is a very calm morning, Murchad.'

The captain nodded but he was not pleased. They were two days out from Ushant. He indicated the limp sail.

'Too calm,' he complained. 'There is hardly any wind. We are making no headway at all.'

Fidelma gazed out across the flat surface of the sea. She, too, was making no headway. Having escaped from their pursuers, they had paused to commit Toca Nia's body to a watery burial. It was Brother Dathal who said that the voyage was turning into a voyage of death, as if the ship was that of Donn, the ancient Irish god of the dead, who gathered the lost souls on his ship of the dead and transported them to the Otherworld. Dathal's comparison brought swift criticism from Brother Tola and Sister Ainder, but nevertheless produced a feeling of gloom among the remaining pilgrims.

Time and again, Fidelma turned the facts over in her mind, trying to find one tiny thread which might lead her to solving the problem. As for the murder of Toca Nia, Cian swore that he had left the ship just after midnight when the last of the passengers and crew had returned from the island. Gurvan clinched the matter by maintaining that he had looked in on Toca Nia well after that and found him peacefully asleep. If Cian was telling the truth about the time he had left the ship, then he was innocent.

Fidelma looked up at the limp sails and made a decision.

'Perhaps we can put this weather to good use,' she said briskly.

'How so?' enquired Murchad.

'It has been a couple of days since I bathed. I had no time on Ushant and I feel dirty. In this calm sea I can take a swim and at least get the grime from my body.'

Murchad looked uncomfortable.

'We sailors are used to roughing it, lady. But we have no facilities for a woman to go bathing.'

Fidelma threw back her head and laughed.

'Fear not, Murchad, I shall not offend your male sensibilities. I shall wear a shift.'

'It is too dangerous,' he protested with a shake of his head.

'How so? If you sailors swim to keep clean in such calm weather, why not I?'

'My sailors know the vagaries of the sea. They are strong swimmers. What if a wind springs up? The ship can move a fair distance before you could swim back to it. You saw how quickly poor Brother Guss was left behind.'

'That danger must be so, whether one is a sailor or a passenger,' countered Fidelma. 'What do your men do?'

'They swim with a rope tied around them.'

'Then that is what I shall do.'

'But . . .'

Murchad caught her eye and saw the stubbornness in it. He gave a deep sigh.

'Very well.' He called to his mate. 'Gurvan!'

The Breton came forward.

'Fidelma is going to take advantage of the calm weather to take a swim near the ship. Make sure a rope is tied around her waist and fastened to the rail of the ship.'

Gurvan raised his eyebrows and opened his mouth as if to protest but then decided to remain silent.

'What point do you wish to swim from, lady?' he asked with resignation.

Fidelma smiled: 'Which is the leeward side? Isn't that what you call the sheltered side of the vessel?'

Gurvan's facial muscles twitched and for a moment Fidelma thought he was going to return her smile.

'That is so, lady,' he replied gravely. He indicated the starboard side of the vessel. 'You will find the waters sheltered there, although there is no wind blowing at present. However, I expect when the wind does come, it will come upon the port side of the vessel.'

'Are you a prophet, Gurvan?'

The Breton shook his head. 'See those clouds to the north-east? They'll bring along a wind soon, so do not delay too long in the water.'

Fidelma stepped to the railing and looked down on the waves. They seemed tranquil enough.

She started to take off her robe, but paused at the sight of Gurvan's anguished features.

'Have no fear, Gurvan,' she said merrily. 'I shall be keeping my undergarments on.'

Gurvan seemed to be flushing in spite of his dark-skinned complexion.

'Is it not considered a sin among the religieux to strip oneself in front of others?'

Fidelma grimaced cynically and quoted: '"But the Lord God called the man and said to him, 'Where are you?' He replied, 'I heard the sound as you were walking in the garden, and I was afraid because I was naked, and I hid myself.' God answered, 'Who told you that you were naked?'" I believe that what God was saying is that the sin is in the mind of the beholder, not in his eye.'

Gurvan looked uncomfortable.

'Anyway, as I said, I shall not be naked. Now, let me have my swim before this wind comes upon us.'

And without more ado, Fidelma took off her robe. She always wore undergarments of *sról* – silks and satins imported from Gaul merchants. It was a habit that she had grown accustomed to as a member of the royal house of Cashel – the only luxury clothing Fidelma indulged in, for nothing was so pleasant than the texture of the foreign material next to her skin. Those of wealth and rank could, of course, luxuriate in buying fine materials. Others, she knew, used wool and linen undergarments.

When she was a young student, under her mentor the Brehon Morann of Tara, Fidelma had been surprised to learn that there were even laws relating to dress. The *Senchus Mór* laid down the rules relating to the dress laws of children in fosterage. Each child had to have two complete sets of clothes so that one might be worn while the other was being washed. The clothes of the sons and daughters of kings, then chiefs . . . going down to those of the lower ranks in society, were all enumerated according to their social grades and, while in fosterage – the form of receiving education – children had always to be dressed in their best on festival days.

Fidelma caught herself musing on these things and suddenly felt a pang of isolation. How she *wished* that Eadulf were here! At least she could talk with him about such matters, even if they did tend to disagree. She badly needed his help in trying to solve this puzzle. Perhaps he could see something which she had overlooked.

She saw that Gurvan was standing with a long length of rope, his eyes averted from her.

'I am ready, Gurvan. I swear, I am decently clothed.'

Gurvan reluctantly raised his eyes.

It was true that Fidelma's garments were not outrageous but neither did they entirely hide her well-proportioned figure; a youthful form that seemed to vibrate with the joy of a life at odds with her religious calling.

He swallowed nervously.

'Show me how to tie this rope around me,' she coaxed him.

He moved forward, the rope end in his hand.

'It is best to fix it round your waist, lady. I shall tie a secure knot that is also easy to undo – a reef-knot.'

'I have seen how it is tied. Let me try it and you can check that I have done so correctly.'

She took the rope end from his hands and placed it around her waist and then, concentrating, she turned the rope.

'Right over left and left over right . . . isn't that the way?'

Gurvan examined the knot and gave his approval.

'Exactly right. I shall tie the other end by a similar knot to the rail here.'

He suited his words to action. The rope was long enough for her to swim the entire length of the ship and back.

Fidelma raised her hand in acknowledgement, went to the rail and dived gracefully over the side.

The water was colder than she was expecting, and she came up from the dive gasping and almost winded at the impact. It took her a few moments to recover and grow used to the temperature. She took a few lazy strokes. Fidelma had learnt to swim almost before she had begun to toddle, in the Suir River, called the 'sister river', which flowed a short distance from Cashel. She had no fear of water, simply a healthy respect for it, for she knew what it was capable of.

Among the people of Éireann, it was a curiosity that while many of the inland folk learnt to swim in the rivers, most of those who lived in coastal fishing communities, particularly along the West coast, refused to learn. Fidelma remembered asking an old fisherman the reason for this because if their boats sank, surely it was necessary to be able to swim? He had shaken his head.

'If our boats sink, then better to go straight to a watery grave than die a longer and more agonised death trying to survive in these seas.'

It was true that the brooding, rocky coastline with its frothy, angry waters was no place to go swimming. Perhaps the old fisherman had a point.

'If God wants us to live then He will save us. There is no use struggling against fate.'

Fidelma had not pursued the conversation for it was not a subject of which most fishermen would speak. Indeed, the greatest curse that anyone could pronounce among these coastal folk was 'A death from drowning on you!'

Fidelma lay back, floating on the rippling waters. The great black outline of *The Barnacle Goose* loomed high above her; the great sail was still hanging limply from the yard. She could see the dark form of Gurvan peering over the rail at her and she raised a languid arm and waved at him to indicate she was all right. He nodded and turned away.

Sighing, she closed her eyes, feeling the soft warmth of the sunshine on her face. The saltwater dried on her lips and she resisted the temptation to lick it off. She knew how incredibly thirsty it would make her.

Now she began to cast her mind over the situation but, try as she would, she could not concentrate entirely on the loss of poor Sister Muirgel. Instead, Cian came to mind. Cian! It was strange that immediately, words from the Book of Jeremiah came into her mind. 'You have played the harlot with many lovers; can you come back to me?' She shivered slightly. Why had that come to mind? Well, she knew that the words were apposite, but why quote Holy Scripture at all? There had been enough passages from Scripture quoted on this voyage! Perhaps it was catching.

She felt a moment of sympathetic sadness for Cian over his wound which had prevented him pursuing the profession of a warrior. She knew how his life had been governed by his physical prowess. He was vanity itself; vain of his body, vain of his ability with weapons, and vain of his belief that youthfulness was immortality. Wasn't it Aristotle who had said that the young are permanently in a state of intoxication? That was the very word to describe the youthful Cian. He was intoxicated by his own youth, for youth was immortal; only the elderly grew old in his world.

That was what had attracted her to him. His youth. His power. He had few intellectual attributes. He knew how to ride well; he knew how to cast a javelin with great accuracy; he knew how to thrust and parry with a sword and use his shield to protect his body; he knew how to shoot an arrow from a bow. The only intellectual pursuit he had come close to following was stratagem in warfare.

Cian never tired of telling the story of the High King Aedh Mac Ainmirech who, sixty years before, had been defeated by the Laigin King, Brandubh, who had smuggled his warriors into the High King's encampment concealed in hampers of provisions.

Fidelma had not been especially interested in the story, but had tried to persuade Cian into playing games of Black Raven and Wooden Wisdom, with the idea of using these games to explore military strategy. Even that had not interested Cian. Such board games were a matter of frustration for him.

Now with his useless right arm, he could no longer be a warrior. She had seen he was unable to adjust and cope with his new role in life. The idea of Cian as a religieux was inconceivable. He had already demonstrated his bitterness and anger at his misfortune. His silly attempt to assert his idea of his masculinity as a compensation was pathetic in her eyes. That was not something that Eadulf would have done. The words of Virgil's *Aenid* drifted into her mind. *'Tu ne cede maluis sed contra audentior ito'* – yield not to misfortunes, but advance all the more boldly against them. That would be Eadulf's attitude, but Cian with his useless arm . . .

Her body stiffened in the water.

His useless arm! How could Cian have left the ship at midnight and rowed himself to the island all alone? It would have been impossible to row the skiff with one arm. And the skiff! Dear Lord, what was happening to her powers of observation? If he had, by some miracle, managed to propel the skiff to the island from the ship, how had the skiff been returned to the ship? Someone had rowed Cian to the island and then returned to the ship.

Eadulf would have spotted that. Oh God, how she needed him. She had grown so used to talking things out with him and considering his advice.

She stirred self-consciously as she realised in what direction her thoughts were travelling. She should have thought of this before, instead of day-dreaming. The effect of floating in the gentle waves was too soporific and . . .

It was then she realised that the waves were not so gentle as they had been. They were becoming much more choppy and she heard a distant crack. She opened her eyes and blinked. The great sail of *The Barnacle Goose* was beginning to billow out. The promised wind was rising and the ship was beginning to move. She turned over and began to take a few strokes.

The realisation hit her like a cold shock.

The rope attached around her waist was not taut. It was floating, that part of it which was not soaked by the sea and therefore made heavier. The rope was no longer attached to the ship's rail.

She gave a cry for help.

She could see no sign of Gurvan or anyone else at the ship's rail. *The Barnacle Goose* was moving away from her with gathering speed.

She began to swim for dear life now, but the waves were rising and it was becoming difficult to swim at speed. She knew, even as she began to strike out, that it would be impossible for her to reach the side of the ship before it vanished, leaving her alone in the middle of the ocean.

Chapter Twenty

The sibilant sounds of the sea, the soft whistling of the wind over the frothing waves, which from her viewpoint seemed to be gigantic, vicious and powerful, drowned out all other sounds. She thought that she heard distant shouting but, head down, she was striking out for all she was worth. Then someone was in the water beside her.

She looked up, startled. It was Gurvan.

'Grab hold of me!' he shouted, his voice almost drowned out as the waves washed over him. 'Quickly!'

Fidelma did not argue. She grasped him by the shoulders.

'For the love of Christ, do not let go!' yelled Gurvan.

He turned and now Fidelma saw that he had a rope attached to him which was beginning to pull them both along at speed. Dark figures on the side of the ship were struggling to haul on the rope and she realised that slowly, agonisingly slowly, they were being pulled up the side of the ship by the sheer muscle of the crewmen hauling on the rope.

An awful thought came to her mind. Dangling helplessly as they were by the side of the speeding vessel, if the men above let go of the rope, the momentum would pull them both under the ship itself. Their death would be certain.

Then they were being lifted clear of the water.

'Keep a tight grip,' yelled Gurvan.

Fidelma did not reply. Her hands automatically tightened on the mate's clothing.

Moments later they were pulled upward with the sea almost reluctant to let them go, the white-capped waves catching at them like faltering fingers, enticing them backwards into the dark maw of the waters.

Fidelma closed her eyes, hoping the rope would not break. Then hands were grabbing at her wrists and arms. They heaved her up over the rails and she collapsed on the deck, gasping and shivering. Young Wenbrit hurried over and threw her robe around her shoulders. His face was concerned. She glanced up and tried to smile at him in gratitude, unable to speak for lack of breath.

It took some time before she could rise unsteadily to her feet. Wenbrit caught her arm to prevent her from falling. She realised that Gurvan was now on board leaning against the rail and also trying to catch his breath. Had he been a moment or two later in his rescue bid, there would have been no hope. The ship was fairly cutting through the waves now. The sail was straining against the yard as the wind came up. She held out her hand to Gurvan in silent thanks. She could not trust herself to speak for a moment or two and then she said: 'You saved my life, Gurvan.'

The mate shrugged. His features mirrored his concern. He, too, finally found voice.

'I should have been more vigilant when you were in the water, lady.'

Murchad came hurrying along the deck to them, glad to see that Fidelma was not injured.

'I did warn you, lady, that it was dangerous to bathe in this manner,' he said sternly.

'Look.' Gurvan stood aside and pointed at the rail. 'Look, Captain, the rope has been cut.'

The rope's end was still tied there, but only a short length of rope was attached to it.

Fidelma tried to see what Gurvan was pointing at.

'Is it frayed?' she asked. But she realised it was a silly question for now she could see that the rope was cut, the strands sliced through as though by a sharp knife.

'Someone tried to kill you, lady,' Gurvan told her quietly. There had been no need for him to make the point. It was all too plain.

'After I went into the sea,' she said to Gurvan, 'how long were you standing by the rope?'

Gurvan considered the question.

'I waited until I saw that you were swimming comfortably. You waved to me and I acknowledged. Then Brother Tola distracted me. He asked me who was swimming and he started to ask me about the dangers of the water.'

'Did you move away from this spot for any amount of time?'

'For no more than a few minutes. I turned astern to speak with the captain.'

'Was no one else on the deck then?'

'A few of the crew.'

'I don't mean crew. I mean passengers.'

'There was the young religieuse, Sister Gormán, and there was Sister Crella together with the man with the useless arm, Brother Cian. Also the taciturn one – Brother Bairne.'

Fidelma glanced around and saw that most of them were gathered some distance away watching her uncomfortably. All had been spectators of the rescue.

'Was any one of them close to the rope?'

'I am not sure. Any one of them could have been. I came back as soon as I felt the wind coming up. Then I saw that the rope had been cut. I called to a couple of crew; we seized another rope and the rest you know.'

Fidelma stood in silent thought.

'Lady.' It was young Wenbrit. 'It is best for you to get out of those wet things.'

Fidelma smiled down at him. She realised that the sodden silk was clinging to her body like a second skin. She pulled her robe more closely around her shoulders.

'A drink of *corma* will not go amiss, Wenbrit,' she hinted. 'I'll be in my cabin.'

She hurried across the deck as crew and passengers broke into groups, talking with one another in passionate but quiet voices.

It was half an hour before Fidelma, warmed inside by the fiery spirits of the *corma* as well as outside by a vigorous rub and some dry clothes, came aft to join Murchad in his cabin. The captain was still looking disturbed by the event, realising just how close the sister of his King, Colgú of Cashel, had come to her death.

'Are you all right now, lady?' he greeted her as she entered the cabin.

'I am feeling like a fool, that is all, Murchad. I forgot that a person who kills can sometimes acquire a taste for killing.'

Murchad was startled.

'Are you saying that we have a homicidal maniac on board?'

'To actually set out to kill someone is always the sign of a disturbed mind, Murchad.'

'Do you still suspect Brother Cian? After all, no one else could gain by the killing of Toca Nia. Therefore, he must have killed Sister Muirgel and then attempted to silence you.'

Fidelma gestured negatively as she sat down facing him.

'I do not think the logic follows. It might be that the person who killed Toca Nia is not the same person who killed Muirgel. There is also the murder of Sister Canair to bear in mind, but to which we only have the word of Brother Guss. I am afraid that now Guss is dead, his word as sole witness is worthless. The same criterion which prevents the arrest and prosecution of Cian applies to the matter of Canair . . . where is the witness? However, the law aside, I am prepared to believe that Guss was speaking the truth.'

'Do you mean that you believe that Sister Crella is the guilty party?'

'She may well be. The inconsistencies in her story certainly point to it. But why tell me something that would be contradicted immediately? Was she lying, or did she believe it to be true? The one problem that I cannot resolve is the motive.'

'How could this thing happen?' Murchad wondered. 'A life at sea makes one always close to death, but never death in this fashion. Maybe this voyage is a doomed one. I heard that young religieux, Brother Dathal, saying as much. That this is like the voyage of Donn, god of death . . .'

Fidelma smiled thinly.

'Superstition, Murchad; it imprisons the world with fears. Reason is that which opens the cage. There is a logical answer to every mystery, and we will find it. Eventually.' She paused and then said: 'Did you remain on deck all the while I was bathing?'

'I did. I saw Gurvan tie the rope around you and then around the rail. I watched you dive into the sea. Don't think that I have not tried to rack my memory to recall if I saw anyone go near the rope.'

'Gurvan came and spoke with you at some point?'

'Exactly as he said. He waited a while at the rail. I saw him raise his hand. Then Tola, who was walking on deck, engaged him in conversation. The wind began to freshen and he came to discuss it with me. I warned him to pull you in for I knew we would soon have steerage way.'

'You did not notice anyone else on the deck near the rope?'

'A couple of the crew were in the yards. I have already spoken to them while you were changing. They saw nothing. As we were expecting a wind, they were there to adjust the sail when it arose. There was someone else though . . .' He frowned, ruffling the hair on the back of his head with his right hand. 'I cannot say who it was.'

'Surely you can describe the person?'

'That I cannot say, for they were well for'ard and they had their hood-thing, you know . . .'

'The cowl?'

'Whatever you call it; the hood covered their head.'

'So it was one of the pilgrims? Can you say whether it was a man or a woman?'

'I couldn't even say that, lady.'

'Did you notice them go near the rail?'

'They might have done so. There was no one else there at the time. The wind caught and I called on the crew. Gurvan went back to the rope at that time and realised something was wrong. The figure of the religieux had disappeared and I assumed that whoever it was had gone below.'

Murchad suddenly looked at her as though he had remembered something important.

'I know they did not come back through the stern companionway.'

Fidelma was puzzled.

'Where could they have gone then?'

'Probably went through the for'ard hatch.'

'But surely there is no access to the lower decks that way, is there?'

'There is a small hatchway just outside your cabin door, but no one uses it. At least, none of the passengers would as it only leads down to the storage areas through which they would then have to make their way into the other areas of the ship.'

'But there *is* a way of going below decks there and reaching the passengers' cabins?' When he confirmed it, she rose and said: 'Let us examine it.'

They needed a light, for the small passage that separated Fidelma's and Gurvan's cabins on either side, and the head at the end of it, was dark. Fidelma went into her cabin to fetch a lamp. The furry black bundle of Mouse Lord, the cat, was curled up asleep at the foot of her bunk. Fidelma lit the lamp and joined Murchad who was levering up a small hatch from the floor. She had certainly not noticed it before. It was only big enough for one person to ease down at a time.

'You say that this is not used often?'

'Not often.'

'And we can move from here the length and breadth of the ship?'

Murchad uttered an affirmative.

They halted at the bottom of the wooden steps in a small storage space. There was scarcely room to stand up. Fidelma raised the lamp and peered round.

'Plenty of dust,' she muttered. 'I presume this is not often used as a cabin or even storage?'

'Hardly ever,' Murchad said. 'The next cabin is where we keep our main stores.'

Fidelma pointed to a series of footprints on the floor.

'Doubtless, Gurvan searched the space when he was looking for

237

Sister Muirgel on the second day out.' When Murchad agreed, she added: 'Then he would check after the storm in case of damage to the hull?'

'Of course.'

She held the lamp close to the steps down which they had descended and bent down to examine them.

There were some brown stains on the boards and below the bottom step on the deck itself was a clear imprint of a foot.

'What does it mean?' asked Murchad.

'I expect that you and Gurvan are the same size and build, aren't you?' Fidelma asked.

'I suppose so. Why?'

'Place your foot beside that print, Murchad. Beside it, mind you, not on it.'

Murchad did so. His boot was large by comparison.

'That shows me that the print does not belong to Gurvan made at the time he discovered the body of Toca Nia.'

'So?'

'This is where the killer of Toca Nia came during the night. They moved silently through the ship and came up these steps. They disturbed me and I awoke, thinking, stupidly, it was rats or mice and pushed Mouse Lord out. But it was Toca Nia's killer who went into his cabin and stabbed him in a frenzy of hate. So much so that blood spilt onto the cabin floor and their foot was covered in it. I noticed the footmarks and saw they led out into the passage, trying to separate Gurvan's prints from them. They seemed to end and I thought the murderer must have wiped off the blood, not knowing of your hidden hatch. I now realise that it was by this route that they returned to their part of the ship.'

Murchad shook his head, perplexed.

'But those stains can't tell you much.'

'On the contrary, the footprint at the bottom here tells me a lot.' She pointed to the print with exhilaration spreading through her for the first time in days at finally finding a tangible piece of evidence.

'What does it tell you?'

'The size of that print tells me much about the person who killed Toca Nia. And now I am beginning to see a faint connection. Perhaps coincidences do not happen so frequently as we think that they do. The peson who killed Toca Nia is the same person who slaughtered Sister Canair back in Ardmore and stabbed Sister Muirgel. Perhaps . . .' Fidelma fell silent, considering the problem.

'I would be careful, lady,' interposed Murchad anxiously. 'If this person has attempted to kill you once, they may well try again. They obviously perceive you as a threat. Maybe you are close to discovering them.'

'We must all be vigilant,' Fidelma agreed. 'But this person likes to kill in secret, of that I am sure. There is also one other thing that we may be sure of.'

'I do not follow.'

'Our murderer is one of only three people on this ship and that person, I believe, is insane. We must, indeed, be vigilant.'

That evening the winds began to change again. After the somewhat strained atmosphere at the evening meal, served as usual by Wenbrit, Fidelma went out on deck to join Murchad and Gurvan by the steering oar.

'I am afraid we are in for another blow, lady,' Murchad greeted her morosely. 'We have been more than unlucky this voyage. Had the calm weather continued, we would be two days out from the Iberian port. Now we must see where the winds take us.'

Fidelma glanced up at the skies. They did not seem as bad as those harbingers of the storm during the first night out. True, they were dark-tinged, but not rushing across the sky as she had seen them on the previous occasion.

'How long do we have before it strikes?' she asked.

'It will be with us by midnight,' replied Murchad.

At that moment Fidelma noticed the ship was positively cleaving the waters, sending a white froth washing by on both sides of the vessel. Everything looked so calm and peaceful.

By midnight, Fidelma could not believe the sudden change of weather. Heavy seas were running now and the wind was changing direction so often that it made her dizzy. Fidelma had been sitting on deck, her mind going over all the facts and incidents, analysing and sorting them in her own mind. She stood up, feeling the deck beginning to pitch under her. Gurvan was busy supervising some of the sailors fastening the rigging.

He came across to her.

'The safest place will be in your cabin, lady, and don't forget to—'

'Stow all loose objects,' ended Fidelma solemnly, having learnt the lesson during the previous bad weather.

'You'll become a sailor yet, lady,' Gurvan smiled approvingly.

'Is it going to be as bad as last time?' she asked.

Gurvan replied with a non-committal gesture.

'It doesn't look too good. We are having to beat against the wind.'

'Wouldn't it be easier to return and go with the wind, even if that blows us back on our course?'

Gurvan shook his head.

'In this sea, to head to the wind would have those heavy seas pouring over us the whole time. We might even be driven under the waves by the force.'

As if to emphasise his words, the spray was beginning to fly over the deck and Fidelma could see the waters around them start to boil. In fact, the wind had increased so severely that the mast, thick and strong as it was, began to groan and bend a little. To Fidelma, it looked as if the wind was threatening to tear the mast itself from its well. The leather sail was thrashing about and appeared to be in danger of splitting.

'Best get inside now!' urged Gurvan.

Fidelma acknowledged his advice and, head down, she moved cautiously along the main deck to her cabin.

There was nothing to do but ensure everything movable was stowed away again and then sit on her bunk and wait out the storm. But the storm did not abate quickly. The hours gradually wore on and there was certainly little doubt in Fidelma's mind that the weather, if anything, was worsening.

At some point she hauled herself from the bunk and went to the window. She peered along the deck but could see nothing. It was black as pitch and the rain – or was it sea spray? – was pouring down in sheets across the ship. It was almost as if *The Barnacle Goose* was totally underwater. As she stared out, the wind sucked the sea from the wave-tops and gathered them to sluice the water across the ship; it lashed into her face and eyes, drenching her.

She turned back into her cabin.

Even above the noise of the wind and seas she heard a strange groaning sound. It seemed to be coming from the side planking in her cabin. Without warning, a geyser of seawater shot through the planks, frothing and bubbling.

Fidelma stared at the water and the splintered wood for a moment in horror, then grabbed at the blanket from her bunk and began to stuff it desperately into the crack. She could feel the splintered wood moving underneath her hands. Everything was becoming soaked – her clothes, the straw mattress, the blankets. And the sea was so cold that her teeth began to chatter.

She tried calling but the noise of the wind and sea simply drowned

240

out the sound of her voice. She did not know how long she stayed there, praying that the wood was not going to splinter further. It seemed like hours, and her hands grew numb with the chill.

Eventually she became aware that the cabin door had opened and closed behind her. She glanced across her shoulder and saw the soaked figure of Wenbrit, holding a bucket and something else under his arm, staggering in.

'Is it bad?' yelled the boy, putting his mouth close to her ear that he might be heard.

'Very bad!' she yelled back.

The boy put down his bucket and the other objects he was carrying. Then he removed the blanket to inspect the damage.

'The sea has splintered the planking of the hull,' he shouted. 'I'll try to strengthen and caulk it as much as I can. It should hold for a while.'

He had some pieces of wood under his arm and proceeded to hammer these over the damaged area. Then he plastered it with the soaked hazel leaves. The gush of the seawater died away to a tiny trickle.

'That will have to do until the storm passes!' Wenbrit had to shout again to make himself heard. 'I'm afraid we will all be wet until then. The sea keeps breaking over the ship and everyone is soaked.'

An hour after he had left, Fidelma gave in to her exhaustion and tried to doze on the sodden straw. Dimly aware of a loud 'Miaow!' she realised that Mouse Lord had been crouching, terrified, under the bunk all this time. Sleepily muttering encouragement, she felt the cat spring up onto the bunk beside her. His warm body curled up on her chest with a deep, contented purring sound. The cat was cosy and comforting on her saturated clothing and she eventually fell into fitful doze.

The pain was sharp.

The tiny needles in her chest were excruciating. Then there was the most appalling cry, almost human, a cry that Fidelma associated with the wail of the *bean sidhe*, the woman of the fairies, who shrills and moans when a death is imminent. It took a moment for Fidelma to realise that Mouse Lord was standing arched on her chest, fur standing straight out, claws digging deep in her flesh. He was emitting a piercing wail. Then he leapt from the bunk.

Adrenalin caused Fidelma to swing quickly from the bunk, gasping in agony.

She became aware of a figure at the door – a slight figure, framed for only a moment. Then the cabin door slammed shut. The ship lurched, sending Fidelma off-balance. She scrambled to her knees. A dark shadow, she presumed it was the cat, streaked under the bunk. She could hear his terrible wail. Then she grabbed for the door and swung it open.

There was no one there. The figure had gone. Holding on with one hand, she closed the door and looked around, wondering what had happened.

The cat had stopped its fearful cry. It was too dark to see anything, although she had a feeling that dawn was not far away. The ship was still pitching and bucking. She staggered back to the bunk and sat down.

'Mouse Lord?' she called coaxingly. 'What is it?'

There was no response from the cat. She knew he was there because she heard his movements and his breath coming in a strange rasping sound. She realised that she would have to wait for daylight to find out what was wrong with him. She sat on the bunk, unable to sleep, watching the skies lighten but without the wind abating. When she finally judged it light enough, she went down on her knees and peered under the bunk.

Mouse Lord spat at her and struck out with a paw, talons extended. He had never behaved in such a manner to her before.

She heard a movement at the door and swung round. Wenbrit entered carrying something covered in a small leather bucket.

'I've brought some *corma* and some biscuit, lady,' he said, not sure what she was doing on her knees. 'There'll be no meal today. It's the best I can do. This storm will not blow itself out before this evening.'

'Something is wrong with Mouse Lord,' Fidelma explained. 'He won't let me near him.'

Wenbrit put his bucket down and knelt alongside her. Then, glancing at her robe, he frowned and pointed to it.

'You seem to have some blood on your robe, lady.'

Fidelma raised a hand and felt the sticky substance on her chest.

'I can't see any scratches,' Wenbrit observed. 'If Mouse Lord has scratched you . . .'

'Can you get the cat out from under the bunk? I think he must be hurt,' she interrupted as she realised that the blood could not have come from the puncture marks the cat had made when he had been frightened during the night.

Wenbrit went down on his knees. It took him some time before the cat allowed himself to be taken hold of. Wenbrit was finally able to get near the animal, having made sure that he held the front paws together to stop Mouse Lord scratching. Making soft reassuring sounds, the boy gently extracted Mouse Lord from underneath the bunk and laid him on the bedding. Something was obviously hurting the animal.

'He's been cut.' The boy frowned as he examined the animal. 'Deeply cut, too. There's still blood on his hind flank. What happened?'

Mouse Lord had calmed down as the animal realised that they meant him no harm.

'I don't know . . . oh!'

Even as she spoke, Fidelma understood the meaning of her painful awakening during the night. She leant over the straw mattress of the bunk and saw what she was looking for immediately. It was the same knife which Sister Crella had given her; the one Crella claimed that Brother Guss had planted under her bunk. It was smeared with blood: Mouse Lord's blood. Fidelma cursed herself for a fool. She had brought the knife from Crella's cabin and put it in her baggage and it had disappeared before Toca Nia's death.

Wenbrit had finished his examination of the cat.

'I need to take Mouse Lord down below where I can bathe and stitch this cut. I think the creature has been stabbed in the hind flank. Poor cat. He's tried to lick it better.'

Fidelma glanced at Mouse Lord in sympathy. Wenbrit was fussing over the cat, who was allowing the boy to stroke him under the chin. He began to purr softly.

'How did this happen, lady?' asked Wenbrit again.

'I think Mouse Lord saved my life,' she told him. 'I was asleep with him curled up on my chest. Someone came to the cabin door. Perhaps Mouse Lord sprang up when the killer entered. They obviously didn't see the cat. I must have been lucky for they threw the knife instead of moving to stab me as I lay. Whether the cat's move deflected it, I am not sure, but poor Puss caught the blade in his flank. The cat's reaction woke me and scared the attacker.'

'Did you recognise the person?' demanded the boy.

'I am afraid not. It was too dark.' Fidelma gave a shudder as she realised how close she had come to death for a second time. Then she pulled herself together.

'Look after Mouse Lord, Wenbrit. Do your best. He saved my life. We'll have some answers before long. *Deo favente*, this storm must moderate soon. I can't concentrate with it.'

But they were without God's favour, for the storm did not moderate for another full day. The constant noise and heaving had dulled Fidelma's senses; she became almost indifferent to her fate. She just wanted to sleep, to find some relief from the merciless battering of the weather. Now and then the ship would heel over to such an angle that Fidelma would ask herself whether it would right itself again. Then, after what seemed an age, *The Barnade Goose* would slowly swing back until another great wave came roaring out of the darkness.

At times Fidelma believed the ship to be sinking, so completely immersed in seawater did it seem to be; she even had to fight for breath against the lung-bursting bitter saltwater that drenched her. Her body was bruised and assaulted by the constant tossing of the ship.

It was dawn the next day when she drearily noticed that the wind was less keen than before and the rocking of the ship less violent. She made her way out of her cabin and looked around. The grey morning sky held a few tattered storm clouds, low and isolated, sweeping by amidst a layer of thin white cloud. She even saw the pale, white orb of the sun on the eastern horizon. Not a full-blooded dawn but with just a hint that the day might improve.

To her surprise, she saw Murchad coming along the main deck towards her. He looked utterly exhausted after the two days of severe storm in which he had been mainly at the steering oar.

'Are you all right, lady?' he asked. 'Wenbrit told me what happened and I asked Gurvan to keep a watch on you just in case you were attacked again.'

'I have felt better,' confessed Fidelma. She saw Wenbrit occupied further along the deck. 'How is Mouse Lord?'

Murchad smiled.

'He might limp a little but he will continue to hunt mice for a while yet. Young Wenbrit managed to stitch the wound together and he seems none the worse for the cut. I don't suppose you saw who threw the knife at you?'

'It was too dark.' Then she changed the subject. 'Are we through the storm?'

'Through the worst of it, I think,' he replied. 'The wind has moved southerly and it will be easier for us to hoist the mainsail once again and keep to our original course. I think this is one voyage that I shall not be sorry to end. I'll be glad to find myself in the arms of Aoife again.'

'Aoife?'

'My wife is called Aoife,' Murchad smiled. 'Even sailors have wives.'

A thought nagged at Fidelma's memory. Suddenly the words of an old song came into her mind.

'You who loved us in the days now fled
Down the whirlpool of hate, spite fed,
You cast aside the love you bore,
To make vengeance your only law!'

Murchad frowned.

'I was thinking of the jealous lust of Aoife, the wife of Lir, the god of the oceans, and how she destroyed those who loved him.'

The captain sniffed disparagingly.

'My wife Aoife is a wonderful woman,' he said in a tone of protest.

Fidelma smiled quickly.

'I am sorry. It was merely the name which prompted the thought. I did not mean anything against your wife – but it has brought a useful memory back to me.'

What was the Biblical verse that Muirgel had mentioned to Guss when she told him that she knew why she might be the next victim?

. . . jealousy cruel as the grave;
It blazes up like blazing fire
Fiercer than any flame.

She looked across to the sea. It was still white-capped but not quite so turbulent now, and the great waves were becoming smaller and fewer. At last it all made sense! She smiled in satisfaction and turned back to the weary Murchad.

'I'm sorry, Captain,' she said. 'I was not concentrating.'

It was then that Fidelma focused on the mess that the storm had created on the ship. The deck was strewn with splintered spars, the water-butt appeared to have shattered into pieces, ropes and rigging hung in profusion. Sailors seemed to have collapsed where they stood, in sheer exhaustion.

'Was anyone hurt?' Fidelma asked in wonder at the debris.

'Some of my crew have a scratch or two,' Murchad admitted.

'And the rest of the passengers?'

Murchad shook his head.

'Not a hair of them was harmed, lady – *this* time.'

To Fidelma it was a sheer miracle that in the two days the little ship had been tossed hither and thither on the rough seas, no one had been injured.

'Tomorrow, or the day after, I expect to sight the Iberian coast, lady,' he said quietly. 'And if my navigation has been good, we shall

245

be in harbour soon after. From that harbour it is but a short journey inland to the Holy Shrine.'

'I shan't be sorry to escape from the confines of your ship, Murchad,' Fidelma confessed.

The captain gave her a bleak look.

'What I was trying to say, lady, is that once we reach the harbour, there will no longer be an opportunity to bring the murderer of Muirgel nor Toca Nia to justice. That will be bad. The story will follow this vessel like a ghost, haunting it wherever it goes. My sailors have already called this a voyage of the damned.'

'It shall be resolved, Murchad,' Fidelma reassured him confidently. 'The mention of your good wife's name has just settled everything in my mind or, rather, it has clarified something for me.'

He stared uncomprehendingly at her.

'My wife's name? Aoife's name has caused you to realise who is responsible for these murders?'

'I do not think that we need delay further before we identify the culprit,' she replied optimistically. 'But we will wait until all the pilgrims are gathered for the midday meal. Then we will discuss the matter with them. I'd like Gurvan and Wenbrit to be there, with yourself. I might need some physical help,' she added.

She smiled at his bewildered features and laid a friendly hand on his arm.

'Don't worry, Murchad. By this afternoon you shall know the identity of the person responsible for all these terrible crimes.'

Chapter Twenty-one

They had gathered as Fidelma had requested, seated on each side of the long table in the central cabin with Murchad lounging against the mast well. Gurvan was seated uncomfortably to one side while Wenbrit perched on the table at which he usually prepared the food, legs swinging, watching the proceedings with interest. Fidelma leaned back in her chair at the head of the table and met their expectant gazes.

'I have been told,' she began quietly, 'that I am someone who knows all by a kind of instinct. I can assure you that this is not so. As a *dálaigh*, I ask questions and I listen. Sometimes, it is what people *omit* in their replies to me that reveals more than what they actually say. But I have to have information laid before me. I have to have facts, or even questions, to consider. I merely examine that information or ponder those questions, and only then can I make a deduction.

'No, I do not have any secret knowledge, neither am I some prophet who can divine an answer to a mystery without knowledge. The art of detection is like playing *fidchell* or *brandubh*. Everything must be there, laid out on the board so that one can choose the solution to the problem. The eye must see, the ear must hear, the brain must function. Instincts can lie or be misleading. So instincts are *not* infallible as a means of getting to the truth, although sometimes they can be a good guide.'

She paused. There was silence. The others continued to watch her expectantly, like rabbits watching a fox.

'My mentor, Brehon Morann, used to warn us students to beware of the obvious because the obvious is sometimes deceiving. I was taking this into account until I realised that sometimes the obvious is the obvious *because it is the reality*.

'If you meet someone running down the road with their hair wild, dishevelled eyes and contorted features, screaming with white froth on their lips, an upraised knife in their hand which is bloodstained and there is also blood on their clothes, how would you perceive such a person? It could be that they have contorted features and are screaming because they have been hurt; that they have the bloodstained

247

knife because they have just slaughtered meat for their meal and have been careless enough to get the blood on their clothes. There are many possible explanations, but the obvious one is that here is a homicidal maniac about to do injury to those who do not get out of his or her way. And sometimes the obvious explanation is the correct explanation.'

She paused again but still there was no comment.

'I am afraid that I was looking at the obvious for a long time and refusing to see it as the truth.

'When I traced everything back, there seemed one person to whom all the events were linked – one common denominator who was there no matter which way I turned. Cian, here, was that common denominator.'

Cian rose awkwardly to his feet, the rocking motion of the ship causing him to fall towards the table, saving himself from disaster by thrusting out a hand to steady himself.

Gurvan had risen and moved behind him, and now put a hand on his shoulder.

Cian shook it off angrily.

'Bitch! I am no murderer! It is only your petty jealousy that makes you accuse me of it. Just because you were rejected—'

'Sit down and be quiet or I will ask Gurvan to restrain you!'

Fidelma's cold tone cut through his outburst. Cian stood still, defiant, and she had to repeat herself.

'Sit down and be silent, I said! I have not finished.'

Brother Tola looked disapprovingly towards Fidelma.

'*Cum tacent clamant*,' he muttered. 'Surely if you do not allow him to speak, his silence will condemn him?'

'He can speak when I have finished and when he knows what there is to speak about,' Fidelma assured Tola icily. 'Better to speak from knowledge than to speak from ignorance.' She turned back to the others. 'As I was saying, once I realised that Cian was the common denominator in all these killings, then they began to make sense to me.' She raised a hand to silence the new outburst from Cian. 'I am not saying that Cian was the murderer, mark that. I have only said, so far, that he was the common denominator.'

Cian was now clearly as puzzled as everyone else. He relaxed back in his seat.

'If you do not accuse me of murder, what *are* you accusing me of?' he demanded gruffly.

She eyed him sourly.

'There are many things that you can be accused of, Cian, but in this particular case, murder is not one of them. Whether or not you are the Butcher of Rath Bíle is no longer my concern. The accusation died with Toca Nia.'

She looked at the others, who now sat mesmerised, waiting for her to continue. She paused, examining their faces in turn. Cian stared back at her in defiance. Brother Tola and Sister Ainder shared a slightly sneering, cynical expression. Sister Crella and Sister Gormán sat with downcast looks. Brother Bairne's expression was one of a caged animal, his eyes flickering here and there as if seeking a means of escape. Brother Dathal was leaning slightly forward, returning her gaze with an almost enthusiastic expression as if waiting with anticipatory pleasure for her revelation. His companion, Adamrae, was gazing at the table, impatiently drumming his fingers silently on it as if he were bored by the proceedings.

'There is no need for me to tell you, of course, that a very dangerous killer sits among us.'

'That much is logical,' Brother Dathal agreed, nodding eagerly. 'But who is it, if not Brother Cian? And why do you call him the common denominator?'

'This killer has been known to you ever since you started out from the north on this pilgrimage,' she went on, ignoring him. 'The first victim of the murderer was Sister Canair.'

Sister Ainder exhaled sharply.

'How can you possibly know that?' she demanded. 'Sister Canair simply did not turn up when the tide forced this ship to sail. What makes you think she has been murdered?'

There was a muttering of agreement.

'Because I spoke to someone who saw the body. Brother Guss saw it, as did Sister Muirgel.'

Cian gave a cynical bark of laughter.

'Convenient, isn't it, since both Muirgel and Guss are now dead and cannot support your claim?'

'Very convenient,' agreed Fidelma. 'Muirgel was also murdered while Brother Guss . . .' She shrugged. 'Well, we all know what happened. He fell overboard because he was driven by fear.'

All eyes turned to Sister Crella.

'There was only one person from whom Guss was backing away in fear at the time,' Brother Dathal commented.

Sister Crella sat hypnotised like a terrified rabbit. She was deathly pale and could only shake her head from side to side as if in denial.

'Sister Crella?' Brother Tola pursed his lips thoughtfully. 'I suppose it makes some sense. There are rumours that she was jealous of Muirgel.'

'Brother Guss told me that he firmly believed that Sister Crella was the person who had killed Muirgel,' Cian offered, glad that the responsibility had apparently shifted from his shoulders.

'Jealousy? Lust!' sneered Sister Ainder disapprovingly. 'The greatest sin.'

Sister Crella started to cry softly. Fidelma thought she should intervene again.

'Sister Crella was only the *unwitting* cause of the death of Brother Guss,' she revealed. 'Unfortunately, Brother Guss did have that unshakable belief that Crella was the guilty person. He was young and fearful – and don't forget that he had seen what the killer had done to both Canair and Muirgel. He was afraid for his life; frantic with a fear that caused him to lose his reason. When Crella came towards him, he thought she was going to strike him down and he backed away in fear, only to fall overboard. His death was caused *not by Crella* – but by the person who had engendered such a fear of death in him.'

There was another, long silence. Sister Crella was staring at Fidelma through her tears, not really understanding what she had said, simply registering that Fidelma was not accusing her.

'Are you playing games with us, Sister?' Sister Ainder turned angrily towards her. 'You accuse in one breath and then you acquit in another. What do you mean by it? Can you not simply tell us what the motive for these killings was, and who is responsible?'

Fidelma kept her tone reasonable, as if discussing the weather.

'You, yourself, have told me the motive.'

Sister Ainder blinked.

'What?'

'You told me – it was one of the seven deadly sins, the sin of lust.' Fidelma paused to let her words sink in before continuing. 'In any investigation the first question that needs to be asked is the one which Cicero once asked of a Roman judge. *Cui bono?* Who stands to gain? What is the motive?'

'Are you saying lust was the motive?' Brother Tola interrupted, his voice full of derision. 'How was the death of that Laigin warrior, Toca Nia, attributable to lust? Or are you treating his murder separately? To me it seems obvious that he was killed because of his accusations against Cian there. Only Cian stood to gain by *his* death.'

There was clearly no love lost between him and Cian.

'You are right,' agreed Fidelma calmly. 'Toca Nia was killed to protect Cian.'

Cian tried to rise again but Gurvan pressed him back in his seat.

'So you are accusing me, after all?' he said bitterly. 'I did not—'

'Did not kill him?' interrupted Fidelma mildly. 'No, you did not. I said he was killed to protect you: I did not say he was killed *by* you. But the motive for Toca Nia's death was the same as the motive for the deaths of Canair and Muirgel and the two attempts on my life.'

'Two?' frowned Brother Dathal. 'Someone has tried to kill you twice?'

'Oh yes,' nodded Fidelma. 'A second attempt was made in my cabin last night during the storm. I owe my life to a cat.' She did not bother to explain further. There would be plenty of time later on.

'So there is one killer and one motive? Is that what you are saying?' Murchad asked, trying to follow her reasoning.

'The motive being lust,' she confirmed. 'Or rather, I should say, a belief that they were in love with Cian, to the extent that all sanity was driven from their minds, leaving an obsession that they must protect him and drive out any who tried to win his love.'

Cian sat back, white-faced and shaky.

'I don't understand what you are saying.'

'Had Toca Nia harmed you, then you would have been denied to this person, who wanted you for themselves.'

'I still do not understand.'

'Easy enough. I said that you were the common denominator. Weren't you the lover of both Canair and Muirgel at various times?'

Cian's face was defiant.

'I do not deny it,' he said shortly.

'There were several others also whose affections you won in your insatiable appetite for young women. Were you trying to compensate for what Una had done to you?' She could not help the malicious twist

'Una has nothing to do with it,' Cian swore.

Sister Gormán leant forward anxiously.

'Who is Una? We had no Sister Una at Moville.'

'Una was Cian's wife. She divorced him on the grounds that he was sterile,' Fidelma said with an unforgiving smile. 'Perhaps Cian was compensating for that degrading position by finding as many young lovers as he could.'

Cian's face was working in anger.

'You . . .' he began.

'One of those lovers could not abide the idea that you had loved others,' went on Fidelma. 'Unlike most of your loves, this person was unbalanced. Insane, we might say, with jealousy. You did not realise what a cauldron of jealousy and hate you were stirring. How fortunate, Cian, that the hate was not directed at you but at the other lovers you took.'

As if she had poured ice water on his anger, Cian had become suddenly still. He was sitting with his mouth partially open; his mind appeared to be working rapidly as he thought over what she was saying.

Brother Tola bent towards her.

'If I have understood you correctly, Toca Nia was killed because he was threatening Cian; and this person, insanely determined to protect Cian, simply saw him as a threat, to be removed in the same manner that his lovers were.'

'The person wanted Cian for themselves,' agreed Fidelma.

'Apart from Crella, there was no one else I had an affair with,' Cian stated, 'other than . . .' He stared with wide-eyed suspicion at Fidelma; a flicker of fear came into his eyes.

Fidelma chuckled sardonically as she realised what was going through his mind. That he could accuse her was ironic in the extreme, but it followed his natural arrogance that he actually believed that she would have retained an intensity of feeling for him after all these years.

'I have to confess that when I was eighteen I might have become a victim of that same insanity,' she admitted to them all. 'Youth intensifies such emotions, and sometimes we are not mature enough to control them. Yes, it is to the instability of youth that we must look in this matter. But you delude yourself, Cian, if you think that you still have any ability to rouse such emotions in me. You don't even arouse my pity.'

Brother Dathal, eager and ferret-like, asked, 'Why, surely *you* were not Cian's lover, Sister?'

Fidelma grimaced resignedly.

'Oh yes. I, too, came under Cian's spell ten years ago when I was a young student at the college of Brehon Morann at Tara.' She gazed thoughtfully at Cian. 'It was a youthful, immature affair on both sides,' she added with a maliciousness she did not realise that she possessed. 'I grew up. Cian didn't.'

'Well, how would this insane lover realise that?' asked Brother Dathal intrigued. 'If your affair happened ten years ago, it was before Cian joined the religieux at Bangor and doubtless long before any of us knew him.'

Fidelma shot him a glance of appreciation.

'You ask a good question, Brother Dathal. You all became aware when I first came aboard that I had known Cian before. One person was very interested in that fact. That same person overheard Cian and me discussing our sad little affair.'

She swung round abruptly to Cian.

'I am sure that you can work things out for yourself. You admitted to me that you had affairs with Canair, Muirgel and Crella.'

Before she had finished speaking, Brother Bairne had leapt from his seat opposite Cian and flung himself across the table. He was brandishing a knife.

'Bastard!' he cried, grabbing Cian by the throat and raising the weapon.

Gurvan had reached forward in front of Cian and grabbed Bairne's wrist with the weapon in it in a vice-like grip, thrusting the wrist back in a painful bend. With a scream Brother Bairne's fingers let the knife drop through onto the table. It fell with a clatter and Brother Tola had the presence of mind to scoop it up and hand it to Murchad.

Brother Bairne was no match for the stocky and muscular Breton seaman. Even as they struggled, while Cian slipped back out of the way, Gurvan hauled the flushed-faced, frenzied young man across the table and twisted his arm behind his back. The young monk went suddenly limp; all the fight seemed to have left him.

Fidelma regarded him with disapproval.

'That was a silly thing to do, Brother Bairne, wasn't it?'

'I hate him!' the young man whimpered.

'Hated but lusted for him?' Sister Ainder was aghast. 'I don't understand!'

'Brother Bairne, explain why you hated Cian,' Fidelma invited patiently.

'I hated Cian for taking Muirgel from me.'

Cian laughed harshly.

'Madness! Muirgel was never yours to take from you, you stupid child.'

'Bastard!' cried Bairne again, but was still firmly held in the grip of Gurvan.

Sister Crella had recovered some of her spirits now.

'Cian is telling the truth. Muirgel wanted nothing to do with Bairne. She thought he was weird, an effeminate dreamer. And she *did* have an affair with Cian.'

Cian nodded agreement.

'But Muirgel and I ended that relationship just before we set out from Moville. Muirgel had found another lover and I had found Canair. It was as simple as that. Muirgel told me that, against all the odds, she was in love with Guss.'

'Guss?' Crella stared at him confounded. 'Is it true? It can't be.' She raised a hand to her cheek as the horror of her denial of her friend's involvement with the young man grew.

'It is true,' Fidelma told her. 'Muirgel really did love him and only your dislike of Guss kept you from believing it. Your refusal to believe that Muirgel was in love with him, made me suspect Guss for a while but, at the same time, your dislike of him, which seemed like jealousy in his eyes, caused Guss to believe that you were the killer – hence his great fear of you, which led to him falling overboard.'

Brother Tola was shaking his head in perplexity.

'I still cannot see why Brother Bairne would kill Toca Nia if, as he says, he hated Cian. Surely the arrival of Toca Nia was the answer to Bairne's dreams – the best way to get rid of Cian?'

Fidelma was impatient.

'You have missed the point. Bairne did not kill anyone. He was not competent enough. Look at the feeble attempt he made just now! Let me get back to what I was saying before he made that stupid display. I was suggesting that Cian was well able to work things out for himself. He had admitted to affairs with Canair and Muirgel. He even admitted to a brief affair with Crella. But there was still one more person on this ship with whom he had an affair, the only person who overheard us arguing about our youth.'

Sister Gormán had risen from the table, for already a look of horror had spread over Cian's face and he had turned to her, memories flooding back. Gormán's features were not reflective of guilt but defiant, and there was a curious glint in her eyes. Her jaw stuck out aggressively. The laugh she gave sounded slightly hysterical, a high-pitched chortling sound, the tone close to malignant triumph. As Fidelma gazed on her face, she was completely confirmed in her estimation that Gormán was, indeed, insane.

The young girl glowered in defiance at all of them.

'I have committed no crime,' she spoke scornfully. 'Does not the Book of Genesis say:

> 'I kill a man for wounding me,
> A young man for a blow.
> Cain may be avenged seven times
> But I seventy-seven!'

Fidelma corrected her gently.

'You are quoting from the Song of Lamech, son of Methushael, whose endless desire for vengeance was transformed by the words of the Christ. Remember what Christ told Peter according to the Gospel of Matthew? "Then Peter came up and asked him, 'Lord, how often am I to forgive my brother if he goes on wronging me? As many as seven times?' Jesus replied, 'I do not say seven times; I say seventy times seven.'" Let Lamech's shade die with his vengeance, Gormán.'

The girl turned furiously towards her.

'Do not be clever with me, whore of Babylon! I would have killed you too but you were able to thwart me twice. You will be punished yet. ". . . I saw a woman mounted on a scarlet beast which was covered with blasphemous names and had seven heads and ten horns. The woman was clothed in purple and scarlet and bedecked with gold and jewels and pearls. In her hand she held a gold cup, full of obscenities and the foulness of her fornication; and written on her forehead was a name with a secret meaning: *Babylon the great, the mother of whores and of every obscenity on earth.* The woman I saw was drunk with the blood of God's people and the blood of those who had borne their testimony to Jesus".'

'The girl is raving!' Sister Ainder muttered uneasily, rising and edging away from her.

Murchad glanced towards Fidelma as if to ask what he should do.

Cian had relaxed now and was sitting with his hands resting on the table. He regarded the girl with complete indifference.

'Thank God this matter is resolved,' he said to no one in particular. 'This insanity has nothing to do with me. I am not responsible for the madness of this girl. *Dominus illuminatio* . . . Why, I only ever slept with her once.'

Sister Gormán wheeled round on him, eyes blazing.

'But it was for you I did it, for *you* – don't you understand? I did it to save you! So that we could be together!'

Cian smirked.

'For me?' he sneered. 'You are crazy. What gave you the idea that I wanted anything more to do with you after that night? You women always want to turn everything into permanent ownership.'

Sister Gormán jerked back as if he had struck her across the face. A bewildered expression crossed her features.

'You can't mean that. You said that night that you loved me.' Her voice became a soft wailing sound.

Fidelma found compassion welling for the young woman as the memories of her own youth drifted through her mind again.

'Cian loves only Cian, Gormán,' she said sternly. 'He is incapable of loving anyone else. As for you, Cian, you may claim that you are not responsible for these atrocities, and you are correct so far as the law goes. However, the law is not always justice. You cannot neglect that moral responsibility which you bear. Your selfishness, your manipulation of people's emotions, especially the emotions of young women, are your responsibility. You must answer for it eventually, if not soon then at some later stage in your life.'

Cian flushed in annoyance.

'What is wrong with grasping at pleasure in this life? Have we all to become Roman ascetics and go into the desert as hermits? Why can't we continue to live our lives filled with enjoyment?'

Brother Tola's face mirrored his anger.

'Thou shalt not kill, is the Commandment of the Lord. The woman is condemned but you, Cian, you have been the cause of this madness and you must stand condemned alongside her.'

Cian turned to him with derision.

'Under whose law? Don't dictate your narrow morals to me. They do not apply.'

Gormán stood with hunched shoulders, like a whipped dog; her arms wrapped round her body as if they gave her some comfort. She was rocking back and forth on her heels, sobbing.

'I did this for you, Cian,' she crooned softly. 'Muirgel . . . Canair . . . I even killed Toca Nia to protect you from his wicked accusations. I would have killed her – Fidelma – and then Crella. They both meant you harm. You had to be protected. Without them we could have been together. They interfered with our happiness.'

Fidelma spoke softly, almost kindly, to her.

'Perhaps you will tell us how you killed Sister Canair. I know part of the story from Guss; I would like to know the other part. Can you tell us?'

Gormán giggled. It was a chilling sound for it was the giggle of an innocent young girl.

'He loved me. Cian loved me – I know it. "I will betroth you to me for ever; I will betroth you to me in righteousness and in justice, in steadfast love, and in mercy. I will betroth you to me in faithfulness . . ."!'

Fidelma dimly recalled the words. She thought they came from the Book of Hosea. There had been many quotations from Hosea.

'Even if he denies it now, he loved me as I loved him. We would have married if . . . if these others had not ensnared him with their lust, and . . . and . . .'

Cian shrugged diffidently.

'She is clearly demented,' he muttered. 'I wash my hands of this matter.'

'Gormán!' Fidelma turned sharply to the girl. 'Tell us of the fate of Canair. When did you kill her?'

Somehow Fidelma's coaxing tone pulled Gormán back from whatever darkness she was descending into and there came a few moments approaching sanity.

'The night before we sailed, I killed her in the tavern at Ardmore.'

She gave the statement coldly, without emotion now, standing quite still, her eyes suddenly devoid of feeling as they stared at Cian.

'All because Canair was having an affair with Cian?' interposed Brother Tola.

The girl had a curious smile on her face.

> 'Persuasively she led him on,
> She pressed him with seductive words.
> Like a simple fool he followed her,
> Like an ox on its way to the slaughterhouse,
> Like an antelope bounding into the noose,
> Like a bird hurrying into the trap,
> He did not know that he was risking his life . . .'

'Stop that rubbish!' Cian cried. 'I have had enough of these nonsensical ramblings.'

Sister Ainder bent forward and chided him with a frosty look.

'The Book of Proverbs is not rubbish, Brother Cian. You are unworthy to hear those words and not fit to wear the habit of a religieux.'

'Do you think I ever wanted to wear these stupid rags?' Cian shot back at her.

'What I have heard today is disgusting,' replied Sister Ainder. 'If nothing else, I shall give all the details to the Abbot of Bangor. When you return to your Abbey, you will suffer by bell, book and candle, if I have anything to do with it.'

'If I ever return to Bangor,' sneered Cian.

Sister Gormán, in the meantime, was continuing to speak as if she had become oblivious to her surroundings.

Fidelma bent forward and spoke to her slowly and clearly.

'Why did you kill Sister Canair?' she demanded.

'Canair seduced him, lured him away from me,' she replied diffidently. 'She had to die.'

Cian opened his mouth to protest but Fidelma waved him to silence and addressed the girl.

'How did it happen? From what I know, Canair had left your

257

company before you reached Ardmore. The group all went on to the Abbey of St Declan to stay the night. You went with them, didn't you?'

'I overheard Canair arranging with Cian to meet him in the tavern later.'

Fidelma glanced back to Cian who simply shrugged.

'It is true,' he admitted. 'Canair said she would be at the tavern after midnight, after she had seen her friend. That was the principal reason why she did not come to the Abbey. She went to see a friend who dwelt nearby. It was as an afterthought that we made arrangements to meet.'

'Did you go to the tavern, Cian?'

There was a silence.

'Did you go to meet Canair?' pressed Fidelma.

Cian sullenly nodded as if reluctant to admit the fact.

'What then?'

'I reached the tavern when there were still people about. I wasn't sure whether Canair had arrived and while I was hesitating outside I saw Muirgel and Guss arrive. From the way they were behaving, it seemed they had the same intention as Canair and me.' Cian sniffed. 'It was no business of mine. As I said, my affair with Muirgel was long over.'

'Go on,' Fidelma pressed when he paused.

'I waited. The hour was late and Canair had not turned up. I decided to go back to the Abbey. That's all.'

Fidelma waited expectantly.

Cian sat back and folded his arms with an air of finality.

'You say that is all?' asked Fidelma, slightly incredulously.

'I went back to the Abbey,' repeated Cian. 'What else would I do?'

'You weren't worried when Canair did not turn up at your rendezvous?'

'She was no child. She could make her own decisions as to whether or not she turned up.'

'Didn't you think it strange when Canair did not appear at the quay either, to take the boat the next morning? Why didn't you raise an alarm?'

'What alarm should I raise?' he asked defensively. 'Canair did not turn up, either at the rendezvous or at the quay, so what was I to do about that? It was her decision. I had no idea that she had been killed.'

'But . . .' For once Fidelma was left without words at the self-centred attitude of Cian.

'Anyway, what alarm was there to raise and with whom?' he added.

Fidelma turned back to Gormán.

'Can you tell us what happened at the tavern?'

Gormán looked at her with dull, unseeing eyes.

'I was there as the right hand of God's vengeance. Vengeance is—'

'Did you go there to kill Canair?' Fidelma interrupted her firmly.

'Canair came to the inn. I was hiding in the shadows. She stood in the doorway for a while, looking about. She was waiting for Cian but he had already gone back to the Abbey. I watched him go. Then Canair seemed to make up her mind and she went in. I heard her ask in the tavern if anyone had asked for her, or if a religieux had taken a room. She was told that a male and female religieux had taken a room but when she was given a description, she lost interest. I stayed in the shadows listening. Eventually she took a room and went to it. I stood in the inn yard, wondering what to do. Then I saw a light at an upstairs window. There was Canair looking out, still hoping that Cian would turn up. I slid back into the shadows. She did not see me.'

Suddenly Gormán had become alive, alive with an expression of malicious elation as she told the story.

'I waited a while and then, when the inn was quiet, I entered. It was quite easy.'

'A curse on the law which forbids innkeepers to bar their doors to prevent travellers seeking rest,' muttered Sister Ainder. 'The same law leaves us unprotected.'

The girl continued without paying attention to her.

'I went up to Canair's room. The whore was asleep and I killed her. Then I left as silently as I had arrived.'

'What made you take her crucifix?' demanded Fidelma, holding out the cross that had fallen from the hand of the dying Muirgel.

Gormán giggled again.

'It was . . . so pretty. So pretty.'

'Then you went back to the Abbey?'

'The next morning Muirgel and Guss were at the Abbey, breakfasting as if they had not left it. Well, I could punish Muirgel later. And so I did.'

'And so you did,' repeated Fidelma. 'So Canair's body remained in the tavern, presumably undiscovered, until after we had set sail?'

Her remark was not expressly addressed to Gormán and it was Murchad who answered.

'It would seem so,' he said, rubbing the back of his neck with his hand. 'I know Colla, the owner of the inn. He would have raised the alarm immediately he discovered the body.'

'Muirgel and Guss were in the next room and heard the dying moans of Canair. So Guss told me,' Fidelma explained. 'They saw her body and stupidly decided to return to the Abbey and say nothing. Only when she came aboard did Muirgel see Gormán wearing Canair's crucifix. It was Muirgel who worked out why Gormán had killed Canair, and she realised that she was going to be next. That's why she pretended first to be seasick and then to be washed overboard. But Gormán stumbled on her as she left Guss's cabin and killed her. Muirgel seized the crucifix that Gormán had taken. Muirgel was still alive when I saw her and tried to warn me . . . but all she could do was attempt to press Canair's crucifix into my hand.'

'So Canair, Muirgel and Toca Nia have all fallen to this madness,' muttered Sister Ainder. 'The girls because they had the misfortune to be seduced by this,' she jerked her head at Cian, 'this degenerate wretch, and the Laigin warrior because he accused Cian of high crimes and misdemeanours, and this insane creature saw that as a further danger. What madness and evil is here, brethren?'

Cian stood up angrily.

'It seems that you are putting the blame on me rather than on this stupid bitch!' he snarled.

Once again, Gormán's head jerked back as if he had physically assaulted her.

> 'Deserting me, you have stripped and lain down
> On the wide bed which you have made,
> And you drove bargains . . .
> For the pleasure of sleeping together
> And you have committed countless acts of fornication
> In the heat of your lust . . .'

Then her hand reached inside her habit and something flew from it. Murchad, standing near to Cian, reacted quickly and shoved the former warrior to one side. A knife embedded itself a wooden beam just behind Cian.

With a cry of rage at having missed him, Gormán seized the opportunity offered by their confusion and indecision, to turn out of the cabin and scamper up the companionway to the deck above.

Fidelma was the first to recover her senses and start to rush after her, but Murchad held her back.

'Don't worry, lady,' he said. 'Where is she going to flee to? We are in the middle of the ocean.'

'It is not fear of escape that concerns me,' she told him. 'It is fear of what she might do to herself. Madness acknowledges no logic.'

As they tumbled onto the deck, Drogon, who stood at the steering oar, cried out to them; he was pointing upwards.

They looked up.

Gormán was swaying dangerously from the rigging at least twenty feet or more above them.

'Stop!' cried Fidelma. 'Gormán, stop! There is nowhere to run to.'

The girl kept climbing up the swaying ropes.

'Gormán, come down. We can find a resolution to the problem. Come down. No one will harm you.' As Fidelma called, she realised how hollow her assurances sounded, even to someone whose mind was so damaged.

Murchad, standing at Fidelma's side, touched her arm and shook his head.

'She can't hear you for the wind up there.'

Fidelma continued to stare up. The wind was whipping at the girl's hair and clothing as she clung to the rigging. Murchad was right. There was no way sound could carry up.

'I'll go up,' Fidelma volunteered. 'Someone needs to bring her down.'

Murchad laid a hand on her arm.

'You are not acquainted with the dangers of being aloft in a strong wind on shipboard. I'll go up.'

Fidelma hesitated and then stood back. She realised that it would need someone more sure-footed than she was to bring the insane young woman down.

'Don't scare her,' she instructed. 'She is completely mad and there is no telling what she is liable to do.'

Murchad's face was grim.

'She is only a slight young girl.'

'There is an old saying, Murchad. If a sane dog fights a mad dog then it is the sane dog's ear that is likely to be bitten off.'

'I'll be careful,' he assured her and started up the rigging.

He had hardly reached it when Sister Ainder gave an inarticulate cry of warning which made Fidelma look up.

Gormán had missed her footing and was hanging desperately onto the ropes with one hand, reaching out, trying to grasp hold of the rigging with the other.

261

'Hold on!' yelled Fidelma, her cry disappearing into the wind.

Murchad, too, had seen the slip and launched himself into the rigging. He had hardly risen a few feet when Gormán's grip relaxed and she fell, crashing down onto the deck with a sickening thud.

Fidelma was the first to reach her side.

There was no need to check for a pulse. It was obvious that the young girl had broken her neck in the fall. Fidelma leaned forward and closed Gormán's staring eyes while Sister Ainder began to intone a prayer for the dead.

Murchad dropped back to the deck and joined them.

'I'm sorry,' he panted. 'Is she . . . ?'

'Yes, she's dead. It's not your fault,' Fidelma said, rising from the deck.

Cian was peering over the shoulder of Brother Dathal, gazing down at the body of the girl.

'Well,' he said with relief in his voice. 'That's that.'

Chapter Twenty-two

Fidelma stood on the quay in the warm autumnal sunshine, inhaling the exotic scents of the picturesque little port which stood under the shelter of an ancient Roman lighthouse known as the Tower of Hercules. *The Barnacle Goose* was tied up in the harbour against the quay. Her remaining passengers had dispersed inland on their pilgrimage towards the Holy Shrine of St James. Fidelma had refused to continue in their company, using the excuse of writing a report of the voyage for the Chief Brehon of Cashel so that Murchad could take it back on his return voyage.

Within an hour of *The Barnacle Goose* easing into the port on the north-west coast of Iberia, perhaps one of the very ports from which Golamh and the Children of the Gael had sailed to Éireann over a millennium ago, the final drama of the voyage had been played out.

Cian had disappeared from the ship once more, but this time along with Sister Crella. Fidelma was not unduly surprised.

'Don't you remember when Cian fled from the ship at the island of Ushant?' she asked Murchad. 'It was obvious that he had help.'

The captain was puzzled and said so.

'It was evident that a man who did not have the use of his right arm could not row a skiff to the island, let alone bring the skiff back to the ship.'

Murchad seemed chagrined that he had not considered the fact.

'I had not thought of that.'

'He had to have an accomplice. He persuaded Crella to help him, as he has persuaded her now. Perhaps I should have tried to warn her about further involvement with Cian, but I doubt if she would have taken any notice of me. He always had a way with women. He can charm the birds from the trees when he needs to.'

'Where will they go now? They surely can't go back to Éireann.'

'Who knows? Perhaps he will continue his journey to Mormohec the physician to see if his arm can be healed. Perhaps not. I feel sorry for poor Crella. She will be in for a rude awakening one day.'

'What made her return to him if he had rejected her as a lover once before?' demanded Murchad.

'Maybe she has never learnt that if one is bitten once, one should be careful about being bitten twice. He will discard her when he feels that he has no more need of her. We will probably never see him back in Éireann but not from any feeling of guilt of what has happened on this voyage. His arrogance would not allow him to accept any culpability there. He will avoid the land of his birth to avoid any further witnesses who might charge him with being the "Butcher of Rath Bíle".'

'So he will go free and unpunished?'

'In these things, it is often the person who holds the real guilt who goes free while those they use as mere tools or dupes are punished.'

Not long after, the surviving band of pilgrims had set off from the port under the charge of Brother Tola. She had watched Brother Tola and Sister Ainder leaving with the less willing company of Brother Dathal and Brother Adamrae. Brother Bairne accompanied them, but he seemed as reluctant to go with them as they were to have him. Forgiveness did not seem to be a feature of the Faith shared by their little band.

Fidelma stayed in the port while *The Barnacle Goose* had its storm damage repaired. She took a room in a small tavern overlooking the harbour, resting and readjusting to the feeling of land under her feet and writing her report. When she heard that *The Barnacle Goose* was preparing to sail, she went down to the quay.

She went on board to say her farewells, especially to Mouse Lord with a gift of fish bought on the quay. The cat was limping slightly but recovering well from the knife-wound. He let her stroke him and purred for a few moments before turning his attention to more important matters, such as the fish she had laid down on the deck before him.

On the now familiar stern deck she had a final word with Murchad.

'When do you set off to the Holy Shrine, lady? There have been several bands of pilgrims passing that way already since we docked. I would have thought that you would have gone by now.'

Fidelma was not worried about finding a suitable group to accompany.

'There is an old proverb, Murchad. Choose your company before you sit down. I would not have chosen the travellers you had to transport as companions, had I known what was going to happen.'

Murchad chuckled broadly but he was still worried for her.

'Do you intend to travel alone? I have a saying for you: is it not said that a healthy sheep will not spurn a scabby flock for company?'

Fidelma allowed one of her mischievous grins to mould her features.

'I think you have reversed it, Murchad. The proverb is: there never was a scabby sheep which did not like to have the flock for company. But I thank you for the thought. No, I shall wait here for a few days, for there are many sheep coming through this port. I shall see if there is a flock that appeals to me. I might, as you say, even go on the journey alone.'

'Is that wise, lady?'

'They tell me that the bandits on the road between here and the Shrine are not many. I am sure the dangers of the road will be fewer than those I encountered on *The Barnacle Goose*.'

Murchad shook his head.

'I still do not see how you finally realised that it was Sister Gormán who was the guilty one. Nor what my wife Aoife had to do with it.'

'It was not your wife – I told you. It was the name Aoife and the story of Lir. Aoife who was the second of the three daughters of the King of Aran, in the story of the Children of Lir. Aoife was beautiful but Lir, the ocean god, married her young sister, Albha. Albha died and Lir then married her eldest sister Niamh. Niamh also died and finally Lir married Aoife.'

'I vaguely remember the story,' Murchad said, but without conviction.

'Well, you will then remember that Aoife became jealous of those who were close to Lir, even though Lir did love her. It grew into such an obsession that she became full of bitterness and brooding evil and set out to destroy everything that loved Lir so that she could have him for herself. The barb of unreasonable jealousy lodged in her heart and she had to destroy. "Jealousy as cruel as the grave", as Muirgel put it.'

'I can see how that fits with Gormán but how . . . ?'

'I was curious that Gormán seemed so interested in how long I had known Cian, almost as soon as I stepped on the ship. Then Crella told me that Cian had slept with Gormán when I questioned her on the second day out. I dismissed these things from my mind. But a good *dálaigh* must be possessed of a retentive memory. I stored the facts. It was when I kept hearing those Biblical quotations about lust and jealousy that I started to realise that the answer must lie in that direction. Yet only when you mentioned the name of your wife, Aoife, and I thought of the jealousy of the character, did I realise what I should be looking for. An unreasoning, insane jealousy.

'Cian slept with her one night and, in his arrogance, did not even remember it until the last moment. Like Aoife, the wife of Lir, Gormán was unbalanced. That fact, her undisguised hatred, was so obvious that I had initially discounted her as a suspect.'

'It was a pity that Sister Gormán escaped justice, then,' reflected Murchad.

Fidelma considered the comment before replying.

'Not so. She was demented. Taken by an illness that is just as debilitating as any other fever. I believe I can understand the depths of jealousy that are aroused in a woman if she feels that she has been betrayed by a man she has come to believe loves her.'

Fidelma flushed a little as she said it, remembering her own feelings.

'Yet she killed. Should she not be punished?'

'Ah, punishment. I fear that there is a new morality coming into our culture, Murchad. It's the one thing that worries me about the Faith. The Penitentials of the Church are preaching punishment instead of compensation and rehabilitation as our native law states.'

'Yet it is the teaching of the Faith.' Murchad was bewildered. 'How can you be a Sister of the Faith and not accept that teaching?'

'Because it is a teaching of vengeance and not an act of justice. Our laws call for justice, not revenge. Juvenal said that vengeance is merely a joy to narrow, sick and petty minds. Blood cannot be washed out by blood. We must seek compensation for the victims and rehabilitation of the wrong-doer. Unless we do so we may enter into a continuing cycle of vengeance for vengeance and blood will continually flow. Those who make their laws a curse shall surely suffer from those same laws.'

'Would you have preferred, then, to have the girl escape?'

Fidelma shook her head.

'She would never have been able to escape from herself. Her mind was too far twisted by her madness so that I think, in this instance, she suffered an act of mercy.'

Gurvan came up and looked apologetically at them.

'Tide's on the turn, Captain,' he told Murchad.

Murchad acknowledged him.

'We must sail, lady,' he said respectfully.

'I hope your return to Ardmore will not be so adventurous as the journey here has been.'

'I would not have become a sailor had I been afraid of storms and pirates,' grinned Murchad. 'However, it is not often that I have experienced murder on board ship. Will you be long in this land,

Sister? Maybe, on your return, you will come back on my ship? I am frequently coming to and fro to this port.'

'It would be a pleasure. Yet I am not sure what my fate will be. Perhaps our paths will cross again. If not, may Christ sail with you. And look after that boy, Wenbrit. He may yet grow to be a fine captain of his own vessel one day.'

She went down to the main deck and bade farewell to Gurvan, Wenbrit, Drogan and the others members of the crew before climbing down onto the quay. Murchad raised his hand in salute.

She watched as the gangplank was hauled back onto the quay and the ropes were untied to allow *The Barnacle Goose* to ease away. She waved energetically at them all, and was then overcome with homesickness so that she began to walk slowly back to the tavern where she was staying. In spite of her sadness, she also felt relief. She had set out on this pilgrimage with two major intentions and she realised that she had resolved one of them. There was no longer any conflict between her place as a religieuse and her role as a *dálaigh*. Her passion for law left her with no other choice: she would always put law before any contemplative life. By the time she had reached the tavern, the sail of *The Barnacle Goose* had been set and she was drifting out of the harbour.

Fidelma sat down on a wooden bench under the shade of a vine tree and stared out thoughtfully across the blue waters of the bay, watching the disappearing vessel.

The tavern-owner came out to her, bearing a glass filled with a drink made from freshly squeezed lemon and cold water which, in the short time she had been there, Fidelma had learnt was the best way to quench her thirst and stay cool in the heat. Then, to her surprise, he handed her a piece of folded vellum. She could not quite understand what he said but he pointed to a sleek-looking vessel which had only entered the harbour within the last hour.

'*Gratias tibi ego.*' She thanked him in Latin, the only language in which they could share a few words in common.

She held back her curiosity for she wanted to watch Murchad's ship leaving harbour. She stayed for some time sipping her drink and watching *The Barnacle Goose* sailing along the estuary, which was locally called the *ria*, until it disappeared beyond the headland. It was comfortable sitting in the warmth of the sunshine. But, again, she suddenly felt enveloped by a tremendous sense of loneliness. She paused to consider her feelings. Was loneliness the right word to describe her emotion? It was better to be alone than in bad company – she certainly had no wish to be in Cian's presence ever again. Yet there was a positive side; she was glad that she had met him again.

For all these years, Cian had been a thorn in her flesh, for she had still recalled all the anguished emotions and passions of her youth. Now she had been granted a meeting with Cian in the maturity of her experiences, and had seen him from the perspective of that maturity; had examined him and realised the folly of the bittersweet intensity of her young love. She had no qualms at all about bidding farewell to Cian and acknowledging that what was past was past. It was to be seen as a growing experience instead of a heavy burden of regret to be carried on her shoulders for ever. No; Cian had no hold on her any longer and she felt no sense of loss in that respect – just an enormous weight falling from her shoulders.

Somehow her mind came back to Eadulf with an abruptness that made her start momentarily, so that her drink shook in her trembling hand.

Eadulf! She realised that he had been a dim shadow during the entire voyage. An ethereal wisp haunting her path.

Why did the words of Publilius Syrus, one of her favourite writers of maxims, come to her mind?

Amare et sepere vix deo conceditur.

Even a god finds it hard to love and be wise at the same time.

She suddenly remembered the folded vellum and reached forward to pick it up. Her eyes widened in astonishment. It was a note written by her brother, Colgú, at Cashel, the day after she had set sail. As she absorbed the few words it contained, a cold feeling of shock hit her, to be replaced by a panic that she had never experienced before. The message was terse: *Return at once! Eadulf has been charged with murder!*